THE TESTIMONY OF DANIEL PAGELS

The Testimony of Daniel Pagels

Vickery Turner

CHARLES SCRIBNER'S SONS
New York

MAXWELL MACMILLAN INTERNATIONAL
New York Oxford Singapore Sydney

Copyright © 1991 by Vickery Turner

Charles Scribner's Sons
Macmillan Publishing Company
866 Third Avenue
New York, NY 10022

Macmillan Publishing Company is part of the
Maxwell Communication Group of Companies.

Library of Congress Cataloging-in-Publication Data
Turner, Vickery.
    The Testimony of Daniel Pagels/Vickery Turner.
        p.   cm.
    ISBN 0-684-19366-3
    1. Indians of North America—Fiction. I. Title.
PS3570.U748T4   1991   91-24515 CIP
813'.54—dc20

10 9 8 7 6 5 4 3 2 1

Printed in the United States of America

To Michael and Caitlin

THE TESTIMONY OF DANIEL PAGELS

Prologue

The suspect, a sixty-four-year-old Native American named Lawrence Pagels, was barbecuing fish when the arresting officers pulled off the Simi Valley Freeway. It took the officers some time to find the exact position of Pagels' motor home, which was hidden among a grove of fan palms in the foothills of the Santa Susana Mountains, near Topanga Canyon Boulevard.

Pagels saw them but his grandson, Daniel, was too busy coaxing their small fire with a stick to pay attention to the procession of cars below them.

The child played a mock sword fight with sparks he produced. "Am I six now, Grandpa?"

Lawrence Pagels brushed oil on the fish. "Yes, I guess you've turned six now, if you want to count."

He looked down the hill and saw the police cars making awkward turns along winding tracks below. The cars disappeared behind small hills, then reappeared. They turned back on themselves, went in circles and stopped. He saw the police officers get out of the cars for a conference. Then they began to circle again.

They found a new track and came closer. Now the police could see the smoke from the fire and headed toward it with more assurance.

"What's wrong with counting?" the boy asked.

"You get stuck with a number when you count. You say you're

six then you're tied to being six, which is pretty good in some respects but kinda dull in others. There's a lot of things six-year-olds can't do."

"Can I do more than other boys of six?"

"I don't know. I'm not going around comparing. Comparing is a really deadly occupation."

The child jumped through the sparks from the fire. "I guess I have a birthday every day."

Lawrence smiled. "I guess you do. That's a good way to think about it, because counting's a real waste of time. People have all kinds of theories about when you get smart, when you get pimples, when you slow down. Don't pin any years on yourself and you won't get stuck in any pigeonholes. You live outside of birthdays. Way above them."

The sun, which had been blinding the police drivers, went down behind the big rocks at Stoney Point. Pagels' fire immediately grew brighter in the remaining shadows.

Moments later twenty-five police officers with guns drawn appeared over the brow of the hill.

Lawrence Pagels was taken to the Devonshire Division Police Station in Northridge, booked and printed, the prints rolled and stamped, twenty in all. He was Mirandized (given his rights) and questioned by Detective John Starbeck. After each question Pagels was asked if he understood. He said O.K. he understood, waived his rights, and was put in a holding cell for the night.

The following day Pagels was brought before Judge Alma Denman and charged with one count of violation of section 187 of the California Penal Code in that on April 12 he murdered John Wilson Nields.

Pagels, who had no funds for an attorney, was represented by Jeffrey Meacher from the Public Defender's Office. He pleaded not guilty to the charge.

After the arraignment he was transported from the courthouse to the Men's Central Jail on Bauchet Street, Los Angeles, where he was booked in at the Inmates' Reception Center. He was deloused under a shower of disinfecting agent and strip searched.

Officer Jay Pilbey gave him the rules of the jail. There were twelve or thirteen simple rules, the main ones being, "Keep your mouth shut" and "Address every policeman as mister, officer, or deputy." He then put a color-coded band on the suspect's wrist.

Due to overcrowding, he slept for two nights on the concrete floor but on the third night he was assigned a bunk in a cell with two other men.

————

Daniel Pagels was taken to McLaren Hall Juvenile Detention Facility. The child had no relatives other than his grandfather and two weeks later he was put into foster care with Don and Sandy Leutwiler of Granada Hills.

Mrs. Joan Briese, an official from the county department of social services, who made the difficult journey up to the motor home with Daniel, was unable to find many clothes or toys belonging to the child. When Daniel arrived at the Leutwilers', all his possessions were in a brown paper bag. There were a few items of clothing and a stick which the child said he used for snakes.

"He's devoted to that stick," Mrs. Briese told the Leutwilers.

The child watched them with big, attentive eyes.

Sandy Leutwiler was acquainted with the ponderous workings of the legal profession and knew that it would take months, perhaps years, for the case to come to trial. And from the look of things, it seemed that Daniel's grandfather was guilty and might get a life sentence.

She prepared herself to take on the boy for an indefinite period.

————

In the spring of 1988 the Van Nuys courthouse in the San Fernando Valley gave itself over to the pursuit of greater security, to grapple with the challenge of murder actually committed rather than recounted within its sanctified precincts.

A man had run into a courtroom and attempted to shoot a lady attorney. While the attorney ran for cover he had wounded a bailiff who had, in turn, shot and killed him.

It was at the time of a rebuilding and expansion program and some of the municipal courtrooms were in prefabricated buildings placed like gypsy encampments round the old courthouse, which was straining at the seams. It was difficult to provide security because of the odd, scattered nature of the courthouse. There was no central place where a scanner could be placed to uncover a hidden weapon. Perhaps a few more justices and attorneys placed pistols inside their jackets. Perhaps the bailiffs steeled themselves for another savage encounter but there was little else they could do but trust to providence.

They were not to know that the nature of the next assault they would receive would be of a completely different nature, one that would set the courthouse in a far greater turmoil than death would bring. One that, in some cases, divided families and caused civil war of the mind. And they were not to know that it would come in the shape of a penniless gardener from Chatsworth, Lawrence Pagels.

During the first few months that this potential troublemaker languished among the dope pushers and gangland assassins in the Men's Central Jail, Pagels had only one visitor, his court-appointed attorney, Jeffrey Meacher.

Pagels found it hard to believe that his visitor was not, in reality, working for the district attorney. Meacher's too-brief moments with his client were spent presenting the people's case. He would describe in glorious detail what the prosecutor was planning to throw at Pagels and then conclude that they would have to come up with something to give him, for Mark Boyman, the prosecutor, was a plea-bargain man.

Jeffrey Meacher would say later in his own defense that Pagels was not in the general line of murderers, for those who committed murder had a certain psychic smell, the stench of a killer. This man, he said, had none of this but neither did he have the sweet smell of innocence. It was as if such measurements did not apply to him. He said this as an indication that he noted something different about the guy, that he had not "slotted him away." These words stuck in Meacher's gut for many a long year as the result of an editorial in the *Los Angeles Times*.

The article stated, "Pagels' court-appointed attorney slotted him away as just another indigent killer. This was partly a racial decision as Pagels is of American Indian descent."

Meacher pleaded, "He didn't look all that Indian to me. It wasn't a racial decision. I was just so busy I didn't have time to piss. How could I know this thing was going to blow up so big?"

Toward the end of the fourth month of his incarceration Pagels received a visit from an attorney from Sacramento who was traveling through Los Angeles at the time.

The story of how Edgar J. Stassen became involved in the Pagels' case would later become the subject of myth. It obtained its myth-like proportions because few could explain why he took on Pagels and why he took the quantum leap into the unknown some time during the following weeks.

Perhaps it was the fact that Stassen's wife had just died of a sudden illness and he could not face going back to the house in Sacramento that they had shared for twenty-odd years.

This may have explained his prolonged stay in Los Angeles but it did not explain why he endured the mental turmoil the Pagels' defense brought him.

Ostensibly nothing in Stassen's life had prepared him for what he was to take on. An unremarkable career had resulted after he scraped through law school in Louisville and caught a Greyhound bus to California. It was on this bus that he met his future wife, Patti.

He was fired from his first job in the probate department of a San Francisco law firm and from several jobs thereafter because problems always arose. It always amounted to the same thing— plain, some said simple-minded arrogance. He was incapable of treating a senior partner as such.

By the time he shuffled into the attorneys' room at the Men's Central Jail to meet Pagels, Stassen had been working for himself for sixteen years.

Stassen was an untidy hulk of a man, whose shirt burst open just above his belt to reveal a bulging sliver of white flesh adorned with black hairs. His briefcase was an antique, stained by splashes of coffee and other indeterminate liquids, which he held before him like a tray because of its split sides.

He dropped his briefcase in front of Pagels and took a sip from his Styrofoam cup of coffee, which was spilling over his hand.

"Uh . . . Mr. Pagels. How ya doin'?"

This was a rhetorical question. He was not looking for an answer nor did he acknowledge the fact that Lawrence Pagels rose to attention when he walked into the room.

Pagels was a tall graceful man with a solid rocklike head, large forehead, deep-set eyes chiseled by a stonemason it seemed, and dark straight hair. In spite of a certain meekness he appeared to be in possession of the place.

If it were not for the words LA COUNTY JAIL stamped in large black letters on his back, he could have been a prison governor receiving a traveling salesman. He bowed his head politely and did not sit down until his visitor was seated.

"Let's see what we got here." Stassen produced a set of papers, waved them aloft in a theatrical gesture and set about squinting at them while he fumbled for his glasses. "Here you go. Pagels. Lawrence Pagels, right?" He looked up uncertainly.

"That's right."

Pagels observed that for a lawyer intent on procuring a new client he seemed curiously vague about the facts of the case.

"I wanna take this over from Jeff Meacher. You see him yet?"

"A few times."

"How long you bin here?"

"Four months."

Stassen scribbled on the back of an envelope and handed it to his client.

"Be careful what you say. This place could be bugged."

Pagels read it without changing his expression and handed it back.

"You're sixty-four, right?"

"Could be."

"Born in Ventura County?"

"Yes."

"Race. Native American." Stassen took off his eyeglasses and looked at him. "Pagels. That ain't Indian. You don't look Indian."

"My father's parents were from Amsterdam."

"Holland?"

"Yes."

Pagels noted that the attorney's fingers were browned by tobacco and his tie, like his briefcase, was flecked with coffee stains. He wondered how much of this man's down-home speech and his shabby appearance was an affectation.

Very little, he concluded by the end of their meeting, and he was not to change his mind. For he was about to get to know this man as well as anyone would ever do. It appeared that education, legal or otherwise, did not necessarily instruct a man on a tidy appearance or better speech. Edgar J. Stassen was a genuine slob who could, on occasion, feign gentility.

The accused murderer was also curious about Stassen's motives for coming to him. He did not seem like a philanthropic man but here he was offering his services free of charge. It was a mystery.

The prosecutor, Mark Boyman, was heard to remark later on, "That son-of-a-bitch tries to come across like Clarence Darrow defending the little man, but he's nothing but a fucking weasel."

Without the benefit of such professional insight Pagels was relying on the legal instruction he received from his fellow prisoners.
He had learned that a trial could be a gold mine to an ambitious
attorney if it was widely publicized. It would put him in the public
eye and even if he gave his services free of charge it would assure
him an abundance of future clients. Pagels' case, however, had not
exploded in the media. The fact that Stassen had first discovered
the case by reading about it in the newspaper proved only how
thoroughly he searched every page. Pagels' arrest had been covered
in a few lines hidden among other court reports in the Valley edi-
tion of the *Los Angeles Times*.

A fellow prisoner remarked to Pagels, "My man, you don't have
nothin' to offer this guy. I don't know why he's hangin' around
you unless he's queer for Indians. . . ." He laughed. "For old Indians. It's weird man."

To his credit Stassen had tried to clear up the enigma but his
explanation had been rejected by the jailhouse lawyers.

"Do you wanna know why I'm takin' this on?" He had asked
as he was on his way out the door.

"Yes."

"Because of the child."

Pagels' mouth quivered but he made no response.

"Normally you get fingerprints or fibers. But here you have a
six-year-old kid."

"Five. If you're counting years. He was five when it happened.
Just before his birthday."

"Right. Well a five-year-old kid found alone in a house at two
o'clock in the morning. Nothing else. No other evidence. A child
is the incriminating evidence."

Pagels stared mutely.

"First time I've heard of anything like that. Sort of hypothetical
shit you discuss in law school."

Stassen moved back into the room. "I suppose I should ask you
this. Did you go to the victim's house on er"—He fumbled through
his papers—" on April 12, 1988. Did you get into a fight, hit him,
and then panic and leave your grandson behind?"

"No."

On his second exit Stassen accepted several sheets of a yellow
legal pad on which Pagels had written in an elegant script his
account of what happened the night John Nields was murdered.
He had also included a detailed game plan for his defense.

"Please read this. It's all in here." He gripped Stassen's hand and would not let it go until he had received an assenting nod.

Even so, it was some weeks before it occurred to Stassen that Pagels' instructions could be in any way useful.

———

At an eleven-minute hearing on August 22, 1988, Edgar J. Stassen substituted for Jeffrey Meacher as defense counsel in the case of *People of California* v. *Lawrence Pagels.* And there were no questions asked.

No one was interested. It was just another case among thousands that steamed through the California courts, where judges handed out sentences like bored tour guides, where the drama was hidden behind the procedural process, where the stage and set never changed and the actors were all typecast.

———

Mrs. Sandy Leutwiler wore gold hoop earrings to accentuate the gypsyish style of her dark curly hair. She fiddled with the earrings and sat with a tight, nervous smile as Daniel Pagels conversed with his grandfather at the Men's Central Jail. She had placed herself at a small distance in an effort to give the child some privacy.

It was the first time in four months that Lawrence had seen the child. He looked intently at the child who had his nose pressed to the glass division.

"I'm going to get you out of here, Grandpa."

"Use the phone. Hold it closer to your mouth."

"I'm going to get you out of here, Grandpa."

"Good. I want to get out."

"I waited for Mrs. Leutwiler to bring me. It was a lot of waiting. Sheila was sick. Jason broke his toe. I had to wait."

"You do it their way. You be polite."

"I am polite."

"Good. So what's it like living in a real house?"

"They have a piano!"

"A piano. Oh boy."

"And four bathrooms!"

"That's nice." Pagels watched the boy's face with a joyful curiosity, as though he were a new pupil before a great teacher.

"Mrs. Leutwiler has a big pink bathroom in her bedroom, it's all pink and they have pink towels with flowers on."

"Oh boy." Pagel raised his eyebrows and his usually contemplative face broke into a smile.

"I wish you could come over and have a bath in that big pink tub."

"So do I, Danny."

"Are you sad here?"

"I'm busy with my thoughts like I always am. No one can lock my thoughts up. So tell me about the other bathrooms."

"O.K. Are you ready for this? Sheila has a bathroom all to herself and nobody's allowed in there."

"Incredible."

"She's a junior in high school and she has to spend a lot of time on her hair."

"Does she have a lot of hair?"

"Not really, but she's devoted to it."

"That's two bathrooms. How about the rest?"

"O.K. That's two. The third one has green and white tiles and it's Jason and Gregory's. And that's the one I use. It's a mess. No one flushes the toilet and we leave towels on the floor in puddles. Mrs. Leutwiler goes berserk about it."

"Do you flush the toilet?"

"Jason says it's not cool to flush the toilet."

"Do you have an opinion about that?"

"My feeling is, it's better to flush it."

"But you want to be cool?"

"No, I want to be with you."

Daniel's face lost the will to be cheerful. He began to cry.

Sandy Leutwiler looked very concerned. She had not wanted to bring the child here. She appeared to be on the verge of taking the boy in her arms and rushing out.

Lawrence Pagels spoke sternly. "Don't start crying. There's nothing to cry about. You know better than that. This is all gonna work out. You've got to help the Leutwilers. They're doing their best. Right?"

"Right."

"There's one more bathroom."

"O.K." Daniel gave it some disciplined thought. "There's one downstairs, and it has black tiles and black walls and gold taps shaped like swans. It's for visitors."

"You live in a palace, Danny."

Daniel looked glum. "I guess I do."

"What's Mr. Leutwiler like?"

"He's real big, as big as you but he has a lot more body. His arms and legs are real thick. He wears a red bathrobe and smokes a cigar."

"What does he do?"

"He owns restaurants. Not a lot. Maybe two."

"Do you get time to be peaceful?"

"Not really. The television is always on in the den. I've seen a lot of TV because that's what they do a lot."

"Before you go to sleep at night you can be quiet."

"I try to, Grandpa, but I'm in Jason's room and it's real hard. Jason's always talking about how good he is at Nintendo."

Before he was lead away by a relieved Sandy Leutwiler, Daniel took his final instructions from his grandfather.

"Hang in there, Danny."

"I'll try."

"We'll get out of this one way or another, right?"

"Right!"

———

Edgar J. Stassen had been driving down to Mexico in his Winnebago motor home when he read about Pagels' arrest. The newspaper article didn't say much, just that the body of John Nields had been found dumped on the Winnetka off ramp of the Simi Valley Freeway. Lawrence Pagels had been arrested and charged with his murder because a spot of the victim's blood had been found on the tailgate of his pickup truck and because his five-year-old grandson had been found alone in the dead man's house about four hours after the murder had taken place.

Stassen was on sabbatical from his Sacramento office. He took the newspaper down to Mexico and sat on a beach for a few months staring at the article from time to time. How could a man commit a murder, dump the body, and forget that he had left his grandchild behind in the victim's house? He had heard of people stopping at gas stations and driving off without their children. He had heard of one couple who left their baby on their car roof and drove off. But he had never heard of anyone committing a murder and leaving a child behind. It was unprecedented.

On his way back through Los Angeles Stassen decided to stay. He contacted the Public Defender's Office, drove up to the northwest San

Fernando Valley and parked his motor home on a burned-out lot in Chatsworth, hometown of the accused. And the rest was history.

Stassen was probably the only attorney in Los Angeles living in a Winnebago and this domestic arrangement had given rise to a lot of jokes about one guy in a trailer defending another guy in a trailer, that he wanted to get the guy off so they could open a Winnebago dealership . . .

His decision to stay in his motor home rather than rent an apartment or stay in a hotel was an economy measure, one of many economy measures in a situation that was about to balloon into a massive expense. His first move had been to set up the Lawrence Pagels' Defense Fund. It took him about a week to realize that the Lawrence Pagels' Defense Fund was a dead duck and would probably remain so. What seemed of interest to a lawyer looking for an excuse not to return home was not necessarily of interest to others.

Lawrence Pagels had no assets, no bank account, no money. His only possessions were his motor home and his 1969 pickup truck, neither of which could be turned into cash as they were of no use to anyone except Pagels himself.

The pickup truck had the added disadvantage of being held in a police garage in Van Nuys.

And as for the motor home, Stassen winced when comparisons were drawn between his polished, brand-new, Winnebago and Lawrence Pagels' almost medieval hut on wheels, which appeared to be welded into the earth. After only one visit Stassen realized that Pagels' vehicle was stuck there for all eternity. Over the years shabby pieces of timber and plastic sheeting had been tacked on to it, so that any signs of the original structure had gone. If any motor home was going to be sold to raise money for the defense fund, it would be Stassen's.

As another economy measure he put an advertisement in several campus newspapers requesting the aid of competant law students. The ad explained that those selected would receive invaluable experience but it made no mention of financial remuneration.

There was an immediate response from a dark-haired, skinny USC student who parked a new white Ford Mustang convertible with soft leather upholstery in the driveway. Her name was Ida Letherbridge. She wafted into Stassen's motor home in an elegant, understated silky beige suit and sat listening with exquisite politeness.

"You understand I can't pay you." Stassen explained.

Ida made no comment.

He looked out of the window at her car. "It doesn't look like it'd be a problem for you young lady. This"— he gestured around him—"is gonna be our office. No fancy high-rise in Century City. But let me tell you, you're not gonna meet a lot of lawyers like me." He said this as if it were more than compensation.

"You wanna work with an old sharpshooter like me, you have to give up your boyfriends, your weekends at the beach, your visits to the movies."

"O.K." she said crisply.

"It's not such a bad deal. There are a lot of kids who'd pay for the experience."

Ida gave him one of the cool looks he was to come to know so well. "Now that, I wouldn't do."

As soon as the preliminary interview was over and terms were agreed on, she found herself a seat in a corner and read through the prosecution briefs. Stassen chose her for her positive attitude, her calmness, and her efficiency.

However he needed two assistants and no one else answered his ad for the next two weeks. He had reached the point where he would accept anybody no matter what he thought of them, so that when Max Haydn turned up he was compelled to take the boy on in spite of everything.

A stocky, smartly dressed young man from Cal State, Northridge, he sauntered in for his interview and having been told the facts of the case said, "What is this? One old man in a trailer defending another old man in a trailer."

Edgar Stassen was fifty-one years old. He looked the young man up and down as though he were figuring out where to punch him. "Yeah, us old men stick together."

"I guess that's why you parked here." Max Haydn, unimpressed, pointed to the retirement home through the trees.

Stassen took an instant dislike to this cocky kid.

After Max had reluctantly agreed in theory to nonpayment for his services, he sat down in Stassen's chair and asked, "So did he do it?"

Stassen scowled. "He says he didn't do it."

"I was taught in my freshman year not to believe what people tell me."

"He says he didn't do it. I'm defending him."

"He says he didn't do it. But there's a universal truth here. Did he do it or didn't he do it?"

Stassen gave what appeared to be a small snarl.

"What've you been studying, cake decoration? Universal truth is a myth. As far as I'm concerned there's only my truth. In law you can be kept from telling everything you know. The jury doesn't judge the truth, they judge what they are told. It's my job to prevent the jury from hearing what I don't want them to hear."

Ida looked up from her notes. "But there is such a thing as truth and there are facts. And they will come out one way or another."

"I love facts," Stassen said. "Facts are like clay to me. I can make anything I like out of facts. Do you think I'd have sent both my sons to Princeton if I was held back by facts?"

"So he's guilty." Max said.

"He looks guilty. You got a guy who was in a dispute with the victim. You got the victim's blood in his truck. And you got the icing on the cake, his own kid left at the scene of the crime. And that, as Lady Bracknell would say, is a real fuck up. You don't leave your kid behind when there's a dead body around."

"He sounds guilty to me. Why don't we all go home?" Max leaned back and put his hands behind his head.

"So he looks guilty. You catch someone with cherry pie round his mouth you can figure out what he's been eating only if you're the district attorney. If you're defending you say . . ." Stassen waved his hands around wearily.

" . . . that someone threw it at him," offered Ida.

"Does anyone else look guilty?" asked Max.

"His wife maybe. The victim liked girls. She could have been brooding about it . . . who knows?"

Max shook his head. "Who are you kidding? Your guy's in deep shit."

"No he's not. I defended a man in Sacramento who hacked his wife to death in front of fourteen witnesses and the jury was out for more than nine and a half hours." Stassen held out his arms. "He's got me. That makes him innocent."

———

"How long have you been working for that turkey?" Max asked Ida as they walked down the weed-bordered path to their cars in the driveway.

Ida stopped and looked back at the speckles of evening sunlight gleaming from the Winnebago. The motor home had been driven squarely on to the place where a home once stood. Now there was nothing but rubble, blackened grass, and shrubs to testify to the catastrophe that took place there.

"I've been here two weeks," she said.

"I bet he doesn't even have permission to park that thing there."

"No, he probably doesn't."

"And why's he doing it? He wants us to work for nothing. He's working for nothing. What's in it for him?"

"It has something to do with his wife. She died a few months ago. And he took a year's sabbatical. That's all he's told me. I mean, he talks a lot, but he doesn't talk about that."

"And you're gonna work here until the trial? Do you know how hot it gets here in the summer? It can go up to a hundred and ten."

"Uh huh." She opened the door of her car.

Max looked the vehicle over. "How much did this set you back, twenty thousand? No wonder you're working for nothing."

Ida put the key in the ignition. Max leaned in the window.

"Do you know anything about him? What's his track record?"

"My father knows Joseph Lentner. . . ."

"Who the hell's he?"

"He's a municipal court judge who used to work in the district attorney's office in Sacramento. He told my dad that Mr. Stassen's O.K., not brilliant but he works hard."

"Did he say when he developed the neurosis about not paying his employees?"

"His only criticism was about his clothes. He ran into him the other day and he says he's gotten a lot worse. He thinks maybe it has something to do with his wife dying."

"What's wrong with his clothes?"

"Didn't you notice? Joe Lentner said he looked like an eccentric street cleaner. He thought Mr. Stassen might be making a social statement or something but it really didn't wash with most judges."

"You call him Mr. Stassen and he's not paying you a cent?"

"What would you call him?"

"For that money, 'hey you!' "

———

Once Max Haydn signed on to work for Stassen there were constant arguments about how much he would be reimbersed for expenses incurred in research—for gasoline, parking, stamps, stationery, etc.

Stassen's munificent gesture in waving his fee for the first time in his life made him stingy in all other areas. He would seldom provide money for coffee and donuts: he would play a waiting game, hoping that one of his assistants would weaken and bring in provisions. And usually it was Stassen who won that particular battle and it was Stassen who ate the lion's share of the donuts and who drank the most coffee.

Of the two assistants Ida Letherbridge would be the more notable. It was Ida Letherbridge who provided the odd mental insight that turned the whole case around.

And Ida was not, at first sight, the kind of girl one would think capable of making the amazing mental jumps that she made. She came from a wealthy family in San Marino who paid for her expensive clothes and cocooned her from many of life's problems. But the cocoon had not cut her off from herself. She was unique.

And although she never got the credit for it, it was Ida alone who caused the Pagels' defense to take its historic swing. Without her it would never have happened.

Max Haydn, on the other hand, came from a long line of bakers in Reseda. He was the first lawyer in the family and had his eye on future employment. Unlike Ida, he was concerned about public opinion. He had no wish to go down in the record book as a simple-minded fool and end up back in the bakery. He was one inch shorter than Ida and Napoleonic and controlling in his approach to life and the law.

That Ida Letherbridge prevailed over Max Haydn in persuading Stassen to take the course he did says less for her powers of persuasion than for Stassen's free-floating mentality at that particular time. With the death of his wife, his two sons in college, the abandonment of domestic life, a consciousness that had been relatively confined had, with a mixture of sorrow and relief, thrown off some of the old tethers.

One could say that a peculiar act of destiny had prepared Stassen to take on the Pagels case and he was ready when the time came. Though it must be said that Stassen did not see it like that then. He had to go through a lot of arm twisting. When Ida Letherbridge first approached him with the idea for the Pagels defense he thought it was cockamamie nonsense, the result of the heat of the valley summer sun—it was always hotter in the valley than in the cooler, richer areas over the hill.

It started when Ida found Pagels' statement and instructions written in his elegant handwriting on the yellow legal pad pages. It was the unique character of the aristocratic scrawl which caught her eye in the first place.

"What is this?" she asked Stassen.

"Pagels wrote that out. I couldn't make sense of it. I'm fighting the temptation to make a plea of mental incompetence. Anyone who reads that will think the guy's deranged."

Ida photcopied it and took the copies home with her. A few days later she made an appointment to speak to a physicist at UCLA. After that she contacted more than thirty leading physicists in the United States. These were the first steps in what later became known as the Quantum Trial.

Meanwhile Max Haydn was sent out every day to interview Pagels' and Nields' neighbors, to look for more witnesses, and to collect police reports. According to him, if he had not been so tied up, perhaps he would have been the one who turned the case around.

Whenever she heard this from Max, Ida, as all women do with men smaller than themselves, would smile benignly and never once call it Monday morning quarterbacking.

The Trial

Van Nuys Superior Court, October 1989

1

Mark Boyman, the prosecuting attorney, was a powerfully built man with the eyes of a starving ferret, in fact the eyes of a prosecutor. He wore dark colors, mostly navy blue in a subtly different variety of fine and wide pinstripes. They emphasized his dark and somber purpose. He was approaching forty but looked older. With his thick dark eyebrows and sleeked down shiny hair, he looked like a hired assassin. His only outstandingly human quality was his descent into frequent bouts of inarticulateness. For a successful prosecutor he was surprisingly unable to ask the most simple questions. Members of the jury who had watched many courtroom dramas on television were accustomed to hearing the prosecution throw incisive, quick questions at the witnesses. They were bewildered by Boyman's occasional meanderings.

He would later ask Graciella Sanchez, the Nields' maid, "Was the demeanor of the defendant of such a nature that would indicate, or from which you would construe er . . . some kind of stress indicative of, or let's say, resulting from some kind of altercation about the transfer of land or property?"

Miss Sanchez who had difficulty understanding any English, let alone Mr. Boyman's, chose to answer "Yes." She shrugged helplessly at a fellow Hispanic in the jury.

The prosecutor could also be obtuse about simple details. The layout of the victim's house caused him surprising difficulty and he took the best part of a morning trying to establish where the kitchen was in relation to the bedroom.

"You mean that bedroom A is on the upper floor, fifteen yards to the southeast of the kitchen?"

"No, you are looking at it upside down," he was told several times.

By the end of the morning the learned counsel was almost standing on his head but was still none the wiser.

Curious onlookers from Chatsworth sitting in the front row, unacquainted with the processes of law and knowing only the methods of Charles Laughton, Spencer Tracy, and a host of television actors, assumed that Boyman was employing a brilliant delaying tactic. It simply did not occur to them that Boyman's steel-trap mind had a few spongy areas and that he used one of them to understand maps and graphs.

The members of the jury quickly concluded that Stassen was no match for the prosecutor in appearance. His bow tie and beige corduroy suit with flared trousers legs were objects of derision. The suit, an antique from the early seventies when he had been decidedly slimmer, fitted neatly under his belly. Over the course of the trial the jury would take bets on how long it would take each day before his white hairy stomach would protrude through his shirt, another antique. There was even talk of clubbing together to buy him a shirt that would fit but they decided their five dollars a day jury payment would not stretch to cover that.

Stassen's hair was a frizzy gray entanglement and his gray-black bushy eyebrows grew like unchecked weeds on the coarse, flushed skin of his face. His briefcase was now new and expensive, purchased by Ida who had grown sick of the old one, but he still carried it like a tray in front of him as though expecting its contents to spill. The jury presumed that Stassen's appearance was a ploy, a means to put them at their ease. An attorney who looked like an old English sheepdog must be honest, reliable, and represent honest men. If asked about this, Stassen would have taken credit for it, but his appearance was something he never gave any thought: as so often happened the jury was overestimating the tactical abilities of the legal profession.

Halfway through the first morning of the trial the judge called for a ten-minute break and Stassen strolled out to the men's room. Once there he rushed to a toilet bowl and vomited.

Joe DeRosa, a bailiff, watched curiously as Stassen emerged from the stall.

"Hi," said DeRosa. "How are you doing?"

Stassen walked carefully to the sink. "I'm not doing too good."

He washed his hands and splashed water on his face. "You know what I'd really like to do? I'd like to fake a heart attack and get carried out by the paramedics."

He filled his mouth with water, swilled it around and spat it out.

"Because you know what? The victim isn't the victim. I'm the fucking victim." He pulled out a paper towel and dabbed it on his face and mouth. "I've been taken for a ride by my own client."

"No kidding."

"This is the end of me. I'll never work in this state again."

He threw the paper towel in a bin and left.

In the courtroom Lawrence Pagels appeared contemplative and removed from all the accusations made against him. He looked handsome in the new suit Ida had bought for him and knew nothing of the dissension it had caused. Stassen had been disturbed that Ida had bought the most expensive suit she could find instead of going somewhere reasonable like C and R Clothiers. So far he had refused to pay the bill.

Max Haydn repeatedly told her, "Get the money out of the bastard. Sue him."

The Van Nuys courtroom was not paneled with dark polished walnut grains but was lined with what looked like strips of plastic wood pressed into walls of dull mustard. The seats for the witnesses and trial watchers were the hard swing-type found in some extremely shabby old movie theaters.

Under the judge's podium, a raised altar, was not written "GOD IS LOVE" but "COUNSEL STATE AND SPELL YOUR NAME FOR THE RECORD." On one side was a witness stand, simply a chair on a platform. Behind the judge were the United States flag and the California state flag. And in the corner some unattractive filing cabinets that were used for leaning on by the bailiff. The jury sat on the right hand of the judge facing the filing cabinets. The courtroom had all the charisma of a dentist's waiting room.

The jury selection had been a long and arduous process and being selected felt, as one prospective juror remarked, like getting an Academy Award. There were not as many blacks and Hispanics as Stassen would have liked and there were not as many white

Republicans as Mark Boyman would have liked, but there were some of each.

There were five women and seven men chosen: of these, four were black, two Hispanic, and the remaining six were white.

They were: Angela Barry, clerical supervisor. Doria Rudell, housewife. Bruce Halpin, post-office worker. Alfred B. Turner, telephone maintenance man. Jorge Ramirez, refrigerator repairman. Antonio Rocha, employee of a water purifying company. William Perrott, lunch-wagon operator. Jake Schroeder, clothing store manager. Jane Sue Rodofsky, accountant. Bradley Ryker, retired Marine. Donna Fabry, dog breeder. Elvie Richter, receptionist, children's dancing school.

During the voir dire the two attorneys had phrased each question to prospective jurors to plant useful seeds in their minds.

"Do you," Mark Boyman asked each of them in turn, "understand that in order to find a defendant guilty you only have to find him guilty beyond reasonable doubt. That does not mean beyond any doubt whatsoever but just beyond reasonable doubt."

And the defense counsel Stassen said, "Have you read statistics that state that most murderers are under thirty-five years of age?"

The first day presented no surprises. The same procedure. A little more alterness. New faces. New jury.

The judge, William A. Conan, fifty-eight years old, balding, fit but already bored, explained the purpose of the opening statement to the jury. The outline of the case given by the counsels should not be taken as evidence per se but merely as a preview. Evidence could only be given by witnesses.

Mark Boyman's opening performance, for that's what it was, a performance rather than a statement, was funereal. He mourned the death of John Nields at the hands of an assailant whom he would prove, beyond reasonable doubt, to be Lawrence Pagels. He ennumerated the many witnesses who would convince the jury that Lawrence Pagels was the murderer. By the end of his oration the jury were glaring at Pagels with dull, accusing eyes.

Lawrence Pagels looked up as though in prayer to some higher force than the State of California; Edgar Stassen popped a breath mint in his mouth, shuffled his papers, and prepared to speak.

Unlike Mark Boyman, who strutted in his smart, sophisticated way up and down in front of the jury and spoke in his fifth-generation California accent, a comfortable, assured speech learned in the private schools and yacht clubs around San Pedro and Long Beach, Stassen leaned on his table like an old farmer and chatted to the jury. He was a neighbor in the next-door yard, he was everybody's "ole Stassen." And by the time he had finished the jury were beginning to think that a sweet old man like Lawrence Pagels was incapable of bludgeoning to death a weevil, let alone John Nields.

———

Daniel Pagels was brought into the courtroom by Sandy Leutwiler. He was wearing a J.C. Penney suit unwillingly loaned for the occasion by her younger son Jason. When Daniel climbed onto the witness stand, a smaller chair was provided, so that his feet could touch the ground.

Mark Boyman approached with a cheery smile that did not suit him.

"Hi, Daniel."

"Hi."

"How are you?"

"I'm fine."

"How old are you, Daniel?"

"I'm seven."

"Do you understand why you're here?"

"Yeah, you're going to ask me questions."

"Right, now I want you to answer in a big loud voice so everyone can hear, O.K."

"O.K.!"

"Not shouting though, just a big voice, O.K."

"O.K."

"Right, now can you remember the night you went over to Mr. Nields' house? It was over a year ago."

"Yes."

"Can you tell the time?"

"Yes."

"Can you remember what time it was then?"

"It was just after George went by."

"Who's George?"

"George has a German shepherd called Lady and he walks her up near our place every night."

"Did George see you?"

"Yes, he waved to me."

"Where was your grandpa?"

"He was asleep."

"Where?"

"In the bottom bunk."

"And you were in the top bunk?"

"Yes."

"Why were you awake?"

"I got up to go to the bathroom and then I couldn't get back to sleep."

"Why was that?"

"Because I wanted to see the puppies."

"What puppies?"

"Mr. Nields' puppies."

"How did you know Mr. Nields had some puppies?"

"Because me and Grandpa saw them."

"When did you see them?"

"In the morning."

"You and your grandpa went over earlier the same day?"

"Yes."

"And that's when you saw the puppies?"

"Yes, they were real cute. Their mother's a Labrador but I don't think their father is because Mr. Nields said she got out and he doesn't know who the father is. And he said I could have a puppy but he said he was going to have them put to sleep too. I guess he couldn't make his mind up."

"Do you know why your grandpa went to see Mr. Nields?"

"I guess so."

"Can you explain it to me?"

"I guess he wanted us to move our motor home."

"Was it a friendly meeting?"

"I don't know. I was in the kitchen with the puppies."

"Did you hear your grandpa and Mr. Nields shouting at each other?"

"Objection."

"Sustained."

"How was your grandpa after the meeting?"

"He was O.K."

"Happy? Sad?"

"Objection."

"Sustained."

"So what did you do after you waved to George?"

"I got out of bed."

"And what was your grandpa doing?"

"He was asleep."

"And then what did you do?"

"I went to see the puppies."

"How did you get there?"

"I just went."

"Mr. Nields' house is about ten miles away from your place. That's a long walk isn't it?"

"Not really."

"Did you have any shoes on?"

"No."

"What were you wearing?"

"My pajamas."

"Did you go down Topanga Canyon Boulevard?"

"No."

"Then how did you get there?"

"I can't remember, I just went."

"How long did it take you to get there?"

"Not long."

"And you went alone?"

"Yes."

"And where was your grandpa?"

"He was asleep."

"How did you get inside Mr. Nields' house? Do you remember when the police came in and found you there, they set off the alarm. How come you didn't?"

"Well I guess I'm small."

"How did you get in?"

"I just went in."

"Through a door or a window?"

"I don't know. I just wanted to see the puppies."

"Did you see Mr. Nields?"

"No, he wasn't there."

"Who was there?"

"Nobody. Just the puppies."

"How did you know there was nobody there? It's a big house."

"Because the dog barked and got real excited when I came in. She made a lot of noise and nobody came."

"Are you sure this all happened Daniel? Do you think maybe you just dreamed it?"

"Objection."

"Sustained."

"Thanks, Daniel, you can get down now."

2

There are those who do not count Van Nuys as part of California. When the wind drops and the temperature rises, the downtown air is so thick with pollution you could cut it with a knife. On a good day the palm trees look as if they are made of brown plastic: the rest of the time they are grayish black, like the shadows of palm trees. Van Nuys is a place people get out of.

One who escaped from Van Nuys returned to hear Daniel Pagels testify. A girl with white-blond hair parked her battered Pinto outside the house she used to live in as a child. She had been looking for a place to park and suddenly realized that she was driving along her old street. She thought it ironic that this familiar place was only ten minutes walk from the courthouse.

She gazed at the simple one-story structure with thin walls and the decaying porch where she used to sit and plan her getaway. The lawn was still dried out, probably because the owner wasn't any better off than they had been and could not afford to water it. The garage roof was still showing large patches of black roofing paper. It was seven years since she had left that house and very little about it had changed.

The girl stood for several minutes staring at the house before she walked over to the courthouse. She took the elevator up to the sixth floor and attempted to slip unnoticed into the back row of the courtroom, but her white-blond hair and her pale round face transfixed the attention of the bailiffs. She was one of five spectators in court that day.

After Daniel had testified he walked toward her seat in the rear of the courtroom and the girl leaned in toward the aisle to get a better view, her face exhibiting a pinched intensity.

Daniel stopped next to the row she was in, and turned to look back at his grandfather. The girl watched his back as closely as she had watched his face, and when he was out of the courtroom she studied the door he had gone through with equal vigilance.

She spent the night at a Van Nuys motel and the following day, Saturday, she joined the long line of prisoners' relatives and friends waiting to give their applications to officials at the Men's Central Jail. After an hour and fifteen minutes she went into the meeting hall and faced Lawrence Pagels through the glass partition.

Pagels stared earnestly at the girl for several seconds before he picked up the phone and spoke to her.

"I saw you in court."

She laughed painfully and then spoke with a nervous, breathy voice.

"It seems like it should be the other way round."

Pagels paused again to study the girl's white, bloodless face. His eyes were deadly serious.

"Where were you, Rhonda?"

She hesitated. "I . . . was all over. I've been up in Washington for a couple of years."

"Then you heard about this."

"Then I heard about this. I got myself ready. I wasn't going to come if I didn't feel right. I'm down to coffee and tobacco. Next it'll be one cup of tea a day. I'll be a princess."

"You've always been a princess."

"I just feel a little . . . raw. . . . Why have they got you in here?"

"I don't know. I've been trying to figure out if there's a purpose to all this. There should be. I can't see it yet. But I'm working on it."

There was another moment's silence. Then she attempted a smile. "I saw the old house yesterday. It's still the same old dump. Do you remember that hole in the ceiling?"

He shook his head. "I never got past her front door . . . your mother was a very literal woman. When she was young, she was quiet and I thought that meant she was a thinker." He shrugged.

"Well she's gone now."

He sighed and nodded. "She didn't tell me she was sick. She kept it to herself."

"She was always saying the last thing she wanted was you coming around being all spiritual."

Pagels smiled for the first time. "She didn't say that. You said that. You were always saying that."

They were silent again.

Rhonda touched the glass as though trying to get through. Daniel had done the same when he had visited the jail.

"I want to help but I don't know what to do."

"You need to look after yourself, Rhonda. Do you want to see Danny? I can give you his address."

Her eyes filled with panic. "Oh no! I mean, that's why I'm here I guess. I'm here for him. But he doesn't want to see me. I'm like . . . a last resort."

"No you're not, Rhonda."

"No, I guess. I'm not," she repeated without conviction.

"Edgar Stassen's been asking about you a lot. Is it O.K. if he calls you?"

"Sure."

"Do you have a number?"

"It's the Oasis Motel in Van Nuys. I don't know the number." She fumbled through her bag.

"That's O.K. Oasis. He can find it."

She looked up. "Are you scared?"

"I get scared."

When it was time for her father to go, Rhonda was reluctant to let him out of her sight. She remained in her chair, staring after him until an officer asked her to leave.

———

After Daniel's visit to the court Sandy Leutwiler could see that he was withdrawn and upset. The sight of his grandfather being escorted into the court by the burly bailiff with the gun in his belt had disturbed him. He was silent in the car on the way home and when they walked in the door he stood in the hallway looking trapped and alien, as though her house was the last place in the world he wanted to be.

"Play the piano again, honey. You did real well when you played it before."

Daniel hung his head and concentrated on moving one foot against the other.

"Do you remember how you used to play that tune you heard on the radio? The first couple of weeks you were here you played it all the time. Why don't you do it again?"

"I don't know."

"How come you don't know?" Sandy bent down and looked into the child's face. "Why don't you go and play with Jason?"

"He says he's too old for me."

"He's nine. What's so old about nine?"

"I don't know."

"And you're a real smart kid. You know a lot of stuff Jason doesn't know. And you can tell him I said so."

"I don't want to tell him. It'll only make him mad."

"Yes, you're right Daniel. You're smarter than me, too . . . well, what are we going to do about you?"

"Go and get Grandpa."

"I can't do that honey. I wish I could. Let's make some cookies. You can lick the bowl out. We won't tell Jason."

Sandy Leutwiler took the child's arm and tried to pull him toward the kitchen. He neither resisted nor went willingly, which was the way he did everything in the Leutwiler's house.

This rare moment of quiet companionship was blown to pieces by the arrival of Jason. Sandy had managed to assemble the ingredients for chocolate chip cookies and had persuaded Daniel to sit with the bowl and supervise the mixing, when Jason appeared. He eyed the paraphernalia on the table as though it were a plot against him.

"Can I lick out the bowl?"

"We'll see."

Jason moved close to the mixing bowl and stood guard.

Two minutes later Don Leutwiler, a big, muscular man, sweating and red-faced from the heat outside, came in and collapsed on a chair next to Daniel.

"How was the trial? Did Daniel give evidence?"

"Yeah, it was O.K. What are you doing here?" Sandy looked at him suspiciously.

"What am I doing here? I live here don't I?"

"Is something wrong?"

"I had to take the car in. I'm going to have to use yours tonight."

"How did you get here?"

"I walked. I left it down at the Exxon station. It's hot out there."

"What about Jason's soccer practice?"

"Sheila can drive him."

"Oh God. You try to pin down Sheila. Look at your hands. Are you going to wash them?"

"It's from the engine."

Jason inspected his father's hands. "You know Dad never washes his hands. He doesn't even wash his hands after he takes a shit because he was in Vietnam."

"When I was nine I didn't talk like that in front of my father." Don Leutwiler dragged himself from the chair and walked over to the refrigerator.

Jason smirked, pleased to notice that he had gained Daniel's attention. "Well let's face it, Dad, you rolled around in all that mud waiting for the Viet Cong. There weren't any washbasins or towels. So you just got out of the habit."

"Right, Jason."

"I'd like to get out of the habit."

"You weren't in Vietnam, Jason." Don Leutwiler took some orange juice out of the fridge and swigged straight from the carton.

"Mom won't let me do that," said Jason resentfully. "I have to pour it into a glass. But because you were in Vietnam you can get away with it."

"Right. You weren't there, Jason."

"I expect when you were out there rolling around in the mud with the Viet Cong you didn't have time to pour your orange juice into a glass. So you kind of got out of the habit."

"Right."

"I'd like to get out of the habit."

"You'll have to go to Vietnam first."

"Mom says that's why you're so mean."

"I did not say that."

"Yes, you did. You said being in the army made Dad mad and he's been mad at people ever since."

"That's right, Jason. The army is about a bunch of mentally deficient assholes telling you what to do every second of the day. It turned me into a killer."

"Did it make you want to go and get the Viet Cong?"

"No, it made me want to go and get everyone in the army. I wanted to kill the army."

Jason's eyes opened in amazement and he began to laugh. He banged his fist on the table and said, "Yeah!"

Daniel, imitating the older boy, laughed and banged his fist too, although he was not quite sure what was so funny.

Sandy Leutwiler was grateful to see that Daniel's eagerness to be like Jason, to have Jason like him, had made him forget the pain of his grandfather's trial. She hoped that this need to be accepted would help him forget his grandfather too, because she saw no future for them together.

———

Later that day Rhonda was chauffeured to Stassen's office by Max Haydn.

"Get her here before she disappears again," Stassen had said.

She arrived wearing loose black clothes and carrying a large and bulky cloth shoulder bag.

When she stepped inside the main room of the Winnebago, Ida was attempting to push several stacks of books out of the way in order to make room for the visitor.

Rhonda picked up one of the books, then another, and examined the titles.

Stassen came in from the adjoining room, drinking coffee and spilling it on his front.

"Why are girls wearing these baggy clothes? What happened to shape? Sit down, Rhonda. Nice to meet you at long last."

Rhonda was aware that she was being studied by these three people as she had never been studied before. She felt self-conscious and bent down to pick up another book.

"Physics. These look familiar. What are you doing with his books?"

There was a collective intake of breath from the three.

Stassen's eyes were popping. "Physics. He told you about the physics?"

"Yeah. He told me. But I didn't listen."

"You don't remember any of it?"

"No. I tuned out."

"Huh." Stassen looked frustrated. "So where have you been?"

"Oh . . . around."

"Why didn't you get in touch?"

"I couldn't ... I mean ..."

Ida bent over Rhonda as though trying to protect her from Stassen. "Can I get you anything?"

"Do you have a soda?"

"So Rhonda ... ," said Stassen. "Tell me about your dad."

"What do you want to know?"

"Who is he? What is he? Where's he from? Why does he think the way he does? Everything."

"Hasn't he told you all that?" She accepted a drink from Ida.

"Oh yes." Stassen rolled his eyes. "Your dad's a talker. But I want to hear it from you."

Rhonda looked blank.

There was an extraordinary tension in the air. Max Haydn was leaning against the wall, alert, on guard, like someone waiting for an assailant to spring out of the darkness. Stassen was drinking black coffee frenetically, his eyes boring into her. And Ida looked under threat, afraid of something.

"Is your father crazy?" asked Max. Ida frowned.

"No," said Rhonda. "He's not crazy. And he wouldn't kill anyone."

Stassen leaned in. "You're Danny's mother, right?"

She lowered her eyes. "Yes."

"When did you hand him over to Lawrence?"

"When he was two weeks old."

"How old were you then?"

"Seventeen."

"You haven't contacted him since?"

"No."

"Why not?"

She did not answer.

"You thought it was O.K. to leave him with your dad?"

"Yes."

"Was he a good father to you?"

"Yes."

"You ... er ... you've been in trouble with the law?"

"A couple of times."

"So you take after your father?"

"No."

"Why did you come back here?"

She looked uncomfortable. "I want to help."

Stassen poured himself some more coffee. "You want to help. How are you gonna do that?"

"By being here."

"You think being here is gonna help?"

"Why not?"

"Have you turned out the way your father wanted you to turn out?"

"Obviously not."

"Why do you think that is?"

"How should I know?"

"I guess it must have been tough stuck up in the hills in that old trailer?"

"I was only there on the weekends. I lived with my mom."

"How old were you when they separated?"

"Three."

"So there you were, on the weekends. Boring, huh?"

Rhonda frowned. "I guess so."

"What did you talk about?"

She didn't answer.

"Are you still into drugs, Rhonda?"

"Not any more."

"You're clean?"

"As a whistle."

"Rhonda ..." Stassen put his hand on her shoulder. "We're grateful for your input ... but ... we suggest you don't come to the trial anymore."

She looked startled. "You don't want me around?"

"We'd love to have you around, but it's better for your dad. You know ... we want to show how he's a good father ..."

"And I make him look bad?"

"No ... but look at it from Lawrence's point of view."

"He wants me there." She spoke in an emotionless, buttoned-up voice.

"He may want you there but he's not thinking of what's best for himself. If the prosecution finds out you're here, they'll go to town on your drug record, giving away the baby ... all that."

"But that's me. It's not him."

"They'll call it his bad influence."

"But it's not true."

"Honey, I'm asking you to stay home. Wait till it's over. Give your dad a break."

Rhonda stood up and walked to the door. Her mouth was tight.

"I'll drive you home," Max said quickly.

"No, thanks."

Ida stood up and put her arm round Rhonda. "I'll take you."

The two young women went out to Ida's car, which was parked at the end of the weed-covered drive.

Max watched them through the window.

"She doesn't like men," Max told Stassen.

"She doesn't like you," Stassen retorted.

3

The next witness for the prosecution was Mrs. Sharon Nields, a large blond woman in her fifties, the widow of the victim. She described her husband as a property developer. Her last conversation with her husband was on the morning of April 12, 1988, the day of his death. He kissed her good-bye and left their Palm Desert home at 6:30 A.M. to drive up to Los Angeles to inspect a development of new town houses in Encino. He had not been happy with the builder's work and had insisted on some alterations. He was going to stay overnight at their house in Bell Canyon and then return to Palm Desert the following day.

He was also planning to have a meeting with Lawrence Pagels.

"Why did he want to meet with Lawrence Pagels?"

"Because he wouldn't move his motor home."

"He wouldn't move his motor home off the wild ground near the freeway in Chatsworth?"

"No, he refused to move."

"Why did your husband want him to move?"

"He was building ten luxury homes with gates and a security guard."

"Had he started work on the building?"

"No, he couldn't with that darned motor home right in the middle of everything."

"Had your husband offered him money to move?"

"He'd offered him everything."

"Your husband had bought the land around the motor home?"

"Yes."

"Does Mr. Pagels own his piece of land?"

"So he says."

"You don't know for sure?"

"No. He said it was Indian land and the city was looking into it but they were taking their time, and meanwhile my husband was losing a lot of money."

"You didn't believe it was Indian land?"

"Johnny didn't. He said maybe it was once but the Indians all left years ago. And this guy's not even a whole Indian. And who's to say he's from some Chatsworth tribe? How could anyone know. They all died out years ago."

When Mark Boyman sat down Edgar Stassen stepped forward, laid his hand gently on the witness stand, and expressed his deep sadness at the untimely death of her husband. Then he bowed regretfully, the niceties being over, and commenced his cross examination in a more gentlemanly, less down-home speech than he had used for his opening statement. "Did your husband know anything about the history of Indians in Los Angeles?"

"No. Well, no more than anyone else."

"Did he know if Mr. Pagels was descended from a Chatsworth tribe?"

"No, but he knew he was half Dutch."

"Did he think that Mr. Pagels was an unusual man?"

"No. He never said that. Well, maybe he thought he was kind of weird living out there the way he did."

"And what did you think of Mr. Pagels?"

"Objection. That's irrelevant."

"Sustained."

"Would you say that your husband was a friendly guy?"

"Oh sure."

"I notice that he lost a few secretaries over the past few years. Was he bad tempered and critical?"

"Objection."

"Sustained."

"He used to have a partner? What happened to his partner?"

"They parted company."

"A disagreement?"

"Sort of."

"Wouldn't you say that your husband was difficult to get along with and had made a lot of enemies?"

"Objection!"

Stassen and Sharon Nields were natural enemies.

To be stuck on that stand while Stassen threw bricks at her was more than she could handle. Many times during the hour-long cross examination she scratched her long red fingernails on the edge of her chair as though it were Edgar Stassen's cheek. But Stassen thrived on her annoyance.

"How long were you and Mr. Nields married?"

"Twenty-six years."

"Did you telephone him on the night he died?"

"Yes, I did."

"What time was that?"

"About six o'clock."

"And how long does it take to drive from Palm Desert to Bell Canyon?"

She looked offended by the implications of that question.

"About two or three hours. It depends on the traffic."

"About two hours late at night, wouldn't you say?"

"Yes."

"Did you drive anywhere on April twelfth?"

"I did some shopping and I went to the car wash."

"And in the evening?"

"Ray wasn't feeling well so I gave him an aspirin and he went to bed early."

"And then what did you do?"

"I stayed in for the rest of the evening. I was worried about Ray."

"Ray?"

"My son."

Sharon Nields did not look at Stassen as she left the witness stand but she did throw a bitter, accusing glance at Lawrence Pagels. Then she fell into the arms of her burly son, Raymond, and was half carried from the courtroom.

The next witness was Gregory Lipman a seventeen-year-old student from Chatsworth High School who literally tripped over the body of John Nields on the Winnetka off ramp of the Simi Valley Freeway. At 1:10 A.M. on April 13 Lipman had abandoned his car after running out of gas. The Winnetka off ramp, where he came to a halt, was built in 1982, but was never opened because the wealthy residents of the nearby Monteria Estates did not want public traffic through their private avenues.

Lipman ran to the Monteria Estates and reached the first house about 1:25 A.M. and rang the doorbell. He shouted that there had been a murder but no one came to his aid. He went to several other houses but received the same treatment. Finally he ran a mile or so down to the phones outside Ralph's Supermarket on Devonshire Boulevard and called the police.

Several police and forensic experts testified. It was established that the murder had been committed roughly three hours before the discovery of the body. The victim had been killed at another location and then dropped at the Winnetka off ramp, an area seldom frequented by cars or people. There were no detectable tire tracks that could be said to have been made by the defendant's car.

Dr. Harish Patel, who had performed an autopsy on the body, stated that the victim was a white male sixty-nine inches tall, weighing 182 pounds. There were two head wounds, one of which had pierced through both layers of skull into the cranial vault. The victim had also been stabbed once through the left side, penetrating a major subclavian vein to the heart.

Officers Jerry Henderson and Wayne Burg testified that they went to the victim's home in Bell Canyon at 2:15 A.M. and assumed the house was unoccupied until they saw a light coming from what turned out to be the kitchen. Looking in the window they saw a small boy, Daniel Pagels, with a Labrador bitch and her three part-Labrador puppies. The child could not open the complex lock on the kitchen door to let them in and when they made a forced entry the burglar alarm was set off.

There were no other occupants in the house at that time. In the den on the other side of the house there were signs that a struggle had taken place and there was blood on the carpet and desk.

———

Sharon Nields had always gone to the Bell Canyon house under protest. She preferred their other home in Palm Desert. She loved its flowers and fountains, the more exotic attractions of life in a desert oasis. The rugged hillsides around Bell Canyon were too primitive for her. John Nields had liked it. The house had been a useful base for his business negotiations. But his wife had prayed for the day when he would confine his business deals to the Palm Desert area. That, of course, was now immaterial.

She had come up to Los Angeles for the trial and she would return as soon as it was over. She had no desire to live in that house any longer than necessary.

It had been unoccupied since the death of her husband. The gardeners had hosed the leaves off the tennis court, the pool man had swum in the pool with his girlfriend, and the maid had dusted and vacuumed, but no one had lived there during that time. It had a serene, well-kept appearance and gave no hint of the violent death that had taken place within its white-walled Spanish splendor.

The brown stain of John's blood was still on the carpet. They had argued about that carpet. She had said that white was impractical for a study because it would show the marks.

"Well, I was right," she thought.

The Bell Canyon house was alien to Sharon. One of John's designers had furnished it according to her own taste not Sharon's, so there were none of the cherry pink couches and leopard skin cushions she favored but pieces upholstered in rather more muted tones, soft grays and whites which blended in with the gentle white curves of the Spanish architecture. Some liked it. She found it too bland.

The house was on two floors. On the ground floor was a large hall, the size of a small ballroom. The upper story landing circled the hall, and the four upstairs bedrooms, each with its own bathroom, had doors opening out onto the landing.

In the master bedroom, unslept in since John Nields' death, everything seemed waiting for his return. His shaving kit was by the sink, his bathrobe hanging on the door.

There was a bottle of Shalimar perfume in the cabinet.

"It's not mine," she told Raymond.

In the walk-in closet were two dresses that did not belong to her.

"Did you tell the police about these?" she asked him.

"Sure. I told them they were yours."

He spoke in that childish, resentful way he reserved for her. He had difficulty establishing his manhood around his mother. It did not help that at twenty-three his fleshy, round face revealed few signs of adulthood. A photograph of him at age nine, which was on the piano in the Palm Desert house, showed a face almost identical to the one he had now.

"This one's not mine. Neither is this. I couldn't get into them. You should have told them that."

"You were there. Why didn't you tell them?"

"I couldn't think. Maybe I did tell them. I don't know what I said."

"You didn't tell them anything. All you did was say 'Oh God' a million times over."

"Did I? Did I? Oh, Ray . . . who would ever think this would happen to us?"

"I'm not going to tell the police about this. It won't make any difference. Everyone knows about Dad."

"What do you mean?"

"Oh come on. It's no good pretending he's a saint just because he's dead."

They went downstairs. Sharon insisted on going outside and touring the tennis courts and the lawn at the back.

"Not a scrap of crabgrass," she noted approvingly.

The trees that lined the front driveway needed trimming. They were hanging over the drive making it almost tunnellike in some parts.

"John would have told the gardener about that," she said to her son but by that time he had gone back into the house.

She noted that the large white boulders that were gathered in clusters at the foot of the trees were spattered with sap from the conifers.

She stared at the boulders with growing consternation.

"Oh my God," she said.

———

A forensic expert, Dr. Jason Phinney, told the court that John Nields' blood had not only been found on the carpet and desk in his study but also a small amount, an eighth of an inch square, had been found on the tailgate of Lawrence Pagels' pickup truck.

There was no evidence that the body had been dragged out of the house so he concluded that it was carried to an awaiting vehicle. There were very few fingerprints in the study as someone had wiped all the surfaces carefully, but a clear print of Lawrence Pagels' had been found on the arms of a wooden captain's chair.

Police Officer Roy Picardi testified that he drove up to Lawrence Pagels' motor home in Chatsworth at 3:05 A.M. He knocked on the door and looked through the window and saw that the defendant appeared to be sleeping.

Boyman asked him, "Did Mr. Pagels seem surprised to discover that his young grandson, who was only five years old at the time, was not at home sleeping in his bed?"

"No, sir."

"How would you describe his reaction?"

"He seemed to accept it."

"And what did he say when you informed him that his grandson had been abandoned at the scene of a murder?"

Stassen waved his hand. "Objection. There is no proof that he was abandoned."

The objection was sustained.

Boyman tried again. "What did Mr. Pagels say when you informed him that his grandson had been found at the scene of a murder?"

"Sir, he said, 'Hold on, I'll get my pants on.' "

Much laughter in court.

Judge Conan leaned forward over the bench and warned everyone present that they were not watching a television situation comedy. This was the law. This was real.

George Lejeune, a partner in a prosperous Canoga Park plumbing firm, was the next witness. A small plumpish man, close to retirement, he would glance over at the defendant from time to time and smile.

Boyman asked, "Are you acquainted with the defendant Lawrence Pagels?"

"Yes, I see him every day. That is, I used to see him."

"What time of the day?"

"Around eleven thirty at night. I leave home at eleven and take my dog for a walk up in the hills near his motor home."

"Every day?"

"Just about."

"Can you cast your mind back to the night of the Nields' murder?"

"Yes, it's very clear in my mind."

"Can you remember anything specific about that night?"

"Yes. When I got to their place Mr. Pagels had gone to bed and the boy was awake."

"How did you know this?"

"I went up to the window and looked in. I always do."

"And what did you see?"

"I saw Mr. Pagels asleep in his bunk and the boy sitting up on his bunk with his legs dangling over the edge. He was swinging his legs like kids do."

"Was Mr. Pagels under the covers?"

"Yes."

"He appeared to be asleep?"

"Yes."

"Could you know for sure that he was really asleep?"

"Looked like it to me."

"Could you see what he was wearing?"

"No, he was under the covers."

"So he could have been wearing day clothes?"

"Objection, he's leading the witness."

Judge Conan sustained the objection.

"What was Daniel Pagels wearing?"

"Pajamas."

"Did he see you?"

"Yes, he waved to me."

"And did you speak to him?"

"I said it was time he was asleep. I looked at my watch and told him it was exactly eleven thirty."

"And what did the boy do?"

"Nothing. He just went on sitting there swinging his legs. When I left, that's just how he was."

After the direct examination, Mark Boyman sat down, content to have established that as late as eleven thirty on the night that John Nields was murdered, a witness had seen the defendant and his grandson together.

Stassen walked up to the witness stand for the cross and stood with his hands in his pocket, his shirt pulling open a fraction at the stomach, and his bow tie dipping to one side. He looked like an attendant at a second-rate carousel.

"How ya doin', Mr. Lejeune?"

"Oh fine."

"Now let's see here. You said it was eleven thirty P.M. when you went up to the trailer that night."

"Yes it was."

"How can you be so sure?"

"For several reasons. It takes me exactly thirty minutes to walk to their motor home from my house and I leave my front door every night just as the eleven o'clock news is coming on. And that particular night I made a special point of looking at my watch when I got up there."

"Why was that?"

"Because I was surprised to see the child awake."

"He was usually asleep at this time?"

"Yes. Sure. A five-year-old kid is usually asleep at that time. I showed him my watch through the window, it's a digital watch, and he read out the numbers. He said, "One, one, three, zero." That's how I remember it was exactly eleven thirty."

"How do you know your watch is accurate?"

"Because I always check it every night when the eleven o'clock news comes on."

"Did you see Lawrence Pagels the next day?"

"Yes I did. He wasn't asleep the next night, he was sitting on the steps of the motor home, I reckon he sat there all night."

"Did he discuss the murder with you."

"He said he had no idea why anyone would want to murder John Nields."

"Did he say anything else?"

"Yeah, he said something like . . . er . . . life was eternal and Mr. Nields had been pushed violently on . . . and . . . er . . . he was on a voyage of discovery. And he said that he and Daniel would pray for Mr. Nields."

"What else did he say?"

"Well, he said a lot of stuff along those lines. I can't remember all of it. But he said Mr. Nields was a man who thought too much of money and profit and in his future existence he'd have to struggle with that for a while until he could see his way through it."

"Did he tell you how his grandson got to Mr. Nields' house?"

"No sir, he did not."

"Did you ask him?"

"Yes I did. And he said it was a mystery."

"A mystery to everyone including himself?"

"He didn't say."

The next witness the prosecution called was Mrs. Arlene Tullis who lived in the Bell Canyon home adjacent to the Nields' house. Mark Boyman remained seated while his fellow prosecutor

Harvey Marlatt stood for the direct examination. Marlatt was a thin, prematurely balding graduate of New York University Law School. He had something of the appearance of a dried cockroach, one who had crawled into an old Bible, been pressed between the pages and had all the juices drawn out of him. Whenever he sat down, he flattened into the chair and became part of the wood.

He approached the amply proportioned, red-haired Mrs. Tullis as though she were a frog about to be dissected.

"Mrs. Tullis, were you acquainted with the deceased, John Nields?"

"Yes, I was."

"And you can see his house from where you live?"

"Yes we're on a hill that looks down over the Nields' house."

"On the morning of April 12 did you see Mr. Nields?"

"Yes, I did. I was in my bedroom putting on my makeup by the window and I saw Mr. Nields opening the front door and some visitors leaving."

"And who were these visitors?"

"They were that gentleman there and a little boy."

"May it be recorded here that the witness pointed toward the defendant Lawrence Pagels. . . . Mrs. Tullis, can you describe the departure of these visitors. Was it pleasant, friendly?"

"No it was not. It seemed like they were having an argument."

"What gave you that impression?"

"John Nields was waving his arms at Mr. Pagels and he had a real angry look on his face."

"And how was Mr. Pagels responding?"

"He seemed calm."

"Was there any physical violence between the two of them?"

"No. Mr. Pagels just took the little boy's hand and walked away to an old pickup truck and drove off."

"Was that the last time you saw Mr. Pagels and his grandson that day?"

"Not exactly. Just before I went to bed I went to close the curtains and I saw that the Nields' house was in darkness except for some Malibu lights round their pool. Then a light went on in the kitchen. It was sudden. It caught my eye."

"Could you see anyone in the kitchen?"

"Well, just about the same time as the light went on, the dog started barking. Then I saw a little boy in pajamas."

"What was he doing?"

"I couldn't see."

"Do you know if Mr. Nields had a burglar alarm in the house?"

"Yes, he did. It seemed to be easily triggered. They were always setting it off by mistake."

"Then the boy could not have climbed through a window without setting off the alarm?"

"Oh definitely not."

"Someone must have let him in?"

"Well, I guess so."

"Thank you, Mrs. Tullis."

Edgar Stassen stood up for the cross examination. He nodded appreciatively at the splendid Mrs. Tullis.

"Ma'am, do you remember what time the Pagels left Mr. Nields on the morning of April 12?"

"Not really. I guess it was between nine and ten."

"You say you saw John Nields waving his arms excitedly?"

"Yes, he seemed upset."

"Did you notice if he pursued Lawrence Pagels' pickup truck down the driveway?"

"I couldn't see everything that went on down there."

"Did you see him take hold of Mr. Pagels' pickup truck in an attempt to stop him driving away?"

"No, I didn't see that."

"Are there several tall trees obscuring your view along the driveway?"

"Yes, there are."

"So what can you see?"

"I can see the front door. Then there are some trees and after that I can see the end of the driveway."

"Did Mr. Nields walk or run toward the truck?"

"He was moving very fast."

"Did he have his hand toward the truck?"

"He was waving his hands."

"In the direction of the truck?"

"Yes."

"And as he moved forward he went behind the trees and out of your sight?"

"Yes."

"And the truck was also behind the trees?"

"For a while, yes."

"And then the truck appeared?"

"Yes, it came down the driveway and pulled out onto the street."

"And Mr. Nields came back into your view and returned to the house?"

"Yes."

"Was he holding his hand in any way to indicate that he might have injured it, cut it perhaps, when he caught hold of the moving truck?"

"Objection, Your Honor. He's conjecturing about something that went on behind a tree."

Boyman grinned slyly at the jury and Judge Conan looked at his watch.

"Confine yourself to what the witness saw."

Stassen was not deterred. "Was he holding his hand ... in an unusual manner?"

Mrs. Tullis looked apologetic. "I can't remember ... I mean I wasn't paying attention to every little detail."

"You can't remember." He stared meaningfully at the jury. They all stared back.

Stassen paused for a few seconds to allow the information to sink in and then he moved on.

"That night, when you were standing at the window, the Nields' house was in total darkness?"

"As far as I could see it was. It's a big house."

"What rooms can you see from your bedroom window?"

"The house is down the hill and at an angle to us. So I can see the front door and above that the main bedroom and below it, round the side, I can see the kitchen door and window."

"So there was a house in total darkness and all of a sudden a light went on."

"The light went on and almost simultaneously the dog started barking."

"How long did the dog bark?"

"Quite a while."

"Long enough to wake anyone in the house?"

"Absolutely, that dog was making a racket."

"Did lights go on anywhere else in the house?"

"No."

"Did anyone come to the kitchen?"

"No. Just the boy."

"Can you remember what time the light went on and the dog barked?"

"It was when the Johnny Carson show started."

"Can anyone back you up on that?"

"Oh sure. My husband and my son were just about to turn off the TV downstairs when the Johnny Carson show started and the barking started at the same time. So they went outside to check if there were any strange cars around."

"And did they see a car?"

"No. So I shouted down to them that I thought the little kid was just a house guest."

"You thought that kid was a houseguest?"

"Sure I did. He was in his PJ's."

"And you're convinced it was exactly 11:30 P.M. when all this happened?"

"Yes. Because my husband was yelling at my son that he should be in bed before the Johnny Carson show. And Ed McMahon was yelling, "Here's Johnny!" And my son was yelling back that it was not so terrible to be out of bed. And the light went on and the dog started barking, all at the same time. So I remember it very well."

"Thank you kindly, ma'am. We all appreciate ya comin'."

4

Rhonda Pagels withdrew quickly from the courtroom, hoping to avoid any further orders from Edgar Stassen. Her need to be out of the building fast was overcome by a greater need to get a light for her cigarette. She unwisely stopped an elderly woman in a pink jogging suit in the hall.

"Do you come everyday, honey?" the woman asked. She was one of a group of senior citizens who dropped in on trials from time to time; this time it was the Pagels trial. She offered Rhonda a dog-eared book of matches.

"Yes . . . I'm a journalist."

"Uh huh." She was unimpressed. "I come here for the exercise. I walk here, walk round the halls, walk home. I've been trying to figure out what that attorney was getting at. He's saying the little boy was seen in two places at once."

"Oh no," Rhonda said quickly. "I don't think so."

"Then what's he getting at? I can usually figure it out but this I don't get."

Max Haydn was coming down the hall toward her.

"No," Rhonda edged away. "Neither do I."

She moved toward the elevator and caught one as it was closing. She saw Max Haydn's hand grabbing for the doors but he was too late.

She was determined to be in court every day. She had been preparing for this for a year. She had bought a classic gray suit and a briefcase from a thrift store and looked, as far as she was concerned, subdued and creditable. They could not keep her away.

She needed to get an evening job in a restaurant or a bar to keep herself going. She also wanted to buy Daniel a present. She remembered Lawrence once made her a doll of straw and brightly colored pieces of cloth, brilliant turquoises and flashy reds and all kinds of yellows and oranges. She loved that doll. But when she went to live in Van Nuys with her mother she saw other children with dolls from Sears and K mart and grew to be ashamed of that doll. She stuffed it in the spokes of her bicycle and rode it to death. The straw flew in a thousand directions.

Rhonda wanted to get something for Daniel that he would be proud of. She would buy him a good truck and send it without signing her name. She knew she was nothing to him. She was invisible. Incognito. A fly on the wall.

——

At night, after each day of the trial, Lawrence Pagels sat in his prison cell and thought of his grandson in the house with all the bathrooms. Daniel had been there for over a year now. Too long. The boy needed his freedom. So did he.

He sat and waited. He wanted to be with his grandson again, wanted to see him grow. It was the greatest need and pleasure of his life.

If he could come through these days in court and remain unmarked by it, he would be a better man. He chose to lift his thoughts each day, to rise above the powerful personalities in the courtroom. He was there but he was not there.

But he did see Rhonda. It was hard not to see the mass of white-blond hair, the pale plump face. She had come back and he was grateful for her presence. He knew what it had cost her to be there.

In his cell he prayed. And when he was not praying he thought of the motor home and the untouched, wild land around it that he and Daniel loved so much.

His mother had told him many stories about that land. She was part Gabrielino, part Fernandino though she called herself a Tong-va Indian. Lawrence Pagels remembered her old face becoming fiercely animated as she recounted what she had been told about the Indians of Los Angeles County. One story she used to tell was of a young boy, the son of a chief, who lived over two hundred years ago in an Indian village in the hills above Chatsworth. His title was Tomear. At night he would lie down to sleep within yards of the spot where Pagels' trailer was now situated.

The young Tomear used to run over the curved and fantastic shapes of the rocks and look down on what is now Chatsworth Park. Where joggers run with their Walkmans and teenagers throw beer cans and buy drugs, then there were deer and antelope running through the wilderness.

The boy lay naked on the rocks and watched the rabbits. He had no clothes for not one of the boys or men in his tribe wore them. They were only for the women who wrapped grass aprons around their waists. Sometimes he went to soak himself in the sulfur springs. His skin was of the palest brown, not as dark as the adults in his tribe and not nearly as dark as the smiling woman who sat under the tree all day and who was said to be one hundred and thirty years old.

The child loved the sun as it was a sign to him of the Great Spirit who smiled down on him. All things were given by the Great Spirit and yesterday and today and tomorrow were all as one to him.

In this timeless existence the young Tomear bathed and laughed until one day, which has gone down in history as August 5, 1769, three Spanish padres came into the San Fernando Valley. They had camped in the Indian village of Yang-na, which is today called Los Agneles, and then climbed over the mountain and saw below them a vast expanse, an enormous, beautiful valley encircled by mountains.

Tomear, who was at that time eight years old, went with his father to present gifts to the visitors. News had traveled swiftly round the valley of these strangers who were not white men as such. Born in Spain with dark hair and olive complexions, their skin beaten by the winds and sun in their long journey from Mexico, they were by no means pale. They did not look unlike the Indians if one were to judge by skin.

But there the resemblance stopped. They were steeped in a concept of life that made them like remote black holes to the Indians. The Spanish padres came to clothe the naked bodies of their hosts and to teach them they were guilty by the very fact of their birth. They told the Indians that the Great Spirit who had always smiled on them would not now smile on them unless they repented. And the Indians, including Tomear, bowed to the superiority of these elegant men from the south and became convinced of their own sinfulness.

Though sometimes Tomear would run over the rocks and feel the sun on his back and he would wonder how this could be.

Lawrence Pagels remembered this story of the young Tomear and he noted that this child and his family were destroyed by the men who called them sinners. He could learn from that. They had not been prepared but he would be. Lawrence Pagels vowed that his own sense of justice would not be crushed by another man's. He would not be destroyed.

––––

The first witness for the defense was Jayne Niemann, a former secretary of John Nields who had dark bobbed hair, a round face, and small deep-set eyes that looked like raisins in a piece of raw dough. Accompanying her were eight members of her family, several of whom had the same doughlike face with the very same raisins. They filled two benches of the small courtroom and sat in petrified, silent awe of the proceedings.

Edgar Stassen approached the wittess box with the assurance of a fox in an overcrowded chicken house. He was wearing a large maroon bow tie and a crumpled cream linen jacket that looked as if it had come out of an old theatrical truck. He smiled at the witness.

"How ya doin', Miss Niemann?"

"Fine."

"Miss Niemann, when did you work for John Nields?"

"Almost four years ago."

"How long did you work for him?"

"About six months."

Stassen raised his eyebrows in astonishment. Like all good attorneys he never asked a question to which he didn't know the answer. But that did not prevent him from feigning surprise.

"Only six months? Was there some disagreement?"

"I guess you could say that, yes."

"What kind of relationship did you have with Mr. Nields?"

"Not the sort he wanted to have."

"Could you explain."

"He was always a toucher, you know what I mean. He'd ask you to do something, you know, like type a letter, and he'd touch."

"What would he touch?"

"Objection. This is prurient."

"Confine your questions to what's relevant Mr. Stassen," said Conan.

Stassen did not let it go. "Was it your decision to stop working for John Nields?"

"Yes. On account of the touching and because he'd make you work late and he wouldn't pay overtime."

Boyman was annoyed. "Objection, Your Honor. This relationship is too remote to have any relevance."

Judge Conan agreed. "I don't see any point in going on with this."

Stassen, content with having presented the deceased as a lascivious skinflint, asked Miss Niemann to step down.

The next witness was Deborah Hillier, a tall woman in her forties with blond hair styled in a neat pageboy: she wore modest clothes and had the shyly enthusiastic manner of a nineteen fifties' coed.

"Mrs. Hillier, ma'am, were you John Nields' secretary at the time of his death?"

"Yes, I was."

"How long had you been working for him?"

"For three years."

"And where did you work for him?"

"Sometimes in his office in Encino, sometimes in the house in Palm Desert, sometimes in Bell Canyon."

"Were you present on the morning of April twelfth when he met Lawrence Pagels and his grandson Daniel at the house in Bell Canyon?"

"No, I was not."

"Did he tell you about it?"

"Yes, he did. He told me that Mr. Pagels was being stubborn."

"Were those his exact words?"

"No. He said 'hard-assed.' "

"And did you get the impression that the two men had been involved in a violent argument?"

"No, not exactly. Mr. Nields was a man with a . . . well, he was expressive, you know, he waved his arms around a lot. Everything was an event. He could get excited about a sandwich."

"So maybe this meeting between Pagels and Nields was not so hostile? Would you say that when Mr. Nields was waving his arms about and shouting on his doorstep as Mr. Pagels was leaving . . . would you say that he was simply expressing himself normally?"

Boyman objected. "He's asking for a personal opinion."

Conan upheld it.

"Mrs. Hillier, ma'am," Stassen asked. "In the course of your work did you often meet Mrs. Nields?"

"Yes. I saw her sometimes in the Encino office and when I went down to Palm Desert.

"Was Mr. Nields relationship with his wife explosive like all his other relationships?"

"Well, yes."

"And would you say that Mrs. Nields was a similarly explosive person, someone who enjoyed an argument?"

"No, she looked like she got real upset. Mr. Nields was a lot to handle."

"Why was he a lot to handle?"

"He was . . . he er . . . he did what he liked. For the first year I worked for him Amy Deerborn was living in the house and Mrs. Nields didn't like that too much."

"Who was Amy Deerborn?"

"She was a business associate, I guess. She'd been in real estate and he used to consult with her about property."

"And was Amy Deerborn an attractive woman?"

"Objection. This is irrelevant. He's wasting the court's time."

Conan drawled, "Get to the point Mr. Stassen."

Stassen got to the point. "Why was Amy Deerborn living in the house?

"Because Mr. Nields liked to have her there."

"And this arrangement upset Mrs. Nields?"

"Oh sure."

"And why did Amy Deerborn leave eventually?"

"Because she got married and moved to Canada."

"And Mrs. Nields was relieved?"

"Yes, I believe so."

"Would you say that she was deeply resentful?"

"Objection, Your Honor. Mrs. Nields is not on trial."

The judge agreed. "Mr. Stassen, confine your questions to Mr. Pagels and his defense. What you're trying to inject into the proceedings here has no relevance. It's collateral. You will not refer to it again."

"I apologize, Your Honor, I'm only concerned with giving Laurence Pagels a fair trial."

"So are we all, Mr. Stassen."

Stassen turned back to the witness. "Ma'am, am I right in thinking that Mr. and Mrs. Nields were partners in his business."

"Yes that's correct. Although she didn't do very much."

"But I guess you were working for both of them?"

"Yes, in a way I was."

"So why did Mrs. Nields dismiss you immediately after her husband died?"

"I have no idea."

"Did she dismiss you because she didn't want you to know too much?"

The deputy district attorney shot up from his seat and seeming unable to pick which of a thousand angry words he wanted to spit out, stood before the defense attorney jabbing his finger and mouthing wordless abuse.

Judge Conan, showing first signs of real anger, sustained Boyman's silent objection.

Stassen was fined four hundred dollars for contempt of court and threatened with a night in the county jail if he continued to make insinuations about Mrs. Nields.

As far as Stassen was concerned the day had been a triumph. He had removed the picture of a grieving widow and shown the jury a woman harboring considerable resentment for deep indignities she had suffered at the hands of her husband. He had shown them someone who had more reason than the defendant to hate John Nields. It was worth every cent.

———

The bailiff, Joe DeRosa, caught Rhonda before she scooted out of court.

"Are you a relative of the deceased?"

She answered, "No, of the about-to-be deceased."

That made DeRosa curious so she said quickly, "Really I'm just here to observe."

DeRosa was willing to accept anything Rhonda told him just as long as he could stand there with his thumb in his gunbelt and look her over. From afar she was blond and beautiful, but at close range her face appeared more intelligent and less alluring. Even so, it provided thoroughly pleasant viewing and he was being eyed enviously by another bailiff.

DeRosa had dark hair with a small belly protruding over his belt, not as big as the defense attorney's but noticeable. Rhonda had observed him staring down at his gut and pulling it in for a few seconds until he forgot about it and let it flop out.

Rhonda pointed to the door that her father had just been taken through.

"What's behind that door?"

He smiled secretively. "What do you think?"

"I was thinking maybe it lead to a trapdoor and they drop the defendant through it every night. Maybe he sits in a cage at the bottom of a pit until they haul him up in the morning."

"You've got quite an imagination."

DeRosa was not willing to let her out of his sight and offered her a ride.

"I'm going to Canoga Park. Where you going? I'll drop you off."

Rhonda considered the offer.

"I took my car in this morning. I have problems with the radiator."

DeRosa shook his head doubtfully. "Oh boy. If you get a radiator replaced, you're talking at least three hundred dollars and with labor, it'd be five hundred at least."

Rhonda frowned. "I'm not putting five hundred dollars into my car. I don't have five hundred dollars."

"O.K. So where do you want to go?"

"Chatsworth."

It was a whim on her part. She was supposed to go straight to her first evening as a waitress at Le Bon Café in Encino.

He drove across the valley along Sherman Way and then turned north on Canoga. They went past West Valley Auto Body, Foreign Dismantling, New and Used V. W. Parts, Lumber City, long rows of storage units, car dealerships with hundreds of colored flags fluttering away in hot clouds of dust.

Rhonda took it all in with a kind of loving fervor. "This is my favorite street."

"Canoga?" DeRosa said. "Are you nuts?"

"Yeah. I used to ride my bike down here when I was a kid. I liked it because it was dusty and mean."

"Uh huh."

"And I used to think that it didn't matter how ugly it got because it always had the mountains behind it. I thought that the snow on top of the mountains looked like little mobcaps on giants' heads. The giants were lying down behind the foothills spying on the people below. And I thought that one day they'd stand up and crush the valley under their giant feet. I always wanted them to crush Van Nuys first and then North Hollywood and Pacoima."

"There you go with your imagination again."

Where the railroad tracks started to run parallel to Canoga the roadside flattened out into a wide dusty area. An old overturned car lay in the dirt with nothing but its shell remaining, picked clean by human vultures. A Mexican woman with her two children sat nearby. The orange-pink on the cheeks of the Mexican children shone like fat shiny bubbles in the dust.

Across from the railroad tracks elegant places like Cinderella Shoes for ladies with small feet, and the Western Trimming Corp., and a store advertising a linen sale were all lined up.

"Those stores pretend they're not on Canoga. They act like freight trains aren't rattling by," said Rhonda.

Canoga came to an end here so they had to continue north on Owensmouth. The route became cuter with neat little apartments, trees, and flowers. Someone had even painted a fire hydrant red, white, and blue. They crossed Devonshire and came to Chatsworth Street.

"Did you know that some guy who liked British dukes named this after the Duke of Devonshire, who had a palace called Chatsworth?" Rhonda told her driver.

"Huh?"

"It was a hundred years ago when it was a whole bunch of ranches. It didn't look much like a British duke's place then, I bet."

"And it sure as hell doesn't look like one now."

"Maybe not, but it's close. They have money around here."

The farther north they went the richer the area around them became. There were houses with white picket fences, stables, and horse trails, and bales of hay piled up in paddocks. There were some of the original ranch houses sitting snootily in the middle of upstart track homes; the new houses had been humble when they were first dumped in the middle of bald patches of earth but now they'd been landscaped with rows of Italian cypresses and palm trees that shot up like weeds. Rhonda had seen those palm trees grow so fast that their roots pushed up the concrete round the swimming pools. Decorated with evergrowing foliage, the track homes had become highly desirable and expensive.

"When I lived here everyone had old Fords and Chevys. Now you get all these BMW's and Mercedes in the driveways."

"You don't live here now?"

"I've been away. I'm coming to see my . . . parents."

"And what did you say you were doing at the courts?"

"Observing. Writing."

"Who for?"

"I'm . . . freelance."

"Why did you choose the Pagels' case?"

"I find it interesting."

"There's a better one on the seventh floor. I'll take you up there tomorrow."

"No. I've started this one . . . I . . . have a lot of notes."

"Uh huh . . . It's nice around here. Really pretty."

"It's pretty but windy. Everyone wants to live here because you get less smog. But that's because the winds blow through the mountain passes so hard that everything that's not tied down gets blown to kingdom come."

DeRosa had not stopped looking curious since he met her. "You know, you sound like a preacher when you talk."

"I do not!" She was thoroughly annoyed.

"You don't like that? You don't want to sound like a preacher?"

"No. Here! Could you drop me off here."

They had reached the corner of Chatsworth and DeSoto.

"I'll take you to the door."

"No. This is fine. Thanks for the lift."

"What's your name?"

"Rhonda."

"Rhonda what?"

"Just Rhonda."

"Well, Rhonda, I'd like to see you again. I'm Joe DeRosa."

"You'll see me. I'm there every day. . . . You know that route we just came. Daniel Pagels could have gone that way. He could have gone down Canoga and taken a right on Sherman Way, up to Valley Circle Boulevard, and straight to Bell Canyon. It was a direct route. A boy who lived in the wilds would be used to walking."

He said, "Are you kidding? That boy never walked anywhere. He was only five years old. Five-year-old kids don't walk. They run around a lot and then they fall down. They have no stamina for walking. When they found him he wasn't wearing shoes and his feet weren't dirty. It's impossible for a small kid to walk ten miles across the valley in the dark. So how did he get there? His grandpa drove him over. Who else?"

She made no response.

"Did you ever see Pagels when you lived around here? He was always driving around here in his truck."

"No."

After waiting for his car to turn the corner she headed up toward the hills.

———

Edgar Stassen was annoyed that Rhonda continued to make her daily appearance at the trial.

"She's not hurting anyone," said Ida. "She's hiding in the back of the courtroom. Nobody knows who she is."

"Hiding! She stands out like a lighthouse!" Stassen shouted. "I don't want her in court. Talk to her."

"You talk to her."

"Aah!"

———

Rhonda came to a place where the road ended. Beyond that was wasteland leading to an unused freeway bridge. She remembered that there was no freeway when she was a child running round those hills. Now the new freeway had made Chatsworth a desirable place for homeowners and robbers. Drivers could get in and out of the area speedily and did not have to spend hours on local streets.

The freeway bridge was a big concrete structure, wide enough to take automobiles, of course, but it lead nowhere and was impossible to reach except on foot. It was grown over with weeds in some parts: few people used it because they did not like walking where they would not see a human face. Crossing the bridge was like falling off the edge of the world. On the other side there was nothing to hold on to. It was too raw for the people of Chatsworth who liked nice safe sidewalks where there was no danger of rattlesnakes. Even the teenagers preferred a nice neat row of ivy to throw their beer cans into.

The only people to be seen on the other side of the freeway were mad bikers kicking up the dust or oddballs like George Lejeune who walked his dog in the dark.

Near the bridge Rhonda saw a mattress and some old carpet dumped near the path but the farther she climbed into the hills the more untouched and prehistoric it became. People were too lazy to cart their trash up a hill.

Lawrence's motor home was among a grove of fan palms, carefully hidden, he always said, so that it would not offend the locals, just as the San Fernando Valley was hidden by hills and mountains so that it would not be an embarrassment to the people of Bel Air and Beverly Hills.

By the time she had reached his place the hum of the freeway had completely disappeared and it was totally silent. That was what she remembered most, the silence. It used to drive her crazy.

The motor home looked like a bunch of old plastic panels and driftwood tacked together. Lawrence used to boast that he could drive it away anytime he wanted and, to this end, he constantly tinkered with the engine. He would turn it over and it would sound like an engine to Rhonda but she could never see how the cabin would get over the first bump without falling apart. It seemed to her that fifty yards down the road the back wheels and the roof would fall off.

She sat down on the steps of the motor home and smoked her first joint in three months. She was ninety-nine percent drug-free but she felt that one little joint didn't count. According to Lawrence, marijuana had no more effect than she allowed it to have, which put a dint in her enjoyment of marijuana. She made up her mind that it was going to relax her whatever Lawrence said. She needed to relax.

She sat down for no more than thirty seconds and then jumped up and looked through the windows. It was so dark inside that she could only see her reflection. When her eyes grew accustomed to the darkness inside, she could see the stove. Lawrence used to make her cornbread in that stove: it would come out hot and crumbly and she would eat it with butter. He made it from a mix because he was not concerned with gourmet cooking. He used to tell her that people like himself who don't drink alcohol, tea, or coffee should mind that they don't get to love their groceries too much.

She could make out one of Daniel's drawings pinned on the wall. It was a picture of a woman, simple but perfect. The woman had large slanting eyes and a long slim face. She wondered who the woman was. Perhaps it was herself. Perhaps Lawrence and Daniel talked about her. The woman wore a black blouse. Rhonda had always loved to wear black. Did Lawrence tell him that? Or was it some other woman?

She drew back a little from the window and saw her own reflection again. And she saw another reflection. There was someone standing a few yards behind her, watching and waiting. It was someone who could climb up the hill and through the bushes without cracking a twig or rustling a leaf.

It was Daniel.

The first thing she did was throw away the joint. She dropped it quickly as though Daniel were a police officer about to arrest her. She found that she was unable to move. She became a spider who does not know which way to run to avoid getting squashed under a large foot. And Daniel stood there and looked at her as children look at adults who mean nothing to them. It was a blank, not too involved, look.

Rhonda knew she was not the woman in the picture.

She noticed that he was dressed like a little rich boy in expensive casual clothes, an elaborately designed sweatshirt, matching pants, brilliant white socks, and new Reeboks. He did not look like a wild trailer kid.

And Rhonda did not feel like his mother. Not the mother of this child. True he had her blue-gray eyes and fair skin. But he was like a symbol of perfection. He was how she should be. She had nothing to teach him.

She felt sick with the urge to throw herself at him. But she was held back by the knowledge that the last thing in the world the child needed was a problem like her.

So she ran. She turned and ran up the next hill, in the direction of the mountains. Then she ran along a gulley and then up another hill. She ran for about twenty minutes which was challenging because she was out of condition. Her saliva tasted like blood in her mouth. When she thought it was safe she ran back toward the freeway and crossed the bridge. Daniel was nowhere around.

5

All the members of the jury now considered Pagels to be guilty. The prosecution witnesses had convinced them of that. The defense witnesses had so far done nothing to remove that conviction. DeRosa told Stassen that only Donna Fabry was waivering but the old Marine, Brad Ryker, would rally her round.

DeRosa had taken to leaning on the defense table and giving Stassen advice. "They need some more evidence. They're saying 'Why doesn't he make it more difficult for the prosecution?' They like Pagels. They'd like to vote not guilty. But they need some help."

Stassen did not take kindly to being told by a bailiff how he should run things. Nor did he take kindly to being given ultimatums by the defendant.

"Bring in the physics," Pagels told him.

"Conan's not going to allow it. We'd be wasting our time."

"If you don't want to do it, we'll have to part company. I'll do it myself."

"Conduct your own defense?"

"Yes."

They were in the attorneys' room at the jail, the room that made Stassen so paranoid. His eyes were constantly surveying the room in a search for hidden microphones.

"Now Lawrence . . ." Stassen used to call him Larry but now it

66

was Lawrence. "I'd like to do it for you. I know you and Ida have poured a lot of passion into it, not to mention myself. We could all get Ph.D.'s . . . By golly, I'd like to do it . . . but I can't. I can't. There isn't a lawyer in the country who would. It's like going out there and committing suicide. You're asking me to kill myself in front of a judge and jury."

Pagels had no patience for Stassen's histrionics.

"Do you believe I'm innocent?"

"I can't believe . . . knowing you as I know you now . . . that you'd do a thing like that."

"You can't believe I could do it but you won't help me."

"I'm sorry Lawrence. No one would do what you want me to do."

Pagels looked away and listened to the hollow sounds of the jail. He seemed to have moved on from Stassen.

The attorney fidgeted with a pen. "It isn't as if I haven't thought about it. I've rolled it around in my mind. I want you to know I've tried. I've given over a year of my life to this. I've sat sweating in that Winnebago when it was a hundred and ten degrees. . . ."

"Don't apologize. I knew you couldn't go through with it. I saw it in your eyes the first day I met you."

"You saw it in my eyes. You saw that I didn't like making an asshole of myself?"

"I saw that you went with the crowd. Your bow ties. Your fancy ways. They're painted on."

"So I'm a phony on top of everything else?"

"You've used me, Mr. Stassen."

"Used you for what? What about your using me?"

"I knew from the start that you'd trip over your own ego. I knew you weren't the man. I kidded myself that you'd change."

"Well, fuck you!"

"The same to you, Mr. Stassen."

As he drove away from the jail Stassen thought about Patti. She was always in his mind one way or another. Dropping the case now meant that Stassen would have to fall into an abyss he had been avoiding. He would have to go back to the house in Sacramento: back to Patti's clothes, her hair left in the brush, maybe even her perfumed soapy smell. He had walked out the day after the funeral and he was still in desperate need of an excuse not to go back.

How long did it take to get over a thing like this? He knew old men who'd lived alone for over twenty years, pining every second. Was he going to be like that?

He had even talked about her to Max Haydn, a dumb idea he realized immediately but he couldn't stop himself. He needed to talk about her just as much as he needed to get away from the house that was full of her.

And for the first time ever Max was embarrassed.

"You know, when somebody dies," Stassen told him, "you lose things they do and say, and you lose their attitude to certain things. And with me and Patti, if she did some things, thought certain things, well that let me off the hook. I left it all to her. You know it's like all those guys down in South America who don't go to church. They feel O.K. because their wives go."

"Uh huh." Max had never looked so uncomfortable. In fact, as far as Stassen could see, the kid had never known what uncomfortable was until this very moment. Now he was discovering that for Max it was discussing a dead wife with her husband.

"And you could say I was doing something out of character by doing a charity case like this, but I'm not, because I was only the sort of person I used to be, when Patti was alive. Do you get what I mean?"

"Uh . . . you mean that you've changed."

"Yeah, I've changed because . . . one of the reasons I could be a bastard was because Patti was so good. She would've wanted me to take on Pagels, she was always asking me to take on guys like him but I didn't because she was there. We didn't need two saints in the house. And you know what? Even the goddam physics . . . she would have gone along with it. She was that kind of person."

"But she wasn't an attorney."

"No. But she was always around when I was an attorney. Now I'm an attorney without Patti, that makes me a different kind of attorney."

Max chose his words very carefully, another new experience for him. "I don't know because I've never been married, but I'd say that the way you are is the way you are, it's like, you know, written in concrete. And you might be feeling like this because it's . . . it's new, you know."

Stassen shook his head, "No I don't buy that. It's something to do with the balance of nature. You can't stop it. It happens. You'll find it out one day. One of these days you're going to forget about just getting laid and you're gonna love some woman just because she's the way she is. Then you're really stuck because if you lose her it's like you lose an arm or something."

Max Haydn had learned his lesson. In the future, whenever Patti's name came up, he rushed to fix the air conditioning or went to the store to get some paper clips.

As far as Stassen could see now, it was a major mistake getting talked into all that physics research. He could make excuses for himself and say he was in shock after his wife's unexpected death. She'd been ill one day, dead the next. Maybe the ability to reason correctly left him for a while. He could make all kinds of excuses but the fact remained he'd let it in.

It had all started when Lawrence Pagels handed him that yellow legal pad. He read the long complex notes and thought nothing of it; they seemed like the meanderings of a lonely old man.

Max Haydn read them and laughed. "What's old Pagels been smoking?"

Stassen cackled. "He's been growing magic mushrooms in his cell."

Ida read the notes, made photocopies, and took them home. She made it her project. She said she needed to do some research and it was generally understood that Pagels' notes were "Ida's project." She studied Pagels' books. He had a considerable collection of books on quantum physics and she went to the university library in search of more. Some days she was gone all day and Stassen began to wonder what he'd hired her for. He complained to Max who pointed out that if he paid Ida she might be more compliant.

Then a couple of months later she made an appointment for Stassen to meet Dr. Irving Walkman at UCLA, a reluctant Dr. Walkman. He had expected to give Stassen a little scientific advice and was profoundly disturbed when he was asked if he would go on the stand as a witness.

Despite the extraordinary mental leaps that Ida Letherbridge made during those few weeks of research, she always asserted that she was doing nothing but following the logic of Pagels' arguments and requests and that her services were merely secretarial.

Whatever Ida said, her efforts threw the rest of the year in that motor home into chaos. Capturing physicists to testify became a main objective. They contacted almost every university and research center in the United States. The papers and books piled up. The debates went way into the night. Max gave up trying to get home and brought a sleeping bag. Ida, like a homing pigeon, always touched base once a day, even if it was not until four o'clock in the morning.

It seemed to Stassen that they had spent that crazy summer looking toward some kind of oasis on the road ahead of them. Now they had reached what they had been looking at. And there was nothing there but humiliation.

After the final split with Pagels in jail, Stassen had to go back to his office and explain it to Ida and Max.

Ida was more than angry.

"Pagels can't do it alone."

"Maybe he can. He's a smart guy."

"You're going to drop it now, after we've done all this research?"

"Yes."

"Why?"

"Conan won't allow it."

"How do you know?"

"I'm sorry, Ida. I know you had your heart set on it."

Ida's face grew red with fury. "Don't say sorry. You can't do this. I won't let you. You owe it yourself. You owe it to Lawrence Pagels. And you owe it to me. You're not going to drop it just like this."

They discussed it until well beyond midnight. He was not going to change his mind.

"So this is it," said Ida.

"Yes."

Stassen rubbed his back against the door frame in a sort of catatonic, compulsive way while twisting an elastic band into tortuous shapes around his fingers. He wanted to pace the floor but there was no room to move. Every available space was covered in books on physics, overflowing files, and notes.

There was one chair left uncovered and Max, dressed in a T-shirt and shorts lolled across it. He had his feet over the arm of the chair, displaying a pair of muscular, hairy calves and torn tennis shoes.

Ida, in jeans and a striped gray-and-white shirt, sat on the floor, rubbing at the dark circles under her eyes. She pulled off her earrings and stared at them listlessly.

"All that work and now we won't use it."

"Can I go home now?" Max asked. "I'd like to sleep in my own bed just once."

Stassen groaned. "I can't believe this kid. No emotion. He's moved on. All he ever thinks about is eating, sleeping, and getting laid."

Max put his feet up on his employer's desk and regarded him insolently. "You know where you made your mistake? In letting the first physics book past that door. You would have slept a lot more. You wouldn't have broken down in the men's room."

Ida gasped. She never failed to be astounded by how crass he could be. Her gasp was a reprimand.

Max shrugged. "I think we should discuss it."

Stassen stared at him. "I what?"

"Some bailiff's going around saying you broke down in the men's room."

"He's saying I broke down in the men's room?"

"He's saying you were talking about faking a heart attack."

"I made a joke. Can't I make a joke?"

"What do they call those kinds of jokes? Gallows humor? I think it's interesting because I think it shows you were getting serious about the physics. My God, we were that close." Max laughed.

Ida said again. "I can't believe we put in all this work and we're not going to use it. I can't believe it."

"Oh come on," Max laughed again. "It was like playing Trivial Pursuit all summer. It was a mad, intellectual game. Some people go to see the Lakers or go to the movies; we farted around with quantum physics." He turned to Stassen. "I knew you'd never put Dr. Walkman on the stand. I knew you'd never screw up that much. You scared yourself real good thinking about it. What a joke. My God, what a joke!"

Max kicked a pile of books off the desk and they went crashing to the floor, some of them hitting Stassen's feet.

"Fucking quantum physics. Man, I wasn't gonna hang around for that!"

Stassen twanged the elastic band so viciously that it caused some pain to the back of his hand.

"Go to hell!"

He pulled at the elastic band violently again and this time it broke and went flying across the room. He stared at the books at his feet.

In a sudden, flashing microcosm he saw the long, hot summer, the physicists, the long debates, he saw Patti, he saw his entire career in court, he saw Ida's face, dejected, destroyed, he saw Pagels' unusual explosion of anger, but most of all he saw Max Haydn lolling comfortably in his chair.

Stassen looked up.

"I'll do it."

There was a momentary silence in the room.

Ida stared. Max's face and body seemed to undergo a temporary paralysis.

"Why not? What am I saving myself for?" asked Stassen.

He looked around for an answer.

"I said, what am I saving myself for?"

Ida came to life. "You're gonna do it?" She screamed with joy.

Stassen shrugged. "Yes, I'll do it.'

By 3:15 A.M. a shocked Max Haydn had handed in his resignation, collected his sleeping bag, and left the Winnebago. He went back to his room on Zelzah Avenue and collapsed fully clothed onto his bed and fell asleep.

Ida drove home to San Marino and grabbed three hours of sleep.

Stassen attempted to get some rest but slept only for the duration of one quick, violent dream just before 6 A.M.

The Quantum Effect

6

The next morning at ten minutes to eight Max Haydn walked through the parking lot at the Van Nuys courthouse carrying his tie in one hand and a cup of coffee in the other. As she was backing her car into a parking place, Ida saw him walk by.

She ran after him to catch up and they walked in silence for a while. The silence was prolonged and did not end until they were going up in the elevator with two police officers.

Then Ida put her hand on his sleeve and asked, "What are you doing here? I thought you'd washed your hands of all this."

"I've come to save you from yourself."

"It's too late."

"Then I've come to see the biggest fucking fiasco in the history of Los Angeles."

"I wish you wouldn't swear."

"You'll be doing more than swearing by the time this is over."

Upstairs on the sixth floor Edgar Stassen leaned over a toilet in the men's room and vomited. He felt marginally better afterward and wiped his mouth with a small sense of relief, a sense which left him when he emerged from his cubicle and saw the bailiff, Joe DeRosa, standing there.

Stassen attempted to appear relaxed.

"Hi. How ya doin'?"

DeRosa looked curious. "Fine. Everything O.K.?"

"Great. Everything's great. Life's a bowl of cherries."

DeRosa remained curious. "I er . . . I remember you saying something about you weren't too happy with this case."

Stassen splashed water on his face. "That's right. I'm not happy. I want to run away to Miami. Get on a boat to the Bahamas."

"That's too bad."

"But you know what?" Stassen dried his face with a paper towel. His hands were shaking. "You watch Boyman's face today. It's gonna go all the colors of the rainbow."

———

In the courtroom Rhonda Pagels was already sitting in her corner seat at the back. She was alone apart from two elderly men across the aisle.

DeRosa walked along the row in front of Rhonda and leaned over.

"Stassen's having trouble again. He was throwing up in the men's room. That's the second time I've seen him do that."

"How come you're always hanging around the men's room?"

"What d'ya mean?"

"I dunno. You seem to be an expert on what's happening in the men's room."

"Are you making fun of me? I drink a lot of coffee. What d'you expect?"

———

When Dr. Irving Walkman stepped onto the stand Edgar Stassen leaned over to the defendant and said quietly, "This is it, so help me God."

Lawrence Pagels looked at him with a sort of patient skepticism. "Don't be nervous Mr. Stassen. My life is at stake, not yours."

For all his doubts about his attorney, Lawrence Pagels appeared more alert and hopeful than he had in weeks. His large, rocklike face with the deep-set, dark eyes was normally set in deep concentration while he communed with some distant voice known only to himself. Today he listened attentively as Stassen went over his notes with Ida. Max Haydn said nothing.

When the defense attorney stood up and adjusted his crumpled jacket several times before moving forward, the tension from the four of them, Pagels, Ida, Max, and Stassen, rose to such a pitch that it almost materialized.

It could be felt by Mark Boyman and Harvey Marlatt who watched with bemused interest. What was going on over there? Dr. Irving Walkman's name had been introduced during pretrial motions. He was to give analysis of the distance between Pagels' place and the Nields' residence. They could not figure out why his presense could cause such jitters in the defense camp.

As if expecting a special occasion, Boyman had picked up a new suit from the tailors that weekend. Navy blue pinstripe of course but with more of an Italian cut. He wore it with a bright fuchsia tie and a shell pink shirt. His shiny black hair was sleeked down to perfection. He was ready for a party.

They watched as Stassen stood there adjusting his jacket one more time and Lawrence Pagels, eyes burning with new intensity, leaned over and talked to his attorney. This was a new Pagels.

Stassen adjusted his jacket one too many times. A button came away in his hands. He stared at it helplessly, as though it were blood. Ida grabbed the button out of his hand and pulled the loose threads from his jacket.

Lawrence Pagels took Stassen's arm and gripped it tightly in a seeming attempt to infuse him with his own strength.

Judge Conan had been kept waiting too long. There was an irritable edge to his voice. "Mr. Stassen."

Ida took Stassen's other arm, the one Pagels was not holding, and gave Stassen a slight push. It had the effect of getting him off his balance; to steady himself he had to take a few steps toward the witness. In order to maintain his dignity Stassen continued in a forward progression. Ida looked as if she had pushed him toward an unexploded bomb. Pagels had no such fears; he had nothing but hope in his eyes. Max Haydn, on the other hand, was not looking up: he had his eyes down on the table.

Dr. Walkman had short-cropped sandy gray hair and gave the appearance of a bespectacled ostrich. About the same age as Stassen, but taller and leaner, he had observed the minidrama at the defense table with a total lack of surprise, but also with a lack of relish. He had been cleaning his glasses obsessively until the judge spoke. Then he stopped suddenly as though obeying military orders. He quickly put his glasses on.

Stassen continued his progression across the short distance to the witness stand and then stopped for a moment to take a breath, rather like an old man climbing a hill. He was pale and perspiring by the time he reached Walkman.

"Dr. Walkman. Any relation to the Sony?"

It was a weak joke but the jury appreciated it.

"Unfortunately not."

"Dr. Walkman, I've called you here as an expert witness to er . . . to er . . . give us some technical information which will er . . . clear up . . . clarify perhaps, some confusion surrounding the movement of the defendant's grandson on the night that John Nields was murdered." He turned to the judge. "To er . . . to do this (cough) we will require some scientific information that might at first seem obscure and unrelated. But I assure Your Honor that it . . . er isn't."

Stassen stopped here and walked back to the defense table to get a drink of water.

Max Haydn groaned under his breath and rolled his eyes heavenward at the delay.

Stassen took one look at Max's cynical face and gained the first modicum of strength he'd felt that day. He returned to the witness.

Harvey Marlatt leaned over to Boyman and whispered, "What's wrong with Stassen?"

Boyman shrugged.

Stassen was now fractionally less pale and ill at ease as he questioned the witness. "Dr. Walkman, sir, where did you receive your training?"

"I'm a graduate of Northwestern University and Stanford, and I'm currently a research scientist at the California Institute of Technology."

"And you are an expert in the field of quantum mechanics?"

"Yes I am."

"I believe you've had several books published on the subject?"

"That's correct."

"Dr. Walkman, we need your help in explaining the movement of Daniel Pagels, then aged five years old, from a motor home in the hills of Chatsworth to a home in Bell Canyon more than ten miles away on the opposite side of the valley . . . er, could we have a blackboard here?" Stassen clicked his fingers at Max Haydn as though summoning a waiter.

Max scowled as he picked up the blackboard and easel from

their resting place against the defense table and set them up between the bench and the jury.

Stassen approached the blackboard with a piece of chalk. "If we call Chatsworth point A, I will mark it here . . ."

He marked a point A with chalk on the board.

". . . and if we call the house in Bell Canyon point B and I mark it here . . . now sir, can you explain the child's movements from point A to point B in terms of quantum mechanics?"

Mark Boyman stood up. "Your Honor, are we to be subjected to an incomprehensible load of scientific data?"

The attorneys were summoned to the bench where the attorney for the defense was able to clear the way for Walkman's evidence. It was an unexpected victory for Stassen, who had clearly been a source of irritation to the far-less flamboyant and down-to-earth Judge Conan. Later in the trial it became known that Conan was a science buff and subscribed to several scientific journals, including the prestigious *Physical Review Letters*, where he had read some of Dr. Walkman's papers.

The defense attorney's question was read out again. "Can you explain the child's movements from point A to point B in terms of quantum mechanics?"

Stassen added, "You have here a child who was seen at both point A and point B at eleven thirty P.M. . . . point A and point B being ten miles apart. He wore no shoes yet his bare feet had not been soiled by walking along streets and dusty hillside paths."

Dr. Walkman had been disturbed by the exchange he overheard at the bench. Now, as he listened to the question, he had the expression of one who would like to go home as soon as possible. He directed his gaze at the blackboard as though seeking inspiration from the chalk and began his "dissertation" as Boyman had insisted on calling it in the hissed discussion with the judge.

"If we see the child as a collection of atoms . . . then it might be helpful to look at what Einstein said about mass and matter. In his famous equation E equals MC squared we see that E stands for energy, M is mass, and C is the speed of light. The most important thing about this equation is that it is correct and was a revolutionary discovery by Einstein."

Stassen stopped him. "You've lost me already. This equation means nothing to me."

"It means nothing to me either, Your Honor," echoed Boyman, who was truly annoyed. "Do we have to put up with this? Is this Physics 101?'

"You know where you're going with this?" Conan was obliged to ask.

"Yes, Your Honor. I er . . . I er . . . You will see. It will become"— Stassen waved his hands in a weak theatrical gesture— "apparent."

Conan showed compassion. "O.K., go ahead."

Stassen turned back to his witness. "Can you explain, in simple terms, what that bit of algebra means?"

Walkman responded, "In the equation E equals MC squared, Einstein showed us that mass or matter, as you may call it, is in fact energy . . ."

Stassen stopped him. "Mass or matter is energy. That's a heavy statement . . . so let's get it straight. Mass is something hard that you can't put your fist through like this table, right?" He strode over to the prosecution table and slapped it hard, right under Harvey Marlatt's nose.

"Yes, it is."

"And energy is something like electricity that you can't see?"

"That's correct."

"And in his famous equation Einstein showed us that mass is energy?"

"He did. In reality mass is nothing but a form of energy."

"And you could say that a human body is matter or mass and therefore also a form of energy."

"Yes. This is something that is not obvious to us in our daily life. However it seems to me that this equation could allow for a case where mass is converted into energy to travel at the speed of light from point A to point B which over a distance of ten miles would appear to an observer to be instantaneous."

"Instantaneous?" Boyman and Marlatt spoke in unison. They looked completely taken aback and hunched together for a hurried muttered discussion.

Coming out of the huddle Harvey Marlatt rose to his feet. "I think it is becoming apparent what counsel is attempting to do here and it has nothing to do with the elemental requirements of this case. Mr. Stassen is putting up a misleading smokescreen of complex scientific evidence to protect his client from the proper scrutiny of the law."

Judge Conan, who had on a wall in his chambers a poster of

Albert Einstein with his immortal words "God does not play dice" printed across the bottom, leaned forward and informed Harvey Marlatt that no defendant in his court had ever been sheltered in any way from the full scrutiny of the law. He instructed the witness to continue.

Stassen asked him, "Dr. Walkman, in this conversion of mass to energy and the transferring of this energy from point A to point B that you were just referring to ... what would be the propelling factor?"

Dr. Walkman frowned. "This is all speculative, of course. But let's say that if you were to walk across this courtroom, Mr. Stassen, you would illustrate several laws of energy and motion, but the factor that would spark the entire operation would be your own desire to get from one side of the courtroom to the other. . . . Your own thought is the propelling factor."

Stassen glanced round at the blank faces scattered around the courtroom and the sea of incomprehension that comprised the collective face of the jury. "I see er . . . well . . . if I've got my facts right here this equation was part of the theory of relativity, which came out in er . . . when was it Dr. Walkman?"

"1905."

Boyman tried once more, "Your Honor, the theory of relativity is not a legal argument."

"If it is not, it should be, Your Honor," Stassen interjected. "It can save an innocent man."

Conan allowed that it was time for a consultation in chambers. As they left the courtroom Boyman and Marlatt moved in on Stassen, hedging him in on either side like a couple of muggers. Stassen, still a little breathless, slipped out of their clutches and went in search of more water. While he was filling a paper cup Boyman came close to screaming at Conan about the deviousness of the defense's use of "scientific gobbledygook." He could not prevent his lip from curling. With his dark hair and fleshy face, he looked like a villain in a very old movie.

Stassen smiled weakly at the judge.

Conan gave him a hard, beady look. "As you can see, Mr. Stassen, nobody wants a physics lesson if they can avoid it."

———

While the judge and attorneys were out of the courtroom, Rhonda Pagels took the elevator down to the canteen on the second floor and bought herself a cup of coffee. She sat at a corner table. Like a small animal trapped in a barn, her eyes darted around nervously, constantly checking every avenue of escape. In order to appear more like a journalist, she had now scraped her frizzy blond hair back into a bun.

Two elderly men dressed in the pastel colors of California sat down at the next table. They were court regulars whom she had seen wandering around the halls in previous weeks. They had been sitting in her courtroom that morning, at the back on the other side. Her view of them was obscured but she could hear them assessing the trial, addressing each other as Hank and Earl.

They nodded politely to Rhonda, recognizing her as a fellow court regular, before they settled down to their coffee and one Danish pastry which they cut in half and shared.

"Here, Earl, I'm giving you the best half." The man who spoke, obviously Hank, had wisps of white hair covering his tanned head. "That's the first time I've heard an attorney talk about the theory of relativity."

"Conan'll throw it out," said his partner Earl, a smaller man who wore prescription sunglasses.

"I don't know. You can never tell with Conan."

"He said a table is energy. What's he trying to prove?"

"Matter is energy. Mass is energy. I don't get it. But I'll tell you one thing, that's the first time I've seen Conan look interested."

"How can you tell?"

"He's leaning forward."

Rhonda stood up and moved toward the door before the old men realized she'd gone. She went back up to the sixth floor and slipped into her seat in the back row. The first thing she noticed was that the judge was leaning forward on his bench and Dr. Walkman was back on the stand.

Joe DeRosa, in his police uniform with the gun on his hip, was standing near the defense table eavesdropping on a conversation between Max and Ida. Across the room a fuming Mark Boyman was tapping his pencil. Stassen had obviously won the last round.

Dr. Walkman was speaking. "From Einstein's relativity theory we learn that moving clocks run slow and that they run slower the closer they get to the speed of light."

"This is a scientific fact?" asked Stassen who looked relieved to be back in the courtroom.

"Yes. If an astronaut left his twin brother on earth and traveled in a spaceship at the speed of light, time would stand still for him. He would not grow older. He would return to earth to find himself younger than his brother."

"You mean if one brother was gone for twenty years he'd come back the same age as when he left?"

"Yes."

"Why wouldn't he get older?"

"Because he was not under our laws of space and time. He would have come under another set of laws."

"Does this mean anything to the man in the street? I mean, it sounds fictional. How can people relate to an idea like that?"

"Well, as I said, it's not merely an idea, it's a scientific fact. When it first came out, relativity theory was only understood by a small group of scientists and mathematicians. They did not and still have not fully grasped its implications. We have all been able to comfort ourselves with the fact that this theory is only applicable to great speeds and seems to have no relevance to our daily life. It . . ."

Boyman jumped out of his chair. "Did you hear that? It's not relevant to our daily life. He's talking about the theory of relativity and it isn't relevant to our daily life and that includes the day that John Nields was murdered."

"Your Honor," Stassen announced wearily, "I am attempting an overview. It will take a little time but it's essential. As I said before, it can save an innocent man, and as far as I'm concerned no stone should be left unturned."

"No stone!" Boyman exclaimed. "How many stones is that? It seems to me that counsel is attempting to dig over the entire universe. That's not within the scope of this court."

Boyman was overruled and warned not to interrupt the witness.

At that moment the senior citizens, Earl and Hank, moved into their seats at the back of the court. They and Rhonda were the only ones who had come to view the procedure that day. Sometimes a small party of Chatsworth residents sat in the front row, but they had not come that day. One half of the courtroom was left for the old men and the other half for Rhonda.

They watched as Stassen laid his hand limply on the edge of the witness stand. "We've all heard the term 'quantum leap' and can make a stab at what it means but hardly anybody knows what a quantum is. Once again I say your explanation will provide us with an understanding of how young Daniel Pagels went to the Nields' house on the night that John Nields was murdered and will show us that he went alone and without adult help."

Dr. Walkman removed his glasses for an instant, and with his sandy gray hair and sandy gray clothes became a California beach pebble. He took a deep breath. "Quantum physics deals with the very small, with particles that are invisible to the human eye. Perhaps I could illustrate with a famous experiment called the double slit experiment."

Once again Stassen clicked his fingers at Max. "Set up that table and the two boards."

Max Haydn allowed himself a couple of seconds to stare sullenly at his superior before bending over to pick up the folded table at his feet. Together with Ida and Joe DeRosa, he set it up alongside the blackboard. Two upright sheets of white board, four feet square, were placed parallel to each other on the table. They looked like two opposing sides of a half-built cardboard house.

Dr. Walkman crossed over and examined the two boards to see if they were to his specifications. Then he looked up waiting for instructions.

"Go ahead, Dr. Walkman," said Judge Conan expectantly. He had moved his chair so that he could see the two boards head on.

Dr. Walkman made a small bow of his head in acknowledging the judge and then addressed the jury as though they were a class of physics students. There was no hint of condescension in the way he spoke.

"As you see, the board in front has two slits in it. If I had flashlight . . ."

Before Stassen could click his fingers Max moved forward smartly and presented a flashlight to the professor.

Dr. Walkman took the flashlight and shone its beam at the front board.

"As I said, there are two slits in the board. If I close one of the slits with my hand, thus . . ."

Dr. Walkman held his hand over the small slit or hole on one side of the board and directed the beam of the flashlight through the other slit.

". . . you will see one line of light projected onto the next board."

The members of the jury leaned forward. Under the fluorescent lights of the courtroom they could barely see the faint line of light on the white board. Dr. Walkman asked the bailiff to turn off some of the lights and it was immediately plain for all to see that there was one thin line of light shining onto the second white board.

"If I remove my hand so that it no longer covers one of the slits and shine the flashlight through both of them you will see a set of striped dark and light lines on the second board."

"Can everybody see it?" asked Stassen.

There were mumbles of assent from the jury.

"The striped dark and light lines show that the two slits of light run into each other and set up an interference pattern."

"An interference pattern," repeated Stassen. "And what does that show us?"

"It shows light behaving in a wavelike manner."

"Uh huh."

"Now, if I were to set up an experiment exactly like this in a laboratory and took one electron, an electron being a particle that orbits the nucleus of an atom . . .

"Could you tell us what an atom is, Dr. Walkman?" asked Stassen.

"An atom is the basic unit of matter. It's what we're all made up of, what this table is made up of."

"What this table is made up of . . . what we're all made up of." Stassen repeated this slowly to the jury to make sure they were getting it.

"Right. If I aim this electron, which is an extremely small particle, through one slit, then it shoots through just like a BB pellet. But if I uncover the other slit and aim it at both of them it sets up a wave interference pattern on the screen."

"Is this surprising?"

"Surprising? It is shocking! It is shocking because it indicates that the electron did not go through one slit, it acted like a wave and went through both slits at the same time! Some physicists prefer not to think about this too much because it shows us a disturbing fact about the essential nature of matter."

"What is this disturbing fact?"

"The fact is that matter is not the solid stuff we've always thought it was. Here you have matter behaving in a mysterious manner in a serious scientific experiment. And that's not all . . . ."

"There's more?" Stassen played surprise for the jury.

"Yes . . . If you introduce a detector into this experiment so that you can observe this little electron approach the two slits, it no longer goes through both slits but behaves like a little pellet and goes through one slit. The act of observation changes the behavior of this subatomic particle of matter!" Dr. Walkman slapped his hand on the table and concluded. Max Haydn signaled the bailiff to turn the lights back on.

Dr. Walkman returned to the stand and Stassen rose slowly from his chair, scratching his head all the while.

"Are you trying to tell me, Dr. Walkman, that a particle changes its behavior when it's looked at?"

"Yes, I am."

"Then why doesn't this table move when I look at it?"

"The only answer I can give to that is, it doesn't move because it doesn't. I personally have no idea why subatomic particles obey the laws of quantum physics and larger solid objects obey the old-fashioned laws of classical physics."

"Then what are we made up of? Are we solid or are we made up of a lot of particles that behave differently if you look at them?"

"These particles are certainly not solid. In quantum physics we say that instead of being definite they exist in a probability of states."

Boyman made another attempt. "Your Honor . . ."

Conan stopped him, but turned to the defense lawyer. "I'm still in the dark about where you're heading, Mr. Stassen."

"Almost there, Your Honor." Stassen talked quickly, realizing his time was short. "Now let's get down to facts, Dr. Walkman and put everyone out of their misery. The results of the double-slit experiment are rock solid, right?"

"Right. The conclusions are scientifically based and inescapable."

"There's not a physicist in the world who would disagree?"

"No. They could not disagree. The conclusions of this double-slit experiment form the basis of quantum mechanics."

"And quantum mechanics is reliable?"

"Quantum mechanics is among the most accurate sciences known to man."

"What's it used for?"

"It's used for making televisions, transistors, calculators, computers. It can predict results up to nine decimal places."

"So it's not a fantasy. It's not bunkum?"

"By no means."

"Sir, you talked earlier on about the possibility of matter being converted into energy and moving from point A to point B at the speed of light. Have you ever known anyone to put this into practice, personally, you know what I mean . . . that is . . . by the way they move about . . . bypassing the laws that everyone else is sticking to, like that little electron in the double-slit experiment . . . and, you know . . . getting to a place real fast?"

Dr. Walkman removed his glasses again and put them right back, like an actor trying to apply some character to his performance. "You mean without any mechanical means of transportation?"

"Yeah. That's exactly what I mean."

"No. I can't say I have."

"Do you think it's possible?"

"My own personal opinion is that given the extraordinary findings of quantum mechanics something of that nature would be possible."

Edgar Stassen wiped his forehead with a piece of a document he was holding. He did not forget to bow. "Thank you very much, sir, Dr. Walkman. It's been a real pleasure."

Mark Boyman and Harvey Marlatt had been conferring, and stood up in unison when Stassen was through. Boyman spoke first. "Your Honor, this is a joke. Irrelevant, misleading garbage. A ridiculous parade of unconnected ideas."

"This is a murder trial not a transistor radio," Marlatt said, acknowledging the jury members who laughed.

Judge Conan looked bemused. "I don't see how you can presume that quantum mechanics are an effective legal argument," he said to Stassen.

"I presume it, your Honor, because it is the truth."

"A scientific truth, yes, but this isn't a laboratory. This is a court of law."

"Since when has truth not been admissable evidence in a court of law?"

Judge Conan concluded that it was time for another discussion in chambers and he recessed the court for the rest of the day. Boyman and Marlatt raced out of the court after the judge.

Stassen, however, seemed glued to the floor. He stood like one wondering how to unglue himself, wide-eyed and startled at the predicament he was in.

Ida put her hand on Stassen's shoulder. "You did it!" Her voice was nervous and breathy.

"Yeah, I did it."

"How do you feel?"

"Like a boiled noodle." Stassen found the strength to move over to Lawrence Pagels who was smiling at him. The last time Pagels had smiled was when his grandson came into the courtroom.

"What d'you think?" Stassen asked him.

Pagels opened and shut his mouth several times as he searched for the right words. He looked almost comic, unusual for a man of such dignity. Finally he said, "I never thought I would see a day like this."

The stenographer, who usually stopped to flirt with Stassen, walked quickly by and gave an embarrassed smile. Stassen watched her go.

"She thinks I'm crazy. She feels sorry for me. . . . Where's that moron Haydn?"

"Here, sir." Max was on the floor folding up the table used in the experiment. He had ducked down there to avoid Stassen.

"Get me some ginger ale or Seven-Up." He placed his hand on his queasy stomach.

"He can't do that," Ida spoke irritably.

"Why not?"

"He's no longer in your employ."

"He's not?"

"Don't you remember? He resigned last night."

"Then why's he been hanging around all day."

Max stood up. "Your extraordinary magnetism, sir."

Stassen was too wound-up to think of an effective way to deal with that. He turned to Ida.

"How do you think I did?"

"You were O.K."

He looked questioningly at Pagels, who gave him a thumbs-up sign.

Stassen picked up his briefcase and readied himself for the confrontation in chambers. As he left he grinned at Pagels.

"It was worth it just to see the expression on Boyman's face."

———

Rhonda Pagels sat with a look of stupefaction on her face, unable to make any sense of what she had just heard. She fiddled nervously with her hair, trying to push it back into a more orderly bun. As her father was led out of court she put out her hand and half opened her mouth as though about to scream something across the courtroom. But no scream came out.

She watched him helplessly. Then she stood up suddenly and ran out of the courtroom, almost crashing into the old men, Hank and Earl, who were making a steady progression through the door.

"Hey!"

"Sorry, sorry."

Earl patted her on the shoulder. "Don't come back tomorrow, honey. The prosecutor's gonna ask for a continuance."

"How do you know?"

The old man smiled. "With that testimony? What d'you expect?"

DeRosa escaped from his duties and went in search of Rhonda. He had exactly sixty seconds to speak to her. He found her in the corridor, fumbling in her bag for a cigarette. She was trembling slightly.

"What's the hurry?" He stood with his stomach pulled in and his thumbs in his belt, a gunslinger's stance. "Are you coming tomorrow?"

"Nothing's happening tomorrow," she said.

He grinned. "I'm happening tomorrow. Meet me downstairs at twelve thirty. I'll take you for a hot dog."

She was still trembling but she managed to look unimpressed. She lit a cigarette and took a deep drag. "No expense spared," she drawled.

"See you downstairs. Twelve thirty. Don't forget."

"Do you know what that professor was getting at?"

"No. Neither does he. I'll explain it all to you tomorrow. Gotta go."

"So he's not serious?"

"Are you kidding? See ya."

Later that afternoon an auspicious meeting took place between Joe DeRosa and Leon Ferguson of the *Daily News* near the elevator on the sixth floor.

Ferguson, a young black journalist, was working on a short feature about new buildings in the valley. He had spent a few hours looking at the new law courts and had strolled over to the old buildings to compare the two. He wore an elegantly styled dark suit, a vest of deep mustard, and a burnt orange tie, carefully thought-out colors.

DeRosa had just finished work. He could always recognize someone from the media and when he was in a good mood he would offer them inside information.

"Hi. How ya doin'?"

"I'm fine thanks."

"You from the *Daily News*?"

"Yes. How do you know?" Ferguson was not a smiler. Premature frown lines marked his forehead. He was two years out of Cal State Fullerton and unhappy that he was assigned small stories.

"I've got my spies out. D'you hear about the Lawrence Pagels case?"

"No what?"

"The defense brought in a scientist to say that his grandson can travel the same speed as light."

"They what?"

Joe DeRosa roared with laughter. "I knew that'd get you. But that's what's happening. I've seen this kind of thing coming for a long time. I knew one day someone would bring in a flying saucer. These guys play games in court. So what do you get? You get something like this."

"Like what? I don't quite understand what you're . . ."

"Got a minute? I'll tell you about it."

DeRosa's wife was not home. He had no desire to go back to an empty apartment. He took Leon Ferguson to a bar on Victory Boulevard. For two hours they discussed the Lakers, women, property prices, and the Lawrence Pagels case.

The Continuance

7

September 1989 is generally regarded as the date that the Quantum War started in Los Angeles. If the introduction of Dr. Irving Walkman by the defense on that date was a kind of Pearl Harbor, then the ensuing confrontation would be, as far as Mark Boyman was concerned, the Battle of Midway.

Mark Boyman and Harvey Marlatt went through the various stages of inevitable emotions that human beings experience after a totally unexpected assault—disbelief, anger, then retaliation. The disbelief lasted longer than usual because they had no idea how to wrap their minds around the problem. They were poleaxed when Judge Conan said that he considered Walkman's testimony valid, and when they asked for a continuance they were even more pole-axed when Conan said he would give them only two weeks.

"Do you know anything about quantum physics?" Boyman asked Marlatt.

"Not a lot. Do you?"

"No."

"What the fuck is quantum physics?" he asked around the office. He was met by blank looks.

One secretary answered, "A quantum leap is a gigantic leap, so quantum physics must mean gigantic physics, I guess."

"Then what the fuck is physics?" Boyman was irritable.

"Physics is physics," another secretary told him.

"Is it single or plural. Do you have one physics or two physics?"

"You can have as many as you like. It's anything that isn't chemistry or biology."

"Aw shit! It's a trap."

Boyman had visions of himself cramming five years of physics into two weeks. He was going back to school because of some idiosyncrasy of the defendant, some strange malaise of the mind that Stassen was unwilling to step on. That old Indian was obviously crazy but Stassen was treating his demented stories as if they were coming out of the mouth of a sane person.

Before the trial started Boyman had heard on the grapevine that Stassen was being pushed into something by the defendant, something that scared him. If it scared him, why was he doing it? Did Pagels have something on him? Was he blackmailing his attorney? What kind of coercion was making Stassen sweat and strain in court over the dumbest fairy tale Boyman had ever heard in his fifteen years in Los Angeles courts?

Why was the District Attorney's Office now ringing with the sound of physics' formulas and odd experiments? Why? Because some idiot old man was using the courts to propagate lunacy.

Stassen had pleaded with the judge to accept an entirely unbelievable story because he himself had to accept it. What sort of an argument was that? He gave Conan a long sob story about Pagels' plan to dump him if he did not present this argument. And Conan had fallen for it.

Boyman had lost all faith in the judge. He had never done anything to annoy Conan, he thought the man was on his side. But there he was, leaning back in his chair and saying, "I understand your anguish Mr. Boyman but this is science. You can't buck science."

"But, Your Honor, he's had a year to cook this one up. We've got two weeks."

They had two weeks to do what? Boyman didn't know where to begin. Did Conan really believe that there was anything to argue about here?

Stassen was calling the motor home in Chatsworth point A and the house in Bell Canyon point B to take them out of the realm of reality. He'd got the jury thinking it was algebra instead of a house and a motor home. He'd made them forget that instead of a piece of chalk traveling from point A to point B in less than one second they were talking about a five-year-old boy crossing the San Fernando Valley at eleven thirty at night.

Boyman moaned to Marlatt, "Lawrence Pagels has been jerking Stassen's chain, and now he's jerking mine. We're all going to be having little debates about some kid flying through space."

They sat down with their assistants and attempted to approach the problem methodically.

"First. The most simple thing of all. Find a hole in the witnesses' evidence. One or other of them must have made a mistake. They could not have seen Daniel Pagels in two places at the same time."

They had an immediate setback. It now appeared that George Lejeune had eight new witnesses to back up his testimony.

When Lejeune returned from seeing Daniel Pagels, he arrived back at his house at midnight. This is exactly the time he would arrive home if he was correct about seeing Daniel Pagels at 11:30. It invariably took him thirty minutes to walk from Pagels' motor home to his house.

As he walked to his front door he noticed that a minivan was parked in the next-door driveway. Fourteen-year-old Janice Hopper, who had been dancing in an amateur musical production at Pierce College, was getting out. There were seven other people associated with the production in the minivan.

Janice had been told by her parents to be back before eleven. She was worried about it and several people in the van checked their watches as they pulled in the driveway and told her it was one minute to midnight. There were some silly jokes about pumpkins.

Everyone in the van and Janice herself could recall George Lejeune walking toward his door with his dog as they were all laughing about the midnight hour. All of them were prepared to swear about the time that George returned from his walk. There were no doubts.

A couple of men were sent from the District Attorney's Office to accompany George Lejeune on a walk from his door to the motor home. The men complained that it was risky for a man of Lejeune's age to negotiate steep hills in total darkness at night. George said he'd been going up there for ten years and hadn't fallen yet. With the added encumbrance of two inexperienced walkers the journey took George thirty-five minutes. The men went with him on a second occasion and this time it took exactly half an hour.

If George Lejeune's testimony was irrefutable, the prosecution reasoned, then Arlene Tullis in Bell Canyon must have been incorrect about the time she saw Daniel Pagels arrive at John Nields' house.

Here the prosecution met a major stumbling block. A Polaroid photograph.

When Arlene Tullis had seen the light go in John Nields' house and heard the dog barking, her husband was downstairs shouting at their eleven-year-old son that he should have been in bed by nine. When he heard the dog barking he had opened the door leading out onto the patio and gone to investigate. The area was well patroled but it was isolated. The Tullis house had been robbed a few months before and they were wary.

The eleven-year-old son, who had been playing with his parents' Polaroid camera all evening, took a photograph of his father as he opened the door to the patio.

The resulting photograph showed a man opening a door. To the right of the door and distinctly in view was the television and VCR. On TV Ed McMahon was standing alone, just as he does every night at the beginning of the "Tonight" show. And on the video recorder was a clock which showed clearly that the time was 11:30.

Mr. Tullis was prepared to swear that the only time he opened the door to the patio that evening was when John Nields' dog started barking.

The prosecution was given a copy of the photograph. Edgar Stassen kept the original.

"O.K. So Stassen has a photo and a busload of witnesses to say they saw the kid in two different places, ten miles apart, at the same time," said Boyman at an early morning meeting with Marlatt and their assistants. "And he's got a scientist to say that kid moved ten miles instantly, or next to instantly. Get me some physics books, I want to see the page where it says that can happen. Get me some scientists. I want to find out how many serious professors think that a human being can act like a rocket."

Mark Boyman's assistant, an ambitious young woman named Mary-Lynn Robbins, went out shopping and came back with fifteen books on physics. Marlatt took three of them, went home and studied them throughout the night. Boyman flipped through a large illustrated volume that still contained a disturbing amount of complex mathematics. He gave up and threw it onto the floor of his office.

"You read it!" he said to Mary-Lynn. "And take notes."

"Notes on what?"

"Notes where it says a kid can move like an atomic particle . . . I don't know . . . notes on anything that's relevant. Use your intelligence."

Mary-Lynn, who with her shiny dark hair and fleshy face, looked like a younger, female version of Mark Boyman, canceled all her appointments, business and social, and sat down to study. She was to discover that the most important difference between her and Boyman was not their gender. It was that she took to quantum physics like a duck to water and he almost drowned in it.

Some went so far as to say later that she was the Ida Letherbridge in Mark Boyman's life. But in fact she was nothing like Ida. She had none of Ida's subtlety and grace. Mary-Lynn was a twenty-six-year old heavyweight computer whereas Ida was a very light but effective piece of machinery. Ida, however, had none of Mary-Lynn's facility with science; Ida understood the whole concept but had trouble with the details, the diagrams and the mathematics. Mary-Lynn's genius lay with the details: she loved the algebra and the convoluted drawings.

Along with Harvey Marlatt, who also had a brain for physics, Mary-Lynn held the prosecution's quantum evidence together while Mark Boyman floated through on bombast alone. He never really understood what he was saying in court. A week after the trial was over, Boyman was unable to engage in an intelligent conversation on the very testimony he had elicited.

Mary-Lynn was not easily embarrassed. She was the one who had to make the difficult phone calls, to handle the prying inquiries, to admit to the press what they were doing. Boyman and Marlatt were both held back by the cringe factor. It was hard for them to admit that they were contemplating what they were contemplating.

Mary-Lynn steamrollered through those phone calls to university physics departments in search of experts. The first one was a major psychological breakthrough for the office.

"Hello, I'm calling from the Los Angeles District Attorney's Office. Could I speak to Dr. Block, please."

"Dr. Block speaking."

"Oh hello, Dr. Block. Well, sir, we need some advice on quantum physics. I'm working for Mark Boyman, the Assistant District Attorney. He's prosecuting a murder case and the defendant is using quantum physics as an alibi."

"As an alibi?"

"Yes, sir. He's using quantum physics as an alibi."

"Any specific area of quantum physics?"

"Well, sir. If you'd let me explain. You see, witnesses in two places ten miles apart say that they saw the defendant's grandson at eleven thirty at night"

"Maybe someone's watch was a little fast."

"No, we've looked into that. They seem to be telling the truth. And the defendant is saying that his grandson traveled these ten miles so quickly that it seemed like he was in two places at once. We'd like to know you're opinion on that.

"I don't have an opinion."

"Oh, I see."

"Why should I have an opinion?"

"Mr. Boyman was hoping you might have a scientific viewpoint on that. The defense have brought in physicists who say that traveling that fast is possible and they're proving it with physics."

"What physicists?"

"Dr. Irving Walkman . . . and possibly Dr. Stefan Zollner."

"Uh huh."

"Do you know them?"

"Yes, I've heard of them."

"Do you know if they have sound reputations?"

"They're O.K."

"How O.K.?"

"I've read some of their stuff."

"You mean their books?"

"Books and papers."

"Would you say that their writings are in any way out of line?"

"Not really, no."

"Dr. Walkman has already given evidence. He says that quantum physics, let me quote here, shows that 'matter is not the solid stuff we've always thought it was.' And he also said 'given the extraordinary findings of quantum mechanics something of that nature would be possible.' When he says something of that nature he means that a small child could travel ten miles instantaneously."

"He said that?"

"Yes, he said that."

"I see."

"Wouldn't you say that's crazy?"

"That's Dr. Walkman's business. It has nothing to do with me."

"Would you be prepared to give us some advice? We wouldn't necessarily ask you to testify in court. We need some strong scientific input and you've been highly recommended."

"I'm very busy right now. I can't do anything this week. Maybe next week. Let me get back to you. I have to go now."

"Thanks you very much, Dr. Block. We'd be real grateful if you do. Bye. Thank you."

Boyman and Marlatt had listened transfixed to Mary-Lynn's end of the conversation.

As Mary-Lynn crossed off Dr. Block's name from her list and prepared to dial again, they watched her nonchalance with envy.

"What did he say?" Boyman asked.

"Nothing much. He's a lost cause."

"But did he react? Did he laugh?"

"No."

"He thinks it's possible?"

"He didn't say."

"He didn't react in any way?"

"No."

"Why didn't he react?"

"He didn't say."

"Is he a friend of Walkman?"

"He didn't say."

Mary-Lynn stared at the men as though they were two troublesome children and went on with her dialing.

Marlatt continued studying the physics books and making notes. Boyman poured over his law books, looking for cases at all similar in nature to the Pagels case, but he knew they would be hard, if not impossible, to find. Where was the case where they had used the theory of relativity to back up an alibi? What was its history in law? Was quantum physics valid evidence if a jury could not understand it? What was the legal history of incomprehensible scientific evidence? Where and when had a paranormal event been found acceptable and valid in any court in California or the United States?

Mary-Lynn soon discovered that her three-day marathon of phone calling was not quite the pioneering effort she thought it was. She was not the first to ask a professor an outlandish question and was following a trail already laid out by Ida Letherbridge. However, Mary-Lynn widened and lengthened the trail. She added a not-insignificant weight to the burden of the Los Angeles taxpayers as her long-distance calls grew longer and more relentless.

Ida, not having the resources of the District Attorney's Office and not wishing to add to her employer's phone bill had made her calls from home. Even though her calls had been relatively short and to the point, she gave her parents a nasty shock when they received their phone bill.

Mary-Lynn kept a physicist from the Massachusetts Institute of Technology on the line for fifty-eight minutes at 11:30 A.M., the most expensive time of day. Boyman and Marlatt watched her in fascination as she sat in her chair, her large thighs bulging out from under her miniskirt, her plump chin resting on thick ink-stained fingers.

She repeatedly said, "What exactly do you mean by that, sir?" or "Would you say that in language I can understand." or "You've lost me! You jumped." With her confidence in her ability to grasp difficult ideas she had no fear of saying she did not understand what the person on the other end of the line was talking about. In subsequent meetings with scientists, when she, Boyman, and Marlatt all sat with yellow legal pads on their laps taking continuous notes, she was the one who would tell a scientist he was not making sense.

By the time she had finished her three days of calls, Mary-Lynn had collected the names of seven physicists who were not only prepared to give the prosecution a physics lesson but were also willing to testify against the propositions put forward by Dr. Irving Walkman.

There was an eighth physicist, Dr. Jean-Paul Chen, who took it upon himself to make an unsolicited phone call to Mary-Lynn. He was to prove himself an angel of light to the anguished attorneys in the DA's office.

8

The morning after his meeting with the bailiff, Joe DeRosa, Leon Ferguson of the Los Angeles *Daily News* drew up a list of people connected with the Pagels case. His feature on new building in the valley was temporarily put on the back burner while he attempted to focus on what had produced this odd turn of events in an obscure murder trial in Van Nuys.

At the top of his list were Dr. Walkman and Daniel Pagels. He was unable to get hold of the child's foster parents that morning so he headed over to Pasadena to find the professor.

Dr. Irving Walkman was heading toward his car when he was waylaid by Leon in the communal garage of his apartment building. It was nine o'clock on Tuesday morning when Leon appeared out of the shadows in the underground parking lot. Dr. Walkman had thought at first that Leon was a student. He seemed youthful enough for it, but he was too smartly dressed.

He was not surprised to discover that Leon was from the *Daily News*. He had expected a certain interest from the press after his appearance in court the day before. He did not like publicity; it was a cross he had to bear but he was ready to accept it. If he was surprised at all, it was because it was almost twenty-four hours from the time he had testified before someone from the media approached him. He had expected to be leapt upon the moment he walked out of the courtroom.

"Dr. Walkman, do you believe that Daniel Pagels could travel ten miles instantly?" Leon had his notebook in his hand.

Dr. Walkman pushed his fingers through his stubbly hair, which was almost short enough to be dubbed a crew cut. "I know very little about Daniel Pagels. I was called as an expert on physics not on Daniel Pagels. Ask his grandfather if you want to know about him."

"Then let's put it another way. Do you think it's possible for a human being to travel in the way that the defense is saying Daniel Pagels traveled?"

"I can't answer that question without using a lot of physics."

"Lay it on me."

"I'm sorry but I have some students waiting." He looked at his watch.

Leon followed him to his car.

"Can I come with you? We could talk in the car."

"Do you have a car here?"

"Yes. It's outside."

"Then how will you get back? It's almost four miles."

"I'll worry about that later."

"Am I what you call a 'hot story'?"

"To me you are."

Dr. Walkman's car was a revamped Volkswagen Beetle which offered the long-legged Leon no more room than his own small Honda. He sat with his knees pulled up toward his chin, his head scraping the ceiling, and scribbled chaotic notes as he received a lecture from Dr. Walkman.

By the time they arrived at the California Institute of Technology, Leon had amassed a good collection of notes and some algebra. Dr. Walkman had not tried as hard as he had in court to make it simple and Leon had great difficulty in understanding seventy-five percent of what he said. Some of it he did grasp and he clung to it as one clinging to a life raft.

Leon went over his notes as he walked the four miles back to his car. He had a quick mind and was able to grasp complex matters with great speed, but he had not been exposed to a great deal of physics in school. He had done the small amount of required physics but it did not sound anything like Dr. Walkman's physics.

Dr. Walkman had said, "I won't insult you by oversimplifying it the way I did in court."

Now Leon wished he'd replied, "Insult me. Insult me."

Why Dr. Walkman assumed he was some kind of science expert just because he was a journalist was a complete mystery to him.

He battled with the weak and strong anthropic principles, with protons and neutrons, with quantum mechanical spin, with spin one-half particles and Minkowskian time-measure. Yet they remained just phrases. And he marveled at the man who had first drawn a correlation between this tangle of incomprehensible physics and young Daniel Pagels' journey to Bell Canyon.

———

Lawrence Pagels had watched Stassen reluctantly following a line of argument that held no meaning for him. His attorney was like a dancing bear waiting for the music to stop. When the words exchanged between him and the witness received a cold welcome from the jury, Stassen showed a touch of relief. In fact, it was apparent to anyone who observed him closely that he half welcomed the prosecution's objections.

A great Indian chief once said that the spirit of the land would always be vested in the American Indian until other men were able to divine and meet its rhythm. Men of such discernment were few and far between in North America. And likewise, Lawrence felt, those who could divine his truth were equally scarce. To comprehend his situation a great purity of mind was required and he could not see it in anyone in that courtroom.

What destroyed the Indian and all but wiped him off the face of the earth was not only the undisputed power of the enemy but also his naive inability to envision greed and determination on such a scale as was ultimately presented to him. Lawrence would learn from that and try to encompass in his mind what the new line of defense would unearth in the enemy. In any victory a complete understanding of the intentions of the opposition was essential and he knew that if Stassen's courage did not fail him and he stuck with it, then it would stir up a hornet's nest.

Stassen was a reluctant crusader but, thank God, he had gone ahead with it. That was the miracle.

It was a year since he had handed Edgar Stassen his full explanation of what had happened on the night John Nields was murdered together with a suggestion of suitable witnesses and defense tactics. He had written it out on a yellow legal pad, precept by precept, line by line. The man from the Public Defender's Office had ignored it and when Stassen took over he did the same. Lawrence had insisted on being heard and brought the whole thing up at every meeting with Stassen, until finally the lawyer had chosen to make fewer visits to the Men's Central Jail.

Ida Letherbridge had come in Stassen's place and Pagels had resorted to telling her.

And Ida was different. She was a transparency.

She reminded him of Daniel, which was strange, because from her background he would have thought she would have been a spoiled girl; but her wealth and privilege had washed right over her and never soaked in, just as all his efforts to teach and elevate. Rhonda had washed right over her.

Ida put up no barriers. She was young but she had surprising strength. If it were not for Ida, Stassen would not have stepped out, sweating and nervous though he was, to present ideas that had never been presented in a courtroom before. The next few days would tell if Edgar Stassen would be a small forgotten blip in the myriad of daily events in the Van Nuys courts or whether he would become one of the most famous attorneys in the history of jurisprudence.

Lawrence returned each night to a cell he shared with Lionel Brown, an overweight, middle-aged black man, who was awaiting trial for armed robbery.

Lionel asked him each night how the trial was going. When he heard about the physicist's testimony he whistled.

"Now you've got 'em by the balls. Man, that's fuckin' beautiful. That's what I need. A physicist. Ask him if he'll tell the jury I wasn't there either."

Lawrence attempted to live in the present because he knew that to live in the past or the future was the path to unhappiness. If he thought back over his past or his ancestry it was as one reading a history book. There were the redoubtable burghers of Amsterdam and Maastricht on his father's side and on his mother's side was Pasegnie, whose name was changed from Tomear when he became chief of the people who lived in the place which is now Chatsworth.

Lawrence's mother had taught him both the familiar and obscure facts about their ancestors. First the familiar. After Padre Junípero Serra, Padre Francisco Gomez, and Padre Juan Crespi made their historic ride north from Loreto, Mexico, a steady stream of white men followed and settled in California. When the priests and the soldiers built the San Fernando mission in 1797 it was named after a respected thirteenth-century Spanish king. The Indians did not offer the white man any immediate names for themselves or their surroundings, so the place where their family had lived for over a thousand years was quickly plastered with Spanish names and Pasegnie found himself to be a Fernandino and the valley around him to be the San Fernando Valley. It was another case of being unprepared.

The more obscure details about Pagels' ancestors were time-honored stories to Lawrence. As a child he learned that Pasegnie was chief of a group of people called the Pasegna, who lived a largely contemplative life and found it hard to communicate with the busy intruders. They were not accustomed to spending more than two hours a day on the work of providing for themselves and devoted the rest of their time to things of the spirit; but the white men prevailed upon them to toil all day long on the building of their mission and the growing of their crops and they had no time left to devote to their sustaining mental life. If the Indian men attempted to run away they were whipped and brought back in irons.

The mission San Fernando Rey de España was built in a place originally called Achoiscomihabit. When it was finally completed it was a very fine building but for Pasegnie it was not as fine as the home in his own village that he had made of sticks and covered in plaited flag mats.

Pasegnie was called upon to teach an industrious and intelligent man, Father Juan Salvideo, the language of the so-called Fernandino Indians and the padre became one of the first white men able to converse in the language of the valley.

Father Juan found Pasegnie eager to learn about the white man's Devil, who appeared to be an amazing character to the Indian; he loved to hear of his great power and exploits. He had nothing like it in his religion and consequently experienced none of the white man's fear. But this Devil was an endless source of amusement as were the white men's church services, which never failed to beguile Pasegnie and his fellows with their seductive array of colors, smoke, and incantations.

"The white men brought their Devil with them," Lawrence's mother told him, "and after they'd talked it up, they went about proving how powerful that Devil was."

A party of soldiers once came upon Pasegnie and his people and tied up all the men. After some whipping and torture they induced the women to appear for the purpose of sexual concourse with their sweaty and unappealing white bodies. The foreigners were hairy and had an unhygenic habit of wearing flannel undergarments, which allowed no air to reach their skin and caused them to smell. Their habit of spitting up obnoxious phlegm was abhorrent to the Indians who had clear pipes and found no need to spit. Many of the foreigners had teeth which were black and rotting, another cause for wonder among Pasegnie and his people, who carried their perfect white teeth to the grave.

Any woman unfortunate enough to conceive and later give birth, took the unwelcome white baby into the thicket, strangled, and buried it.

Sex, Pasegnie discovered from Father Juan, was a dreadful thing, an example of man's great and abiding sinfulness. White men, being in a constant state of sin and being instructed in the forbidden nature of sex, were consequently doomed to be preoccupied with sex and rarely had it out of their minds: whereas the Indian was allowed some respite in his mental life and was free to think of other things.

The prohibition placed on all things sexual served as a wildly effective aphrodisiac, Pasegnie observed, and he saw also that the fixation on sexual matters placed a terrible strain on the relationship between men and women.

The female breasts, for instance, perfectly natural parts of the human anatomy, were kept covered by law. And the white women were not accepted as normal human beings because they carried before them these anatomical threats. Those who had depended for their very life on breasts as babies, turned against them as men, and pronounced them wicked and disturbing.

Pasegnie was amazed that these seemingly intelligent white men had not given more thought to their happiness and peace of mind. To the Indian sex was a rejoicing. It had within it the great gift of birth. But for the white man it was an act of lust, requiring disgraceful thoughts and images to accompany it. The Pasegna had great respect for nature and knew that to disobey its laws was to court disaster. And just as to be gluttonous instead of eating moderately when hungry caused disease, so these white men, hypnotized by the sexual act, sought sexual congress in every place and with every available person and gave themselves diseases entirely unknown to the Pasegna people.

Not only did the foreigners give the Indians food that made their teeth rot but they also gave them their venereal diseases, their influenza, and a host of other infectious illnesses and the Indians, with no protection, died in their hundreds.

Pasegnie's long conversations with Father Salvideo only served to convince him that all white men were quite mad. He never met a sane one. He concluded that the madness stemmed from a misinterpretation of the Great Spirit who made the mountains, the rivers, the wolf, and the coyote and who was the father of all men.

All Indian symbols and ceremonies revolved around the circle. It was a symbol of wholeness and unity and truth. Lawrence Pagels drew a circle on the wall of his cell in the Men's Central Jail as a tribute to Pasegnie and his struggle.

If this circle of truth could encompass his trial then the time would not be far off when he would return with Daniel to the life they had always had. A broken circle, a concept that constantly presented itself, would never be drawn on the walls of his cell. He could not allow it any reality.

———

Leon Ferguson had no luck in getting hold of Mark Boyman. The assistant district attorney was always "in a meeting."

Leon's editor at the Los Angeles *Daily News* told him to keep at it because he'd never heard of an attorney who did not want publicity.

"Its like mother's milk to them. If they turn you down, that's the story. You find out what they're afraid of."

Leon finally caught Boyman's assistant as she was going out to the ladies' room. Mary-Lynn was not intimidated by this tall, intense young man.

"There's no mystery. This isn't Watergate. Mr. Boyman's doing a crash course in physics and he's not going to surface for a while. That's all. I bet you'd be just the same if you were in his position."

Leon stooped a little so he could come down to the level of this small barrel of a woman.

"Physics. Why is he using physics?"

"Because some of the testimony is based on physics."

Mary-Lynn edged herself toward the ladies' room. Leon followed.

"Does he believe that Daniel Pagels has unusual powers?"

"No."

"Does he think that physics will prove that Daniel Pagels is just like the rest of us?"

Mary-Lynn stopped.

"Mr. Boyman has absolute faith in scientific evidence. He knows that it will uncover any fraud."

With that she disappeared into the ladies' room and slammed the door shut.

———

"Dr. Zollner says the theory of relativity and the double-slit experiment are crap."

Max Haydn was resting himself, as usual, on the only available chair in the Winnebago office while his co-workers made do with what was left. The two other chairs had long ago disappeared under boxes of files and notes. A few minutes of attention to the clutter would have cleared the chairs and made the seating arrangement more comfortable, but there were no minutes available for this kind of activity.

Stassen was currently sitting on a stack of books in the corner.

"He what?"

"He says you need Bell's Theorem."

Stassen's jaw dropped.

"Bell's Theorem! We've been meeting this guy all summer. Why didn't he tell us this before?"

Max repeated the question into the phone to Dr. Zollner and listened to a long explanation while his boss tapped at his mouth in an incessant, neurotic motion.

Ida was on the other phone. She held out the receiver to Stassen. "It's someone from the *Daily News*."

Stassen waved his hands. "I'm in a meeting."

"I'm afraid he's in a meeting . . . hold on . . . When will you be free?"

"Not until the trial resumes."

"I'm afraid he won't be available for a couple of weeks . . . Yes, that's correct . . . No, it certainly is not."

Ida put her hand over the receiver. "Somebody in the DA's office called the physics a fraud."

"Uh huh. Uh huh."

"He wants an in-depth interview."

"After the trial."

Ida spoke to the caller. "Mr. Stassen is concerned about the ethics of talking to the press right now."

Stassen rolled his eyes.

Ida went on. "He'll be happy to talk to you when the trial is over . . . Fine, good-bye." She put down the receiver.

Stassen looked at her accusingly, as if it were all her fault. "This is a cause celebre."

"You mean a *cause célèbre.*" Ida pronounced it correctly.

"This Winnebago is gonna be the center of the universe." The idea gave Stassen no joy.

Stassen's once-spacious recreational vehicle looked more like a cramped library storeroom every day. It was getting hard to open the door. Two or three mornings a week Ida would come in with more physics books. Not all of them were read but the presence of so many scientific tomes comforted them. Books were like bullets in the Quantum War.

Stassen pushed some books away from his feet and surveyed the chaos around him. "Somebody should clear this place up."

"O.K., Dr. Zollner," Max said into the phone. He looked over at Stassen. "He wants to discuss it with you."

Stassen had not stopped tapping his mouth. He turned to Ida. "Do you think we should use Bell's Theorem?"

Ida shook her head. "I don't think the jury will understand it."

"Oh shit . . . I don't know . . . O.K. Ask him to come over and talk us through it."

Max smirked. "I thought you understood it. I understand it. How come you don't?"

"Get him over here will you!"

"Dr. Zollner. Could you come over here and talk Mr. Stassen through it? Let me see. It's eleven thirty. How long will it take you to get here? . . . O.K. We'll wait . . . Oh sure. You're our piece de resistance."

Ida made a face. "If you two are going to speak French why don't you pronounce it properly."

Max slammed the phone down. "Because we don't go in for that sissy accent shit. Isn't that right, Mr. Stassen?"

"How long will Zollner be?" Stassen was frowning and looking at his watch.

"An hour or so."

"What's he doing, walking on his hands?"

Max smirked once again. "Well he's not getting here by the Danny Pagels method. You know when this is all over we should market it. We could sell shares in the Daniel Pagels Supersonic Airline, instant travel for the masses. No customs, no crowded air terminals, no fat ladies pushing you out of your seat. The ultimate in luxury travel."

Stassen was still frowning. "He's gonna take over an hour to get here from Westwood? It's practically midnight. There's no traffic."

"Look at it like this, Ed, I bet ol' Boyman's spending a fortune contacting guys all over the world. They can't bike over at a moment's notice whenever he panics. They have to fly in from the East Coast or Zurich."

Stassen started to grin. "You wait till Boyman hears I'm using Bell's Theorem."

Max was delighted that he'd made his boss smile. "Exactly. It's all beginning to pay off. We're so poor we have to use local boys. But who else could get on a bike and be here in an hour?"

Ida was curious. "A bike? Dr. Zollner's not coming . . ."

"Sure, what's wrong with that? You go down Sunset, left on Beverly Glen, into the valley. Fantastic. I'd like to do it."

Stassen lost his grin and began to panic.

"He's coming on a bike?"

"He apologized. But he said he's fast."

"Just my goddamn luck. He wants to introduce another theory. Does he know how long it takes me to get one of those damn things in my head! He won't be here for an hour and a half. He'll get a flat tire! Oh shit!"

While they were waiting for Dr. Zollner to arrive, Ida brought out her notes on Bell's Theorem and read them aloud to calm Stassen and get his mind prepared. She drew diagrams and charts and tried to explain the mathematics, not her forte. It had the effect of reducing Stassen to a greater state of panic.

When Dr. Zollner, a prematurely balding man in his thirties from the physics department at UCLA, arrived wearing bicycle shorts, racing helmet, and a Cambridge University sweatshirt, they were completely unprepared. The Bell's Theorem they had understood in July was incomprehensible in October.

However Stassen, always the actor, managed a smooth performance. He put his arm round the scientist's shoulder and led him to the one available chair.

"Are you hungry, Dr. Zollner? We have some cold pizza."

Ida was apologetic. "We only eat food that can be delivered."

Dr. Zollner had thoroughly enjoyed all previous encounters with this group because of Ida's presence. He smiled a smitten smile and shook his head. "I've told you. Call me Stefan. . . . I'm sorry I didn't get here sooner. But I needed the exercise. I've been sitting at my desk all day."

"O.K., Stefan," Stassen settled himself on the corner of the table closest to Dr. Zollner's chair. "Tell me. Why are you suddenly bringing up Bell's Theorem?"

Dr. Zollner's name had been given to them by Dr. Walkman, as one who would have sympathy and great interest in their cause. They had enlisted the help of other scientists, but Zollner and Walkman proved to be the two with the most open minds and with the greatest ability to simplify physics so that a newcomer could understand it. They were also normal.

Stassen had investigated long and hard to make sure that neither of them had "Ouija boards in the kitchen drawer or aunts who practiced voodoo." They had no loonies, physics, clairvoyants, or mediums in their backgrounds and Stassen was confident that no matter how hard Boyman probed he would find no hint of the occult or the paranormal in these two well-grounded individuals. Dr. Walkman had even coached his son's Little League on a few occasions.

Zollner had met Stassen for question-and-answer sessions almost every week between July and September. At their last meeting they had finalized the points that would be brought up when he testified in court.

They had decided that Dr. Walkman would appear first. The purpose of Dr. Zollner's testimony would be to clarify and extend points already made by Dr. Walkman. Everything he was to say had been gone over with a fine-tooth comb so that Stassen understood what they were talking about. Although the attorney had few of the problems with comprehending physics that Boyman had, he was still no scientific genius, and had to learn some of it by rote. To introduce another theory at the eleventh hour was profoundly disturbing to Stassen.

Stefan Zollner looked around at the three drawn faces, at the purple shadows around the eyes of the two younger people and the pouches under Stassen's sleep-deprived eyes.

"I'm sorry if this is a shock. I was going over what Walkman said." He had been sent a transcript of Dr. Walkman's testimony. "And I was thinking about it . . . what you really need here. You know this is a sort of unique situation."

"I thought we'd gone over it with you." Stassen's voice was edgy. He was punching his fist into his hand, as though preparing to punch the scientist.

"Yes, you did . . ."

"But it didn't sink in?"

Ida moved in warily. She did not want Stassen to scream at Dr. Zollner and blow it. He had been cooperative up to that point but he was not in love with the idea of testifying. He could easily walk off in a huff.

"We know how busy you are, Stefan." She was fully aware of the fact that her soft voice had a soothing effect on Dr. Zollner. Max watched her and whistled quietly through his teeth. "We're really grateful that you came over tonight," she said.

Stassen's eyes darted back and forth for a while. He added nothing to Ida's thanks but at least he kept quiet and Dr. Zollner was happy.

He nodded appreciatively at Ida. "I began to have a few new insights about it and I saw that what you really needed was Bell's Theorem."

Stassen went back to tapping his mouth. "Yeah, but you can't give a demonstration of it in court. I guess my feeling is, you'll lose their attention. I'm not saying the jury's dumb but the prosecution is."

"Maybe so, but when you're trying to prove something so far out of the general experience, then I think you're going to need Bell's Theorem."

"O.K. Let's assume I'm as dumb as the prosecution and explain it to me in real simple language."

"Well, let's see. Do you think the jury and the prosecution could understand the concept of local causality?"

"Refresh us on that."

Max groaned quietly and wiggled his eyebrows at Ida, who frowned back.

"Local causality was something Einstein was trying to hang on to. He got together with two guys called Boris Podolsky and Nathan Rosen and they devised the Einstein-Podolsky-Rosen experiment. It's called the EPR paradox although it wasn't at all paradoxical. I don't think we need to go into it in court but I think it would be enough to say that these guys tried to show that local causality is ... how shall I say ... that local causality is where it's at. Local causality is the idea that something that happens in one place cannot be affected by something that happens some distance away."

"Could you give me a little illustration of that?"

"Sure. Er ... well ... if a bomb dropped in New York. At the moment it explodes it won't have any affect on you. If you hear about it on the radio or by telephone, you hear about it through ordinary causality."

"Uh huh."

"Without going into EPR and confusing everybody we could say that Einstein and his friends came to the conclusion that quantum theory was incomplete. If you weren't prepared to agree with their conclusion then you had to say you believed something really weird and foolish ... you had to say you believed that distant particles could communicate by some kind of telepathy."

Max grinned. "I know which side I'd choose."

Stassen shifted his position on the corner of the table. "Then along came Mr. Bell. . . ."

Zollner looked around at the three oddly matched inhabitants of this paper pigsty. He was not embarrassed about sitting in the only chair.

"Yes, along came Mr. Bell. He was, he is, an Irish guy, Northern Irish, a theoretical physicist who works at CERN. Do you want me to tell the court what CERN is?"

"Will it wake them up?"

Zollner did not get the joke.

Ida frowned. Stassen added quickly, "Sure. I'll ask you."

"O.K. I'll tell the jury that CERN is the European Organization for Nuclear Research, which has a great big high energy laboratory in Switzerland near Geneva. That's as much as I'll say and then I'll move on to the experiment."

Once more Stassen wriggled on the uncomfortable tabletop. "Yeah, as I just said, we looked at Bell's Theorem. We liked it didn't we?"

"Yes, we liked it." Ida spoke automatically. Her beautiful dark hair was now a little unkempt and greasy, falling in loose strands over her pale, tired face.

"We liked the theory but the experiment ... you could explain it to us but the jury wouldn't get it and Boyman would go cross-eyed," said Stassen.

Zollner looked surprised. "The experiment is really simple."

"It may be simple but we didn't like it," the lawyer added.

Max went to the fridge and took out two cans of Pepsi. He slapped one can down in front of the scientist and kept the other for himself. "What he means is, it may be simple but it's not simple enough for him to learn in a few days. It took him six months to learn the double-slit experiment."

Stassen gave Max a killer look, but Max was undeterred and went on.

"And even then, he had to have the definition of an electron written on his cuff when he went into court."

Zollner chose not to acknowledge the joke. "Well, let's deal with the conclusion of the experiment. Take it on trust. The jury accepts gravity. They don't need to see an apple drop on anyone's head. Bell's experiment showed that nonlocal causality is a fact of life. That means he showed that it's possible for one particle that's, maybe, on the roof of this motor home to tell another particle on the moon about a measurement that's being made on it."

Stassen stood up and rubbed his eyes, an action that helped him think.

"I don't really see how it relates to Daniel Pagels."

"It relates because . . . well, look at it like this. We're talking about the most important discovery in physics in this century. It's taken another step beyond everyday reality into quantum reality. Bell's Theorem shows that information travels faster than the speed of light. If you get a pair of particles zooming off in different directions, then what you do to one on earth will instantly affect the other one thousands of miles away. There's no way that information could be sent by any way known to man."

"If it's not known to man," said Max, "then it's a mystery. That means nobody can figure it out and everyone's throwing out guesses."

"Yes, it's a mystery. But that doesn't alter the fact that this weird, seemingly impossible communication goes on. It's a fact. Physics tells us that. Now it seems to me that it could be invaluable to your defense."

Ida had been sitting on the floor, leaning against the door. But she was suddenly charged with new life and she jumped up and stood next to Stassen.

"You're right. It's the distance between the two particles. They act as if there's no distance. They act as if they're right next to each other."

Max grinned slyly across at Ida and crossed his eyes, his usual gesture of total disbelief.

Stassen edged his bottom onto the table once more. "So let's discuss the experiment."

"I think we should rest lightly on the experiment," said Ida, "and emphasize the results. Look at Max now. He's getting bored, he's fidgeting. He's taken in about as much as his brain can cope with. That's how the jury will be. I was watching them when Dr. Walkman was talking and they tuned out. The girl who looks like Diana Ross really paid attention and so did the lady dog breeder and the telephone engineer. . . ."

Max was irritable. "Don't you know their names yet? The girl is Doria Rudell. The telephone maintenance guy is Fred Turner and the dog breeder is Donna Fabry."

Ida nodded. "They paid attention but the others gave up. If you start talking about photons and spins, they'll tune out again. You have to make it entertaining."

Dr. Zollner was astounded. "Entertaining!"

Stassen sighed. "Yes. We're in the entertainment business."

Zollner looked down at his shoes for inspiration and then looked up. "No. I can't make it entertaining."

"I know." said Stassen. "You're not Walt Disney. You're a physicist."

Max spoke in a low voice to Ida. "Walt Disney would make more sense."

Zollner caught it and looked quizzically at Stassen. "You have a little opposition here."

"Yeah. It'll teach me not to be cheap next time. This is what you get when you use college students."

Zollner smiled weakly. "I could show you the general ideas behind the experiment or rather experiments. There have been several since Bell came up with the theory in 1964. I could start by explaining to the jury that . . . well, if you take the case of an atom called a positronium that decays into two photons traveling in opposite directions. I could draw it for them. . . ."

Dr. Zollner bent down and picked up a piece of scrap paper from the floor and scribbled a diagram of a decaying positronium. "There you go."

Max grabbed it. "It looks like tadpoles to me."

Zollner took it back from him and gave it to Stassen. "To cut a long story short, you have the two photons traveling in two different directions and you place a detector in the path of these two photons."

Stassen was staring at the diagram. "What kind of a detector?"

"If I talk about the detector then I'll have to talk about the polarization of the photons."

"Lay it on us."

"The polarization of a photon is the orientation of its vibration in space. Here we have an atom decaying into two photons traveling in different directions but their polarization is identical. If one is polarized vertically so is the other one."

"Polarized vertically?" Max asked.

"Yes. Imagine the photon's holding a baseball bat. If it's vertically polarized then it holds the bat upright. Whatever way this photon is holding the bat, the matching photon will have identical polarization."

Max did a little dance and sang, "The matching photon will have identical polarization. The matching photon will have identical polarization."

The other three stared at him unamused.

He shrugged. "I'm gonna do that for the jury . . . I just thought it was hard to imagine these invisible specks . . . O.K., so tell me where you get a situation where photons fly off like this?"

Ida was annoyed. "Geez, Max! He just explained. And we went over it before he got here. Neon lights, remember? Neon lights contain a gas which emits photons in pairs."

Max clicked his fingers. "Neon lights! Got it. And the photons are like identical twins that fly off in different directions, but they still look alike—they have identical polarization."

Zollner looked relieved. "That's it. You've got it. So if you put detectors in the path of these photons, you'll find that if you line up the detectors so they are identical to each other, the photons will behave identically."

Zollner was holding his hand out to represent the two detectors.

"But if you slightly rotate one of the detectors, you get a situation where . . . I'll draw it for you."

Zollner took his scrap of paper from Stassen and drew a quick sketch of photons approaching detectors, one of which was slightly out of line. The paper was passed from hand to hand around the room and studied with pained concentration.

"You see, one photon will pass through the detector and the other will have its path blocked."

Ida nodded. "Because the detector's been rotated out of line."

"Exactly. Now if I still have you other guys with me. We could say that when a photon passes through the detector we get X, and when it's blocked we get O . . . Oh boy, the most difficult thing of all is trying to make it easy . . . Forget the X and the O . . . Er, let me see . . . Bell discovered that no matter how you set these detectors, the results of passes and blockings correlated too strongly to be accepted as mere chance."

Stassen cracked his knuckles. "Do you know this guy Bell? Is he a friend of yours? Do you think he'd like to come here and testify?"

Zollner looked annoyed. "I have no idea."

Ida moved in to mollify the scientist. "We don't need him if we've got Stefan."

Max made it worse. "We couldn't afford him. I mean if this guy's made the most important scientific discovery of the century . . . phew. And then there's his fare from Geneva. Hotel bills. Astronomic!"

"They're tired," Ida explained icily. "They haven't slept for weeks."

"Uh huh." Zollner looked at them as impersonally as he would look at a graph or a computer printout. "Well, as I said, Bell's Theorem showed that the principle of local causality is mathematically incompatible. You can't beat mathematics. Especially mathematics that are proved by experiments. These photons were communicating at a speed faster than light. Some scientists say this shows that everything is different from the way it looks. I'm one of those scientists. It seems to me that if a photon on the moon can communicate instantaneously with a photon on earth, then . . . as Ida said just now . . . they're acting like there's no distance between them."

"And," said Ida, "if there's no distance for a particle, then what does it say about any distance? What does it say about the distance between Pagels' motor home and Bell Canyon? Maybe distance isn't a rock-solid thing. I mean, maybe it's more negotiable than people realize."

There was a silence. Even Max Haydn kept his face in repose instead of rolling his eyes as he usually did at such a moment.

There had been many such moments as these throughout the summer when the awful truth of what they were envisaging hit them.

Edgar Stassen broke the silence.

"So this Bell's Theorem is a big deal, huh?"

"Oh sure."

"It's the biggest scientific discovery of the century?"

"It's arguable, but, yes."

"So there a lot of people who agree with you on this?"

"I would say that when you have proof like this that the principle of local causality is not an all-encompassing fact of life, then it changes just about everything."

Max Haydn finally allowed himself to slip back into his usual dubious expression. He pushed his hand over his wiry, curly hair, something he did a hundred times a day in a constant, fruitless attempt to straighten and flatten it.

"And local causality is what we all live by, right? Something only has an effect if you can see it or hear it or touch it?"

"Near enough, yes."

"And this isn't the case anymore?"

"It never was."

"But people have been living this way for centuries."

"Oh, sure."

"And just because this happens to some little photon you think it applies to us?" As he spoke, Max's expression of doubt slipped further and became a cynical grin, another of his standards throughout the previous months.

"Yes, I do." Zollner was an even-tempered man but Max was getting to him. "Let's put it like this. Scientists are not too happy about the implications behind quantum theory. You know why? Because it's putting them out of business. If they admit too much they'll have to hand it all over to psychologists. They probed into matter too far and now they're being pushed into metaphysics. They don't like it. They don't like it one bit. They'll tell you that physicists like me are just giving in to wish fulfillment, that we're applying some fancy dream onto the hard rock of science. But I'm not the only one. It's a sort of revolution, you know."

Zollner took a swig of Pepsi and went on quickly. "Time is manmade. It won't be long before everyone realizes that. Everything's changing. There are great revolutions going on in the world. Demographic explosions. Political upheavals. Quantum physics is part of all this. Physicists are scrabbling around, trying to find an old-fashioned, rational explanation for the mind-boggling things that quantum physics have uncovered but Bell's Theorem took the wind out of their sails. And now quantum physics is moving into human experience. I'm damn sure of that, and that's why I'm sticking my neck out like this and helping you out. You asked me and I said I would, and now I'm keeping my word."

Zollner looked at each one of them to see if they understood him. "I'll tell you, it's not going to do me any good. I'm just letting myself in for a lot of flack. I don't even know if Lawrence Pagels is telling the truth. But something strange happened that night. It might not have anything to do with what I'm talking about. But maybe it does. And that's why I'm here. This isn't a joyride for me."

Dr. Zollner sat back, blinking his eyes rapidly.

Max knew that this speech had been directed largely at him. Ida was watching him to see his reaction. He was therefore careful to show nothing.

The to-and-fro of classical reality versus newfangled reality went on for another two hours. A few minutes after three A.M. Stefan Zollner climbed on his twelve-speed bicycle and headed out of the valley, over the hills, and back into Westwood.

Stassen fell on to a bunk bed, relieved by the knowledge that there would be no court the following morning. The continuance was a blessing, or rather it would have been a blessing if there weren't so much ground to cover. He had read physics books all summer and still he knew nothing. He dreamed of Mark Boyman sitting in a vast library with three hundred assistants studying giant law books. Boyman had a long whip and he cracked it over his galley slave assistants as they bent over their books with magnifying glasses. They were searching for loopholes in Stassen's defense. As they found one loophole after another they piled the books onto giant wheelbarrows. Then Boyman cracked his whip and lead the wheelbarrows toward the Van Nuys courthouse.

Max set out for Hughes Supermarket to get some bread and bologna slices. Before he left, he walked Ida to her car.

"Thanks for whining so much," she said.

"I don't whine."

"Max, you really disturb me. What we're attempting is revolutionary and it's so difficult. Poor Stassen is close to a breakdown he's so scared and all you do is whine."

"Oh come on. I have the odd little disagreement. Somebody has to do it. It's the only way I can prove to myself that we're not all Smurfs."

"Max, you can't joke about this."

"Sure I can. I'm working my butt off for no money. I'm gonna get laughed at in court and ruin my future career. I'm eating junk. I'm covered in pimples. My sex life is zilch. Even if I had the time, who'd want a boy with acne? And for what? To prove that some little kid can fly like Superman."

"Goodnight Max."

Ida drove off toward the freeway. Max set out for Hughes Supermarket to join the odd humanity, the night creatures, the cowboys and tattooed people who crawled out of their hiding places into the bright fluorescent lights and did their grocery shopping at three A.M.

9

It was late Wednesday morning when Leon Ferguson finally caught Sandy Leutwiler. It had been a bad morning for her. She had dealt with two traumatic events. First, the swimming pool had to be drained so that the underwater light could be fixed and then Jason had fallen off his skateboard and sprained a wrist.

Jason had taken Daniel out to the driveway before school to teach him acrobatic leaps. Daniel had proved to be a good pupil but the teacher had crashed to the floor after an overly ambitious demonstration.

Don was in bed, dead to the world. Sandy had to beg Sheila to drive Gregory and Daniel to school while she rushed Jason to the emergency room. when she and Jason returned home after half a morning of waiting at the hospital she found that Don had left for work and pool water was flooding down the street in torrents, chlorinating and ruining the neighbor's lawns. The pool men had chosen the quickest means of pool draining and had simply attached a pump to a hose and then stuck the hose out in the street.

Changing the pool light had become a long-running saga. Six days ago two men had appeared to put in a new underwater light. The light was in the side of the pool about halfway down, three or four feet below water level. The men had confidently removed the light bulb casing in two minutes.

When it proved difficult to dislodge the old wiring that was embedded in the concrete, various instruments were brought in. At the end of the afternoon they said they would return with more instruments the following day.

However the next day was occupied with gymnastics. The younger and lighter of the two men would plunge his torso into the pool and tug at the protruding wire while the other would hold his legs to prevent him from falling in headlong. This was accompanied by cursing and shouting from both men.

Two more days of struggle went by, followed by a weekend break. On Tuesday they proceeded to drain the pool. It drained throughout the night down the street at the back of the house. It was not until Sandy returned from the emergency room and drove by the back way that she became aware of the primitive method they had used.

She had phoned Don and he had screamed, "Tell them to use the proper outlet. We've got a drain. Tell them to use it for Chrissakes!"

"It's too late. They've almost finished. It's going to cost five hundred bucks for one little light. They've been here all week."

The men had brought a canister of gas to blow the embedded wires out of the concrete. All the while cursing the man who had installed the old light, they blasted the wire with no effect.

It was at this point that Leon Ferguson phoned.

Sandy was disturbed by the strange note of caution in the reporter's voice. And she was annoyed with herself for not knowing what he was talking about. She had been following the events of the trial by daily phone calls to Stassen's office. But she hadn't called for two days, and she had no idea what had transpired in court. Daniel had been disappointed. He liked to be told what was happening.

"I'm sorry. Are you talking about something that happened yesterday?"

"Monday. What do you think about Dr. Walkman's testimony? What they're saying about Daniel Pagels is . . . quite interesting, wouldn't you say?"

"I don't know. I haven't heard what they're saying."

"Oh . . ."

There were a few seconds silence.

"You haven't heard anything about it?"

"No. The judge doesn't phone me every day."

Ferguson laughed politely.

"I believe," she went on, "Daniel will go in to testify again soon. That's about it. I only go when I have to take Daniel."

"And the defense attorney didn't tell you about it?"

"About what?"

"About what Dr. Walkman implied about Daniel."

"What did he imply?"

Leon Ferguson coughed. "Let me ask you a question. How long has Daniel Pagels been living with you."

"Since June of last year."

"So that's over a year. What do you think of him?"

"He's a nice little kid."

"Does he go off on trips by himself?"

"No he doesn't. He stays put."

"Mrs. Leutwiler, do you think I could get together with you and Daniel?"

"No. We're not looking for any publicity. It wouldn't be good for Daniel. He has enough to cope with."

"Mrs. Leutwiler, I think I should warn you that Dr. Walkman's testimony is going to bring Daniel into the public eye. You're going to hear from everyone in the media."

"There's no law that says I have to speak to them."

"That's true. But I'm about as kind and considerate as they come. I think you'd find talking to me very painless."

"What did you say your name was?"

"Leon Ferguson."

"Well, Leon, I'm going to hang up now. And don't call back. I don't want to hear from you again."

As soon as Leon hung up, she dialed Edgar Stassen's office.

"He's in a meeting," Max told her.

"Then you can tell me. Who is Dr. Walkman? And what did he testify?"

Sandy was unfortunate in having Max Haydn to explain the quantum testimony to her. Although he gave her a model explanation, he made no attempt to make it comforting. He described it as though it were a punishment he was accepting and therefore so should she.

Ida picked up one of the other phones and interrupted. "Mrs. Leutwiler. Don't worry about it."

"Is this a joke?"

"No, it's not a joke."

"You're not going ahead with this are you?"

"Yes, we are."

"Why didn't you tell me before?" Sandy's voice was breathy and weak.

"It's a difficult thing to explain in advance and because it's so difficult, Mr. Stassen was hoping he wouldn't have to introduce it. But we want to get Lawrence Pagels released. I'm sure you do too."

Max grimaced and made a stirring gesture with his hand.

Sandy was not persuaded. "Have you thought what it will do to Daniel? The publicity. I've just had someone calling from the *Daily News*."

"We discussed it with Lawrence. He was concerned but he felt that under the circumstances it was the best thing to do.'

"But of course he'd say that. He wants to get out of jail. He'll say anything. I have Daniel here. I know what it will do to him. He's a very sensitive little boy."

Max spoke up. "Mrs. Leutwiler, everyone's gonna think we're mad or else we have some devilishly clever scheme up our sleeves, they're not going to blame Daniel."

Sandy Leutwiler spent the rest of the day watching her pool refill. The men had triumphed and installed a new pool light. She had planned to photograph them in a victorious pose by the side of the pool but she had lost heart for that.

Instead she toyed with the idea of getting a lawyer to sue Lawrence Pagels' lawyers. She phoned Don, who was in the middle of firing a waiter. He could not understand what she was talking about; he kept having to hang up to get back to work. She phoned him six times until finally he understood.

"Wait till I get back. We'll talk it over. Don't get upset, Sandy."

Jason and Daniel were the first home. Jason, with his arm bandaged, had enjoyed having the morning off from school. He had told elaborate stories about the emergency room.

"Is it true," asked Daniel, "that you get six Hershey bars and a Twinkie if you go to the emergency room?"

Sandy studied Daniel's open, earnest face, as though seeing it for the last time. She put her arm round him.

"Well, if it is true, then Jason should have some chocolate left to give you."

"He said he's eaten it all!" Daniel's eyes opened wide with awe at the thought of it.

"Maybe Jason would like to retell that story."

Jason looked gloomy. "They gave me a candy cane."

"How many?"

Jason glanced at his mother shiftily. "One."

"Just one? Is that all?" Daniel was shocked.

Jason used his good arm to shove Daniel across the room. "Can you believe this kid? He's such a dork. He believes anything you tell him. Dumb asshole!"

As Daniel hurtled toward the door, Don came through it and caught him. Daniel's head landed slap in the middle of Don's stomach, a small battering ram against a beefy, six-four hulk of a man.

"What are you doing here, Dad?" asked Jason.

"I'm checking up on you. What's with the bad language?"

"What do you mean?" asked Jason innocently.

"Why'd you call Danny an asshole?"

"Because he is."

"I don't like you using that kind of language, Jason."

"You say asshole all the time."

"I'm an adult, and I don't call Danny bad names. You don't do it either, O.K.?"

Jason chewed his lip. "I bet you said asshole all the time when you were in Vietnam."

"Maybe I did. But this is not Vietnam. This is Granada Hills. We do things differently here."

"You don't."

"Don't argue, Jason."

Sandy let out a small sigh.

Don went over and put his arm round her. "We'll sort this out. Don't worry about it."

"Worry about what?" asked Daniel, ever alert.

"Nothing," she said quickly. "Daniel got an A in math today."

"Well done, Danny." Don slapped the boy on the shoulder.

Daniel squirmed uncomfortably and looked over at Jason. Getting an A in mathematics was the quickest way of losing Jason's good will.

Sandy stared at Daniel miserably. His painstaking efforts to be accepted as just another kid were about to be destroyed. He was something of a hothouse plant, obviously coached by his grandfather, precocious and advanced for his years. He'd accidentally gotten an A in math. When he was on his guard, he wouldn't let a thing like that happen. Since he had come to the house he had worked hard at establishing a mediocre image for himself. For a child like Daniel, sensitive and loving, the most precious thing in the world was to have friends. He had found out that nobody loves a smart aleck.

Jason was helping himself to some cake from the fridge.

"What have I told you," said Sandy with a hint of hysteria in her voice, "about taking stuff out of the fridge without asking first?"

"Dad does it. So do Sheila and Greg. Even Danny does it."

"He does because he's copying you. You're two years older than he is. You should be a good influence."

"He's got a mind of his own. He can make his own decisions."

"I don't know why Danny does it, but I do it because I was in Vietnam." Don tried to take the tension out of the air with the running gag. "We were so busy running around the swamps with our M-16's that we just didn't have time to ask permission to open the refrigerator."

"Gee, I wish we could have another war. It's not fair."

Jason grabbed an imaginary machine gun and, with the accompanying loud rat-a-tat sound effects, slaughtered everyone in the kitchen. Daniel obligingly crashed to the floor in a dramatic death.

Sandy made the boys sit down at the table while she inflicted healthy raw vegetables on them, which they endured until the special allowance of two Oreo cookies each.

Daniel, who could sense any change of mood a mile off, was aware that Don and Sandy were studying him with the sort of close attention they rarely had time for. They had given him that kind of attention when he first arrived but it had soon worn away. Now it was back again. He watched them watching him.

Gregory came home and he went outside with the two younger boys to watch the pool refill.

"I'll talk to that asshole. See what he's playing at." Don retired to his study, shut the door, and phoned Stassen.

Stassen was still "in a meeting." Don got no more out of Max Haydn than Sandy had.

"We do know what we're doing," said Max. "It's a valid defense based on a lot of heavy research."

Max was closing ranks. He'd either have to stay with Stassen and voice the party line or leave. He had made his choice.

"You're not serious. You don't really believe that a little kid could move like that."

"Is that a statement or a question?"

"I'm asking you!" Don was beginning to shout.

Max sounded cool. "As I said before, we wouldn't be going ahead with this if we didn't consider it be a valid defense."

"Do you personally believe that the kid could do it?"

There was a pause.

"Yes," came the eventual answer. "I do believe it. I wouldn't be here if I didn't. I believe in the truth."

"You do, huh? God almighty! What's happening to the fucking world. My wife's practically having a breakdown over this. You tell your boss that he's an idiot. You tell him that there's a child here. Has he thought of him? We've been trying to give that kid a normal life, and now that's all going to be screwed up by some moron who wants to make a name for himself. He's turned Danny into a joke. The newspapers have started coming round. He'll be on the front page of the fucking *National Enquirer*. He's not the kind of kid who can handle that. You tell your boss to think about this again. You tell that asshole to think it through."

Don always knew when shouting would prove effective. He had screaming down to a fine art. But as he put the receiver down, he knew that he'd been whistling in the wind.

He stepped out of the study and looked round at his beautiful home with its paintings by California artists, its polished wooden floors, oak beams, vaulted ceilings, brick fireplaces, its kidney-shaped pool and Jacuzzi. The house was his accomplishment, his badge of merit.

He'd always known what to do in school, in the army, how to handle Sandy, how to run two restaurants. But he had no idea what to do now.

He went to look at the water shooting into the pool, which was by now half full. Jason had pushed Daniel, fully clothed, into the water. Sandy was helping the giggling boy out. She was not angry. She did not shout. She simply removed the wet clothes and wrapped the boy in a towel, hugging him to her as if he were a baby.

If Daniel was aware of the approaching storm he showed no signs of it. He wriggled out of Sandy's arms and went back to Jason by the side of the pool, where they watched the gushing water with unequivocal joy.

———

Leon Ferguson drove up to the Nields' house in Bell Canyon after a long argument with a security guard. He had made an appointment with Sharon Nields but she had done nothing about informing the officious man at the gate. Phone calls to the house were being picked up on an answering machine and the guard was not going to let anyone through who had not been given a personal go-ahead from Mrs. Nields.

"They had a murder up there. We've got to be careful."

"I'm not going to murder anyone, I'm from the *Daily News*."

Press card, driver's license, car registration, credit cards—nothing had any effect. Leon even produced his gas bill, but the guard, an over-the-hill surfer with a blond mustache, would not let him pass. Leon was not a violent or quick-tempered man. But what he lacked in temper he made up for in determination. Few people escaped Leon. He was prepared to wait.

Finally another guard was dispatched up to the Nields' house, while Leon sat in his car and watched numerous people sail through the gate. He got out of his car and stood under the blazing midday sun and looked at the bare hillside around him. It seemed wild and uncivilized to him. He lived in a small bachelor apartment in Studio City, close to Ventura Boulevard, where there were all-night coffee shops and everything was within easy reach. He couldn't understand why rich people had to live out in the wilderness and suffer inconvenience.

The guard returned with word that Leon could go through the gate. Leon blew the guards a kiss and drove past.

Leon had not yet met a brick wall in his career in the newspaper world. He had worked on papers in one way or another even when he was in high school. In college his journalism teacher had recommended him to a newspaper in Orange County and he had worked on it during the four years he was in college. He'd been given a lowly position on the *Daily News* but here he was working on a valley trial, and he had a gut feeling that this story would get a lot of attention.

He was an agnostic from a profoundly religious family. He felt that the jury was still out on God. Journalism was his god. To him truth was everything. He despised reporters, either in print or television, who did not get the facts right or twisted facts for the sake of a good story. He was about to struggle with a story that would offer him a variety of truths and his faith in an absolute journalistic truth was to be tested.

The route to the Nields' house led past grand palaces built into the raw hills: Tudor mansions, Mediterranean villas, gothic castles, ranch houses with white picket fences, corrals, and stables, everywhere the California dream.

Then the road wound through a wild area where the native hills had maintained their ascendency and no building had been attempted. Mrs. Sharon Nields lived a mile or so beyond this, on the other side of a hill, on a curve in the road where several mansions had been built to form a palatial village.

Mrs. Nields was sitting at a front window when Leon drove his car up the driveway to the white-walled Spanish house and stopped by the great wrought-iron front door. He was looking for a bell among the wisteria growing over the door when Mrs. Nields came out. She appeared distracted and made no mention of the fact that he had been left at the gate for twenty minutes while she ignored the phone.

She stared at his car which he had parked near the front door.

"If you park there, the trees will drop sap on your roof."

As she made the remark, a momentary flash of terror appeared in her eyes.

"That's O.K.," he told her calmly. Leon had a way with nervous women. His girlfriend was prone to fits of anxiety and he handled her as he was now handling Mrs. Nields, by not reacting.

As soon as he walked in Leon saw that it was impossible to break into that house. Every window had fancy wrought-iron bars and the outside doors had double locks and a decal indicating an alarm system connected to the police. The murderer had not broken in the night he attacked John Nields. He was invited in. There was no way he could have penetrated this fortress.

"I'm here on my own. The maid's not here and my son is off somewhere. He said he'd be here to give me moral support but . . . I guess he's busy making money. . . . You're lucky to catch me here. I don't like Los Angeles."

She led him across the polished wooden floor in the front hall into a large room with soft white carpets and white sofas. Leon noticed that her hands were shaking. A gaudy woman with overperoxided hair and too-garish makeup, she was not necessarily a tough one. She was more tasteless than tough.

Because of her obvious fragility he was cautious with his questions.

"How do you feel about the new evidence they're bringing up in the trial?"

"The new evidence? I . . ."

The sound of the front door opening alerted them both. While Mrs. Nields fumbled for her lighter with trembling fingers, Raymond Nields entered the room. He was wearing a double-breasted business suit and carrying a briefcase.

"Hello, honey, this is Leon."

"Hello."

Raymond gave Leon a half smile. He rested his briefcase neatly on a side table and shook hands. It was obvious that he had things on his mind and meeting the reporter was a distraction.

"Leon's writing about the trial, honey."

Raymond nodded. "I always wanted to be a journalist but I can't spell."

"Neither can I," said Leon.

They laughed politely.

"You've heard about Irving Walkman's testimony," Leon asked him.

"Sure."

"Have you been going to the trial?"

"No. My mother finds it too upsetting."

"I went to testify," Mrs. Nields said. "But I thought I was going to die. I couldn't take it."

"Mr. Boyman would like her to go," said Raymond.

"Yes. He keeps asking me to sit there. He said that the jury should see the widow sitting there every day. It makes them realize he was a human being with a family."

"She can't go. It makes her ill."

"I come out in a rash. I can't sleep. I get headaches. I want to forget all the horror. I want to sit in a rocking chair and knit."

"But," asked Leon, "you must have heard about Walkman's evidence on Monday?"

"Yes."

"Ray thinks it's a joke." Mrs. Nields tapped some ash from her cigarette. "They're playing games. They don't seem to remember that my husband's dead. Nobody's thinking of John."

"We're not used to trials," Raymond added. "We didn't know that lawyers could do things like this. It's a farce."

"You don't take it seriously."

Raymond drummed his fingers on the sofa. "Are you kidding? They said the Pagels kid got to this house from Chatsworth the second he thought about it. That's what they're saying aren't they? They're talking about . . . thought travel. My father died and they're turning it into some kind of space movie. Oh boy. . . ."

There were a few seconds of silence. Mrs. Nields stared at her cigarette. Raymond continued to drum his fingers. Leon pretended to write notes.

Finally Raymond asked, "What's your angle on this piece you're writing?"

"You sound like my editor."

Mrs. Nields patted her son's knee. "He's fascinated with journalism. When he was a kid he used to make his own newspaper and deliver it to the neighbors. . . ." She stopped suddenly, lost in thought.

"What kind of man was Mr. Nields? Do you mind if I ask you that?" asked Leon.

Mrs. Nields came out of her revery. "He was a real man. And he used to make me laugh."

"My father was a practical joker," said Raymond.

"Oh, yes," she laughed. "He was a terror. Nobody was safe. And he loved to talk . . . always talking. I mean, you think I'm talkative but I couldn't get a word in around John."

"A big personality," said Leon.

"You better believe it." Mrs. Nields eyes were getting teary.

Leon stayed for another half hour. He found them polite but without a clue about the quantum defense. They had no special insights to offer.

Raymond saw him to the door.

"My mother is a little tense," he said apologetically.

"That's understandable."

Leon was aware of the fact that Raymond and Mrs. Nields watched him until he was clear of the long driveway and out on the road. He could see their faces at a front window. They stood like stone statues, motionless and solemn. And they were still there when the house disappeared from his view in the bend of the road.

———

Rhonda was having dreams about Daniel. She would see him coming toward her with his arms outstretched and then some unseen force, a gust of wind or a flock of giant birds with great flapping wings, would take him away. She would feel the wind that these wings created but she would never get to touch her son.

She remembered that when Daniel was two weeks old he was no longer than the distance between Lawrence's wrist and his elbow. She figured that between that particular wrist and elbow was a good place for him to be.

She had forfeited her rights to her son. She had heard about women who turned up to claim their kids after they had avoided them for years. As far as she was concerned, women like that were cheating.

She distrusted the dreams she was having. She could control emotional thoughts about her son when she was awake but they got at her when she was asleep.

There was no trial on Tuesday but Rhonda turned up at the courthouse anyway so that DeRosa could take her to lunch. She had not planned to go. But the appearance of that scientist in court had unnerved her. Now she needed to stay close to the trial and having lunch with a bailiff was about as near as she could get while it was in recess.

DeRosa was downstairs in the lobby talking to two other bailiffs. They all looked over at Rhonda as she stood at a discreet distance waiting.

He approached her with a big grin on his face.

"Do you see the guy with the blond hair? He says he saw you talking to Lawrence Pagels at the jail."

Rhonda looked down and adjusted a button on her cuff.

"He did?"

"You really got a scoop there. You could sell that. You know Leon Ferguson of the *Daily News*? He's onto this. You should try and sell it before he gets to Pagels."

"Uh huh."

He took her to a restaurant on Victory Boulevard.

She was wearing her plain journalistic clothes, white blouse and a white headband. But this did not prevent DeRosa from looking at her with admiration.

"I guess everyone tells you you're pretty."

"No."

"Oh come on! With your looks . . . You're not eating. Aren't you hungry?"

"Oh . . . yes." She picked up a fork.

"I have to eat fast. I don't get a lot of time." He shoveled some food into his mouth.

"You said you'd tell me about that scientist. What was he saying about the little boy?"

"Who knows what he was saying? He was a smoke screen. They brought him in to confuse the jury. And when they're confused they can't get a consensus. You should have heard them moaning about it."

Rhonda frowned. She had been trying not to look anxious but she had lost the battle. "Do lawyers often do things like this?"

"Not like this. No." DeRosa laughed. "This is the weirdest evidence I've ever heard."

"It's crazy."

He smiled. "Yeah it's crazy. . . . Are you going to eat any of that?"

"Oh . . ." She pushed the food around the plate.

"Tell me something. How did you get to see Pagels?"

"I just asked."

"I heard Pagels' attorney telling him not to talk to anyone. You got an exclusive."

"Yes, I suppose I did."

"You suppose you did?"

Rhonda took a sip of water and then rubbed her eyes as though trying to remove the weariness and anxiety. "They're saying that Daniel, the little boy, got across the valley in no seconds flat, like instantly."

"Right. You got it. Only in California."

"My God."

"It's just tactics. Stassen's testing the system."

"But why would he use a little boy for that?"

She said this with a depth of feeling that caused DeRosa to look at her quizzically.

He touched her hand. "He used him because he was there. . . . Look, all I'm saying is, I shot my mouth off to a guy from the *Daily News* last night. I wasn't thinking. . . . You've been sitting in on that trial every day like clockwork and he was just passing by. Now you've got competition. I'm sorry, it's my fault. But I guess I heard that testimony and I got a little excited and I wanted to tell somebody . . . my wife's walked out . . . she's always going off . . ."

"Does she come back?"

"Yes. I don't know why she bothers."

"Maybe she needs a break. That's how I am. I'm taking a break."

"From men?"

"Yes."

DeRosa's face fell.

"Huh . . . So, anyway, what I really wanted to say about, you know, this story you're working on . . . you better move fast because maybe it'll blow over in twenty-four hours."

"I hope so." She spoke from the heart again and received another curious glance from DeRosa.

He walked her back to her car.

"Do you wanna give me your phone number?"

"I don't have one. I'm in the process of moving."

"Where to?"

"An apartment on Sherman Way."

"So I could call information."

"No . . . it's not my apartment. And I can't remember the number."

"Then keep in touch. I'm here every day."

As she was driving away he wrote her license number on the back of his hand.

———

"Edgar Stassen's office."

"Can I talk to Mr. Stassen."

"Who is it?"

"I called before. I'm Leon Ferguson from the *Daily News*."

"I'm sorry he's in a meeting."

"Yeah, I know. He's been in a meeting for two days. Tell him I've got some new evidence."

"About what?"

"About the Pagels case. Does he want to meet me somewhere?"

"Hold on . . . it's not convenient for Mr. Stassen. Why don't I get together with you?"

Max Haydn met Leon Ferguson at Carrow's Coffee Shop on Devonshire Boulevard. Carrow's was one of the last bastions of old Chatsworth, where men in cowboy hats stopped to get their pancakes and bacon before returning to their old pickup trucks. From there they would go off to some rugged existence not too visible from the standpoint of Mason and Devonshire, with its fancy mini-mall, video rentals, and frozen yogurt. Ranches and citrus groves that once covered the whole of Chatsworth and miles beyond were now pockets of antiquity, hidden from the main street and known only to these cowboys from Carrow's.

Leon was already sitting in a window seat drinking coffee when Max arrived. They were the only men in Carrow's wearing suits and ties. Leon's serious brown face, creased into its permanent frown, made him appear older than his years and gave him an immediate edge over Max. This advantage did not go far against the younger man's unbreakable ego. Max was impervious to the fact that Leon was taller and more expensively dressed than he was. The law student's wiry hair had been cut the night before and looked sleeker and more restrained than usual. It made him feel immeasurably smart.

Max ordered coffee and got down to business. "So Leon, what's this about new evidence?"

"I went to see Sharon Nields yesterday."

"Uh huh."

"Nice meeting. Upset about her husband. Son trying to hold her together. I gave her a card with my number on it and when I got home she called me."

"What did she say?"

"She went on about her house in Bell Canyon. She wants to sell it but her son says the market isn't good right now. She said she doesn't like the house and she wasn't there very often when her husband was alive." Leon consulted the shorthand notebook on the table in front of him. The phone call with Sharon Nields had been recorded in hieroglyphics that were indecipherable to Max.

"Yeah, we know that," Max said cockily.

Leon looked up. "She's found two dresses belonging to some other woman in the closet in the master bedroom."

"This is the first time she's looked in her closet? It's nineteen months since her husband was killed."

"It upsets her to go in the bedroom. She's been sleeping in another room. Nobody goes there except the maid."

"The police went through that closet."

"Yes. I mentioned that. She said the police don't know she can't get into a size eight."

"So how come she's going through her closets now?"

"I don't know. I just thought you'd be interested to know that

John Nields had a girlfriend in the house the night he was murdered."

Max corrected him. "He had a girlfriend's clothes in the house."

Leon shrugged. "If you like."

"I don't get it. It's not in her interest to tell a newspaper about this. Stassen's already brought in witnesses for the jealousy motive. He can use this against her."

"She didn't think that. She thought that the girlfriend might have had a husband or a boyfriend who came round that night and found them together."

"She's always acted like she's a hundred percent sure that Lawrence Pagels did it."

"Maybe she's changed her mind."

"Did she say anything else?"

"No. That was it."

"Why didn't she call the police?"

"Instead of me? I don't know. She likes me. She wanted to tell someone friendly like me."

A skinny blond waitress poured more coffee into their cups. The two young men examined her in a distracted manner.

Leon picked up his pen. "Can I ask you about the unusual scientific evidence you're bringing in?"

Max looked at his watch. "That was the carrot to get the donkey, huh?"

When Max returned to the Winnebago, Stassen was not impressed.

"So a girlfriend left her clothes in the closet. So what. Find me her jealous boyfriend, get me his address, and a couple of fingerprints, then come and tell me about it."

"Maybe she's been put up to this by Boyman. Maybe he's hoping that if we have this we'll drop the scientists," said Max.

"Boyman's not that smart."

"Call him and ask him."

"No, I'll let him stew."

———

Sandy was reliving every single visit to the Winnebago motor home, going over every conversation she could remember. Could she have made more effort to find out what was going on? Could she have done more to protect Daniel?

Don said that to prepare a defense with scientists saying what they said, Stassen would have had to do "a mountain of work and some pretty weird mental gymnastics, real mind-fucking stuff."

When had Max Haydn taken his feet off the desk and started racing around university campuses and research labs looking for a scientist who would say what they wanted? What had they asked Daniel when she'd been off on her shopping trips?

"The same old questions," Daniel always said. He'd never given her any intimation that they were trying a new tack. He was as quiet as a mouse about the whole thing. He was only a kid but he must have had some idea of what was going on. Maybe he didn't. No, he couldn't have known. He wouldn't have understood it even if they'd explained it to him.

But shouldn't they have told her? She was the foster mother. She was going to have to deal with this.

Don had said, "I see now why Stassen's defending Lawrence Pagels for nothing. He's crazy."

"Why didn't he tell me about a stunt like this? I'm his foster mother. He should have told me. I was dragging the kid to his office all summer. Why didn't he tell me? I had a right to know."

"Not if he's crazy he shouldn't have told you. The guy's flipped out."

Sandy had always thought that Edgar Stassen, with his crumpled white suits and bow ties, was flamboyant and a man of many personalities. One minute he'd be shouting into the phone, "If you don't move your ass over here in the next five minutes, I'll . . . sure I'm threatening you." And then the next minute he'd be the old-fashioned gentleman, smiling and bowing to her and Daniel.

The unorthodoxy was accepted by her as a requirement of a complex legal mind. It had not occurred to her that it might be a sign of instability.

She should never have gone off and left the child unprotected in that man's office like that. She had been using Stassen and his cronies as a babysitting service. How did that happen in the first place?

It was Ida who suggested it. She must have been in on the whole thing.

"Why don't you take a break." Ida had said. "I'll keep an eye on him. I love children."

And she fixed up a Nintendo for Daniel and after that he couldn't wait to get there. He was crazy about computer games.

Sandy had always known about muggers and rapists but she'd never thought she had to protect her children from attorneys. If she hadn't left the child alone in Stassen's office maybe they wouldn't have been able to devise this crazy scheme. Because it was a scheme that centered around Daniel and would require some sort of cooperation from him. He was going to have to testify again. What did they talk to him about? What did they tell him to say?

It was too late now. It would be in the papers. Everyone would read about it and it would make life hell for Daniel. He had just started second grade, was just getting to know his new teacher.

"Don't start punishing yourself," Don told her. "What makes you think you could have changed anything? You're dealing with attorneys. They spend years and years learning how to lie and cheat. You're a tadpole to them. This guy obviously has some idea and he's gonna use a lot of people to work it out, that's all. Don't worry about it. Danny's a smart kid. He'll get over it."

"How do you know?"

"He'll get over it because he's a survivor. Look what he's been through already. He's doing great."

"He's only seven years old."

"Sure he's only seven years old, and his grandpa's got a mad attorney, but so what! The kid'll get over it."

They were in the kitchen. Jason was sitting at the table with earphones on listening to heavy metal. Its throbbing beat spilled out of the earphones and made a tinny, rhythmic noise like several dancing grasshoppers.

When Daniel came into the kitchen Jason said, "Your grandpa's attorney's flipped out."

Sandy was upset.

"Were you listening, Jason?"

Daniel was alert. "Flipped out? What means flipped out?"

"What means flipped out?" crackled Jason. "He acts like a visiting Martian. Don't you know anything? This is a fork, get it. And this is a knife. *Comprendo?*"

"Cool it, Jason."

"But how can he be so dumb?"

"Cool it, I said."

"Dad kicked me."

"I tapped your foot."

"You kicked me."

"One man's kick is another man's tap."

"Mrs. Johnson told fourth grade that if our parents hit us too much we should report them."

"Who to?"

"To her."

"You're gonna tell Mrs. Johnson that I tapped your foot?"

"I'm gonna tell her you kicked me."

"You're gonna tell Mrs. Johnson. Well while you're about it, ask her if she knows what a book is. Spell it for her. B-O-O-K book."

"No I'll tell her you killed so many people when you were in the army that you don't know how to stop, and now you're killing me."

"Right tell her that. Tell her that I don't want to lose my touch so I like to work out on little kids and dumb schoolteachers."

Daniel heard none of this. He went over to Sandy. "What means flipped out?"

Sandy cupped his cheeks in her hand. "It means gone crazy."

"Why has he gone crazy? Does Grandpa know?"

She saw that Daniel's solemn face looked more disturbed than she'd ever seen it before.

"Don said he'd flipped out. But you know Don."

"But he must have had a reason for saying it. You don't just say it."

Sandy took Daniel by the hand, lead him into the study, and shut the door.

"They're going to write about your grandpa's trial in the *Daily News*. And it's all because Mr. Stassen has brought in some scientists to explain how you could get to Mr. Nields' house real fast, faster than its really possible for a person to get there. They're saying that because people saw you at home and at Mr. Nields' house at the same time."

Sandy watched the boy carefully to see if he had known this was going to happen or whether he was surprised or disturbed. But there was nothing in Daniel's eyes but concern. And that told her very little.

She went on. "Don and I were talking about it. You know we were kind of surprised to hear about it and Don said he thought

Mr. Stassen had flipped out. It was a kind of joke. I'm not a lawyer so I don't understand how they work things out, but maybe Mr. Stassen has a clever plan and he's playing a trick on everybody. I know he wants to get your grandpa out of jail. I'm sure that's the most important thing to him."

"And what did Grandpa say?"

"About the scientists?"

"Yes, about what they said."

"He hasn't said anything yet. I expect he'll be a witness soon and then he can say what he thinks about all that."

Against the dark wooden beams and the brick fireplace of the study Daniel's pale face and his blue-gray eyes had a silvery, moon-like quality.

"Did Mr. Stassen tell you he was going to get those scientists to say those kind of things, Danny?"

"No."

"What did you talk about when you went to see him all those times?"

"He asked questions."

"Is that all? He didn't tell you anything?"

"No."

"Did he tell you what to say in court?"

"Yes."

"What?"

"He said, say 'Sir' "

"Anything else?"

"No."

She drove the children to school and watched Daniel run through the gates and toward the other children. He was very much a people person which was surprising for one who had lead such an isolated life. If he came across a group of children on the beach, in the park, on the street, he did not hang back shyly but would move in and watch their play doggedly, laughing at their jokes, running where they ran, until he was an accepted member of the group. Then he would quickly become the ideas man, thinking up things for them to do, arguing for the right to do it. He was always hungry for play with other children. Whereas her own children would just as soon watch television, Daniel would always prefer the interaction of a game. The relationship between Daniel and Jason fell down over the amount of time they should devote to the television. The older boy complained that he could no longer sit on the couch in peace.

Daniel's teacher said that he was too bright for second grade but he was getting along well with his classmates and she did not think it a good idea to move him to a higher class. She also said he spoke quite freely about his grandfather's trial. He had told the class that his grandfather was innocent and that he would soon be free. The teacher thought that much of Daniel's well-being seemed to spring from the conviction that he would soon be back with his grandfather. She had cautioned Sandy that it might be a good idea to get Daniel to consider the idea that his grandfather might be in jail for a very long time.

There was a danger that Daniel could lapse into a serious depression at a later date if he did not now begin to think about the idea of a life permanently apart from his grandfather.

Sandy tried to approach the idea with Daniel on several occasions but she met a complete mental block. She would suggest that perhaps the jury would not be very understanding and perhaps they might be hard on Lawrence. His jaw would tighten and he would say, "Grandpa didn't kill Mr. Nields." He would not respond to any suggestions that his grandfather might be in a difficult situation.

The day was not far off when they would all have to deal with the verdict. Daniel did not seemed perturbed by the odd turn in the defense lawyer's tactics. Perhaps he did not yet fully understand its implications. Perhaps she didn't either. It was quite possible the whole thing might blow over very quickly instead of turning into something that would damage Daniel. What did she know?

One thing was certain. Daniel was determined to remain a child as long as possible. It seemed to her as if Daniel had the choice to be anything, but to be a child was his choice because . . . well, because he was one.

His model of perfection was Jason. His two-years seniority made him a powerful influence. Sheila and Gregory were a little too old, too far out of his sphere. Jason set the standard. Daniel had discovered that piano playing was unacceptable to Jason and he had immediately given it up. He had stopped drawing as stylishly and accurately as before. If he did draw, he drew like Jason, big untidy sketches of planes and ships, spindly-legged dogs, crooked cats.

Daniel watched carefully, saw what was going down, and then

did likewise. He had never complained until he'd listened to Jason a few times. But now he could do a perfect imitation.

"Mom, there are nuts in this ice cream. Yuk!"

"Yuk! Nuts in the ice cream." And he would get the pitch of the whining voice with the accuracy of a professional impersonator.

Daniel was learning well.

10

Mary-Lynn Robbins had given a copy of *Physics Made Simple* to Mark Boyman. During lunch, as he prepared to have his first meeting with a physicist, he studied the book for three-quarters of an hour and then went in search of a chocolate bar.

"Are you telling me," he asked Mary-Lynn as he unwrapped a Three Musketeers, "that this book is for high-school kids?"

"Yes"—she read out the words on the cover—"it's a complete guide from Newtonian physics to nuclear fusion."

"Uh huh. Then if its so complete why do I keep on thinking I've missed something? This professor who wrote this wrote it for himself. Every so often he'll assume something that he hasn't told anybody about and then he throws in a bit of algebra and after that you could be reading the telephone book."

"You have to stick with it and then it all makes sense."

"How can it make sense? It's like a foreign language. I'm going along fine for a couple of paragraphs and then he changes the rules."

"He doesn't change the rules. If you think he's changed the rules, you haven't really understood the first two paragraphs."

Boyman threw *Physics Made Simple* off his desk and it joined all the other physics books that had been similarly treated by him. He went to the window and looked down on the street below where a youth was levering a car door open with a chisel. He observed the scene objectively as though watching a spider climb up a wall and marveled at the combination of stupidity and chutzpah which would bring someone to rob a car in broad daylight when they were within spitting distance of the District Attorney's Office, City Hall, the Criminal Court buildings, and the Police Department. He turned away and went back to his desk, kicking *Physics Made Simple* as he went.

"There's nothing in that book about the experiment with the board and two holes. And even if it was there it would not make any sense. The jury didn't understand it. Nobody understands it."

Mary-Lynn had been caught as she was halfway out the door. She turned. "I understand it."

"Explain it to me."

"Explain what?"

"Anything. Explain it."

"Look. If you want to understand the double-slit experiment, it's easy. A particle went through two holes at once. It should be impossible but it isn't."

"Maybe it broke in half."

"No, it didn't."

"It didn't?"

"No. And when you put a detector on it, it only goes through one hole."

"So what?"

"So what? That's it!" Mary-Lynn held her hands out. She was wearing another of her many miniskirts which had trouble getting round her ample haunches. She wore it with a Ralph Lauren shirt and an Indian conch belt, which was straining to do its job of holding things together. She was an expensive bundle. "That's what it's all about. I think you should stop trying to understand the whole of physics because you're not going to make it. And you should just study that one experiment."

Mary-Lynn reminded Boyman of his mother. And their relationship was growing to be more and more like the one he had with his mother. She hectored him with the same kind of authority.

"I get that," he said irritably. "I don't have any trouble with that. I've never had any trouble with that. I just want to know why Stassen thinks he can stand up in court and say it has a connection to Daniel Pagels."

"He's saying if a little thing changes when you look at it then a big thing changes when you look at it."

"Like what?"

"Like the little boy. I think they're saying he changed himself . . . something like that."

Harvey Marlatt walked in. "No. They're not saying that. They're saying things are only there if you look at them. He forgot to look so *POW*, he was there in a flash!"

Marlatt grinned and waved his arms around like a ghost on Halloween night. *"Wooooh!"*

Boyman was not amused. "Mary-Lynn, study that experiment again. I want fifteen clear reasons why it has absolutely nothing to do with human experience. Bring them to me as soon as you're finished."

He pushed past Marlatt and went in search of another chocolate bar.

———

Max Haydn phoned Rhonda at the Sherman Way apartment.

"Hi, Rhonda. It's Max From Edgar Stassen's office."

"What do you want?"

"I just wanted to say hi. See if you're O.K. If you need anything, give us a call . . . and . . . if you're planning to see your dad at the jail again, Mr. Stassen thinks it would be better if you waited a while."

"I can go and see who I like when I like."

"Of course. Absolutely. It's a free country."

"I'm a human being. I'm not a disease."

"I agree, Rhonda. I'm with you all the way. But if you're interested in helping your dad, don't go to the jail that's all. Give him a break."

"Why was that scientist saying those things about Danny?"

"To help your dad."

"Did he ask you to do it?"

"He's not against it, Rhonda. He's for it a hundred percent."

"Can you tell him to get in touch with me?"

"No, Rhonda. Not right now. Be patient. Wait till after the trial and you can talk to him twenty-four hours a day."

"In jail?"

"You've got to hope for the best."

Max put the phone down and groaned.

"I hate this job."

_____

Article by Leon Ferguson in the Los Angeles *Daily News*.

The attorney for accused murderer Lawrence Pagels now on trial at Van Nuys courthouse has brought in Dr. Irving Walkman, a Caltech physicist, to offer some bizarre scientific evidence in Pagels' defense. Dr. Walkman said that it was possible for the accused man's grandson to move through space at the speed of light.

Lawrence Pagels, a 65-year-old Chatsworth gardener, is accused of murdering wealthy property developer, John Nields on April 12, 1988. Pagels' 5-year-old grandson Daniel was found abandoned in John Nields' Bell Canyon home a few hours after Nields had been murdered there. Also a small trace of the victim's blood was found on Lawrence Pagels' pickup truck.

Assistant District Attorney Mark Boyman is convinced that these two pieces of evidence prove that Lawrence Pagels killed John Nields.

Defense attorney Edgar Stassen says that the blood was left on the truck when John Nields grabbed hold of it during an earlier meeting with Pagels. He insists it has no connection to the murder.

He called Dr. Irving Walkman to testify that it is possible that the child could have traveled by himself at the speed of light to the Bell Canyon home instead of being taken there by his grandfather. Witnesses have testified that young Daniel Pagels was seen simultaneously at his home in Chatsworth and also ten miles away at the house in Bell Canyon. He was witnessed in both places at 11:30 P.M., which was around the time John Nields was murdered.

Stassen says that the child was not taken to Bell Canyon by his grandfather. He insists that this seeming presence of the child in two places at once indicates that he traveled from one place to the other with superhuman speed and that he traveled there alone. The child told the court that he went to John Nields' Bell Canyon home to see some puppies he had played with earlier in the day.

Dr. Walkman, who was brought in to testify to the possibility of superhuman travel, is a respected physicist at the California Institute of Technology and has written several books on nuclear physics. He believes that quantum physics reveals extraordinary facts about the nature of life and that everything that we have always accepted as normal in daily life has to be reevaluated in the light of quantum physics. Quantum physics is the branch of physics based on quantum theory, used for interpreting the behavior of elementary particles and atoms.

Sandy Leutwiler, foster mother of Daniel Pagels, is skeptical of the strange claims made for the child and feels that the publicity will be harmful to him. She told the *Daily News* that Daniel is a normal child without unusual abilities.

The murder victim's family are disturbed at the inclusion of this bizarre proposition in the trial. John Nields' son, Raymond, does not take the defense's proposition seriously. He labeled the idea "a farce" and says that it has had a harmful effect on his mother. She is so shocked by it that she is no longer able to leave the house or lead a normal life, he claims.

Max Haydn, the defense attorney's assistant, insists that there is no hidden motive behind the introduction of quantum physics testimony. He said, "We are absolutely convinced that there is a strong scientific basis underlying this. Daniel Pagels went to the house alone and there is sufficient evidence to prove this. We are serious. There is nothing frivolous about what we're doing."

This is the first case of its kind. Quantum physics has never before been used in a California court to prove unusual human abilities. Mark Boyman, the district attorney, had no comment on the defense assertions, but it is thought that the prosecution will introduce physicists who will ridicule the defense's claims.

The trial resumes in Van Nuys on November 6.

On the morning that the article appeared in the *Daily News* there was a flurry of phone calls to the District Attorney's Office and to Stassen's Winnebago in Chatsworth. The calls were from two local television stations, as well as the *Los Angeles Times* and several San Francisco and San Diego newspapers.

Mark Boyman wrote out a statement which Mary-Lynn read to everyone who called. Her first moments of stardom came when she read it out, on camera, to a Channel 7 reporter.

Edgar Stassen followed Boyman's example. Max and Ida were kept busy on the day of the publication of Leon Ferguson's article, but the next day, the siege stopped almost as immediately as it had started. A few calls dribbled in over the weekend. There was a phone call from the BBC in London and a telex from a television station in Australia, but on the whole things quieted down. There was a spurious sense of peace but no one took it at face value.

The sudden attention had thoroughly unnerved Stassen and the ensuing quiet made him more nervous still.

"It's not going to be the same in that courtroom. News editors all over the world are sitting with that article on their desks and they're asking themselves 'Is this guy for real.' And they'll say, 'Well, what the hell, let's put someone on that.' Do you remember those news reports about flying saucers landing in the Soviet Union and everyone said 'this is a joke, but they reported it in *Pravda* so let's send a camera crew out there to film that hole in the ground and talk to those people who saw the big green men.' That's how they're gonna be with this. 'Where the fuck is Van Nuys' they'll be saying. 'Get someone out there. They're going to put on a show.' They'll be coming from all over. They'll be hanging from the rafters. I'm glad we have reserved seats."

"Oh shit," Max whispered to Ida. "I wish I'd never got involved with this turkey."

Sharon Nields received few calls from the press. Those that did come were deflected by Raymond Nields. "My mother finds it disturbing to talk about this," he told reporters. As for himself, he said that he would not make any comment until the trial was over.

The Leutwilers were not surprised when a couple of reporters appeared on their doorstep in Granada Hills. They had anticipated this reaction to the article and had worked out a plan of action. They had determined not to answer the door and the reporters eventually tired of ringing the doorbell and went away. Don retired to his office at the back of his restaurant and did paperwork. Sandy monitored all calls on their answering machine and kept Daniel away from school for the week. She took to driving past the house before she parked the car. If she saw anyone suspicious, she drove right past, parked around the corner, and climbed over the back wall.

"It's a one-day wonder," Don announced the following day when the street was clear.

"Don't count your chickens," said Sandy. "I want you to put a step ladder by the back wall."

————

Leon Ferguson wrote a short follow-up article in the *Daily News* about the discovery of the dresses at Nields' house. With its slight flavor of sexual scandal it served to stir up more interest in the Pagels case.

Raymond Nields was bitter about it and complained to Leon. "My dad is dead. He can't protect himself from all these innuendoes. And you've taken advantage of my mother. She didn't know what she was doing when she spoke to you."

Whether she knew what she was doing or not, Sharon Nields received a muted reprimand from the DA's office.

"Hello, Mrs. Nields. This is Mark Boyman."

"Oh."

"How are you?"

"I'm trying to cope."

"That's good. I know it's a difficult time for you."

"Yes, it is."

"I'd like to help you if I can, Mrs. Nields, that's why I'm calling. Mary-Lynn is on the other line."

"Hello, Mrs. Nields. How are you?"

"I've been better."

"If you're worried about anything, call Mary-Lynn. Talk to her first before you do anything. You've got us all very upset here because you've been talking to the press."

"Uh huh."

"We realize you're under a lot of stress. But so are we. You'll make things a lot easier for us if you don't go around talking to reporters. Do you understand that?"

"Oh yes. I'm not stupid."

"I know that, Mrs. Nields."

"I know what you want to hear and what you don't want to hear. But this information has to come out. Those dresses. They're important. There was a woman here . . . jealousy is a terrible thing. Perhaps her husband was here that night. She was a small woman. Slim, size eight."

Boyman sighed. "Yes, we know all about it. We're looking into it. Don't worry yourself about it."

"And I've been thinking about Lawrence Pagels. How could he forget that boy? Nobody's ever murdered someone and left their child behind. I'm a mother. I know what it's like. You don't forget."

"Lawrence Pagels killed your husband, Mrs. Nields. Trust us. We've been working on this for a long time."

Boyman pulled a despairing face at Mary-Lynn. He remembered the Mrs. Nields who had come in to testify. She exuded hatred for the defendant. What had happened to change her?

"I'm asking you a special favor, Mrs. Nields. Don't talk to anyone else, please."

"O.K."

"Good. I'm going to hang up now, Mrs. Nields. I thought you'd like to have a chat with Mary-Lynn. It might help to have a long talk. Feel free to call her anytime. She's there to help. Good-bye."

Sharon Nields talked to Mary-Lynn for forty-five minutes about John Nields and his affairs.

"He had a lot of energy. He was a powerful man. And men like that have to express themselves. I didn't like it. But that's the way things are with men like that. You learn to accept it."

She talked about life without him. "It's like a bubble burst. I miss him every minute of the day."

About her son. "He's driven. Just like his father. Very ambitious. What he is, is what John made him. It's John's fault."

About their two houses. "As soon as the trial is over we're selling the Bell Canyon house. I don't care if there's a slump in the market."

Mary-Lynn reported in to Boyman. "She talked, but you know what? She's still got something on her mind that she's not telling us."

"Whatever it is," Boyman told her, "I don't want to know."

———

Max Haydn was convinced that if he could find the female who had left her clothes in John Nields' closet, he could also find another suspect. Her boyfriend, her husband, anybody strong enough to batter Nields to death, carry his body to a car, and dump it out onto a freeway. And if he could find another convincing suspect, someone who would plant seeds of doubt in the minds of the jury members, then maybe Stassen would call off the dogs, throw out all the scientists and the quantum physics and stop embarrassing himself and everyone working with him.

That, at least, was the hope.

To find the owner of those dresses was theoretically not difficult. Previous testimony had pointed out that John Nields had been ostentatious about his liking for women. He was like a kid in a candy store around anything female. He propositioned, he pinched secretaries, he made sexual jokes. But many felt that he did it to impress men in business circles. They were not sure that he followed up on too many, if any, of his advances.

The dresses in the closet put paid to that idea. John Nields had at least one women in his bed in Bell Canyon. And that woman, if he could find her, could take the heat off Lawrence Pagels, and consequently take the heat off him. He, Max, could have a future instead of being a joke for the rest of his life.

There had also been the odd domestic arrangement with the female business partner who lived in the house with Nields and his wife. Max checked up on her. She was now living in Canada. When he surprised her by calling to ask her measurements, she told him she wore a size fourteen. That was the wrong number, she could not have squeezed into those size eight dresses.

He talked to Graciella, the Nields' maid. She came in between nine and ten in the morning and left at five o'clock. She said she saw no girlfriends. If they were there, she said, they left before she arrived in the morning.

Arlene Tullis, the curious neighbor up the hill from Nields' house, said that she never saw any young women go into the house.

"They have a garage around in back. He always drove straight in and went into the house through the garage. He had those dark windows on his car so you couldn't see who was in it. He usually drew most of the blinds except in the kitchen. I never saw a young lady in the kitchen. But I'm not on duty at my window twenty-four hours a day, I could have missed something."

A waiter in an Italian restaurant on Ventura Boulevard in Encino said he had seen someone like John Nields in his restaurant with a dark-haired young woman. But he could not be definite about the date or give an exact description of the woman. It was, after all, now nineteen months since John Nields had been killed.

Max went through all Nields' diaries and appointment books for the tenth time. But he could find nothing that was not connected with his family or business. If John Nields finagled, he had never made a note of it in writing.

"Neither would you," Stassen shouted at him. "If you were screwing around on your wife, you wouldn't write in your diary 'See Maisy Bell tonight.' "

It seemed to Max that his pursuit of the dress-in-the-closet mystery was seen as another vote of no-confidence in the quantum defense. He was getting to think that all Stassen and Ida cared about was quantum physics and that it was more important to them than getting Pagels out of jail.

He felt that if he suddenly dropped the real killer on the doorstep of the Winnebago, they would be more than disappointed, they would be devastated. It seemed as though the trial had become all about proving that Daniel Pagels had abnormal abilities and nothing else. Because, he thought, if they really wanted to defend Pagels they would be more interested in the dresses in the closet.

"What would you do if I walked in with a signed confession?" he asked Stassen. "Would you call up Dr. Zollner and tell him to forget it?"

Stassen did not bother to answer. He gave him the finger.

When Max was alone with Ida he said, "You two are obsessed. All you care about now is quantum physics."

"That's not true, Max." She spoke as one speaking to a small and not too intelligent child. Or as Max saw it, in the manner that obsessed people speak to those without their vision. It made him angry.

"Don't even try to deny it. I see the changes going on around here. First Stassen was scared shitless of the whole idea of using quantum physics. Now he's had a little publicity. He's beginning to like it. It's subtle but I see it."

"So what if he likes it? What's so bad about that?"

"It's bad because he likes it so much, he'd shoot the guy who came in here and confessed and he'd shoot me for bringing him in. He wants to bring in those scientists."

"That's your impression, Max. It's not mine. What's so bad

about wanting to keep Lawrence out of jail? He's doing his job. And anyway . . . he doesn't love the physics. He's still tortured."

"Maybe so. But I see someone who's beginning to enjoy the torture."

———

Joe DeRosa checked Rhonda's license number on the computer and discovered that her name was Rhonda Moor Pagels.

"Pagels!"

He sat down to think about it.

———

In defiance of the assistant DA's orders, Sharon Nields invited Leon Ferguson up to the Bell Canyon house for a second visit. She told him to bring a photographer with him.

When she met them at the door she appeared to be a little unsteady on her feet, as if the strain of it all was now sapping her muscular strength.

"You didn't have any photographs with your article. Don't you think you should get some pictures of the woman's clothes? If you put them in the paper somebody might recognize them."

"I'm not sure I could get them in the paper."

Leon was, unusually for him, wearing jeans that day. But when Leon wore jeans, he looked like other men do in suits. He certainly looked smarter than the photographer, who was in sports jacket and tie.

She lead her two visitors up to the closet and had them photograph the dresses front and back.

"Get the belt," she urged. "It's the main feature."

She held the dress out with unsteady hands.

Leon watched her curiously. "Why are you doing this, Mrs. Nields?"

"Because if I don't, nobody will. It'll be a mystery. Like the Sphinx."

She produced the second dress. "It's hand-finished. I bet he paid a bundle for this. It has something on the label but I don't know what it means. You should follow this one up because the other one could have been bought anywhere."

Leon took the photographs over to Max. He wanted to get the defense opinion on this. The two of them trekked round several department stores showing the photos. Finally one young assistant buyer pointed out that the odd design on the label was actually an N superimposed on an H to form a geometric pattern.

The NH stood for Nana Hobbs, a new designer, who had a small showroom and workshop on Melrose Avenue.

"I have absolutely no idea who bought it," Nana Hobbs told Leon and Max. She offered them several boxes of invoices and receipts.

It took them only an hour to find a copy of a receipt made out to John Nields. A note scrawled in pencil on the bottom read, "To be picked up by Jennifer Perry."

Max was jubilant. "Jennifer Perry! I know her! I interviewed her last year. She worked for Nields. My God, I spoke to her!"

At this point Max called Detective John Starbeck and informed him of the discovery.

Starbeck was cool. "I'm not working on this case anymore. Tell the girl to pick up her clothes. Don't tell me about it."

Jennifer Perry had assisted Deborah Hillier at Nields' Encino office in 1987. She was not happy to see Leon and Max on her doorstep.

"Please go away," she whispered. "My husband doesn't know about it."

She had the appearance of a ballet dancer, with small wrists and ankles, and dark hair pulled back in a bun.

"He doesn't know about any of it?" asked Max.

"No. Now go, please!"

They did not go.

Leon was convinced that this was an occasion when truth was more important than keeping secrets between husband and wife. Max did not even consider an alternative. Nothing would prevent him from talking to that woman.

Jennifer Perry's husband came to the door and when he discovered why they were there, he attempted to shut the door. It was immediately apparent that he knew all about his wife's relationship with Nields.

"Why don't you leave her alone?"

"Did you know John Nields?" Max asked.

"No, I did not. She wants to forget about all that. Go inside, Jenny."

Jennifer went inside the house and left her husband, a dark-haired, wiry man in a T-shirt and sweatpants, to face the two men.

It was obvious at this point that he was about to punch either Max or Leon, so they left.

In talking to the Perrys' neighbors, they discovered that Bruce Perry had been laid off from Hughes Aviation around the time that John Nields was murdered. During that period he had suffered from bouts of depression and drank excessively. Now he had found other employment and his disposition had improved. Though not that much. He overreacted to any complaints about his dogs, two Great Danes, who repeatedly fouled neighbors' lawns.

"He acts like he's going to punch you," Max and Leon were told.

"Yeah, we know," they replied.

Max called Stassen, who said he would use the information about Jennifer Perry "if he needed it." He also left a message with John Starbeck giving him an update but he did not return the call. Max was more disturbed about that than Leon. Given time, Max knew he could get their attention and find a possible way out of looming disaster. But Max had run out of time.

The Trial Resumes

11

The scene on the sixth floor of the Van Nuys courthouse was totally
unlike anything that had gone before. An obscure murder trial in
a city of many murders had become the instant focus of media
attention. In the hallway outside the courtroom there were two
television camera crews and six or seven reporters, plus a throng
of hopeful members of the public who wanted to see for themselves.

Joe DeRosa stood at the doorway of the courtroom ushering
people in one by one. He beckoned to Rhonda Pagels who was at
the back of the crowd and pushed her through the door.

He whispered, "You're a surprising girl, you know that?"

She looked startled. "What do you mean?"

"Tell you later."

DeRosa went back to corralling the press. He sent a group of
reporters, Leon Ferguson among them, to one side of the courtroom. At Judge Conan's insistence, he ordered the television cameras outside. Earl and Hank squeezed in with two of their friends.
When all the seats were full, he advised the remaining members of
the public to leave the building, but many of them refused to go
and waited outside in the hallway with the television cameras.

When Judge Conan came in and saw the packed courtroom he
paused for a moment and considered what the quantum defense
had wrought. He appeared taken aback although he must have
suspected something like this. He made a short speech about court

behavior in which he asked for absolute quiet and no laughter. They had not come here for entertainment but to hear a trial for a brutal murder. They were not watching a television show.

It was déjà vu for the attorneys on both sides. There was Stassen in his crumpled white linen jacket, looking nervous and ill; Max, tight-lipped and depressed, disassociating himself from the proceedings and Ida, a combination of wary and helpful. The prosecutors, Mark Boyman and Harvey Marlatt, were a touch more apprehensive than they had been last time, a little more clued in to what was going on and hence a touch more like Stassen in mood.

As before, Lawrence Pagels was hopeful and alert. He even nodded affably to the witness Dr. Stefan Zollner, a move which made the witness distinctly uncomfortable.

Only the jury had changed and they had changed considerably. They were electrified. They had become twelve instant stars in a media event and they were wide-eyed and bolt upright.

Dr. Zollner brushed his thinning hair back with fidgeting hands and took the oath in an almost inaudible voice. Stassen watched him apprehensively, wondering if the usually confident Dr. Zollner was going to crumble now that his moment had come.

The appearance of so many spectators in the courtroom gave Stassen a sense of occasion and gave him a buzz, an extra charge of adrenalin that helped rather than hindered him. It removed some of the paralyzing nervousness, some, but not all of it. The sheen on his forehead and the breathiness in his voice gave him away.

Having a considerably larger audience, Stassen started by recapitulating. His preliminary questions covered the same ground that he'd gone over with Dr. Walkman two weeks before, so that the newcomers could get the picture and the jury could acquaint themselves once more with the unsettling conclusions of quantum physics. Then he moved on to fresh territory. He was going to ease gradually into Bell's Theorem.

"Dr. Zollner, you told us that quantum mechanics are real accurate. Does this show us that the world is orderly and easy to measure?"

"No. According to Heisenberg's uncertainty principle you cannot make a completely accurate prediction."

"Can you explain that sir?"

"Werner Heisenberg was a German scientist who formulated his uncertainty principle in 1926. We learn from it that we can't measure the position and velocity of a particle exactly. The more we know about one, either its position or velocity, the less we know about the other. The act of measuring affects the particle."

"The act of measuring affects the particle." Stassen repeated the words and turned to the excited jury to see if they got the meaning.

"Yes, it does. It affects the particle." Zollner was trying hard to make his meaning clear. It was difficult for any advanced scientist to accurately predict the degree of incomprehension in average members of the public.

William Perrott, the lunch-wagon operator in the middle front row of the jury, was smiling at the meaningless of it.

"I know," said Stassen turning to face Perrott and the rest of the jury, "that the very mention of these words, particle and velocity, makes your eyes glaze over. So perhaps I should ask Dr. Zollner if the ladies and gentlemen of the jury are made up of particles?"

"Yes, they are."

"Is the judge made of particles?"

"Yes, he is."

"Is Mr. Boyman over there made up of particles?"

"Yes, he is."

"And perhaps you could explain the meaning of velocity in case anyone here has any confusion about it."

"It's the rate at which something moves. Speed, if you like."

"Speed. Even a dummy like me can understand that. Speed. I got it. . . . So let's go back to Heisenberg's principle. He said that the act of measuring a tiny particle of matter, which means a tiny particle of a hat or a cup or a human being, affects it. Is that what you said?"

"Yes, I did."

Stassen went over to the blackboard which had been set up well in advance by Max to avoid any peremptory clicking of fingers by his superior.

The attorney picked up a piece of chalk. "I'll mark a point A here. If you have a subatomic particle here at point A . . . and don't forget this courtroom is made up of atomic particles. I'll draw a point B here. Now what happens, Dr. Zollner, if you observe the fact that this little particle is sitting on point A?"

"If you measure its position at point A then you cannot measure its rate of motion as it changes position and moves to point B because the act of location itself alters the position of the particle in an unpredictable way."

"So are you saying that once you've acknowledged the fact that the particle is at point A, then there's no way in the world you can tell how long it takes to get to point B?"

"It's uncertain. That's the uncertainly principle."

"And if you measure its velocity, then what happens to point A and point B?"

"They become uncertain."

"How does the particle know what you've measured?"

"It can't know. It's mindless."

"Is the uncertainty in the particle or in us?"

"It's not in the particle. A particle can't think. It doesn't know how to be uncertain. The uncertainty is in us."

"Why don't we have this uncertainty problem in our everyday life? How come, if I cross this courtroom, you can measure my position and momentum at the same time?"

"I can only speculate on that. It seems we've all agreed on certain overall definitions of things which we all abide by."

"And this uncertainty principle, this absolute fact of life, was discovered by Werner Heisenberg in 1926?"

"That's correct."

"When he came up with this, didn't it make everyone get a little nervous?"

"Very few people understood what he was getting at."

"Didn't they understand that when you measure a small particle you immediately affect it in a drastic and amazing way?"

"Only a few scientists understood it then. And generally only scientists understand it today. It isn't talked about in the media. People don't worry about it."

"And what would you say is the consensus among scientists today about this amazing phenomenon?"

"They avoid too much concern about it mostly by saying that the uncertainty principle only refers to subatomic life and has no meaning on the large scale of things. But I think everyone would agree that generally speaking, if things happen in a small way in the small scale of things, then they must happen in a colossal way in the large scale of things. The uncertainty principle presents enormous philosphical problems, which are not being met by scientists. They are able to use quantum mechanics successfully but they are not able to explain the shattering implications behind it."

As he neared the end of his speech Stefan Zollner's voice developed a slight squeaking rasp not unlike a chisel scraping against stone. He needed water.

"So let's have a little recap," said Stassen. "You get a particle, and then once you've looked at it you've kind of interfered in the situation by looking in on it and saying 'hey there, little particle, I see you're at point A'?"

"You could say that, yes."

"And after you've done that, this little particle is no longer under the laws that you and I know in everyday life. This little particle could travel from point A to point B in any time . . . or no time at all?"

"That's correct."

"And if we measure its volition, that is, the time it takes to get from point A to point B then we can't be certain it was traveling from point A?"

"Objection, Your Honor." Boyman was grimacing. "Mr. Stassen is going over this to the point of tedium."

Conan waived Boyman's objection. Judging from faces in the jury, tedium was not yet a problem.

Stassen took a little walk over to the jury and back to the witness. "O.K., Dr. Zollner. Tell us ignoramuses what exactly is quantum mechanics?"

"Quantum mechanics is a science which uses the uncertainty principle. It states that as particles have no definite position and velocity, they have a quantum state, a state that combines position and velocity."

"So I'll ask you the big question. Why don't we human beings who are a collection of these particles that obey these strange laws, why don't we have a quantum state so we can move about like the particles we're made up of?"

Dr. Zollner laughed, "The answer is . . . we do but we don't."

"Why don't we?"

"Nobody knows why. You're getting into big unanswerable areas. We only know how, not why."

"If a small boy were to move very fast one night, so fast that it appeared he moved from one place to another instantly, then is there a scientific principle, a law whichwould explain this movement?"

"There is a quantum law that could explain it on a quantum scale. But there isn't a classical law on the level of everyday reality."

"So every little particle in that kid's body was obeying these laws, which allowed him to travel instantly from one place to another . . . but his whole body put together did not have an official endorsement from science ... an endorsement that said he could do it?"

"That's about it."

"Knowing what you know about the dramatic discoveries of modern science, would you think it strange or impossible for a child to move instantly like that?"

"To me, no, it would not seem impossible to me for anyone in this courtroom to move around like that. I think we all have the ability in us. It seems logical to me. What's illogical to me is that we don't. It seems illogical to me that we still behave according to the laws which Isaac Newton presented to the world over three hundred years ago. Our movements are sluggish, weighed down. Energy has been frozen into matter for some reason that's inexplicable to me. But I think as science continues in its failure to find a reasonable excuse for the solidified, sluggish behavior of the classical world, then new movement, new abilities will be discovered."

Mark Boyman leaned over to Marlatt and said in a whisper that was clearly audible to the jury, "Where does he get these guys?"

For that he had to spend some time in chambers with a piously indignant Stassen.

———

During the break Max Haydn went outside and met Leon Ferguson. The reporter was leaning against one of the great, high windows that gave a flattering panoramic view of Van Nuys.

"Do you smoke? No, you don't smoke. I think I need a cigarette," said Max.

"Sorry."

"Hell. You don't smoke. Maybe I'll talk to somebody else. What do you think of Zollner?"

"I think he's great. Stassen's an incredible guy."

"You think that?" Max looked astounded. "What are you going to say about him?"

"I don't know yet."

"You could say, 'Today at the Van Nuys courthouse I saw a bunch of insane assholes. They're gonna put Pagels in jail for the rest of his life. Why didn't they forget all that shit and just plea bargain?' "

Leon indulged himself in a something approximating a smile.

164

Max went on, "Come on, what are you going to say? What's your boss saying about this?"

"He's saying 'Thank God I've got Leon off my back. That guy was driving me crazy moaning about doing lightweight stuff. Now he's got a murder case maybe he'll shut up.' "

Max stared gloomily out of the window at the scene below in distant Van Nuys, at the faraway palm trees scattered along the stringy boulevards and poking up out of tiny backyards.

"Do you think people are walking about down there who murdered somebody and they're just going to work, driving along Victory—you know, just getting away with it because the law is very tidy. You know, it's like a fussy old lady. It can't cope with too much information. It likes one suspect at a time."

Leon looked out of the window and thought about it. "Who knows?"

"Thanks for the input, Leon."

Max sighed and turned to go. He stopped to say, "That was off the record. I never said anything. Don't let me down, Leon."

As Leon watched Max's drooping shoulders moving back into the courtroom, he heard a fellow reporter say to another, "That's Leon Ferguson."

They came over to Leon.

One of them asked, "Does he work for Stassen?"

Max heard them and ran back into the courtroom.

"Did he tell you anything, Leon? What's Stassen's motive?"

"I haven't the foggiest."

"What's he hoping to get out of this?"

"Don't know."

The other reporter said, "I think he's serious. And you know, strange things happen. We all know that. Things happen that we can't explain. And you have to give him brownie points for trying to explain it."

"Is Stassen serious, Leon?"

"How should I know?"

"Is it a hoax?"

"Why don't you ask him?"

"He's not here. He beams himself over to Malibu during the breaks."

When everyone returned to the courtroom Stassen was standing in front of the witness consulting a heavy wad of notes, leafing through them rapidly, too fast to allow for any kind of comprehension to take place. His face had assumed its usual pink, sweaty glaze.

"Now before we move on I'll just recap on the Heisenberg uncertainty principle. Is it correct, Dr. Zollner, that when we step into the arena and observe the position of a particle, we have an amazing effect on that little particle?"

"That's correct."

"And in the double-slit experiment, which I went over with Dr. Walkman, we discovered that a particle of matter went through two slits at once. A particle of matter behaved like a wave of light. Do you know of that experiment, Dr. Zollner?"

"Of course. It's basic to quantum physics."

"And would you say, sir, that the double-slit experiment indicates that the stuff human beings are made of can behave like light beams?"

"It opens up a lot of speculation about the nature of matter. It would seem that it's not the solid stuff we think it is."

"And wouldn't you say, sir, that it seems like this solid stuff we call matter can be moved about in a drastic way just by the act of observation."

"It would seem that way. Yes."

Stassen consulted his notes again. He grabbed at several pieces of paper and mumbled to himself while the court waited. His hands were shaking slightly.

Pagels whispered to Ida, who was darkly intense and nunlike in a gray crepe dress, "He's afraid for himself. If he could forget himself he wouldn't feel so much fear. He needs to be objective."

"I can't tell him that."

Pagels rose slightly as though about to speak to Stassen. Ida quickly put her hand on his arm. "I don't think you should tell him either. He wouldn't be able to . . . act on it."

"He wouldn't?" Pagels seemed surprised.

"You have to make allowance for the fact that everyone isn't as . . . quick as you are at using information like that. To some people it's just words."

"It's never just words."

The two of them looked over at Stassen who was now back on track.

"The act of observation . . . I wanted to ask you about the act of observation in the double-slit experiment." Stassen smiled delightedly now they he'd recovered his train of thought. "In that experiment the particle only behaves like a wave, like a beam of light, when it is not observed. As soon as it's observed it goes back to behaving just like a pellet, in fact just like us. It no longer goes through two holes at once, it goes through one hole. It's like it says, 'Whoops, you guys saw me! Now I'd better behave myself.' And it conforms. What does this tell us, Dr. Zollner?"

"It tells you whatever you want it to tell you. Many physicists are comfortable with the idea that these extraordinary facts about subatomic particles have no relevance to our everyday life. They say there are rules for particles that somehow, in some unknown way, are not relevant to collections of particles like ourselves. They don't explain how or at what point the rules stop applying. They just point to the fact that everything seems really solid in the every-day world. That's the usual cop-out."

"You say many physicists think that. But what do other physicists think?"

"There are almost as many theories as there are physicists. But some physicists like myself have concluded that the act of observation, that is, the action of the mind plays an extraordinary and powerful influence on what we experience. We collectively measure ourselves and obey certain classical laws as set down by Sir Isaac Newton, laws of gravity, time, and space that set the boundaries of our everyday life. We ourselves have set these boundaries and we experience what we observe, rather than the other way round."

Stassen gave the jury a wan, helpless grin. "I'm not making this up, guys. This is the way it is."

Boyman stood up. "Objection, Your Honor. This is not the way it is. This is the way his witness says it is."

Judge Conan admonished Stassen to differentiate between scientific fact and the interpretation of those facts.

Stassen looked at his notes again.

"Ah . . . Dr. Zollner. Have you heard of something called Bell's Theorem?"

Dr. Zollner allowed that he had.

"Will this take a long time?" asked Judge Conan.

"Er . . . yes, Your Honor."

"Then let's break for lunch."

During the lunch break when the spectators and journalists

fanned out over Van Nuys looking for places to eat, the conversations among them turned to either charlatinism or the nature of reality versus nonreality.

Rhonda Pagels was one of those who did not move far from the courthouse. She sat on a low wall just outside the main door and had her usual lunch when alone, a can of soda. Joe DeRosa found her there.

"Is that all you're having?"

She lifted her eyelids slowly in a way that tantalized deRosa. "Uh huh."

"You wanna have lunch with me again?"

"I'm not hungry."

"You just gonna sit there?"

"Yes."

"Hold on then. I'll join you."

DeRosa dashed off and came back with a sandwich and a bag of tortilla chips.

"What d'you think?" he asked her.

"I don't know what to think. I'm just like everybody else. I hear them saying the attorney's out of his mind or he's clever or he's stupid. I don't know what to think. It's crazy."

"All trials are crazy."

"As crazy as this?"

"In a way. Law is crazy."

Rhonda swept a lock of white-blond hair out of her eyes and frowned at the sunlight hitting her face.

"Doesn't it make you scared? The idea of it?"

"You mean if it was true? Nah! . . . I'd be the first one out there, speeding at a billion miles an hour. No traffic jams. It'd be great. Just imagine Victory Boulevard in the rush hour. There'd be no cars. No accidents. Everyone'd just zoom off home from the spot they were standing on. Pow! Wham!"

DeRosa roared with laughter and showed a mouth full of tortilla chips.

"By the way," he said, "why didn't you tell me your name was Pagels?"

Rhonda stopped breathing for a few seconds and then flicked a glance over his shoulder as though planning an escape route.

"That's . . . private. My name is private."

"Why don't you want anyone to know?" He went on stuffing tortilla chips into his mouth.

She didn't reply.

"So you're not a writer?"

"I guess not."

"Is he your uncle, your father, what?"

"My father."

"What's so bad about that? You ashamed of it or something?"

"No. They're ashamed of me."

"They?"

"The attorney."

"Why?"

"Oh because."

"Well don't look so down about it. It's not the end of the world. I didn't tell you about my wife right off."

He smiled.

"And the boy. Are you his cousin or something?"

"How could I be his cousin?" She looked at him with great annoyance.

"Oh . . . you're his mother. I get it. You're his mother."

She did not answer.

"Then what kind of kid is he? He's coming into court again. Is he gonna go along with this?"

"How should I know?"

Her face showed such pain that he was momentarily embarrassed.

"You don't know . . . well . . ."

DeRosa ate some more chips. They sat in silence for a while.

"So there you are," he said finally. "Your secret's safe with me. I won't tell. I like you. I won't tell."

———

After lunch Stefan Zollner submitted to questions on Bell's Theorem. The jury struggled painfully with the concept of particles communicating instantly with one another when they were thousands of miles apart. Only Bradley Ryker, the retired Marine, managed to maintain a calm, almost supercilious, expression while listening to the bewildering, mad facts of life presented by quantum physics. Jorge Ramirez, the refrigerator repair man, stared at Dr. Zollner's drawings on the blackboard of particles and detectors as though they were missives from the Devil.

"Are you telling me," said Stassen employing a look of absolute astonishment, "that if you get a pair of particles zooming off in different directions, then what you do to one on earth will instantly affect the other one thousands of miles away?"

"That's what I'm saying."

"This information travels faster than the speed of light. How can it do that?"

"It's impossible by every law and standard that we know in our everyday life but it does happen. The physics tells us that it happens."

"These particles act as if there's no distance between them, as if they're next door to each other. What does that say about distance, any distance, long or short?"

"I would say that space or distance is not what it appears to be."

"Well, thank you, Dr. Zollner. You've been real helpful."

For the cross Mark Boyman had only one question.

"Would you say Mr. Zollner"—Boyman pointedly omitted his correct title—"that you're a little out on a limb with these opinions of yours?"

"Probably."

"Thank you, Mr. Zollner."

———

There was no more time for another witness that afternoon. Judge Conan stood up, looked at the row upon row of curious faces before him with a certain amount of distaste, and headed for the seclusion of his chambers. As soon as the judge left the courtroom the crush of spectators rose in a noisy, chattering mass. Joe DeRosa saw a group of reporters coming toward Stassen and Pagels and he and two other bailiffs quickly formed a human barrier to keep the journalists back.

Stassen, preparing himself for a quick getaway, grabbed his briefcase and thrust it at Ida. He paused momentarily to put his arm around Lawrence Pagels' shoulders.

"Well?"

Pagels nodded. "It's coming along."

"Coming along! Will I ever be good enough for you?"

"You're doing fine. But you'll make things easier for yourself if you lose a personal sense of what you're doing. It's scientific. It doesn't have anything to do with you."

"Give me a break will you? I can't operate without my personal sense. I disappear."

170

Pagels shook his head. "No you don't."

"Believe me, I . . ."

He had no time to argue any further about it because the barrier of bailiffs was broken through and reporters were surrounding the defense table.

Stassen made a dash for the door. He was immediately enfolded in a crush of bodies also heading doorward and he partially disappeared from view. He was squeezed out into the spacious, high-ceilinged hallway and, still camouflaged by bodies, he slipped unseen through the door leading to the emergency stairs with the sound of "Mr. Stassen! Mr. Stassen!" fading behind him.

A statuesque lady reporter with flowing red hair from Channel 7 news was bewildered by Stassen's disappearance. As soon as it was clear to her that he'd flown the coop, she charged into the courtroom and joined the curious group who were still gathered near the defense table engrossed in watching Lawrence Pagels make his departure.

The lady reporter pushed her way to the front.

"Hello, Mr. Pagels, I'm Judy McGinnis, Channel 7 Eyewitness News. Do you really believe that your grandson can teleport himself? Do you believe he traveled ten miles instantly?"

Lawrence Pagels was being led to the side door by Joe DeRosa. They both paused while Pagels looked at her politely, as politely as he would look at someone who asked about pruning the rose-bushes, while DeRosa studied her wonderful red hair with obvious delight.

Max Haydn stepped in.

"What do you need to know?"

The beauteous Judy turned her attentions to Max, giving DeRosa the opportunity to lead Pagels out of the courtroom.

"What's your name?"

"Max Haydn. H-A-Y-D-N."

"May I ask who you are?"

"I'm working for the defense."

"O.K., Max. The camera's outside. Would you care to come out for an interview?"

Max glanced over at Ida, who was sitting at the table stuffing papers into two briefcases. She made a cutting gesture across her throat with a finger. Max nodded but followed the reporter anyway.

171

Outside Max was placed in a good light and the camera started rolling.

Judy McGinnis produced her microphone, "Why are you making such an unnatural claim about a small boy?"

Max said carefully, "It's not so unnatural, Judy."

"How can you say that?"

He put his hand in his pockets and thought for a moment. He was aware of the fact that Ida had taken up a position behind the camera.

"If anyone stops to think for more than five minutes about what they are, what they're doing here"—he stared earnestly into the television camera—"then they'll start considering the idea that there's more to existence than just being a solid body held down by the law of gravity. You know, how you feel in your heart of hearts that it's a kind of imposition." He turned to the immaculately coiffed interviewer. "We all dream about flying. You know, how you're lifted up over rooftops . . . I expect you did, Judy, when you were a kid."

Judy allowed that she had. The interview was over.

"Will this be on tonight?" Max asked.

"I think so," Judy McGinnis told him.

"I'll be glued to my set."

It was on at five, six, and eleven.

Stassen was not impressed. "There are larger things at stake here than being a television star."

It was, however, the last time that Max was permitted to hog the cameras. Thereafter Stassen restrained himself from dashing out of the courtroom and attended to all television interviews himself.

Besides Channel 7, the trial was also reported on the ten o'clock news on Channel 13, and the following morning articles appeared in the *Los Angeles Times* and the *Daily News*. Reports also appeared in San Francisco and San Diego papers and were faxed to Stassen's office later in the day. The news went out on the wires and appeared in a dozen or so newspapers around the world.

———

Sandy Leutweiler watched Daniel carefully as the spotlight that fell upon him grew so intense that it was painful, not only for him, but for all those around him.

She acted swiftly. She took all four children out of school and escaped to the safety of the snow and the mountains up at Big Bear. One of Don's customers loaned them a more than adequate cabin furnished with a wall-sized television and sofas covered with fine white leather. Her first act was to cover the sofas with blankets so that Jason couldn't get to them with french fries and ketchup.

Don joined the family when he could, twice having to foil a car that tailed him. The family spent their days under the piercing blue skies tobogganing and falling down the beginners' slopes, filling their lungs with the sharp, clean air. They watched the proliferating television reports on the trial with a growing bewilderment, as though it were a particularly fanciful miniseries. What did it have to do with them? It was madness.

Daniel's attitude continued to be indefinable. Sandy couldn't make him out. Obviously he did not understand the scientific jargon, even though pundits were called on to explain aspects of quantum theory to television viewers; but any child could grasp its implications. Daniel could not be drawn into a discussion about them.

In the relative safety of Big Bear he did not become more communicative on the subject. The only thing that he made quite obvious was his conviction that he and his grandfather would be together soon.

Sandy felt it incumbent upon her to ease the child gently out of that conviction. She began to see clearly what the second grade teacher had forecast. If Daniel could not envision the idea of a guilty verdict, with all that entailed for himself and Lawrence, then he was heading for a traumatic and highly destructive disappointment.

She did it drop by drop. A little word here; another word there.

"If the jury aren't kind to your grandpa he might stay in jail."

"If your grandpa stays in jail you can record tapes for him every week. You can tell him what you're doing at school."

"Your grandpa wants to get out of jail but the judge might say he has to stay there a long time. Judges can be real mean."

All to no effect. Daniel would simply look at her as if she were out of her mind and needed a little help. He would comfort her in her madness.

"Don't worry," he would say, "He'll be O.K. Don't worry." Sometimes he patted her hand like a kindly psychiatrist with a disturbed patient. And he, in all his seven-year-old wisdom, would gaze at her with gentle, caring eyes.

She discussed it with Don. He felt the only way around the impasse was to scream at Daniel until "the truth got into his skull."

"You try that then. Try it!" She told him.

Don thought about it but he did not try it. He rationalized that even if he screamed until he was blue in the face, there was no guarantee that it would have any effect on the child. They would simply have to await the outcome of events and support Daniel in every way they could. He was going to need a lot of support.

———

Jennifer and Bruce Perry packed up, put their dogs in kennels, and left their house without leaving a forwarding address. They were seen by a neighbor dragging suitcases out of their house at 1:30 A.M. Employers, friends, and relatives were not told in advance of their departure.

When Leon Ferguson informed Detective John Starbeck, he replied, "They got out of town because you've been bugging them."

Leon called Mark Boyman and left the information with the receptionist. He asked Boyman to call him. A secretary from Boyman's office called after two days and thanked him. That was the last he heard of it.

Stassen said the news was useful but not enough to make him change course.

12

The trial on the sixth floor of the Van Nuys law courts had now achieved complete celebrity status. A barrier was erected outside the main doors on the ground floor to hold back the ever-increasing crowd of people wishing to attend the Pagels' trial. A room also on the sixth floor was hurriedly vacated for use by the press and a small army of police officers was recruited to handle the crowds. Joe DeRosa continued to hold his kingpin position in the courtroom itself.

It was because of Joe DeRosa that Rhonda Pagels was still able to get a seat in court. Without his help she, the unknown daughter, would have been left to wait outside all day with the crowds who contented themselves with being in the vicinity of the trial.

The phones had been ringing most of the night in Stassen's Winnebago. He had eventually turned the phones off but the clamor stayed in his head and he was unable to sleep. He could not remember that last time he had slept. When he arrived at the courthouse, he slipped in through a side door and up to the sixth floor with a curious light-headed feeling. Every minute or so, he had the odd sensation of not knowing where he was or what he was supposed to be doing.

The sight of Max Haydn always brought him down to earth. There was something about the sheer vanity of this stocky young man that cleared Stassen's head. It was probably the slight sneer lying in wait at the corner of Max's lips that filled him with a resolve that the kid should not be proved right. That smirking face worked on him more effectively than any gibes or leers from Mark Boyman.

It took some time for the press to settle themselves in the space allotted next to the Pagels courtroom. The lucky few who had been allowed in as spectators and the selected members of the press who were given seats in the courtroom itself, sat quietly while the noisy reporters outside accepted the fact that not all of them could squeeze in.

The morning's proceedings were an hour and a half late in getting started. When Dr. Sheila Mollen, the next witness for the defense, stepped on to the stand, the air was tense with anticipation. And Dr. Mollen was hardly of the appearance to satisfy the expectant courtroom. She was a coarse-skinned, gray-haired neurologist from the UCLA medical school who spoke with a voice so soft that some members of the jury, not to mention the rest of the court audience, had to lean forward to catch her words.

Dr. Mollen listed her qualifications and then, at Stassen's request, gave the court a short course in the constitution and function of the brain. The human brain, they were told, contained 10 billion nerve cells. At birth it weighed about 300 grams and it increased to 1,300 to 1,500 grams in the full-grown adult. At the age of six a child was able to produce an orderly series of mental images, which were the requirements for true thought.

The way information was received by the brain was described briefly. They were told that light traveled from perceived objects to the eye and was transformed into neural codes which were then processed by the brain.

Stassen asked, "Does the scientific community have any knowledge about the exact point where information from something physical like the brain enters something abstract like the mind?"

"A lot of conjectures. No real knowledge."

"I see." Stassen stared meaningfully at the jury who stared back, blank and uncomprehending like a class of bored schoolchildren. "And what do scientists know about the limits of a man's capacity . . . I mean, for instance, if we look at athletics. Men are jumping higher, running faster. What does this indicate?"

"Your Honor, do we have to listen to a discussion about athletics?"

Boyman was overruled.

"Athletics are an interesting example," Dr. Mollen said as Stassen gestured that she should answer his question. "If there's a breakthrough, then it seems to break a mental barrier and a lot of people follow the first man or woman. Breaking the four-minute mile, for example. One man did it and then a lot of men found they could do it."

"What about the development of intelligence? Are there signs that mankind is getting any smarter?"

"We have discovered that I.Q.'s increase by a few points with each generation. This may only indicate an increasing sophistication and understanding of the testing system rather than an actual increase of intelligence, but the data cannot be ignored and more research is needed to fully understand the implications of the results."

"So it's possible that actual genetic intelligence could be increasing with each generation?"

"I would have to wait for further research before I could commit myself to an answer."

"But there is evidence that intelligence has increased in man since he was in a Neanderthal form?"

"Yes. The brain has developed over thousands of years but in recent centuries our progress has been in developing our use of the brain. It is vastly underused, underchallenged."

"Would you say that future generations will find ways of using the brain that have not yet been tried?"

"Yes, I would."

"Do you think maybe we have people among us now who are using their brains in ways that have not been used before?"

"I have seen examples of extraordinary intelligence that might be called freakish or genius."

"Your Honor," Mark Boyman waved a pencil, "this is all very informative but what is the relevance?"

Judge Conan said that the court was prepared to accept this testimony if relevance could be shown.

Stassen rushed his next question, tripping over the words until they were almost unintelligible. "Could you tell us about the phenomenon known as idiot savants? I mean, could you explain to us what sort of people that term is referring to?"

"An idiot savant, a term no longer used by professionals, is generally considered to be someone with a severe learning disability, a mentally handicapped person, who perhaps cannot talk or read, who suddenly shows a great talent or genius in one specific area without having received any instruction."

"What sort of areas would this genius show itself in?"

"It could be in mathematics, or art, or music, any area of ability. I have known instances where severely retarded people have played musical instruments skillfully and they have done it without the usual training and practice required by normal people."

"Can you explain this?"

"No, I can't. But one might say that the person uses the part of the brain that is working effectively with a far greater concentration than is normally employed. Just as a blind person uses the senses of hearing or smell."

Stassen pulled back his crumpled white linen suit coat and thrust his thumbs into a pair of fancy red suspenders. "Or is there another way you could put it: An idiot savant is too stupid to get in the way of his brain."

The members of the jury who were still following the testimony smiled weakly. Mark Boyman frowned and engaged in a prolonged whispered discussion with Harvey Marlatt.

Undaunted, Dr. Mollen continued. "I don't know about that, Mr. Stassen, but I would say all of us have a hundred times more ability than we use. Human intelligence and ability are conditioned by convention."

Stassen paused for thought and a short bout of exercise, that little walk he frequently took from the witness stand to the jury and back.

When he returned, he asked, "Dr. Mollen, do you think that as the human race develops, it will learn to perform feats that are unheard of now, feats that seem impossible to us now?"

"Yes, I believe that."

"And do you believe that we already have the ability and where-withall to accomplish these things right now but don't know it?"

"As I said, human intelligence and ability are conditioned by convention. When conventions change, abilities change."

"And would you say that those of us who are most ignorant of conventions are the most likely to lead the way in showing extraordinary abilities . . . abilities that some might even call miraculous?"

"That sometimes happens."

"And would you say that among those of us who would be most ignorant of convention, a convention that holds back our ability . . . would be a small child?"

"Yes, I think you could say that."

Stassen whistled quietly to himself and paced back and forth for a few seconds. Then he announced that he had no further questions.

Harvey Marlatt, for the prosecution, asked, "Would you agree, Dr. Mollen, that there are millions of children all over the world who are not conditioned by convention?"

"Yes."

"Would you also agree that before this claim about young Daniel Pagels came along, not one of these many million children showed the capacity to travel at the speed of light?"

"As far as I know, yes."

"Thank you, Dr. Mollen."

———

In his report of the days proceedings in the *Daily News*, Leon made reference, for the first time, to Jennifer Perry's relationship with John Nields and her sudden disappearance with her husband. It was picked up by several newspapers and TV stations.

John Starbeck, convinced that they already had the right man in custody, was gratified that there were no follow-up reports. Media attention returned to the trial at hand.

———

Judge Conan's wife, Sonya had noticed that her husband was more than usually tired when he came home. She was not surprised. There was a growing movement in California legal circles calling for the judge's removal from the Pagels trial. There was no doubt that this was an added strain on top of the already burdensome requirements of conducting a singularly unusual trial.

His opponents accused him of squandering taxpayers money to prove the unprovable. They complained that the whole trial had become a farce and was a disgrace to the Los Angeles courts.

The movement to have him removed from the trial grew within days to a movement to have him dismissed from the bench. Every night there were phone calls from fellow judges, some sympathetic, some persuasive, and some hostile, but not many of the latter.

Those who were hostile were not wasting their time on phone calls to the judge, they were concentrating on finishing his career.

Conan had always been a nonconformist. But his nonconformism was having large demands made upon it. Too large, Sonya thought.

"They'll ruin you, Bill. Isn't there a way you can get out of it?"

"No."

"Did you ever think it would turn out like this?"

Conan ran his hand over the remaining hairs on his balding head. His eyes showed a certain hurt, a hint of dismay. "No, I can't say I did. I'm surprised, just like everyone else."

"It looks like they're making a monkey out of you, honey."

"Maybe it does. *C'est la vie.*"

The Conans lived in a house hidden by trees in Hancock Park, the resort of old money and gracious style. One of their three children still lived at home, a nineteen-year-old daughter who was firmly on her father's side.

"These things have to be discussed, Dad. You're right to bring it out in the open. I think people are embarrassed. They want to sweep it under the table."

Sonya nodded vigorously, "Yes, absolutely. I want to sweep it under the table. I want to go on living in this house. I want to go on eating. Call me old-fashioned."

"Don't worry, Mom. You can always get a job at Thrifty's."

Evenings were usually spent in the oak-paneled den, chatting and watching TV. But lately, Conan had more often withdrawn to his study to go over the files on the Pagels case, to read his physics books, and to reacquaint himself with Hegel and Emerson. He took pills for stomach pains.

There was a somber pall over the household.

Sonya waited with as much patience as she could muster for the completion of the trial. She prayed that the forces working against Conan would not strike too deadly a blow. And she hoped that in the coming years she would still be married to a judge and not a man who had made a laughingstock of himself and brought ridicule to the criminal justice system.

―――

The vexing question of whether or not to put Lawrence Pagels on the witness stand was resolved by Pagels' determination to speak up for himself.

Stassen was nervous.

"I'm warning you, Lawrence, Boyman will twist everything you say. That asshole'll make mincemeat out of you."

"That doesn't matter."

Even Ida, arch disciple of the Pagels way of looking at things, thought it was a bad idea.

"Danny can speak for both of you when he testifies again. Boyman won't bully him. He can't bully a little boy."

"Danny can only speak for himself."

Max had a go. He was simple and direct. "Don't do it, Mr. Pagels."

Pagels folded his hands in front of him and looked into the middle distance, a move which they all knew meant that there was no more to be said on the subject.

It took the court by surprise when Pagels was called forward to testify. The prosecution broke into a flurry of hissed whispers. The judge looked amused. And for those in the courtroom who had been examining the defendant's back and wondering about his face, it was now an opportunity to see his angular features and deep-set eyes, and the pale blue tie purchased for the occasion by Ida. It was also the occasion to see how tall he was. The man from *Newsweek* noted that Pagels was one inch taller than the lanky Harvey Marlatt, who managed to be standing as Pagels stepped forward, so that comparisons could be drawn.

Pagels had regained some of the weight he had lost when first imprisoned, and looked fitter than he had in a long time. His black hair, streaked with gray, was slicked back in a manner dictated by Ida. In the suit that Stassen still had not paid for, he appeared too elegant to be the gardener he had been, let alone a prisoner from Men's Central. Lawrence Pagels had sprung to life in this latter phase of the trial.

He was on the stand for two and one half days. Much of the first day was used by Stassen to comb through all the details about Pagels' relationship with John Nields and to bring out the fact that Pagels was not one to bear grudges.

"You were in danger of losing your home, a place you considered important to people of Indian heritage. Weren't you angry with John Nields for threatening to deprive you of that?"

Pagels spoke in a calm, authoritative voice. He had a soft California accent, an accent that lacked any strong identity.

"I never feel anger toward an individual. I don't associate wrong thoughts with the person. They are two separate things."

"You mean you were mad at what he was doing but not at him?"

"That's right. I was not mad at him. I could see his point of view and I could see mine. I told him what I thought about building around my home and he listened."

"You never argued?"

"Mr. Nields was excitable. Very dramatic, like an opera star, so he shouted a lot when I told him that I didn't like his plan."

"That didn't upset you?"

"Of course not."

"You felt no animosity toward him?"

"No. I never feel animosity toward anyone. I have more regard for myself. To hate someone is to hurt yourself."

Boyman held up his pencil. "Objection, Your Honor. We seem to be getting some kind of philosophy lecture."

Conan requested the witness to confine his answers to exactly what was asked.

It was not until Pagels' second day on the stand that Stassen approached the subject of Daniel Pagels' late-night visit to Bell Canyon.

"Mr. Pagels, did you take your grandson to John Nields' house on the night of April twelfth last year?"

"No, I did not."

"You had gone over to Bell Canyon that morning?"

"Yes, I did."

"But you did not return that night?"

"No. Certainly not."

"How did your grandson Daniel get to the Nields' house in Bell Canyon later that night?"

"He went there by himself."

"And he was how old when he did this?"

"He was five years old."

"Do you believe its possible for a five-year-old boy to travel ten miles late at night by himself on a journey he'd only done once before?"

"Yes, I do."

"Do you think there's a scientific explanation for it?"

"Yes, I do."

"Do you think that quantum physics can explain it?"

Lawrence Pagels glanced across at Judge Conan. He wished to answer in detail but was not sure if he would be allowed. He went ahead anyway.

"Quantum physics is as far as people have got now with understanding something like that. One day they'll throw away quantum physics. It'll talk itself out of business."

Stassen had not expected this reply. It had come right out of left field. He took a few seconds to examine his feet and open and shut his mouth like a gasping fish. Boyman and Marlatt were smiling broadly.

Stassen regained himself. "How then, Mr. Pagels, did your grandson get to the Nields' house?"

"He got there the same way he does everything else. People say its a miracle for someone to move around like that. But it's no more a miracle than getting up in the morning or cleaning your teeth. How on earth do you do that? Can anyone really explain it? No one really knows how a snail crawls up a wall, they don't know where he gets his energy or how he knows which direction to go, so how are they going to work out how Danny got to the Nields' house? You might as well . . ."

Judge Conan interrupted, "Thank you, Mr. Pagels, I think we get the picture."

Stassen stood still as a statue, his hands clasped in front of him. Only his eyes rolling from side to side showed that a desperate mind was at work. The court had remained very still and silent while Pagels spoke and now they were equally still as they waited for the defense attorney to come up with something.

"Are you saying then"—Stassen found some words—"that it was simply a natural thing for your grandson to travel in the way he did?"

"Yes. It was the most natural thing in the world."

"Can you do it?"

"No, I can't. My mind's not as free as Daniel's. I'm working on it but it's hard. You have to heave out a lot of garbage."

"What sort of garbage?"

"Oh just about everything you think during an average day."

Stassen coughed. "Now, Mr. Pagels, you're saying it's a natural thing. And scientists are saying it can be explained by quantum physics. Wouldn't you say that's one and the same thing?"

"Oh yes."

"So you're not denying the relevance of this scientific evidence?"

"Oh no. Those scientists are brilliant men."

Stassen looked immeasurably relieved. "And you agree that there is a scientific basis to the kind of movement that Daniel achieved?"

"Yes."

Stassen could have hugged him.

The defense attorney devoted the rest of the day to a long, step by step review of Lawrence Pagels' movements on April 12, 1988.

Pagels told the court that his meeting with John Nields in the morning had been to discuss what he considered to be the boundaries around his home on the Chatsworth hillside. He had brought a map along with him and drew out a plan. John Nields had complained that Pagels' plan gave Pagels too large a share of the land.

"But," Pagels said, "this was not true. My plot of land is very small. He was mad because it was going to be right in the middle of his big houses."

While they were in the house John Nields had taken Daniel into the kitchen to see a Labrador bitch and her three-week-old puppies. Daniel had stayed in the kitchen while the two men had gone into the study.

"Did you sit down while you were in the study?"

"Yes."

"Where did you sit?"

"I sat on the wooden chair with the arms."

"The captain's chair where your fingerprint was found."

"Yes."

Pagels said that they talked for twenty minutes and he went back to the kitchen to get Daniel. John Nields walked with them to the door.

"Was Mr. Nields shouting at you?"

"He was describing this dream he had of building a whole new city up in the Chatsworth hills. And I said Chatsworth had enough people and cars and gas exhausts. I told him his dream was a nightmare."

"Did he threaten you?"

"No."

"Did you threaten him?"

"No."

"So how did you leave it?"

"I said I wasn't moving."

"When you were pulling out of the drive in your pickup truck did Mr. Nields run after you?"

"Yes, he did."

"Did you stop?"

"Yes."

"And what did Mr. Nields do then?"

"He asked me to come by the next day so he could give me some sort of chart that would show where he was going to put his houses. I don't know why. I wasn't interested."

"When he ran after you, what speed were you going?"

"I was just pulling out. Five, ten or so miles an hour, I guess."

"Did he grab hold of the truck?"

"He could have. He had his hands out."

"And when he spoke to you, did you notice if he'd damaged his hand?"

"He wasn't acting like it was hurt but I don't think he'd have felt it even if I'd run over his toe right then. He was really wrapped up in what he was taking about."

"The tailgate of your truck is rough to the touch?"

"Very."

"It could easily break the surface of the skin if grabbed by someone as the truck moved forward?"

"Oh yes."

Stassen paused to let the jury take in the significance of that.

"And that was the last time you saw Mr. Nields?"

"Yes, it was."

Pagels went on to give an account of the rest of his day. He had been to three houses in Chatsworth and two in Granada Hills to do his gardening work. He had bought milk and orange juice at Ralph's Supermarket and had then returned to his motor home with Daniel; the child had spent the whole day with him. After that he had read while Daniel drew pictures. He put his grandson to bed at eight and retired himself at ten thirty. He had missed George Lejeune's arrival at eleven thirty.

"Did you know that Daniel was awake when George Lejeune went by with his dog?"

"No."

"You heard no voices?"

"No."

"Were you aware that Daniel left your motor home?"

"Not until the police were battering on the door."

"What time was that?"

"It wasn't long before dawn."

"Does it worry you that Daniel can leave your home like that?"

"No."

"You don't worry about his safety?"

"Not when he lived with me, no."

Stassen was reluctant to let Pagels go. He would like to have gone on until the following morning so that Boyman didn't have the night to prepare his cross examination, but he was tired. His arms felt like dead weights hanging from his sockets. It was almost impossible to lift his hand to scratch his nose. He thanked Pagels and went back to his seat.

As soon as Stassen sat down a noisy chatter broke out among the spectators. Several reporters ran down the aisles and out the door.

"That's it for today." Conan spoke above the din. He looked gravely around the courtroom. "I don't think it can be said too often that this is a court of law and not a circus. I would ask people who are entering and exiting this courtroom to do so with respect. Not only do I not like pandemonium I also dislike excessive chatter. Remember that. I'll have you all removed if you don't behave yourselves."

———

Joe DeRosa was expecting a reward for his silence and to that end he invited Rhonda to his Canoga Park apartment. He had prepared for the occasion and sprinkled himself liberally with after-shave lotion.

The apartment was furnished in a strongly feminine style which made it hard to ignore his absent wife. The pale mauve drapes she had hung, her ruffled lampshades, her artificial trees of flowering pink blossom and her embroidered cushions made her well-nigh a third presence in the room.

"Would you like some wine?" DeRosa asked Rhonda.

Rhonda was huddled into a corner of a couch. "Do you have any soda?"

"You don't drink?"

"Not anymore."

"You AA?"

"Alcohol was one of the things I never got addicted to."

"Uh huh." He pondered about that for a while. ". . . So now you're a waitress?"

"I'm not a waitress in my soul."

"Not in your soul. You sound like your dad."

She looked surprised. "I don't sound like him. I'm nothing like him."

He poured some grape soda into a glass of ice. "He's a strange dude, your father. I don't like to say this, he's your dad, but if he doesn't change his tune quickly, he's going to spend the rest of his life being laughed at in jail."

He gave Rhonda the glass and sat down beside her.

She stared gravely at the ice and bubbles in the glass. "I can't believe this is happening. I don't know why he's saying these things about Danny. When I was Danny's age he used to tell me everything was consciousness. But it was just something he said. . . ." She looked up helplessly.

He put his arm around her. She looked at the arm as if it were an unwelcome insect.

"What's the problem?" he asked.

"Oh nothing." She tried to smile.

"I'm not after your body," he said. "I can see you've got a lot on your mind. I asked you over here so you can talk."

"You want to hear me talk?" She was suspicious.

"Sure."

"Oh." She looked at the arm that remained firmly around her shoulder. "Well . . . all I want to talk about is Danny."

"That seems like a reasonable thing to do. . . . Don't worry so much. You need to relax." He put a hand on her knee.

She studied the hand seriously. "Do you want to know what Lawrence says about sex?"

"Sure."

"He says sex is sort of hypnotic."

"Oh, don't I know."

"And he says our thoughts about sex get stuck, you know like a cracked record on a turntable, and they go round and round, over and over and they never get anywhere."

"Oh sure. I can believe that."

"You know, we get to thinking sex is our whole identity and

we, like you know, worship it all our lives, sex, sex, sex, when really it's only a minuscule part of our real identity, a part that's there to be outgrown so we can go on to do all these great things, move on to a higher dimension. That's what he calls it, a higher dimension, you know, like we're in a constant state of growth out of ourselves. But it's like, we're on a board game and we never get past go."

"Yeah. I can . . . uh . . . go along with that. That's me. I never get past go. Everyone's like that."

Rhonda looked at a hand-embroidered cushion on the couch beside her.

"Even your wife?"

"My wife?" He groaned. "I can't tell you anything about my wife. She says I don't love her enough. She comes back every six weeks to see if this right kind of love has come down from wherever it's supposed to come from."

"Maybe you don't do what she wants."

"What does she want? I don't understand women."

"They're not so different. They want the same things as men."

"No, they don't. Men want sex and women want men. It's not the same thing."

Rhonda had no answer to that. They were silent for a few seconds.

Then he leaned toward her and kissed her. She did not push him away but she did not respond either.

His hand went in search of the buttons on her blouse. He was brought to a halt by the sensation of tears on her cheeks being transferred to his.

"Hey! What's the matter?"

"Nothing."

"Nothing?"

Rhonda broke down.

"Look don't cry. I won't touch you anymore. I'm moving away."

"I'm sorry . . . I don't want you to tell anyone . . ."

"Tell what?"

"About me."

He stood up. "You think I'm some sort of blackmailer? Is that what you think?"

"I just don't want him to get hurt. I'm not a good person. They'll say it's his fault. I don't want you to talk about me."

"I'm not gonna talk about you. It's your business. God, I've had it with women. I need a beer."

"I'm sorry. It's hard for me. I should be able to work this out . . . but I can't."

"Well don't let me get in your way. I won't lay a finger on you. Sit there and think. Enjoy yourself."

He went in search of a beer.

"And if I find you a place to sit in court," he shouted from the kitchen, "don't think I'm doing it so I can get your clothes off. O.K.?"

"O.K."

13

The following morning Mark Boyman was cautious when he approached the witness Lawrence Pagels.

"Good morning, Mr. Pagels, I hope you slept well last night."

"Yes, thank you."

Pagels was polite to the prosecutor but he looked down his nose as he spoke which made it seem as though he were looking at an annoying ant on the floor in front of him.

"Mr. Pagels, you seem to have a philosophical answer to everything. Do these opinions of yours come from Indian religious beliefs?"

"Not particularly. I read a lot. I take what's good from all types of thinking. If it works, it's good."

"What do you mean, if it works?"

"I mean if a type of thinking brings you peace of mind then it's got to be good. You get peace of mind, you have a free life and good health."

"So you're not a follower of Indian religion?"

"I'm part Indian so I have a lot of respect for the religion, but I don't accept all of it."

"You accept some of it?"

"Well I'd have to argue it with you point by point."

"I think it will suffice to say that your respect for your Indian heritage and Indian religious beliefs caused you to have a passionate devotion to the land you lived on. Is that correct?"

"Not passionate no. I liked the land. I'd lived there thirty-one years."

"Isn't it a fact that John Nields offered you a large sum of money to leave that land?"

"He offered me some money, yes."

"How much did he offer you?"

"He offered me twenty thousand dollars."

"Enough to give you a certain amount of luxury, wouldn't you say?"

"It's nothing. You can't buy a chicken coop in Chatsworth for twenty thousand dollars."

"It's a lot of money to someone like yourself, wouldn't you say?"

"No."

"Do you have a private income we don't know about?"

"No, I don't."

"You just had the money you earned as a gardener?"

"Yes."

"How much was that?"

"I got fifty-five a month from each of my customers."

"How many customers did you have?"

"I had . . . about fifteen customers, sometimes more, sometimes less. I could have had more. I'd sometimes do special work, tree trimming, et cetera, and I'd get more. I got about eight hundred a month. It was enough for me and Daniel. We ate well."

"That's not a fortune, Mr. Pagels. Are you telling me that twenty thousand dollars wasn't a barrelful of money to you?"

"Not if I had to use that money to get another place to live."

"O.K. So you turned down Mr. Nields' offer. Did you feel threatened by Mr. Nields after that?"

"I knew he was upset."

"You didn't answer my question. Did you feel threatened?"

"He wanted me to feel threatened . . ."

"Please answer the question, Mr. Pagels," interjected the judge.

"Did you feel threatened?" the prosecutor repeated.

"Do you mean scared?"

"If you like."

"No, I wasn't scared."

Boyman acted as if he had not lost that round. But he was looking for revenge.

"Let's look at your departure from the house. Can you see the tailgate of your truck in your rearview mirror?"

"No."

"So you could not possibly see Mr. Nields' hand grabbing the back of your truck?"

"No."

"So all this business about his hand touching your truck is mere speculation."

It was not a question and Pagels did not answer.

Boyman spent the rest of the morning trying to show that Pagels was prepared to fight to the death over his land. In trying to show his complete lack of murderous intent, Pagels launched into another long explanation of his philosophy.

Conan cut him short. "We do not need a lecture on the meaning of life, Mr. Pagels."

In the afternoon Boyman finally reached Daniel's trip to Bell Canyon.

"It's a remarkable claim you're making about your grandson's abilities, isn't it, Mr. Pagels?"

"No. I've said before, it's natural. People think they've got to organize everything, measure it, they hold themselves back, they tie themselves up. They have no faith in themselves, so they have faith in machines instead."

"I'd love to believe that, Mr. Pagels. It sounds wonderful. But I'm a little disturbed that your grandson Daniel is the only person in the entire world who's been able to achieve this amazing feat of instantaneous movement from one place to another. Why do you think that is?"

"He's not the only one. You listen to the stories Indians hand down. They talk about people who move faster than the wind. I happen to know about Indians because I am one, but you study any group of people and I bet you'll find they have somebody in one of their stories who, way back some time, moved about like Danny."

"Maybe so. But you're talking about stories and I'm interested in facts. . . . Why do you think your grandson was so special? Why could he do this miraculous thing?"

"I keep trying to tell you. He's not all that special. He's just Danny. But I guess, I didn't realize it till all this happened, but he had a pretty secluded life with me. Nothing ever got in his way. He didn't know he couldn't get to Bell Canyon that fast."

Lawrence Pagels spoke slowly, giving each word great thought.

The look of intensity on his face was something to behold, and was the one thing that prevented spectators in court from laughing at him. Boyman stood there impatiently waiting for him to finish each sentence, almost wriggling with the effort of holding himself back from interrupting. Of the two, Pagels was by far the more pleasing to the eye. For all his fancy dressing, Boyman could not overcome a face that looked, according to Stassen, like a constipated bullfrog.

"He didn't know he couldn't get to Bell Canyon that fast?" Boyman repeated. "What *does* he know?"

"He doesn't know very much. He's innocent."

"Innocent of what?"

"Maybe innocent isn't a word that makes sense to you. Let's say he hasn't accumulated a lot of negatives."

"Negatives? Do you mean negative thoughts?"

"Yes, I do."

"Negative." Boyman rolled the word around his tongue. "Is that the same thing as garbage?"

"Garbage?"

"I believe . . . let me see . . . didn't you tell Mr. Stassen yesterday that this garbage was, I quote, 'just about everything you think during an average day'?"

"Yes. I suppose I must have said that."

"So Daniel could do this and the rest of us can't because we're not innocent like him. We carry this mental garbage around." Boyman's grin grew wider and wider. "Are you accusing the entire world of harboring mental garbage?"

"I don't accuse anyone of anything. You can tell what people are thinking by what they do. You don't have to be a mind reader. And I don't set myself up as a judge of that."

Stassen had been watching this interchange like a hypnotized rabbit looking at a snake. He didn't like it, but he couldn't bring himself to do anything to stop it. All the usual standards that he applied to occasions such as these had gone out the window. Sometimes he wasn't even certain that he was there at all.

Judge Conan had looked over at him several times expecting an objection. But the defense attorney was temporarily unable to protect his client.

"But," said Boyman "you seem to think that what most people have in their minds is pretty disgusting."

"I didn't say that. You should pay attention to what I say."

"I am paying attention, Mr. Pagels, believe me. And what I hear is pretty ridiculous. These negative thoughts, this mental garbage you disapprove of so much, is simply the human thought process. You don't have much regard for humanity. Do you realize that all of modern civilization has been built out of this mental garbage?"

Judge Conan stepped in for the incapacitated Stassen. "Mr. Boyman, this isn't a high school debate we're having here. Mr. Pagels seems to have seduced you into a philosophical turn of thought."

The jury and spectators giggled. Boyman had been maintaining a perpetual grin and periodically shaking his head to indicate total disbelief in what he was hearing. But the laughter in court wiped the grin off his face. He made a half-hearted apology to the judge and then turned back to the defendant.

"Mr. Pagels, you seem to have an extremely objective view of humanity. Did this view extend to your opinion of John Nields? Did you see him as another poor speck of humanity, harboring negative thoughts, with a mind full of garbage? Did you think he should be done away with because he was unworthy?"

The blood immediately flooded back into Stassen's veins. He shot out of his seat, stabbing his pointed finger vigorously at Boyman.

"Objection! *That's* garbage! Now you know what garbage is!"

Conan was relieved to see that Stassen had resumed functioning. He went through the motions of chiding the defense attorney but he upheld the objection.

Boyman returned to the cross examination and avoided Stassen's wrath for a while by haphazard questioning on several subjects. It was not until about an hour after lunch that he returned to the perplexing question of Daniel's late-night presence in the Nields' house.

"Daniel was five years old when this happened. Were you in the habit of sending him to the supermarket to do the shopping?"

"No."

"You always went with him?"

"Yes."

"When you went to John Nields' house in the morning, you didn't leave Daniel behind on his own, did you?"

"No."

"Did you ever leave him at home alone?"

"No."

"Was that because he was only five years old and too young to be left alone?"

"You could say that."

"Then wasn't he also too young to go out across the San Fernando Valley just before midnight? Some areas of the valley aren't the safest places to be at night."

"He wasn't in the valley. He was here and then he was there."

"He was here and then he was there. I can see that being a headline in a few papers tomorrow. Come clean, Mr. Pagels. You're bullshitting us. Why don't you admit it?"

"Objection!"

Boyman was called to the bench, admonished, and given a fine.

By the time that had been dealt with it was getting late. The prosecution was allowed fifteen more minutes before the close of the afternoon session. Boyman used that time to ask some questions about Daniel's mother. Why had she abandoned him? Was she a drug user? Had she been in trouble with the law? (Not to Pagels' knowledge.) Was this evasion of responsibility something that ran in the Pagels family? One of Stassen's series of objections was sustained on that one.

Boyman gave one more of his sly grins to the jury and said he had no more questions.

————

From his cell in the downtown jail Lionel Brown had been following the daily developments of the Pagels trial with a degree of interest he had thus far confined to robbing supermarkets. Distrusting Lawrence Pagels' abstruse depictions of each day's events, he had taken to checking them out by reading the newspaper reports and listening to the radio and television.

"It says you been testifying in court."

"That's right."

"You didn't say nothin' about that."

"I guess I forgot."

"You guess you forgot. How can you forget? Man, you're on trial for killing a man and you can't remember nothin' about it. You ain't in this world, d'you know what I'm sayin'? You're out in space. This mother, Stassen, you tell him I don't got no lawyer. Tell him to come and see me, will ya."

195

Lawrence Pagels studied Lionel's overweight torso as if he were a painter about to depict him on canvas.

"Sure I'll speak to him, Lionel."

"Now don't *forget*. Don't float off somewhere. I wanna get myself a lawyer who can fool the judge real good."

"He hasn't fooled the judge."

"It says here that everyone's listening to all that shit he's layin' on them. They ain't throwing it out of court. Man, that's what I need. You tell that Stassen to come and see me. That public defender, he don't know enough about my case to keep the flies off a dog dick."

"Do you know what punishment is Lionel?"

"Sure, I know."

"It's committing a crime. You punish yourself when you commit a crime. You stop going around robbing people and you set yourself free."

"I see what you're sayin'. There ain't no happiness in bein' a robber. I see what you're sayin'. I'm into that. I like that idea. I used to work for the city. Sanitation. There's big bucks in sanitation. That's a heavy idea. When I have a little more time I might think about that."

Lionel took it upon himself to save any references to Lawrence Pagels that he found in the newspapers.

"Preacher, you're a star! Everyone's talkin' about you. That's fame, man. You don't look like a star, but you are. I told my wife I'm sharin' with Lawrence Pagels and she says, 'No shit!' I mean, I'm famous because you're famous."

"Are you a Californian, Lionel?"

"Sure. I was born in Stockton and then I moved down to Whittier when I was eight years old."

"Then you're a Californian just like Daniel."

"I guess I am, yeah."

"To be born a Californian is a gift."

"Yeah, I guess you could say that. But I'm black."

"Only in certain lights."

"Uh huh."

"In a prism you see all the colors but you don't see black and white. You see violet, indigo, blue, green, yellow, orange, and red. Black absorbs light. White reflects light. You can have a black man in white clothes, a white man in black clothes. And what are they in a prism? Nothing."

"Uh huh."

"In the light of truth there is only that light, Lionel. You have been given a lot. The world is waiting to see what you'll make of it. A Californian leads the way for the rest of the world."

"Uh huh."

"California is a prophecy."

Lionel always turned out when the old man talked too philosophical. He left the old guy to his own thoughts.

And when abandoned thus, Lawrence Pagels would often as not drift off into thinking about the waters of the Pacific Ocean washing over the California shores. Many times he had taken Daniel down to the beach at Trancas or Zuma at sunset. They would watch the sandpipers' courtly dance with the waters, advancing and withdrawing in their rapid nervous motion.

Confined in a jail cell with no view from the window and nothing to see through the bars but more bars, the sights and smells of the beach were still strongly present.

The position of California, with its back on the old Eastern establishment, old world, old beliefs, and its face toward a vast free-flowing ocean gave the state its special liberty, the essence of what Americans meant by freedom. If the Pagels defense were to find a sympathetic ear anywhere it would be in California. Most of its inhabitants were not native-born but they were Californians by choice, eager to turn their backs on old ideas and reach out and up like the giant sequoias in the conifer forests of the Pacific coast.

Edgar Stassen, not a Californian by birth but one by nature and intent, was the man of the hour. He had answered the call in the true spirit of adventure and was leading the history of justice along new paths.

That Stassen had not one ounce of belief in the current line of evidence was transparent to Lawrence but of no concern. He did not require Stassen to believe. It was enough for him that the ideas should be aired and his case considered in a new light by the jury. Beyond reasonable doubt. If there was a seed of doubt planted it was conceivable that they might not find it in their hearts to pronounce him guilty.

And why not? Was that so impossible? Every man and woman in the jury had lived through an age where the impossible became possible. They accepted satellite television, microchips, and computers. Why shouldn't they accept his line of defense? It was just one more barrier to be leapt over. It was an opportunity for mental growth. That was good, that was good ... an opportunity for mental growth. He would write that down. Stassen could use it in his summing up. An opportunity for mental growth.

This kind of thing, this kind of advanced motion was not so advanced. He kept on trying to explain that to Stassen. It was hard to explain anything to Stassen without the man's eyes glazing over. But it was not some miraculous thing they were claiming for Daniel. It was natural to many people. It had not been unknown to the Indians who lived in Chatsworth, for instance. They knew about it. When they went up to work at the San Fernando Mission they told the priests about it. They recounted stories of men who had traveled long distances in a matter of seconds, distances that would normally take an entire day of hard running. The stories angered the priests who accused the Indians of black magic and witch doctoring and the Indians, not wishing to receive any more diatribes, kept those stories to themselves after that.

But those Indians who learned to speak and read Spanish, studied the white man's holy book and found instances of the very same movement they had described to the priests. They read about men who had been instantly in another place, about men who parted seas, and men who escaped from jail by walking through locked doors and past armed guards. These were activities that did not astound the Indians; as far as they were concerned they were quite within man's capacity.

The Indians found it fruitless to draw any comparisons. They were not anxious to be beaten unnecessarily. They kept silent for silence was both their weapon and their comfort. With their silence they kept the white man out.

They kept their visions and their knowledge to themselves. When the Mexicans revolted against the Spanish the flag of the Republic of Mexico flew over the mission. There was a gradual decline in mission life, lands were sold off, and the Chatsworth Indians drifted off in various directions. They did not return to their village and their strong spiritual life was blown away in the dust of the Santa Susana Mountains.

"Did you know, Lionel, that prospectors used to dig for gold in the hills above Chatsworth."

"Now ain't that funny, you sayin' that. I was just thinkin' that what I need is a gold mine. If I ever get out of this place I'm comin' to visit you. You can show me round, know what I mean?"

"The valley is a great place, the best place in the world."

"I'm glad you think so, man, because it ain't right to be ashamed of where you come from. My wife says she'd hang by her thumbs before she'd live in the valley, but what right's she got to say that? She owes five months rent."

"Oh, the valley is a great place. You know where the 101 freeway goes through the Cahuenga Pass?"

"Oh sure. That's where my automobile acts like it won't make it. I floor the damn thing and the whole world is goin' by me up that hill."

"Well, just there on that hill they fought a battle."

"Don't talk to me about fightin'. Where I come from it's Beirut every day, man. It ain't safe to feed the cat."

"This was in 1845. Two armies met in the Cahuenga Pass and people came from miles around to watch. One horse was killed and a mule was wounded, no soldiers were killed."

"Sounds like they couldn't aim straight then. You know what? I was born a hundred years too late. In them days you could go down to the corner, buy a beer, and come back again. Every guy who was tryin' to kill you missed."

"And you know, Lionel, you'd see armies of men on horseback riding down from northern California to fight over what city was going to be the capital, Monterey or Los Angeles."

"And they'd get out their guns and all miss each other. I like that."

"California was part of Mexico in those days."

"Man, that explains everything."

"And then, when was it ... 1847. Yes, that was it. 1847. American soldiers rode into the San Fernando Valley."

"Right. And those guys weren't foolin'. They shoot to kill."

"And three years later California became the thirty-first state to join the union."

"Ever since that day, people in the valley, they been aimin' straight. Where you get a bunch of Americans you get a high body count."

"The Americans came out from the east and they discovered this paradise. But it was a little on the empty side. So they set about advertising it."

"You got it. Killin' and advertisin'. That's the American way."

"But they didn't know what they had here. They still don't know.

People came out to California and they could wash themselves clean. They came here to escape from their lives, to get away from stick-in-the-mud ideas. They came to float free and listen to the wind. You know what, Lionel, anything is possible here. This is California."

"That's for sure. There's a lot of shit in California."

"The worst and the best. It's all here."

"Man, all I want is a good lawyer. That fuckin' public defender, I only seen him once, and he thought I was someone else. He still thinks I'm someone else. He's got his head up his ass. You know what? I wish I killed somebody. I kill a man, I get a real good attorney like you got. But I didn't have no bullets in the gun."

"You think I killed him?"

"I think you fooled 'em all real good. And you fooled 'em so good that you're gettin' to believe it yourself."

"You think I'm fooling myself?"

"That's how it looks to me. I been sittin' here watchin' you day in and day out. I see you wake up. I see you go to sleep."

"What do you think's going to happen then, Lionel? Will I get off?"

"You askin' me? What do I know? I know you got a fancy attorney and that puts you ahead of the game. If that guy would tap dance like that for me I'd have a chance. I know the law don't have nothin' to do with guilty or not. But I ain't a prophet."

Pagels fell silent. Outside the light was fading but they could not see its source. The two men sat and listened to the harsh reverberations of the jail. After Lionel fell back on his bunk and dropped into a heavy sleep, Pagels reflected for some time on his daughter's startled white face at the back of the court. Then he sat with his head bowed until the early hours of the morning. Finally he lay down but he could not go to sleep.

———

By the time Lawrence Pagels stepped on to the witness stand there were few people in Los Angeles County who had not heard of the Pagels trial. It was not uncommon now to see lights in the hills above Chatsworth around eleven thirty at night, the time that George Lejeune habitually arrived at Pagels' motor home. Balancing their cameras and sound equipment, film crews would pursue George on his nightly walk in those once-dark hills. Stumbling in potholes, tripping over rocks, they would be mystified by this choice of a route for dog walking. It seemed to them that a lone man with nothing but the moon to light his pathway could not avoid twisting his ankle or falling down a steep slope.

They were even more mystified at Lawrence Pagels for choosing this desolate spot to live in with his grandson, cut off as it was from amenities and offering no easy access for vehicles. Although the current joke was that the two Pagelses were not so cut off, since they were "less than a second away from any Seven-Eleven."

George Lejeune did not like all the attention thrust upon him. Although he ran a successful plumbing business and could present a sociable face in his dealings with the public, he was essentially a private, solitary man who needed the bleak quiet of his nightly walk. The motor home had always been the exact halfway point of his walk. He would walk silently around it, glance in at the windows to check that the old man and the child were O.K., and go back down the hill. He had no need to pass the time of day with Lawrence Pagels, but if on rare occasions he was still awake, they would exchange a few words.

Now all that was changed. Pagels and the boy were gone and his walks offered all the serenity of a jackhammer. The questions drove him crazy. What were Lawrence and Daniel Pagels like? Were they different from other people? Was he at all disturbed by the fact that he was backing up a fraud and a delusion, a confidence trick being played on the people of Los Angeles? No, he was not. He was telling it like it was. He had nothing to do with the way people chose to interpret it.

Had Lawrence Pagels confided in him? Did he explain the big secret? How did the kid get there? No, Lawrence Pagels had not confided in him. He didn't seem like a guy with a secret. He seemed like an ordinary decent fellow just like any other person. No, he saw nothing wrong in living up in the hills. He'd do it himself if his wife would agree to it.

Was George absolutely convinced he passed the motor home at precisely eleven thirty that particular night? He was tired of telling them he was a man of habit, that he had passed that motor home that exact time every night for almost ten years and he would continue to do so.

Timing George Lejeune became a media game. There were few local television stations, newspapers, and magazines that had not followed George with a stopwatch. As time went on they were succeeded by journalists from the Midwest and the East Coast, until eventually it became an international story and George's nightly walk became, as he complained to his wife, like the Universal Studios tour. At this point he gave up. For the first time since he had moved to Chatsworth, George stayed in at night. He prowled his backyard with the dog like a prisoner in an open jail.

Mrs. Elaine Lejeune was waylaid on her way to her job at an optician's office in Reseda. Was her husband in possession of his normal faculties? Did they have a good marriage? Did George have a history of mental aberration? Did he believe in UFO's. She was pursued home, she was photographed stepping into her Jacuzzi by a man standing on the backyard wall.

"If it's like this for us," she said to George, "can you imagine what it's like for Danny Pagels?"

———

Daniel and Jason had built a fort out of cushions. They sat in it wondering what to do next.

"Let's destroy it," said Jason.

"But I like it," said Daniel.

"You like everything. You're so dumb."

"I'm not."

"When we go to LA on Wednesday I'm gonna go to Orange Julius with Sheila."

"Can I come?"

"No, you dummy, you'll be in court."

"Right." Daniel's face lit up. "I'm going to see my grandpa."

"Do you like answering questions?"

"I don't mind."

"Do they search you to see if you have a gun?"

"Some people. Not me."

"They should search you. You could have a gun so you can get your grandpa out."

"Uh huh."

"What do they ask you?"

"Oh lots of stuff."

"Do they ask you for your autograph?"

"No."

"You should make a video. You could sell a lot of copies because you're famous."

"I don't want to be famous."

"Why not?"

"I just don't." Daniel stepped out of the cushion fort and went to stare out of the window.

14

The first rebuttal witness for the prosecution was Dr. Jean-Paul Chen. He was a small, slim man with a hyenalike laugh which had been ringing around the District Attorney's Office for the previous ten days. He had been dubbed Boyman's fairy godmother because he had the ability to make the attorney look good in a very short space of time. He was Mark Boyman's lifesaver, his great stroke of luck, and he had, in the best tradition of fairy godmothers, appeared without request or forewarning. Or, more accurately, he had phoned Mark Boyman's office and offered his services.

Other scientists were as knowledgeable, other scientists were equally opposed to the Stassen line, but few were able to drill the finer points of quantum physics into Boyman's porous brain at such short notice. He had told Boyman what to think and when to think it. He had orchestrated what would be covered during his appearance in court so that Boyman would never seem to be even minimally unaware of what he was talking about. This at least was the intention.

Harvey Marlatt would have been an easier subject for force-feeding but Boyman had the more effective presence in court. As the stakes grew larger, Marlatt was being pushed farther and farther into the background, his ability sacrificed to Boyman's supposed charisma.

To say that Mark Boyman was nervous as Dr. Jean-Paul Chen

was sworn in would have been an understatement. Boyman was not given to nervousness but he felt straitjacketed. He had to follow the script exactly or, as Dr. Chen had repeatedly told him, he would fall into a black hole.

Mary-Lynn, squeezed into another of her elaborate mini outfits, was sitting at the prosecution table, ready to give Boyman moral support. If he got into difficulties, Marlatt and Mary-Lynn would talk him through it.

For the first time the court would see Mary-Lynn in a role similar to Ida's, the female assistant acting as mental prop. It was a coincidence that did not go unnoticed by the reporters.

In the preceding days and nights of cramming quantum physics, Boyman had begun to have a dull respect for what Stassen had achieved.

"How the hell did he come up with it?"

"He didn't come up with it," Marlatt said. "Pagels did."

"Then how the hell did he understand what Pagels was talking about?"

"Who knows?"

As Dr. Chen settled himself into the witness chair, journalists made quick notes on his slight but athletic build and his somewhat stilted, utterly correct pronunciation of words which indicated foreign birth. In their reports of the day's proceedings much was made of the fact that he had completed the LA marathon in three hours and twelve minutes.

Boyman, face muscles tense, eyes narrowed, muttered to Mary-Lynn and Marlatt, then stepped forward.

Dr. Chen gave his qualifications. Degrees from Stanford and M.I.T. Author of several books on quantum physics, science consultant to high-tech industry.

"Dr. Chen . . ."

Boyman spoke lightly as though this witness were of minor importance. Dr. Chen's presence might appear as an admission that the prosecution took Stassen's silly babblings seriously. He was therefore at pains to appear untroubled. The wild claim by the defense was a fly he would swat quickly and efficiently and then forget. The jury, however, remembering how floor plans had baffled the prosecuting attorney, were curious to see how he would handle quantum physics.

"Do you think," Boyman consulted his notes, "do you think it is possible for any man, woman, or child to move from one place to another at the speed of light?"

"No, I do not." Dr. Chen smiled cheerfully around the crowded court.

"Why is that? And in your explanation, sir, remember that many of us are untutored in physics and would appreciate it if you would take pity on us."

Laughter from the jury. Dr. Chen smiled back.

"No man could travel at such a speed, 186,279 miles per second, very fast you understand. Einstein's special theory of relativity shows us that the mass of a moving object increases as the velocity of the object increases. As the object approached the speed of light it would require more and more energy to speed it up. If this man, woman, or child were to reach the speed of light, by that time the person's mass would have become infinite."

"The person"—Boyman hesitated—"would have become infinite?"

"His mass would have become infinite. And by the equivalence of mass and energy this person would have required an infinite amount of energy to get him to this great speed."

"What exactly do you mean, a person's mass would have become infinite?"

"If you were to work it out in a mathematical equation, that would be the result. Infinity."

Already Boyman had panicked and forgotten the rehearsed script. Haltingly he asked, "If a person's mass became infinite they'd balloon up wouldn't they? They'd wipe out everyone else."

"A lot of things would happen to a human body before its mass became infinite. The whole idea is completely impossible."

"The whole idea is completely impossible." Boyman repeated the idea with relish. This he understood.

"That's right." Dr. Chen smiled again. He was enjoying himself.

"Dr. Chen, perhaps we should examine all the scientific jargon used by the counsel for the defense to prop up this impossible idea."

"Objection. He's leading the witness." Stassen appeared gratified that his objection wiped the smile off Dr. Chen's face.

"Your Honor, I'm only repeating what the witness has said."

Conan overruled the objection.

Boyman was back on track. He had remembered the script.

"Dr. Chen, we have established that man cannot travel at the speed of light. But I believe the defense is making another claim here. When they're not talking about high-speed travel they're implying some kind of instant transmission from one place to another. Have there been any recorded instances where a man, woman, or child has jumped through time and space, moved instantly from one spot to the other?"

"No. It happens with subatomic particles in quantum physics but it has never been known to happen to any human."

"Have you heard of the phrase 'Beam me up, Scottie'?"

"You mean from *Star Trek*? Yes I have."

"Do you consider beaming somebody up to be possible?"

"Well . . . so far we've worked out how to fax documents but I guess it'll be some time before we do it to humans."

Laughter. Conan frowned.

Boyman consulted his notes.

"The defense offered several scientific formulas or propositions for this er . . . what d'you call it . . . er . . . unusual idea . . . the special theory of relativity, described by Albert Einstein in 1905. The double-slit or two-hole experiment. The Heisenberg uncertainty principle. And Bell's Theorem."

Boyman paused, temporarily exhausted, and then went on, "So let's start by looking at the theory of relativity. I believe this is used by some people to explain time travel, sudden leaps, teleportation or . . . translocation . . ."

"Yes, it is. It is not unusual for people to confuse facts with myths."

"Is there such a thing as absolute time? By that I mean . . . if I say to you that I'll meet you at three thirty on Santa Monica Pier, would we ever make contact? Am I kidding myself that there is such a time as three thirty?"

Stassen leaned over to Max Haydn and whispered, "Have you noticed when Boyman uses his brains that his eyes cross?"

Max snickered.

Chen gave a small speech. "Time is relative. Einstein proved that and it has been backed up by proof many times. Isaac Newton taught us that there was a universal flow of time common to all, but when Einstein brought out his theory the old classical attitude to time had to change. It was discovered that different observers witnessed events at different times according to the observer's velocity. So there is no such thing as absolute time."

"You can understand, Dr. Chen, that an idea like that can appear quite disturbing in a court of law, where evidence and alibis often depend on having an absolute rather than a relative time."

"It is not disturbing at all. Relative time is not noticeable in our ordinary daily life. It is only observable at great speeds."

"I see. So you and I could meet at exactly three thirty? We wouldn't have any trouble about that?"

"Sure. As long as we could get through the traffic."

Big laughs from the reporters who had been stuck on the San Diego Freeway that morning.

"And these great speeds you're talking about have no relevance to us here in this courtroom?"

"No and yes. No, in that it is impossible for any of us to reach those speeds and yes, in that we have benefitted and suffered from relativity theory. It transformed modern science but it also helped produce the atomic bomb."

Boyman wiped a few small beads of sweat from his forehead and looked over to Mary-Lynn for support. She raised her eyebrows and nodded like a proud parent watching her child in an egg-and-spoon race.

Comforted, Boyman moved on.

"So this theory may be influential but it has nothing to do with us guys here in this courtroom. It has something to do with moving clocks running faster . . ."

"No. Moving clocks run *slower* and stop altogether at the speed of light."

Mary-Lynn was wincing.

Boyman shrugged, "So they run slower."

"Yes. They run slower and stop altogether at the speed of light." Dr. Chen repeated it, hoping that the attorney would pick up the ball.

He did. "They stop. Time stops?"

"Yes."

"And what happens if the clock goes faster than the speed of light?"

"The clock will go backward."

"Does this er . . . go on? Is it real?"

"Well, there are some so-called particles that travel faster than the speed of light called 'tachyons.' "

"But there are no human tachyons?"

"No, and it does not appear that there ever will be, no matter how technically advanced mankind becomes in the future."

"Why is that, Dr. Chen?"

"No one has ever visited us from the future." The witness grinned broadly.

"That's very interesting, Dr. Chen. So the science-fiction writers have got it all wrong. No one will ever be able to travel through time?"

"That appears to be the case."

"So if, in the next million years or so no one will develop this ability, it's doubtful that a small boy living today could get through time barriers."

"Objection. He's muddled two ideas and he's leading the witness."

Dr. Chen watched with interest as the two attorneys wrangled. Boyman, with his sleeked-down hair and perfectly pressed pin-striped suit could not have been more of a contrast to the disarranged Stassen, whose crumpled cream linen jacket appeared to have developed a couple of soup stains during the course of the trial.

Stassen insisted on a ten-minute consultation with Conan which did little more than irritate the judge.

Boyman returned enthusiastically to the subject of time travel.

"Dr. Chen, without getting too technical could you give us any more reasons why it is not possible to travel backward in time?"

"Certainly. The reason a person could not travel backward through time is because it would result in his meeting himself when younger. And if everyone carried out this activity to excess the world would be filled with hundreds of versions of each person at various stages of his experience."

Stassen was up again. "Objection. They're at it again. They're talking about traveling backward in time. We have made no claim along that line."

Judge Conan called a recess.

The reporters raced each other to the phones. Rhonda Pagels went to the ladies' room for a smoke and, lost in her thoughts, stared past her pale, ghostlike reflection in the mirror. A fat woman, who had stood in line since five that morning to get her seat, pushed past her.

"I've gotta rush. I put my coat on my seat but I don't trust anybody."

Rhonda nodded vaguely and returned to her reveries.

The woman stopped at the door and looked at her curiously.

"You come every day? I saw you here yesterday. What d'ya think of the trial?"

"I think it's great."

"I don't understand a word they're talking about. Not a word."

"Then why do you come?"

"I come to all the big murder trials. And would you believe this one? Three weeks ago I wouldn't have touched it with a barge pole."

"Yes, it's big." Rhonda sighed.

"Yeah," the woman acknowledged the sigh. "The physics is really tough. I used to get B's in math at school but this stuff's going right over my head."

Rhonda looked at her coolly. "It's not that hard. They're bending over backward to make it easy."

"Maybe. Maybe. I just don't know why Pagels thinks he can get away with it. Why didn't he plead insanity?"

"I guess he must think he's sane."

"What does he know? He's got a screw loose. But you know what? I bet he's laughing up his sleeve."

Two women went past her and out the door and the fat women jumped.

"Gotta go. If someone's taken my seat I'll scream bloody murder."

Someone had taken her seat and pushed her coat on to the floor. She settled herself in one of the press seats and refused to move until her own seat was restored. DeRosa was called to sort it out. Diplomacy was not his strong suit and there was a nasty scene before the fat woman got her seat back.

One of the key players in the growing drama of the Pagels trial had not bothered to claim his seat in court that day.

While the throngs of reporters were swapping cigarettes and stories during the break, Leon Ferguson was meeting with Lionel Brown in the visitors' room at the downtown Central Jail.

―――

"I'll help you man, if you give me a little help." Lionel told him, eyeing the reporter's expensive jacket and his designer shirt.

"Like what?" asked Leon.

"You ask Ed Stassen if he'll take up my case."

"I'll try."

"No man. You don't try. You do it. I do something for you. You do something for me."

"O.K. I'll talk to him."

"Tell him to come and see me. Tell him I didn't have no bullets in the gun. I never shot nobody. I couldn't. I don't see too well."

"O.K., O.K. Tell me about Lawrence Pagels. What sort of man is he?"

"Once he gets to know you, he talks a lot. It's a burden I have to bear, because some people he don't like and he don't say a word to them. But he says, 'Lionel, I like you,' and then he talks and talks."

"What about?"

"That's hard to say."

"What did he say this morning?"

"He didn't say nothing this morning. He sits with his eyes closed thinking a lot. In fact that's what he does the rest of the time. If he's not talking then he's sitting there with his eyes closed, getting ready."

"Getting ready?"

"That's right. I ask him why he sits there like that and he says 'I'm getting ready, Lionel.' "

"Uh huh. Has he told you if he killed John Nields?"

"No, he hasn't told me."

"Do you think he did it?"

"How would I know? It seems like he wouldn't have time to kill no one. He's always got his eyes closed or he's talking."

"What does he talk about?"

"He talks about consciousness. I know about unconscious because I've seen a lot of it, but I never thought too much about conscious."

"What does he say?"

"He says you live in your consciousness, Lionel. You can't be taken out of your own consciousness. And I say fine, but how do I get Men's Central out of my consciousness. And he says you have to understand how you're really free. You live in your consciousness. And I say maybe he's living in his consciousness because he's always got his eyes closed, but I'm in a cell."

"Does he seem violent in any way?"

"No. Neither am I. I wouldn't hurt a mouse. Would you go and see my wife?"

Back on the sixth floor of the Van Nuys courthouse, Mark Boyman had returned to resume his examination of his rebuttal witness. He looked pleased with himself, more confident.

"Dr. Chen, the theory of relativity and this quantum theory about particles jumping about mysteriously. How do they hang together? How do they gel?"

"Relativity theory and quantum theory are two of the greatest intellectual achievements of the twentieth century. Relativity is concerned with the force of gravity and the universe on a large scale, anything from a few miles to billions. Quantum physics is concerned with the minute, what is imperceptible to the human eye, subatomic particles that are a millionth of a millionth of an inch. These two theories have proved correct and useful over the past six or seven decades but they are inconsistent with each other."

"You mean . . . that one or other of these theories is wrong?"

"No. It's simply that one theory is not in agreement with the other. Scientists are looking for a unified theory which would include them both and iron out the inconsistencies."

"Would this complete, unified theory explain the mysteries of the universe?"

"There is hope that it would."

Stassen interrupted, "Your Honor, he's wasting the court's time if he's trying to disprove the theory of relativity. He lacks the mental equipment to understand it in the first place."

"Mr. Stassen has proved himself not too well endowed in the brain department, Your Honor . . ."

The remarks were ruled out of order and fines were imposed. Conan warned the counsels to leave out the sideshow or else incur further fines and/or imprisonment.

As the attorneys returned from the bench, two assistants from the DA's office walked into court carrying a movie screen and projector. The sight was highly disturbing to Stassen.

"Boyman got a major motion picture together in two weeks." Max grinned.

"I could have used film," Stassen scowled. "Any asshole can use film."

"So he uses film," said Ida. "What difference does that make? He doesn't have right on his side."

Max and Stassen looked at Ida in amazement.

"Right on his side?" Stassen asked sardonically. "What are you, Joan of Arc?"

Ida looked quickly across at Lawrence Pagels who seemed not to have heard their remarks. Just as his daughter had stared vacantly at the mirror during the recess, so he focused his eyes on something far removed from the courtroom.

"I know, I know," Ida said irritably. "There's no right or wrong. There's only winners and losers. You should have it printed on your stationery."

Getting back to business, Mark Boyman tackled the speed of light once more.

"Dr. Chen, you were saying that light travels at roughly 186,000 miles per second."

"Yes."

"But everyday objects like a chair or a person cannot travel at the speed of light?"

"Light is a wave with no intrinsic mass so it can move at 186,000 miles per second, whereas an object such as a chair is confined by relativity to move at speeds slower than the speed of light."

"A chair or a person is not a wave?"

"No."

"A chair or a person," Boyman repeated for the jury and for himself, "is not a wave and therefore a chair or a person cannot dispatch itself through the air like a beam of light?"

"No, they cannot."

"And that's a scientific fact?"

"It certainly is."

"Would you say, Dr. Chen, that the interpretation of the theory of relativity is affected by vested interests?"

"How do you mean?"

"For instance, paranormal interests?"

"It's possible. It's a scientifically accurate theory but some unscientific claims are made in its behalf."

"And would you say that the same goes for the quantum theory?"

"Yes, I would. It has become a fashionable idea to believe that quantum mechanics will explain paranormal behavior but from what I've seen of it it's merely bending facts to suit the claim."

"So you would say that it's incorrect to use quantum mechanics to explain what we call paranormal behavior?"

"Yes. It's used by every crackpot to back up ESP, spoon bending, all that kind of thing."

"Why do you think they do this?"

"Because they misinterpret the findings."

"Well, let's try and interpret these findings correctly shall we, Dr. Chen? How about taking a closer look at the double-slit or two-hole experiment."

Boyman's well-rehearsed assistants set up the projector and screen. The lights were lowered and Dr. Chen stepped down from the witness chair and stood behind the projector. There was some scuffling among spectators whose sight lines were obstructed by the projector and Dr. Chen.

On the screen were two vertical and parallel white boards as set up previously in court by Dr. Walkman. But these white boards or screens were far larger and easier to see now. Instead of Dr. Walkman's hand-held flashlight, there was a powerful light source sending a clearly visible strong beam onto the first screen.

"As you see," said Dr. Chen, "there is, at the moment, only one hole in the front screen. The beam of light goes through that hole and projects onto the second screen as a single bar of light. If you open up the other hole, thus . . ."

On screen an attractive girl appeared and removed the covering from the hole. Some members of the audience reacted as though she were a magician's assistant and gave low whistles.

"Quiet!" yelled Conan.

"Now," said Chen, "the light is directed through both holes. See what happens. On the second screen you see a pattern of wavy dark and light bands. This is a wave interference pattern. This shows us the light behaved like a wave."

"Which is what you would expect with light," said Boyman intelligently, like a student trying to get his teacher's approval.

"Exactly. In the next experiment we use an electron . . ."

"What's an electron?"

"It's an elementary particle in all atoms."

The screen now moved from real life to animation. And in an attempt to aid concentration, a snappy piece from Bizet's *Carmen* played in the background.

Several comic characters came jumping across the screen: one of them, a pirate with a peg leg, was dragging with him an apparatus that looked something like an ancient cannon.

"To avoid complex explanations about the production of electrons," announced Dr. Chen, "let us just say that they will be shot, one at a time from this apparatus."

Stassen's voice came from the darkness. "Your Honor, the prosecution is being evasive."

Boyman's voice came close to a squeak, "Evasive?"

"Evasive?" echoed Conan.

"It's vital that they tell the jury how electrons are produced for this experiment. Electrons are not mysterious things from outer space. All human bodies are made up of atoms and electrons. Everyone in this courtroom is a seething mass of electrons."

The film came to a halt while Boyman protested.

"Is there a quick, painless way of describing the production of an electron?" asked Conan.

Dr. Chen smiled. "No problem. A hot tungsten filament will boil off electrons."

"Hot tungsten?" asked Conan.

Dr. Chen's smile reached Cheshire-cat proportions as he looked at the uncomprehending faces in the jury.

"Yes, and I would like to add that electrons cannot be seen or touched by any human being. They are unbelievably small. If you were to enlarge a human body to the size of the earth the atoms in it would appear to be about the size of an acorn. If you were to enlarge that acorn-sized atom to the size of the Hollywood Bowl, the electrons in that atom would be no larger than a grain of salt."

"I think we can go on with the film now," Boyman said, more than satisfied.

"And," Chen, who had not finished, went on, "an electron is not a particle in the sense that you and I understand it. It is not so much a thing, or an object. You have to give up thinking of it as a thing."

There were loud whisperings about this between Pagels and Stassen.

The film continued. The pirate dragged a large metallic sheet across the screen and set it upright. After making sure that it would not fall over, he produced a drill and bored a hole through the metal.

"That," said Dr. Chen "is the hole we'll shoot the electron through and beyond that we'll have a screen of electron detectors."

215

The pirate dutifully set up what looked like another metallic sheet covered in small knobs behind the first one.

"If you shoot an electron through one hole it behaves exactly like a pellet."

The pirate aimed the electron apparatus at the metal sheet. An electron shot out and was shown to zoom through the hole and leave one clear impression on the electron detector behind it.

"That is what one would expect of an electron. But if we have two holes and shoot an electron at the barrier . . ."

The pirate drilled a second hole in the metal sheet. Then he pointed the electron apparatus toward the two holes. An electron shot out and went through the metal sheet. A wavy pattern emerged on the electron detecting screen.

"The electron has acted like a wave and gone through both holes at once."

Boyman spoke up. "This is what they all think is such a big deal, huh?"

"Yes, indeed."

"And what happens if you observe this process taking place?"

"We'll see . . ."

An observer appeared in the shape of a lady pirate who stood by the metal sheet staring fiercely, her nose a fraction away from the two holes.

The pirate shot another electron at the two holes. This time there was only one clear impression on the electron detector screen.

"The electron only goes through one hole."

"So when you observe the electron it changes its behavior?"

"That's correct."

"Does this indicate to you that people can effect the movement of an elementary particle by the very act of observation?"

"The act of observation in this case would be to shine a beam of light by the hole and observe how the light is scattered by the electron as it passes through the hole. And yes, it does effect the particle."

"And can you also say that this indicates that . . . on a much larger scale, we can effect movement by observation?"

"No. Certainly not. You cannot confuse the quantum world with the everyday world."

"Could you explain why not?"

"We have shown you an animated cartoon. And as you know,

cartoons show impossible things that do not happen in real life. Electrons, in a way, are impossible. They do not have an objective physical reality in the way that we understand a chair or a human body to have. Electrons only seem to exist when we observe them. Chairs, tables, human bodies, have a physical reality that stays with them whether they are observed or not. Electrons do not."

"So let me get this straight. Just because the act of observation changes the behavior of a subatomic particle, you cannot automatically conclude from that that the act of observation is so powerful in our daily life?"

"No. Not at all."

"And the act of observation or, to put it another way, *the mind itself* does not have the power to move the body in strange and revolutionary ways?"

"No way, José."

There were giggles from the jury and spectators.

Boyman paused as though waiting for an objection from Stassen. None came. Stassen and Pagels were whispering together again.

Conan coughed, a habit of his when he was about to call a recess. He said it was time for lunch and cautioned spectators about unseemly fighting over seats.

———

"Want to go somewhere for lunch?" Max asked Ida.

"What do you mean, somewhere? Where's somewhere?" Ida's eyes had lost a little of their luster. Her ivory skin displayed a slight dullness.

Max himself looked like a child who'd been kicked once too often. "I dunno. I mean what do you want?"

"I just want some orange juice."

"Orange juice. Is that all you want?"

"It's not a sin, Max. Just because I don't want six hamburgers, I won't go to Hell."

"Look. I don't believe in Hell. Have an orange juice. I don't give a shit."

"Where's Stassen?"

"He's a dug a hole somewhere. He's disappeared."

"Then why don't we go to the Subway."

"Sure you can stomach the sight of people eating?"

Ida looked around. "Shouldn't we wait for him?"

"He's not eating."

"He should eat."

"So he should eat. You tell him!"

"Don't shout at me, Max."

"I'm not shouting! I'm not shouting!"

"I don't have to go with you. We're not glued together."

"I'm not asking you to marry me. We're just talking about lunch."

"Yes. I know."

"So let's go."

"We're going, aren't we?"

"You know, Ida, you're not going to make it through this."

"I'm not?"

"I see the hysteria creeping in."

"There's nothing wrong with that. It's quite a rational reaction to what's going on."

"Oh come on. There's never a reason to be hysterical."

"For a bovine person like yourself, Max, maybe not."

"Oh well, pardon me. I'm not a sensitive, finely tuned little instrument like you. I wouldn't know about fainting fits and the vapors."

"No. You'll end up in some greasy little office, making a fortune out of swindling people who can't afford it."

"Sounds good. I suppose you'll be cornering the market on aliens from Pluto."

"Max."

"What?"

"You're not very clever."

"No. If I was clever I wouldn't be here."

———

Boyman, Marlatt, and Mary-Lynn Robbins had a working lunch of club sandwiches and cola in a crowded deli on Van Nuys Boulevard. As they drove there Boyman's voice, which had hoarsened during the previous hour in court, declined to a whisper.

"It's nerves," said Mary-Lynn.

"It's not nerves, it's my voice."

"You'll have to give it a rest."

"Give it a rest!"

When they walked into the deli, customers stared. They had seen

Mary-Lynn on television reading prepared statements, and Boyman and Marlatt giving nervy answers outside the courthouse.

"See how it goes," said Marlatt. "You've got ninety minutes."

"Oh shit." Boyman rubbed his throat trying to find the source of the trouble.

"Don't speak until you get back," Mary-Lynn instructed.

At a secluded table at the back Boyman sat mutely, answering Marlatt with signs and written notes.

"Mrs. Richter doesn't like me," Boyman wrote.

"She doesn't like me either," Marlatt replied. He was beginning to think that Boyman was unduly concerned about the jury.

"But," Boyman wrote, "Bradley Ryker's been with us all the way and you can bet he'll be foreman."

"The rest look as if they've been hit with a wet fish," said Marlatt.

"People are smarter than you think," said Mary-Lynn.

"I hope so." Marlatt bit into a thick roast beef on rye. "Presuming that the smarter they are the more likely they are to vote guilty."

Boyman nodded in agreement to that.

"But we're not using the usual norms here," mused Marlatt. "You're delving into levels you don't usually touch."

"I don't know," Mary-Lynn said practically. "It may all boil down to how much they like kids."

"Or Indians," wrote Boyman.

"Or motor homes. Five of them have RVs. They might belong to some RV organization."

Boyman wrote quickly, "Ryker has an RV and he hates Pagels."

"Yeah," said Marlatt. "But you've got another incalculable. Elvie Richter and Angela Barry are both sympathetic to the kid. They both strike me as bossy women. I don't know how they'd come out in a battle of wills with Ryker."

"He's an ex-Marine," wrote Boyman.

"What's his wife like?" asked Mary-Lynn.

"Dead" he wrote.

"Oh, right, of course. She's dead."

"So they'll feel sorry for him," said Marlatt.

"No way. He's a pig."

"Love him, Mary-Lynn. He may pull us through," wrote Boyman.

When they arrived back at the courthouse, Boyman's voice was no better.

Harvey Marlatt took over for the prosecution. Boyman, alternately spraying his throat and sucking cough drops, watched mutely.

Marlatt had donned a pair of rimless glasses with half lenses. Peering at the jury and Dr. Chen over the top of the glasses gave him some needed authority.

"Now let's go on"—he frowned at his notes—"to the Heisenberg uncertainty principle. It says, I believe, that we cannot measure both the position and momentum of a particle at the same time. They are uncertain until the observer, or rather the observing instruments play their part in establishing position and momentum. Did I get that right, Dr. Chen?"

"Roughly, yes."

"Well, it's good enough for me, Dr. Chen. I haven't done physics since I was a freshman in college. . . . Now, did Einstein, one of the greatest minds of this century, agree with Heisenberg's uncertainty principle?"

"No, he did not."

"Why is that?"

"The uncertainty principle conflicted with Einstein's faith in a God who created an orderly universe. He said, 'God does not play dice.' "

"Was he, in your view, correct?"

"I would say that he was correct on one level."

"What do you mean by that?"

"When we get up in the morning and make coffee and eat toast . . . we are experiencing things according to principles laid out for us by Isaac Newton three hundred years ago . . ."

"But the uncertainty principle . . ."

"The uncertainty principle relates to things that are so small we can't see them. As I said before it's difficult to imagine such smallness. The quantum effects take place on such a minute scale, unobservable to us, that we cannot see these minuscule quantum effects take place in our daily life."

Marlatt paused to reflect on that, staring up at the ceiling. Several jurors looked up at the ceiling too. "You spoke earlier about a particle in an atom being like a grain of salt in the Hollywood Bowl."

"Yes."

"Uh huh." Marlatt stared down at his notes. Boyman stood up and whispered hoarsely in his ear and then the two of them looked down at the notes.

Judge Conan leaned forward. "I'm sure counsel would be interested to know why a particle can go through two holes at once."

Marlatt nodded hurriedly, "Yes, Dr. Chen. In the double-slit or the two-hold experiment, whatever you like to call it, why did the particle go through two holes at once?"

Dr. Chen took a breath, "I don't know."

"Do you know what it means?"

"No."

"Does anyone?"

"No. I don't think that the results of the two-hole experiment should give rise to strange speculations about the nature of matter. I've heard some physicists struggling to explain it and even reaching the conclusion that the photon or electron may be conscious!"

"You mean that a tiny little particle has a mind of its own?"

Dr. Chen laughed loudly. It was a little too ebullient for the court and it made the jury laugh along with him.

"Yes, the quantum world is a mine field. If every subatomic particle had a consciousness of its own the world would be impossibly chaotic. A chair would fall apart because of a disagreement between particles. It is a preposterous idea."

"So you would say that some people misinterpret the quantum theory?"

"Oh yes. It's rich pickings for any crank with any bizarre proposition."

"And this quantum theory is in truth a practical theory used for making er . . . scientific instruments?"

"Quantum theory can be used for precise and accurate instruments like the transistor, even though the theory itself is based on probabilities and uncertainties. It's these uncertainties that the crackpots pick on."

Marlatt had a hurried consultation with Boyman and Mary-Lynn, then he turned back to the witness.

"One last thing, Dr. Chen . . . Bell's Theorem."

"Ah yes. Bell's Theorem." Dr. Chen spoke with relish.

"I don't think we need to go into it in detail . . ."

There was a low sigh of relief from two members of the jury but the witness looked disappointed. This had not been his plan.

To mollify him Marlatt said, "Perhaps you could explain it to us in one or two sentences."

"That's not possible."

"Oh." Marlatt was stymied.

"But I can say," Dr. Chen went on tautly, "that Bell's Theorem shows us that if a pair of particles with identical polarization travel in separate directions, a measurement taken on one will instantly affect the other."

Marlatt was cheered by this. "And one particle could be here in this courtroom and the other one could be on the moon?"

"That's correct. The theory questions the idea of locality."

"What is locality?"

"The idea that influence or information cannot travel faster than the speed of light."

"Which it doesn't here in the real world?"

"Absolutely not. Bell's Theorem is no excuse for claims of telepathy or other psychic nonesense."

"And why is that, Dr. Chen?"

"Because . . . I will say once more, that you are dealing with minuscule particles that are not objects as we know them."

"So we cannot identify the behavior of subatomic particles with ourselves?"

"No. Because to do that you would have to accept a fantasy. The fantasy that these ghostlike particles exist in a definite state. But they do not. The exist as a probablity. They are nothing like ourselves. Bell's Theorem is not referring to local objects."

"And by local objects you would mean a table or a chair or a small boy?"

"Yes, I would."

"Thank you, Dr. Chen."

———

It was difficult for Raymond Nields to avoid his mother. If he arrived back after midnight, two, even three in the morning, her voice would come out of the darkness. "Is that you, Ray?"

"Go to sleep."

"You work too hard, Ray."

She, however, was now working obsessively on the silver and looking for smudges on the walls and light switches. The maid watched curiously as she rubbed at spots actual and imaginary. She exhausted herself but she was still unable to sleep.

When her son came back at four thirty in the morning she emerged from her bedroom and confronted him.

"That little boy. What's he thinking about all this?"

"How should I know?"

Raymond's eyes were half closed, indicating either tiredness or some alcohol or chemically induced state of torpor.

Sharon wrapped her pink silk robe tightly round her thick waist.

"I keep on thinking about him. If Pagels wanted to kill John, then why would he take the little boy with him?"

Raymond's eyelids lowered still further. He patted his mother on the shoulder.

"Don't worry about it. It's not your problem. He took the boy with him because he wasn't planning to kill him. It must have happened by accident."

"Then why did he leave the child in the house?"

"Nobody understands panic. People are very irrational when they're in shock."

"I guess that's how I am. I know things I don't want to know."

"You'll get over it."

"Will I, Ray?"

"Of course you will."

"Uh huh. Do you want a cup of coffee?"

"I'm going to bed."

"Do you think I should go to court? For John's sake."

"Only if you feel up to it."

Raymond had attended the trial three or four times in the early days but had soon, like his mother, chosen to stay away.

"I miss John," she said. "At night. That's when it's the worst. When the daylight goes I get really low."

"But you never saw him."

"That's not true, Ray. He was never gone for more than three days. Now it's . . . it'll be two years in April. I can't believe it. I thought it was supposed to get better. It's the trial that's making me nervous. It's bringing it all back."

"It'll get better. You have to hang in there."

"I can't stop thinking about that little boy. Do you think strange things do happen? When you stare at the back of someone's neck in a crowd, they turn round. You can make them turn round. Why is that?"

"I don't know. I'm going to bed."

"Do you want me to get you up, Ray? I'm always awake."

"No, I have an alarm."

"Goodnight, honey."

" 'Night."

"You seem a little depressed, Ray. You don't seem yourself. I guess it's getting you down too, huh?"

"I'm fine. Good night."

Sharon sighed heavily.

Raymond stopped at his bedroom door. "Let it go."

"I can't let it go, honey."

15

For the cross examination of the rebuttal witness Edgar Stassen was initially noncombative.

"Dr. Chen, I've read some of your books and may I say, I'm a fan."

"Thank you."

"You're welcome." Stassen curled his thumbs under his red suspenders. "As you may realize, Dr. Chen, I'm not a physicist. I have just enough savvy to know I'm out of my depth and I tremble to set my little pea-sized brain against your great mind, but I guess I must. So let me, with great fear and hesitation, ask you about Isaac Newton. Did he set up a bunch of principles that we all observe as correct?"

"Yes, he did."

"And that was about three hundred years ago, right?"

"Yes."

"And then Einstein came along and smashed a lot of those ideas apart?"

"Right, he did."

"And he said, and it's probably driving the jury up the wall hearing it again, that there's no such thing as absolute time. Time is relative. There's a kind of thing called space time. Right?"

"That's right."

"But very few people understood the theory of relativity, did they?"

"No, they did not."

"And everyone went on living according to guidelines set out by Isaac Newton?"

"Yes."

"They went on winding up their clocks and believing that time was absolute. And it worked real well right up to today, everyone's been real happy with it?"

"Yes, they have."

"It's worked real well even though it's completely wrong. We're living a lie."

"No. The theories of Isaac Newton work very well for the zone of middle dimension that we all live in."

"Even though they're out of date?"

"Oh yes. As I've already said several times, the extraordinary anomalies discovered in quantum theory and relativity theory are too small or too fast to apply to our daily experience."

"It's occurred to me, so it must have occurred to you, that what you might call the Newtonian thought processes that we all rest on so comfortably are . . . habits. You might call them addictions, passed on from one generation to the next. What do you think of that?"

"Yes, I've thought along those lines."

"And . . . ? What did you come up with?"

"I think it's sloppy thinking. A hole for letting in a lot of unscientific, unprovable ideas."

"Well, let me ask you this. And I'm just asking you like a kid asking his physics teacher in high school. If there's no such thing as absolute time when you travel real fast and there's no such thing as a real solid piece of matter . . . I mean when you get down to analyzing it up close, there's just little bits of stuff jumping about like light waves one second and then changing to solid particles the next . . . then why can't we do the same? It seems logical to me that we should. I mean if you get one peanut or a hundred peanuts, they're still peanuts. And if you get one electron or a whole bunch of them, they're still electrons. And that's what we are. We're a bunch of electrons. Why can't we ignore time? Why can't we jump about?"

"I can tell you that we don't for the reasons I've already given. If you're asking for the philosophical 'why' behind that, then I can't answer. I have no idea. But it's been proven by common consensus that we don't."

"Common consensus. Right. But what happens if someone comes along who does ignore time, who does demonstrate this particle/wave phenomenon? What do you say to that?"

"That's a hypothesis I can't answer."

"I beg to differ, Dr. Chen. It ain't no hypothesis. We've got someone here who's doing just that."

Boyman, voice croaking, objected. Conan upheld it. The jury was told to ignore Stassen's remark. As Jorge Ramirez, the refrigerator repair man, commented later, "If you're asked to forget a pink elephant, all you can think of is pink elephants."

Stassen tried to rephrase his statement another way.

"All I'm saying is, if we're made up of a lot of stuff that ain't really there. It may be. It may not be. It's in a supposition of states. It's only there when you measure it. First it's here, then it's there. It's floating about and it doesn't settle until we measure it. Then what does that say about us? Are we a collection of wild, free particles that only stay put when they get measured by some observer? And if we are, who's this observer who's keeping us in our place? Are we our own observers? Does the way we look at things have a profound effect on what we experience?"

Dr. Chen smiled compassionately. "No."

Stassen was not surprised. "And why not, Dr. Chen?"

"Because it has been proved not to be the case."

"How do you mean?"

"I mean, look around you, Mr. Stassen. We're all firmly planted on the floor here, we're held down by gravity. At the end of the day we all have to eat dinner and wash the dishes. It never changes whatever wonderful theory anyone comes up with."

"Yeah, well maybe we're all stuck to this floor by ignorance not gravity. Maybe these are the dark ages. Maybe we have abilities we don't use."

"Objection." It was Boyman whispering hoarsely.

Marlatt helped him out. "Your Honor, counsel is asking himself questions and answering them. If he'd like to make a statement he should be sworn in and go on the witness stand."

Judge Conan called a brief recess. There was twenty-five minutes of haggling in his chambers. Reporters drifted out to smoke. By now there was almost a party atmosphere in the halls.

———

Joe DeRosa took Pagels to the holding cell to wait while the attorneys were out. The bailiff stood a head shorter than the defendant but was decidedly thicker round the waist.

"Your Daniel's a good kid," DeRosa told him.

"Yes, he is." Pagels looked at him kindly, grateful for the remark. He remained standing as long as the bailiff was there.

DeRosa scratched his head. "Are you sure . . . er . . . you sure it won't, you know, do some damage. You know what I mean. I mean kids can get twisted around. They don't know what's happening and then, you know, they never get out of it. They're screwed up for life."

"Danny knows what's happening."

"How can you tell?"

"I know Danny."

"I don't know. He's just a kid. Sometimes you can ask too much of a kid."

"Danny will learn from this."

"He'll never be the same after this. He's being talked about all over the world. I saw this Japanese magazine yesterday. He's on the cover."

"The public forgets very quickly. Especially things like this. Their minds are like shallow bowls. It will all flow out."

"Yeah, but is it worth taking the risk? You've got half a dozen easier ways than this."

"There's only two ways. The right way and the wrong way."

DeRosa rubbed his hand across his mouth and shifted from one foot to the other. Lawrence Pagels, by contrast, made very few movements. The stillness of his body gave the impression of one who put all his bodily energy into thinking and wasted nothing.

"I'll say this for you," said DeRosa. "You've put on the biggest damn show I've ever seen. And that's good I guess, if that's what you wanted. But the jury . . . they don't get it. I mean, you're obviously a thinking man, but some of those people, they never put two thoughts together in their life. They've been coping with life. Watching television, going to the mall, they're not prepared for this. You got one or two smart ones there. You got the accountant, Jane Rodofsky, and you got Fred Turner, he didn't go to college, but if you ask me, he's the smartest one there. But the rest . . . it's not looking too good for you there, I gotta tell you."

"Maybe not." Pagels' chin slumped toward his chest. He rarely showed depression, but when he did, this was a sign of it.

"Look at it like this. You go to jail. That's not so great but you'll have this to look back on. You shook up the world. You made a name for yourself. Maybe you can make some money out of it, who knows. Send the kid to college."

Pagels raised his head. "It's strange how these things happen. There's a purpose to it. I know that."

"Do you want a Coke, root beer? I'll get you a Coke."

"No thanks."

"You never give an inch, do ya? I mean, you never let on. You always act like it's the truth."

Pagels didn't reply.

"So tell me one thing. Are you saying that your kid is the only one who can do it? Or are you saying that anyone can do it?"

"It's a gift. It's given. It has a common source."

DeRosa frowned. "Common?"

"Yes."

"Uh huh . . . anyway." The bailiff looked at his watch. "I'll be back."

Still frowning, DeRosa left.

————

During the break Mary-Lynn approached Ida.

"How're you doing?"

"I'm tired."

"Me too. The most I get is a couple of hours sleep. I'm too wired up."

"Same here." Ida smiled.

"I'm so used to working through the night, I got to bed at midnight last night and I was awake till four. Just lying there trying to remember what I hadn't done."

"I don't think I can take much more." Ida pushed her hair out of her eyes.

Mary-Lynn looked at her in an older sister sort of way.

"Sure you can . . . Did you hear some reporter wrote an article about you and me, saying we were the brains behind the scenes, something like that, and it was a battle between the two of us."

"Yes, Max told me about it. I'm getting a lot of flack about it." Ida laughed.

"I'm not." Mary-Lynn grinned. "I don't allow it."

Max moved in. "This is a record. Ida smiled twice in two minutes. She's never smiled once at me and Stassen. She hates us. She loves the prosecution. She's a very confused girl."

Mary-Lynn looked Max up and down. "No, she's not. She's changing the rules. Isn't that what this trial is about? Changing the rules?"

Max raised his eyebrows. "Oh very profound. Too profound for me. I'm not the brains in this operation. I don't go to USC."

Ida looked at Mary-Lynn. "See what I mean."

"Yes." Mary-Lynn studied Max again. "Nip it in the bud. Don't let him get out of hand."

She went off. Max watched her large rear retreating.

"Yuk."

"Max, I wish once in a while you would surprise me. Don't be so predictable."

"All I said was yuk. She's got a fat ass. It's not a pretty sight."

"You're not so cute."

"I didn't say I was cute. I don't have to be cute."

"Neither does she."

"O.K. I defend her right to have a fat ass. It's wonderful, colossal. It's like the Taj Mahal. It's like the Astrodome. It's like . . ."

"Shut up, Max."

———

Back in court Dr. Chen was permitted to respond to Stassen's suggestion that those present in the courtroom were stuck to the floor by ignorance not gravity.

"A nice idea," Dr. Chen allowed. "I've heard them all before. You throw them around in graduate school."

"And what conclusion have you reached?"

"Oh, everyone has his own pet theory but it always comes down to an opinion. No one knows. The questions you are asking are unanswerable."

"Then perhaps I can ask why they are unanswerable. Is it because the idea of living in a shifting reality is kind of unthinkable, kind of scary? You know, like, we say that table is solid and unmoveable because that's the way we like it to be. But really it's just there by agreement, not by actual fact. We could move it, make it disappear, whatever, if we changed our approach to it."

Dr. Chen laughed. "Yes, that idea is a bit of an old chestnut. There was a Bishop Berkeley, who lived in England in the eighteenth century who believed that everything in the universe was only in our minds. He's often mentioned in physics books. Boswell says in his biography of Samuel Johnson that Johnson struck his foot with mighty force against a stone and said, 'I refute it thus.' And the same goes for the table in front of us. If every single person in this court changed his ideas about that table we still couldn't change it into anything but what it is, a table."

"So . . . O.K. . . . we can't move the table. But what if it's our own ignorance that's keeping us from doing it?"

"That's an unanswerable question."

"Then . . . try this one . . . If all these strange rules apply to the quantum world and they don't apply to our world, then where is this Iron Curtain, this Maginot Line that divides us? Where is the line drawn between us guys here and those particles there?"

"There is no line as such, but there is certainly a difference between the subatomic world and our world."

"You betcha there's a difference. And why haven't we been told about it before? This quantum theory has been around for over sixty years. It tells us that the world is made up of stuff that changes if you look at it. That an act of observation can move stuff around. How come we haven't been told that? Your average man in the street knows the expression 'quantum leap' and that's about it. He doesn't know this stuff is going on. Now come clean, do scientists consider this information too frightening for us laymen? Or are they scared of what we'll do with it?"

Dr. Chen laughed loudly and the jury laughed at him, as did almost everyone in the courtroom. His laugh was very catching.

"No. No. No way. It's too hard for people to understand, that's all. The mathematics are so complex. And scientists use it but they don't understand it either." There was more laughter.

"Then maybe I'm a genius after all, because I got it. And the jury got it. They know what we're talking about. . . ."

Boyman wanted to object but he could not alienate the jury by casting aspersions on their intelligence. He kept quiet and Stassen went on.

"It ain't so hard. It seems to me like they don't want us to know about it because it's too hot to handle."

Dr. Chen laughed again. "I like that idea. Very good."

"O.K. Dr. Chen . . . as one who understands the magical quantum world could you tell me why . . . even though we're all frozen into a real limited way of getting around . . . could you tell me why you won't accept the fact that one person at least is not frozen, that one person can move around in a way that seems impossible to the rest of us?"

"Objection! He's doing it again, Your Honor. It's the same question. Leading the witness."

Boyman's face reddened as he rasped out the words with every bit of strength he had, but they still emerged as a whisper.

The objection was sustained and Stassen received another warning from Conan.

The defense attorney was invariably calmed by an outburst from the prosecution. He smiled serenely at Dr. Chen.

"Let's take another look at good old Albert Einstein, perhaps the greatest mind of this century. When he said, 'God does not play dice,' he said it because of the uncertainty principle, is that right?"

"Yes. Einstein believed in a God who had established an orderly universe. The uncertainty principle seemed to deny that."

"Albert came a cropper with that didn't he? The greatest mind of the century was outplayed by some younger men."

"Maybe, maybe not. Things are believed and then they're not believed. Isaac Newton was believed for over two hundred years before he went out of style."

"Albert's theory made it possible to make the atomic bomb, right?"

"Yes."

"But the uncertainty principle brought us the transistor and the computer?"

"That's a vague generalization, but yes."

"So maybe Albert Einstein, even with the most brilliant mind of the century, made a mistake or two?"

"Perhaps."

"Like he didn't accept the uncertainty principle because it interfered with a firmly held belief about how God operated."

"Yes."

"Firmly held beliefs can trip up even the most intelligent people, wouldn't you agree, Dr. Chen?"

"It's possible."

"And you know . . . Albert was a young man when he discovered the theory of relativity, which shattered a lot of firmly held beliefs. Right?"

"Yes he was."

"And Werner Heisenberg was a young man when he presented the uncertainty principle. Right?"

"Yes."

"It takes a young person without many preconceived notions to grasp a great new idea, would you say, Dr. Chen?"

"On the whole, yes."

"What about a very young person, a child? Would you say it's possible that a young child would have so few preconceived notions that the child could do things no one else could?"

"Very young children are limited by undeveloped motor capacity and limited mental ability."

"Maybe so, Dr. Chen. But what if a child knows so little he doesn't even know he's limited. What then?"

"He'd act just like every other child."

"Dr. Chen, is it true that Niels Bohr, the great Danish physicist, said 'Anyone who is not shocked by quantum theory has not understood it'?"

"Yes, he said that."

"And have you heard another frequently quoted remark by a physicist, 'In mathematics you don't understand things you just get used to them'?"

"Yes, I've heard that."

"Good, I'm glad. Thank you, Dr. Chen."

————

Over the next few days the prosecution produced three more physicists to pour cold water on the defense's propositions: Dr. Charles Corrian from M.I.T., Dr. Paul Godowitz from CERN (Conseil Européen pour la Recherche Nucléaire) situated close to Geneva in Switzerland, and Dr. Dorothy Young from Columbia University. As neither the prosecution nor the defense wished to stray any further into the complex depths of quantum theory, they were limited to covering the same ground already covered by Dr. Chen.

The jury members, both nervous and stimulated by the sudden media attention and the instant-star status they had achieved, were nevertheless fuzzy on the whole scientific issue. Their minds were not nearly as blank as they appeared to be to the attorneys, but they were struggling. One juror remarked later that on the several occasions when he had been tempted to tune out he had looked across at Lawrence Pagels, saw the man's fierce concentration, and stayed with it.

16

The last prosecution rebuttal witness was Daniel Pagels, who was being called to testify a second time.

On the morning that he was going to appear in court all three television networks had camera crews and vans outside the Van Nuys court. A jet-lagged BBC news team had arrived overnight from London via Houston, and various other crews from Europe, South America, and Australia were fighting for positions amid a cacophony of foreign languages. While they waited, they filled in time by interviewing and filming each other.

"Where are you from?"

"Amsterdam."

"Oh! Lawrence Pagels' father came from Amsterdam. Did you know that?"

"Oh sure. We're very excited about that."

"Television?"

"No. I'm working for a weekly magazine. You probably haven't heard of it."

"No. I don't know much about Amsterdam except . . . you know . . . drugs, hippies . . ."

Laughs. "Oh yes. It's not so bad though."

"No, right . . . you've got all those tulips, right?"

Passers by were grabbed. An elderly woman with an equally elderly poodle had a microphone thrust under her nose.

"Hi, I'm from the BBC. Do you think they're telling the truth about Daniel Pagels?"

The woman shook her head nervously. "I don't know. Who knows? There's more to life than meets the eye."

"What exactly do you mean by that?" The microphone came closer to her nose. "Do you think we're all capable of zooming about like Danny?"

"I'll tell you one thing," the woman said as she edged away. "If they have evening classes for it, I'll sign up."

A clerk from the local IRS office was waylaid.

"Hi. Do you think they're telling the truth about Daniel Pagels?"

"No. I think they're crazy."

A construction worker in a hard hat sitting on a wall yelled out. "Ask me. I'll tell you. This town doesn't deserve guys like they've got up there on the sixth floor. They should all be put in jail. They're in it for the money."

A girl eating a hot dog was stopped.

"Hi, I'm from NBC News. What do you think about Daniel Pagels?"

The girl giggled. "I think today he'll tell the truth."

"What do you think he'll say?"

She giggled again. "I think he'll say April Fool."

"But it's not April."

"Maybe they should tell him." More giggles.

An editorial in *The New York Times* that morning had commented that the interest that the Lawrence Pagels case had aroused in the public "showed a deep desire to believe that mankind possesses limitless abilities. Whether or not this arises from watching too many fantasy movies or from something more intrinsic in the soul is almost impossible to assess."

The newspaper *France Soir* had its own opinion on that. It said that the American public had fallen victim to the long-standing preoccupation of Hollywood producers with characters such as the Flying Nun and Batman.

The *Independent* of London wrote that "By the use of physics to back up their claims, Lawrence Pagels and his lawyer Edgar Stassen, mistaken or not, have touched a soft spot in the human psyche. Even if these two men are the world's most outrageous liars, they are providing a great show."

Discussion among the waiting journalists centered around who was responsible for coming up with the quantum defense, Edgar Stassen or Lawrence Pagels. Opinion was divided. Stassen had now given a few monosyllabic answers to questions hurled at him as he ran to his car. Max Haydn had been told to keep his mouth shut. Ida followed suit. Mark Boyman and Harvey Marlatt were not much more forthcoming. And Pagels categorically refused to talk to anyone in the media. This left room for a good deal of speculation.

"This isn't penny ante poker," a man from the *Chicago Sun Times* told a lady from the *Washington Post*. "Pagels is gambling with a life sentence."

"He must have high hopes he can pull it off."

"Pull it off!" he laughed. "Let's face it. The guy's a bastard. He's just using the kid."

"But the kid adores him."

"Kids are loyal. They're like dogs that get beaten."

"Are you saying he's abused the boy?"

"He's up on a murder charge. He could be a really scary guy."

"That's not the way I read it."

"It's the only way to read it. You make any other interpretation, you're in outer space."

Those reporters who leaned toward the defense's view of things were labeled the Mary Poppins faction.

———

Daniel Pagels had been brought in through a back door of the courthouse at six thirty A.M. He sat with Sandy and Don Leutwiler in a waiting room and ate an Egg McMuffin given to him by Mary-Lynn Robbins. Sandy was unable to eat or drink anything, the celebrity of the case had unnerved her so. Even Don refused offers of donuts and knocked back cup after cup of coffee and smoked an unending relay of cigarettes.

Daniel, his face pink with excitement, munched at his food and asked constant questions about his grandfather. Was he already in the building? When would they see him? How long would they have to wait in that room?

At eight thirty a bailiff came and escorted them up to the sixth floor where Daniel saw his overjoyed grandfather. According to the California Penal Code and the Bailiff Manual, communication between a prisoner and a witness in court is not permitted. But there was no law against smiles, winks, and thumbs-up signs.

At nine fifteen the attorneys and the judge emerged from a discussion in chambers and at nine twenty-five Daniel Pagels went on the witness stand. It was ten and a half weeks since he had last testified.

———

Mark Boyman approached Daniel cautiously and attempted a smile. Smiling was not his forte.

"It's good to see you again. How are you, Daniel?"

Daniel surveyed the immaculately dressed man from head to toe. "Fine."

Another attempt at an ingratiating smile from Boyman. "There are a lot more people here than last time you came. You don't mind all these people listening to what you say, do you?"

"No."

"That's good ... Now, Danny, we all know that you're seven years old now and we're going to be talking about something that happened almost twenty months ago when you were five. Will you have any problems with that?"

"No. I was almost six then."

"Good. Then maybe I'll begin by asking you all over again what happened that night you were found in the kitchen of John Nields' house in Bell Canyon. Why did you go there?"

"I went to see the puppies."

"Why was that, Danny?"

"I went to check them out."

"What for?"

"Grandpa said I could have one. And Mr. Nields said we wouldn't have to pay if we wanted one because they were just mutts."

"You'd seen Mr. Nields when you went over in the morning with your grandpa?"

"Yes."

"And Mr. Nields was friendly to you?"

"Sure."

"He said you could have one of his puppies and your grandpa said it was O.K. for you to have one at home?"

"Yes."

"Then why didn't you take one home?"

"They were still too young to leave their mother. So I had to wait."

"Did you know which one you wanted?"

"Oh sure."

"Then why did you have to go back to check them out?"

Daniel paused and looked guilty.

Boyman asked again. "Why was that, Danny? This is important. I know it's rather cute talking about puppies. But you know how really serious this is."

Daniel spoke very quietly. "I wanted to be with him."

"With the puppy you'd chosen?"

"Yes."

"Why didn't you ask your grandpa to take you over?"

"Grandpa said we mustn't go being a nuisance to Mr. Nields because he was a busy man. So I thought if I went after Mr. Nields had gone to bed I wouldn't be any trouble."

"You didn't discuss this idea with your grandpa?"

"No."

"Why not?"

"Because I didn't get the idea till after he'd gone to sleep."

"You didn't want to wake him up?"

"No."

"Where were you when you had this idea?"

"I was sitting on my bunk."

Boyman moved closer to Daniel and squeezed his knee. "You were sitting on your bunk dangling your legs, just like you're doing now, when you made up your mind to go and see the puppies?"

"Yes."

"So then what did you do?"

"How d'you mean?"

"I mean, you were sitting on your bunk, right?"

"Yes."

"Did you jump down?"

"No."

"Did you crawl out the window?"

"No."

"How did you get out of your grandpa's motor home?"

"I just went."

"You don't remember if you went out of a door or a window?"

"No."

"You're teasing me, Danny. Just when it gets interesting, you don't remember anything . . . Watch this. I'm gonna show you something."

Boyman walked over to the prosecution table and sat down. "See this. I'm sitting down. Now watch me."

Boyman rose and crossed over to Edgar Stassen and touched him on the shoulder. Stassen sat expressionless and unmoving.

"See what I did, Danny. I'll describe it to you. I was sitting down on a chair next to Mr. Marlatt and then I got up. Then I took a few steps across the courtroom to Mr. Stassen and I touched him on the shoulder. The whole thing didn't take much more than five to ten seconds ... I've described the journey in detail haven't I? The beginning, the middle, and the end of the journey. Right?"

"Yes."

"So, Danny. You were sitting on your bunk and then what?"

"I said to myself, I'll go."

"Just like that?"

"Yes."

"Now, Danny. I want you to think very hard about this. You tell us exactly what you did. You made up your mind to go and see the puppies. It was late at night. Your grandpa was asleep. There was nobody else there. You were sitting on your bed thinking about those puppies and then you made up your mind to go and see them. What exactly did you do to get there?"

Daniel looked thoughtful, strained almost, as he tried to give an answer.

"I don't remember. I didn't do anything. I was just sitting on my bunk thinking real hard about the puppies."

"Did you move around in any special way?"

"No."

"So let's get this straight. You made a decision to go there. Were you planning to walk?"

"No."

"Did you know that you were going there in a way that's impossible for the rest of the world?"

"No. I just wanted to get there as quick as I could."

"So you thought about the speed you would go?"

"I guess so."

"And after you thought about getting there fast, what was the next thing you did?"

"I turned the lights on."

"Where?"

"In the kitchen."

"In Mr. Nields' house?"

"Yes."

Boyman could not resist looking over at the jury with a smirk on his face.

"You got there that fast?"

"I guess so."

"Did you feel the wind whooshing past your ears?"

"No, sir."

"The air is very cold at night, especially up in the hills. Do you remember how cold it felt?"

"No."

"Does your grandpa have a heater in his pickup truck?"

"Yes."

"It would have been warm if you'd driven over there in your grandpa's truck, right?"

Daniel looked at him blankly.

"Do you like movies and comics, Danny?"

"Yes, sir."

"Have you seen *Superman*?"

"Yes sir. I saw it on TV."

"What do you think of Superman?"

"I think he's great."

"Do you think all boys would like to be Superman?"

Daniel shrugged.

Boyman moved on quickly, like a fast-moving mugger.

"So there you were. You landed in Mr. Nields' house. Were you surprised?"

"No."

"O.K. So you weren't surprised. What did you do next?"

"I told Jessie to stop barking."

"Jessie was the mother of the puppies?"

"Yes."

"Now, can you remember the last time you and I talked together when I asked you about how you got into the kitchen?"

Daniel shrugged.

"Maybe you don't remember. I'll remind you. We talked about how Mr. Nields' house has alarms fitted to all the doors and windows. When Officer Henderson asked you to open the door you couldn't undo the lock. Do you remember that, Danny?"

"Yes, sir."

"And when Officer Burg broke the door open, the alarm went off. Do you remember that?"

"Yes."

"How did you get into the kitchen without setting the alarm off?"

Daniel shrugged again.

"Can you give me a proper answer, Danny?"

"I don't know, sir."

"You have no idea?"

"No sir."

Boyman folded his arms, momentarily stumped. "You don't know . . ."

Daniel looked over at his grandfather. Lawrence gave him an approving nod and Daniel responded with a weak, cautious smile, that left his face as quickly as it arrived.

The prosecuting attorney unfolded his arms and adjusted his tie.

"Right. So there you were, in the kitchen. It was eleven thirty at night. But when the police officers found you there it was two fifteen in the morning. How come you stayed so long?"

"I fell asleep."

"Were you asleep when the police came?"

"Yes. But they made a lot of noise and I woke up."

Boyman was taking cautious steps through the mine-field before him. He was aware that the women in the jury were watching him carefully. This child, lying or not, had aroused a lot of maternal sympathy.

"Do you always tell the truth Danny?"

"Yes, I do."

"Do you know what a lie is?"

"Yes, sir."

"For instance, Danny. If I said my hair was pink, that would be a lie, wouldn't it?"

"Yes."

"Why would it be a lie?"

"Because it's not pink."

"It's dark brown isn't it?"

Daniel looked at Boyman's hair carefully. "Not completely."

"It looks dark brown to most people."

Daniel looked skeptical.

"And," Boyman went on quickly, "if I said that lady over there has red hair, I'd be telling the truth wouldn't I?"

He pointed to Donna Fabry, the dog breeder in the front row of the jury, who had flamboyant, obviously dyed hair.

"Yes."

"Do you like to write stories and poems, Danny?"

"Yes."

"It takes a good imagination to write good stories, doesn't it?"

"I guess so."

"Do you think that a lot of grown-ups have talked this over with you so many times, that you've used your good imagination and thought that maybe this really happened, when really it's just a story?"

Daniel shook his head vigorously. "No."

"Do you always do what grown-ups tell you to do?"

"I try to."

"If a grown-up tells you to do something wrong, do you do it?"

"No."

"Do you love your grandpa?"

"Oh sure."

"Would you do anything to help him?"

Daniel gave the attorney another of his blank looks.

Boyman amplified the question.

"Would you do something that you knew was wrong to help your grandpa?"

"No."

The sketch artists were scribbling away producing varying degrees of likeness of Daniel being cross examined by the assistant DA. To a man they produced a small fair-haired boy looking up at a bullfrog in a navy blue suit.

The prosecuting attorney pinched his nose reflectively and a dangerous look came to his eye that made Edgar Stassen squirm.

"O.K., Danny. I'm having a problem understanding exactly how you got to Mr. Nields' house that night. You can't explain it. But maybe you can show us."

Alarm swept along the faces at the defense table. Boyman saw it and went on with increasingly undisguised triumph.

Again Daniel looked over at his grandfather for guidance. Lawrence was unable to do anything but frown at Boyman, in the manner of any parent protecting his child from danger.

Undaunted, Boyman went on.

"It's hard for kids to explain things. But they can always show how they did something. I want you to show us how you did it."

A collective gasp went up from the spectators followed by a flurry of whispering.

Stassen shot out of his chair.

"Objection. Counsel seems to have forgotten that he's dealing with a child. He hasn't ascertained if the child knows how he did it. He can't repeat something he doesn't understand."

Conan's face was a mask. The more fantastical the trial became, the more his face muscles stiffened. He called for a break and instructed the bailiff to quiet down the journalists waiting in the hall outside.

In chambers, Boyman argued for a threefold test of Daniel's abilities.

First a short "hop" to a location immediately outside the courthouse, a journey that would normally take two to five minutes from the sixth floor, depending on the time spent waiting for the elevator. According to claims made for the child he should be able to complete such a journey in a tiny fraction of a second.

If he should accomplish this successfully there should be a test over a longer distance—say to a mini-mall five miles from the courthouse.

"It's slightly over five miles from here," Boyman explained. "But it's exactly five from the corner of Van Nuys and Victory Boulevard. My assistant measured it on her odometer."

Lastly there would be a journey of ten miles, the distance Daniel was claimed to have traveled on the night of John Nields' murder.

"If he went directly south, we figure he would land at a Mobil station just here."

Boyman pointed at a map he'd spread out in front of the judge.

"In each case we plan to take the child to the location first, just like the day he went to Nields' house."

There was an hour-long debate that left Stassen shaking with frustration. But Conan finally agreed to permit this "demonstration."

"It's scientific," Boyman whispered to Stassen on the way back to the courtroom. "You can't buck science."

The jury was reassembled and Daniel brought back. Boyman, with the expression of one who was about to deal a deadly blow to the defense, set about describing the "test." Daniel listened poker-faced. He looked like a boy being told to wash the dishes.

"You remember," said Boyman "that I showed you how I moved

across the courtroom. I went from this table here to that table over there. Well. I want you to do that too, Danny. I know you need a reason, a goal, something to make it worth your while ... so I'll give you something. Do you like chocolate, Danny?"

"Yes."

"Good. I have a Hershey bar here. A big one. I'm going to give it to the bailiff and he's going to go downstairs in the elevator and go to a hot dog stand about twenty yards down the street. If you can get from this courtroom to that hot dog stand the same way Mr. Stassen says you got to Mr. Nields' house, then you get the chocolate bar!"

Another gasp went up from the spectators. The journalists were making rapid notes.

Stassen made objections about the safety of taking the child through the "mob" outside.

Conan wavered on that. For a while it looked as though Boyman might lose the right to his scientific test, but finally the judge conceded that with sufficient police protection there would be no danger or discomfort to the child.

A lanky fair-haired bailiff called Bill Bateson escorted Daniel, along with Sandy and Don Leutwiler, out of the courtroom and attempted to take him toward the elevator.

It was not an easy walk. A cluster of reporters and cameramen acted like crazed dogs in pursuit of a bitch in heat and made movement close to impossible. They pushed their way into the elevator and were pushed out again by the police.

When the doors opened on the ground floor, another crowd was waiting. They swept aside the police and engulfed Daniel and his protectors. More police help was called for and dozens of reinforcements appeared within seconds.

Sandy and Don Leutwiler, tense and grim-faced, shrouded Daniel with their bodies, while four police officers did their best to create a human shield.

Daniel looked up at Sandy. "Is this why they're called press?"

Sandy looked down at his small, flushed face uncomprehendingly. She was horrified by the sheer hungriness of the thronging reporters.

"Because they press so hard," Daniel prompted.

She said nothing. She was thankful for Don's height and his broad back. He was taller than any of the policemen around them.

She silently cursed all those self-serving adults, Mark Boyman, Edgar Stassen, Lawrence Pagels, and others, who would put a child through an ordeal such as this.

"I'll be left to pick up the pieces," she thought.

It was debatable whether the experience was harmful for Daniel. The battle to the hot dog stand seemed to be a matter of interest to him rather than an ordeal. Being not far above waist level he had a restricted view of the proceedings. When asked later what it was like he said, "There were a lot of shoes."

Having checked out the hot dog stand, a cart on wheels with a striped umbrella over the top and a bemused owner, the crowd returned to the sixth floor of the courthouse.

The bailiff, Bill Bateson, walkie-talkie in hand, prepared himself for a long wait on the street. It was notable that few members of the media stayed by the hot dog stand to await the possible return of Daniel Pagels. Nearly all of them went back upstairs. Those who waited with Bill Bateson were mostly California natives. There were two Los Angeles television crews and several reporters from around the state.

"It's true what they say," commented a journalist from Montreal. "They shook all the newsrooms in the United States and all the loonies fell down onto the West Coast."

The area around the Van Nuys courthouse had now been cordoned off. No traffic was permitted to enter any of the side streets which lead in from Victory Boulevard. Traffic was jammed all the way along Victory Boulevard to Van Nuys Boulevard and beyond as curious drivers slowed to see what had caused the large police presence and crowds.

When Daniel Pagels returned to the witness stand a giggly excitement that had filled the courtroom took some minutes to subside and only did so after some sharp words from Conan.

Sandy and Don Leutwiler were angry and silent. Their worst fears had been realized. Don looked as though he were about to cause major injury to the judge and the attorneys. He glared and punched his fist into his hand in a dull, rhythmic motion.

Rhonda Pagels, hidden in the back row, was beyond emotion and sat drained and motionless, her eyes never straying from Daniel's face.

Max whispered to Ida, "It had to come to this. What did you expect?"

And Ida ignored him. Some of her cool exterior had been chipped away by this trial. She looked tired and even a little frightened.

Stassen, exhausted from his frantic efforts to have the test called off, slumped back, defeated, in his chair.

Lawrence Pagels had sat throughout the entire break with his head lowered and his hands covering his face and only when Daniel returned did he raise his eyes and sit up.

Boyman, successfully quelling any desire to smirk, stood up and put his hands in his pocket. His voice was about as gentle and friendly as it would ever get.

"Danny, during the break you went down with Bill Bateson to the hot dog stand. You know where it is, how far it is, and how most people would get there. Is that right?"

"Yes."

Daniel was beginning to look mournful. He pulled at a loose thread on his sleeve, tugging at it and making a hole.

"Now, technically speaking, to get down to the hot dog stand you have to go through two doors, down the hall to the elevator, down six floors to the ground floor, out the main door, right around the courthouse and then out onto the street, twenty-five . . . thirty yards down, there's the hot dog stand. That's how most people do it. If you chose to do it a quicker way then, you have to get through concrete, plaster, wood, glass, and steel . . ."

Boyman paused to let the jury absorb that idea and then went on.

"I'm just an ordinary guy. I have to take the elevator. But I'm real curious about how you got to Mr. Nields' house so fast and without any help. I know it's hard for you to explain. So I'd like you to show us how you did it. First you're here, then you're there! Amazing! I can't begin to imagine how you do that."

The prosecuting attorney checked out the women in the jury to see if he was getting an adverse reaction. They were looking tense. It was neither a good nor a bad sign. He turned back to the witness.

"So when you're ready, Danny. I want you to go down to the hot dog stand. I want you to go the same way you went to Mr. Nields' house. Real fast. If you do it at the same speed you did before, you should be down there in about a tenth of a second. Hold on . . ."

He ostentatiously picked up a walkie-talkie.

"Are you ready, Bill?"

There was a loud crackling on the walkie-talkie but Bill Bateson's voice was audible. "Here, Mr. Boyman."

Outside in the hall cameramen joked about catching "a sudden burst of ectoplasm." But inside the courtroom there was now no need to ask for quiet. It was deadly still.

A momentary flash of misgiving crossed Boyman's face as he looked at Daniel fidgeting in his chair, kicking his feet, glancing back and forth between his grandfather and the expectant faces before him.

"Are you ready, Danny?"

Daniel shrugged.

"Are you ready?" Boyman repeated.

"I guess so." He spoke in a whisper.

"I know you're just a little kid, Danny, but you did it once, right?"

"Yes."

"Then you can do it now. I'm going to call down to Bill Bateson and say you're on your way. O.K.?"

There was no reply.

"O.K."

Daniel's quiet "O.K." was inaudible to the court.

Boyman spoke in to the walkie-talkie. "O.K., Bill. I'm giving him the signal now! Right, Daniel. Go!"

Boyman waved his arm as if starting a motor race.

There was a one minute pause. Silence. No movement. Very little breathing. Two minutes. Three minutes.

Three minutes was an eternity in the crowded courtroom. Every face was turned toward Daniel who looked at his feet and observed their kicking motion back and forth, back and forth.

Boyman stood with the walkie-talkie in hand, his eyes showing something like disappointment that the inevitable had happened.

Finally he spoke.

"Are you going to do it, Danny?"

The child looked up.

"No."

"Why not?"

"I don't know."

"You don't know?"

"No."

Boyman did not smile.

"O.K., Danny. I'll let you go now. Thanks a lot."

As Boyman sat down and Stassen rose for the cross, a slight chatter started in the courtroom. Spectators shifted in their seats and freed themselves of the tension of the last few minutes.

Stassen leaned over Daniel.

"You O.K., Danny?"

"Yeah."

"When you went to Mr. Nields' house by yourself were there a lot of people staring at you?"

"No."

"Were there TV cameras and reporters?"

"No."

"Were there bailiffs and attorneys with walkie-talkies?"

"No."

"Was there a jury of twelve ladies and gentlemen watching every little thing you did?"

"No."

"Have you told any lies this morning?"

"No. I haven't."

"O.K., Danny."

Stassen sat down. Boyman said he had no more questions.

Judge Conan leaned over to Daniel and said quietly, "Thank you, Daniel. I expect Mr. Boyman will arrange for you to get the Hershey bar. You can go."

Daniel looked over at his grandfather and shrugged. Lawrence Pagels gave him a last thumbs-up sign. Neither of them smiled.

To avoid the waiting reporters, DeRosa took Daniel out through a side door, where he was joined by Don and Sandy Leutwiler.

"Are you all right, Danny?" Sandy asked. She had been crying. Her dark curly hair was untidy, one of the results of her battle with the crowd when they went down to the hot dog stand.

Daniel looked solemn and old beyond his years. "I guess so."

"I want you to know," Sandy said, "that what these people did here today, and what they put you through wasn't right. They're in the wrong. You haven't done anything wrong. So don't be upset, Danny. You did really well and we're proud of you."

"Yes," said Don. "You were great. Fantastic. You spoke up like a real trouper."

Daniel looked back at the door that led to the courtroom. "Can we stay for the rest of the day?"

Sandy put her arm around him; her chunky metal earrings pressed against his cheek. "No, honey. We have to get back. We don't want to get into one of those crushes again."

"But I think Grandpa would like me to stay." Daniel put on his most pleasant expression in an effort to persuade them.

"No, sweetheart. We've gotta go."

As the Leutwilers and Daniel escaped from the courthouse by a circuitous route, a rumor arose that their car was parked in a garage on Sylmar Avenue; reporters rushed to investigate. The rumor proved to be false but it allowed the Leutwilers and Danny to make an untroubled getaway.

DeRosa told Rhonda afterward that he had been responsible for the rumor.

"I did it to help the kid. See, I do have a heart. I like him. It's not his fault his grandfather's screwed up."

Conclusions

17

The pool shed was Daniel's favorite place because it had first been, and still was, Jason's favorite place.

It was a haven for black widow spiders and therefore smelled of death and danger. The air hung with the odor of stale, discarded pool chemicals, dry rot, and water that had filtered through the citrus orchard. Every morning after the sprinklers went on, water drained into the pool shed and collected in large puddles on the concrete floor. By noon the hot sun had dried out the wooden slats of the pool shed and the puddles inside would slowly steam away.

From time to time one or other of the Leutwiler children had cleaned it out and turned it into a school, a den, or a hut in the forest.

Jason and Daniel went out there early, just after the sprinklers had gone off.

"They caught you out," said Jason. "You couldn't do it."

"No," agreed Daniel glumly.

"How come you told them you could do it, you nerd. Didn't you know you'd get caught?"

"I guess not."

Daniel poked his foot at the blue plastic wall of a dusty, broken Barbie pool, left there years before by Sheila.

"You can't even jump off the shed without hitting your head."

"I didn't hit my head. I rolled over."

"You hit your head. You dropped like a brick. They should see you jumping off the pool shed, then they'd know you can't fly."

"I rolled. I'll show you."

"No, you dummy. She's looking through the kitchen window."

Sandy Leutwiler was leaning over the sink and staring out the window. She tended to watch the boys more than she used to. She was in constant fear that someone would leap over the back wall and a mob with notebooks and cameras would follow.

She felt guilty about being at the house at all. But she had brought Daniel back there from the Van Nuys court on the theory that no one would hunt for Daniel at home. It had been widely broadcast that they had gone into hiding and the press was busy trying to find out where the hiding place was. She knew they couldn't stay in the house more than twenty-four hours.

Sheila and Gregory had initially gone with them up to Big Bear but they had quickly grown bored. They had insisted on returning to the house in Granada Hills and going back to school. They had their obligations. Sheila had a leading role in a production of *Grease* and Gregory had football. They also enjoyed the notoriety the Leutwiler name now had and they wanted to be around while it was still hot.

Jason, on the other hand, loved any old excuse to stay away from school and bore Daniel no resentment on that count. He also liked the cloak-and-dagger game of running and hiding.

"If a reporter came to the front door now," Jason told Daniel, "I'd jump over into the Taubers' backyard and then I'd jump over six backyards and come out into Scot Hoag's house."

"What about me?" asked Daniel.

"You can follow me. Don't hit your head."

They both listened carefully for the sound of reporters. It was morning. The area was deserted and the only sound came from a distant leaf blower making its ugly noise a street or so away. But on the Leutwiler's cul de sac there was no sound. The houses around them were unoccupied during the day. The entire street emptied every morning as children went to school, babies were taken to day care, and parents joined the long lines on the freeway.

Sandy had been the lone stay-at-home, watching for strange pickup trucks cruising the street, accepting packages from UPS for absent neighbors, chasing stray garbage cans. They always had the strongest winds on the day the garbage was put out.

But now she had deserted her post and was living the life of a fugitive, returning occasionally to the house after dusk and leaving late at night the following day.

"Come on," said Jason. "I can hear someone. Let's go."

Daniel was thoughtful. "What about the Mollers' German shepherd?"

Jason stopped. "Oh shit!"

Daniel was sorry he mentioned it. "He might be O.K."

"Are you kidding! He bit Greg on the leg when he was just walking past the house."

"What are you boys doing?" called Sandy.

Jason looked wary.

"We're planning a way of escape," offered Daniel.

"Nerd," whispered Jason. "Don't say anything."

"Don't leave the backyard. You know what I've told you. If someone comes I'll tell you what to do."

"Dork," whispered Jason again.

Daniel shrugged. An insult from Jason meant only one thing to him. The lines of communication were open. That's all he cared about.

The boys spent another hour devising complex escapes using tunnels and swinging ropes to carry them under and over the Mollers' dog. They went inside for a lunch of Kraft macaroni and cheese, the only kind of macaroni Jason would eat, and played Nintendo and table tennis. They finished the afternoon with a wrestling match. The evening was spent with Sheila and Gregory. Don took some time off from the restaurant to be with them. Just after ten o'clock Sandy took Jason and Daniel back up to the snows of Big Bear.

"Do you think," the television interviewer asked, "that Daniel Pagels is a phony?"

"Sure," replied the lady shopping in the mall. "They asked him to do it and he couldn't. That's proof enough for me."

"What do you think?" the interviewer asked a couple of teenagers in expensive torn jeans.

"He couldn't do it because everyone was looking at him," said one.

"It made him nervous," said the other.

"Do you really believe that or are you just saying it?"

"Everyone's so down on Danny. I think he needs a little support."

"Yeah. We love Danny!"

A smartly dressed Argentinian woman said, "I think it's a publicity stunt. They will use the little boy to advertise things. That's what they do in this country."

A man eating a donut said, "There's no way he's gonna get away with it. I think it's terrible. Somebody's been murdered and they're acting like it's a carnival or something. They should put the guy in jail and forget about it."

On a college campus, physics students were questioned by reporters as they came out of a lecture hall.

"Do you think the Daniel Pagels story is over now?"

"Oh absolutely. They carried out a conclusive test. You have to accept the results."

Another student disagreed. "No. I don't think so. Look at the conditions for the test. They were so different. They're saying that Danny got there by some kind of mental effort. If that's the case you have to look at the mental conditions in each case. And they were wildly different. In physics if there's such a drastic swing in the conditions for a test, then the findings are unacceptable."

"Do you think they can test him then?"

"No. Because the testing process changes the conditions."

A third student said, "I think it's a nasty plot by professors all over the United States to give people a bellyful of physics."

———

Stassen had one member of the jury on his side. Donna Fabry, the dog breeder from Granada Hills. She had even gone so far as to nod in agreement a couple of times when he lodged an objection. Her battered, sun-creased face under the reddened hair with its gray roots watched him intently. He had no trouble getting her attention. She had been like that from the beginning and had not changed when the trial took its quantum turn. It did not seem to surprise or disturb her. She still looked like his number-one fan. Even Daniel's so-called failure to prove his abilities had not affected her.

As for the rest of the jury, it was hard for him to judge. They were as enigmatic a bunch as he'd ever met. Jorge Ramirez, the small guy with the skinny mustache, had looked like he was in a trance since the first day of the trial. There was no way you could read him.

Stassen could occasionally get a smile out of Fred Turner but from what he could gather, Fred was not too happy to be there and wanted to get back to his job with Pacific Bell. Doria Rudell, the pretty one, who looked a little like a plump Diana Ross, was also a smiler. She smiled a lot. But he'd been smiled at before, only to discover that the smiler voted his client guilty. Brad Ryker, the retired Marine, had a habit of frowning when he was paying attention. That was Stassen's interpretation of it. The guy frowned when he was really listening. Whatever it was, he got more of the frowns than Boyman or Marlatt did.

After the first electric shock of becoming media stars, the jury had sunk into their original state of mild disinterest. It was surprising to Stassen how little the general demeanor of the jury had changed since the physicists had been introduced as witnesses. Something that had caused him sleepless nights, a variety of headaches, a near-constant reliance on Rolaids, seemed, if you were to judge from the faces in the jury box, merely another phase of the testimony.

Was it above their heads? Did they have any idea what was going on? Did they get any of it? He had bent over backward to make it as simple as possible. Maybe you wouldn't find too many college degrees in that jury but life was technical and complex for everyone these days. You had to be a genius to assemble a kid's toy at Christmas. And Fred Turner, in his daily work, had to disentangle an embroglio of wires and work out technical stuff that was way beyond Stassen's capabilities. If they gave Ph.D.'s in telephone maintenance that guy would probably be the first to get it. He'd been with the company for years, long enough to write a dissertation that would be right over most people's heads.

Yet during the physicists' testimony the expression on Turner's large brown face was no different from what it was when the Nields' maid testified about grocery shopping or when Boyman questioned a forensic expert for three hours about the varying width and patterns of tire treads. Basically Turner looked bored. He looked like they were reading him the Van Nuys telephone directory. The only thing that cheered him up was the sight of Daniel swinging his legs while Boyman stood there with a walkie-talkie and the entire court held its collective breath. Fred Turner was close to laughing then.

Stassen was in the habit of gearing his efforts according to the degree of support he felt coming from the jury. He could usually get some idea of a mood or detect a dividing line. He would pick out the most forceful personality and if that person looked favorable, Stassen would try to persuade the bailiff to give him or her the voting papers. It was not unusual for the person with the voting papers to be elected chairman and thus become a powerful swayer of votes.

But only Donna Fabry looked favorable, and she was a little eccentric and smelled of dogs, so he'd heard. She did not look like a vote swayer.

During the voir dire, when Stassen had still been clinging to the hope that he wouldn't have to bring in the physicists, he had still asked each potential juror if he or she believed that mankind would do things in the near future that were presently considered impossible. He had made sure that those twelve men and women finally selected had all attested to a strong faith in the present capacities and further development of mankind. That was the least he could do to pave the way for himself.

The only positive thing he could find in all this was that the introduction of the quantum evidence had not turned any of them off. Whether they were taking it in was another matter. He'd make his summing up real simple just to make sure.

———

Ida's car had broken down. Just before midnight Max drove her home after the usual long evening with Stassen in the Winnebago.

"Wanna see a movie?" he asked.

"Are you kidding?" Ida was taking her shoes off and rubbing her feet.

"We could go and see a horror movie and you could scream a lot."

"I can't scream."

"You can't scream about anything? That's useful to know."

"Max?"

"Yes."

"What are your parents like?"

"They argue a lot. It's what they do best. They're unbelievably good at it."

"My parents never argue."

"I guessed that. I bet they have harp music playing all the time."

"They're beginning to argue."

"I know what about."

"My father's on my side. But my mother is just dying over it. They shout at each other and they shout at me."

"This is the one issue my parents have never argued over. They both think I'm a total asshole. I don't go home anymore. I can't take it."

"I wonder why it gets people so mad?"

"I say to them, 'I'm famous. The whole world is coming to this trial. Doesn't that mean anything to you?' And they say, 'that's why we're worried.' . . . There's a pizza place. Wanna stop?"

"No, I want to go home and hide."

"A piece of pizza would improve your morale."

Pizza was out. Max drove her back to San Marino. He had to approach Ida's house with great caution, dropping her off fifty yards from the house in the middle of a long driveway. Ida closed the car door quietly to avoid alerting her parents.

As she crept toward the house, Max rolled down his window and called out in a loud whisper.

"Nice house."

"Is it?"

"Ida?"

"Yes?"

"Do you wish you'd never heard of Daniel Pagels?"

She paused before she said, "No." Then she added, "I know he needs us."

Max rolled up his window and drove away.

———

Mark Boyman, neatly dressed as usual in immaculate navy blue pinstripe, rose for his final argument. He had gained a little weight during the trial; as he puffed air into his lungs he gave the appearance of a pouting pigeon posing before a very weak-willed female.

"The defense has made much of the testimony of Daniel Pagels. In fact, the defense has gone to town on it in a spectacular way." He smiled at the jury. "I only ask you ladies and gentlemen that you do not allow yourselves to be fooled by a parade of mere speculations . . . speculations that are still a matter of debate and much suspicion in scientific circles.

"I've always found that you can't go wrong with old-fashioned facts and the evidence presented. Common sense must rule here. And what is common sense? It's what we know to be true because it's always been true. That's the foundation of the law.

"They say you can prove anything with statistics. Well, it looks like Mr. Stassen has gathered a mishmash of scientific phenomena together, and now he's trying to prove anything with science. And when I say anything, I mean anything.

"But we're not looking to prove anything, we're looking to prove the truth. We are concerned with bringing the murderer of John Nields to justice. There is only one person who went to John Nields' house on the night of April twelfth, 1988, was invited inside, went into the study, and there battered and knifed John Nields in a brutal, murderous attack. This person then removed the body from the house, drove up the 118 freeway and dropped the body on the Winnetka off ramp, a deserted and unused off ramp. And this person is the defendant, Lawrence Pagels.

"We have heard that there was an argument between John Nields and Lawrence Pagels on the morning of April twelfth. We have heard that John Nields was a threat to Lawrence Pagels, that he wanted Mr. Pagels to move his motor home from the land that he had lived on for thirty years, land that some say is ancestral Indian land. Land that is of great significance to Mr. Pagels because he is part Indian.

"The Fernandino Indians lived on that land. There is no longer a tribe of Fernandinos living on that land but Lawrence Pagels could trace his ancestry back to the Fernandinos and he closely identified with them. It would seem that the demand to move his trailer was a threat to his identity, a threat, we have heard by his own admission, which was disturbing to him.

"The police and the district attorney did not get together and prosecute the first person they found who lived near the Simi Valley Freeway. The evidence accumulated against Lawrence Pagels is significant. And it is significant even before you come to the two most compelling pieces of evidence.

"One: John Nields' blood was found on Lawrence Pagels' pickup truck. Blood is not something you sprinkle around as you go through your day. The victim did not leave a spot of blood behind when he was saying good-bye in his driveway. He left his blood behind when he was attacked and killed and dropped into that truck.

"Two: Lawrence Pagels' five-year-old grandson was found alone in the Nields' house at two fifteen A.M. on the morning of April thirteenth a few hours after John Nields had been murdered in that house. According to common sense and a thousand years of experience, five-year-old children are usually taken by adults to locations that are several miles away from their own home. And the only adult who had any responsibility for this child was Lawrence Pagels.

"Now, if you put your mind to it, you could think up a slew of imaginative reasons for that young boy's presence in that house. He was dropped there by aliens from outer space. He flew there on a supersonic time machine. Or, maybe, after he went to the house on the morning of April twelfth his grandfather went home and he stayed there. And the boy witnesses saw leaving the Nields' house in the morning with his grandfather was a clockwork dummy, or a hologram ... the possibilities are endless once you move onto the rarified planes of imagination. You could think up almost anything, which is what the defense have done. They've thrown an Unidentified Flying Object at the prosecution.

"They are asking us to believe that a small child, who up to that point had spent his entire five years in a trailer in the San Fernando Valley, suddenly got up one night and arrived in a place ten miles away at the same time that he left his home.

"Well, what do you say to that? You say pull the other one, it's got bells on. You sing 'Somewhere over the rainbow' and 'We're off to see the wizard.'

"This is not a children's fantasy. This is a court of law. The defense counsel has seen too many cartoons.

"But let me say here, what an imagination! He should drive right over to Warner Brothers or MGM and get himself on the payroll.

"An imagination is a good thing. It's entertaining. It's diverting. It's got this case a lot of attention. Or perhaps I should say *sometimes* imagination is a good thing. It can take your mind off all the pain and suffering in the world. I have nothing against imagination. But it has nothing to do with truth. It's the opposite of truth. It has nothing to do with bringing a murderer to justice.

"We did not come here to be entertained. We came here to serve the cause of truth and justice in the State of California and by God we will do that. No scientific pyrotechnics or mental gymnastics will deter us from that.

"The defense attorney has dragged up one or two little-known scientific facts and stirred them up. This guy's argument in a nutshell is . . . if subatomic particles can jump around, why can't we? The answer to that is we're not subatomic particles. We don't move ten miles in one jump. We walk. We take a bus. We ride a bike. We go in a car. And it takes time."

Mark Boyman strolled back to the prosecution table and took a sip of water. The jury watched with interest as though this action were part of the argument and required observation. Lawrence Pagels alone did not see it. Staring at the wall, he was far away, listening to another voice.

Boyman went on. "The defense attorney, Mr. Stassen, was on a sabbatical from legal work when he read about this trial and decided to take it on. Perhaps Mr. Stassen found out that vacationing wasn't all it was cracked up to be or perhaps . . . who knows? Maybe even Mr. Stassen doesn't know why he took this case on.

"But I'll tell you this, some people get a contact high from being around criminals. A contact high is an interesting thing. You see it in all areas of the law and law enforcement, police officers, attorneys, prison officers. It behooves everyone in the law business to examine their motives and their emotions. We don't need anyone in it who is merely excited by crime, and who uses it like a drug. Because then you get attorneys who prolong trials unnecessarily, who bring up any old fiddle-faddle to keep the party going. . . ."

Edgar Stassen was leaning back lazily in his chair. He raised his hand slightly like a pupil trying to get his teacher's attention.

"Objection, Your Honor, I ask for him to be admonished. What is this contact high? If I needed a contact high from criminals I could just go and stand near the back door of the county jail and breath in the fumes."

The jury tittered.

Judge Conan told the jury to disregard Boyman's last remarks and ordered them stricken.

Boyman continued. "All I'm trying to do is find a reason for such a screwball defense. I don't know. We all sympathize with Mr. Stassen for the bereavement he suffered last year. He lost his wife. It may be that he was looking for something to take his mind off it. It may be that he got carried away. And I guess Lawrence Pagels didn't realize he was being used as therapy . . ."

Stassen's face reddened with anger. His instantaneous leap out of his chair and his roar of objection caused some jury members to jump nervously.

"Objection! This is an unprecedented attack. It's base and improper. I'm not under analysis and I'm not on trial. That guy needs an enema for God's sake."

Conan's voice rose to the same pitch as Stassen's. "Watch your language, Mr. Stassen! This court is not a place for vulgarity. Once again I'm telling the jury to disregard Mr. Boyman's comment and once again it's ordered stricken." He cast a beady eye toward the prosecutor. "I would like you to come up with something we can keep on record."

Edgar Stassen was wandering around like an angry bull, back and forth across the courtroom, toward the judge, toward the jury, back to his table, and then off again. As a precaution Boyman had backed into a corner near the bailiff.

Conan's voice rose to a screech, "Sit down, Mr. Stassen!"

The defense attorney went back to his seat and very slowly sat down.

Boyman adjusted his suit jacket and went on to deal with what he called the defense's "red herring"—the suggestion that Mrs. Nields had a reason to kill her husband.

"It's more wild and desperate speculation. Mrs. Nields was in Palm Desert on April twelfth. And there's not one ounce of evidence to suggest that she arranged for anyone to carry out the murder. There was a strong emotional bond between her and her husband. It was not to her advantage to lose Mr. Nields, a devoted companion and breadwinner, at a time in a woman's life when it is hard to readjust and find a new companion. She had no one waiting in the wings. It is ridiculous to suggest that she would even dream of harming her husband.

"Whereas Lawrence Pagels would have benefitted considerably from the removal of John Nields from the face of the earth. The threat to his home and heritage would have been instantly lifted. Lawrence Pagels is an unusual man but he has one thing in common with a lot of us: one of the most important things in his life is his home. If he had not made the fatal mistake of leaving his grandson in the victim's house, it may be that he would be at home right now instead of in this court, it may be that it would have taken the law a lot longer to catch up with him.

"We come now to the logical reason for the presence of young Daniel Pagels in the Nields' house on that fatal night and we come to the logical explanation of his means of transport. He was witnessed at eleven thirty in the hills of Chatsworth and he was also witnessed at eleven thirty in the hills over Bell Canyon, ten miles away. He was seen in two places ten miles apart at exactly the same time.

"Now if you can find it in your heart to say that he jumped there in an instant like some cosmic frog then I say you have my blessings. You see a strange and charmed world that I and the rest of mankind do not see. I live in the world as it is and that's where the law is. The law cannot reach out into the realm of fantasy and illusion.

"Daniel Pagels, in a simple court test of his so-called abilities, was unable to move the smallest distance in the way the defense has alleged he can move. The child could not do it. That's enough for me. I'm sure it will be enough for you.

"If you want to stay within the parameters of the law then you will have to admit that some of the witnesses made a mistake. It happens. It's no big deal. People make mistakes. Some people are so convinced about things that they'd swear to it in court and yet they can still be mistaken. They swear they saw this or that but they didn't. It happens all the time.

"You will also have to admit that Daniel Pagels was taken to John Nields' house by someone intent on murder. This someone arrived late in the evening of April twelfth and was let into the house by Nields because he was known to him. This someone went into the study with John Nields where he stabbed and battered him to death. This person, being strong and accustomed to lifting heavy loads, was able to carry the body out of the house without dragging it across the floor. This someone was able to clean up most of the evidence of a struggle in the study. This someone was able to set the alarm of the house before he drove off and dumped the body by the Simi Valley Freeway. This someone did not notice the small trace of the victim's blood in his vehicle. And this someone, being in a high state of excitement as is usual when one man kills another, made a highly uncharacteristic move. He forgot one thing.

"When somebody commits a murder he usually leaves something behind. He leaves a button, or a cigarette case, hairs or fibers from clothes or carpeting, or a piece of his own skin, or semen. It's hard to clean up everything after a murder. The heart races, the palms are wet, the mind fogs over.

"In this case it wasn't a button or a cigarette case that was left behind. It was a small boy. Someone forgot that he had come with Daniel Pagels, who was still playing with the dogs in the kitchen. This someone was the only person in the world who would have found it necessary to take this small boy with him when he went to kill John Nields. This someone is the defendant, Lawrence Pagels."

18

Edgar Stassen looked like a man with nothing to lose when he stood up to make his closing arguments. He had been rendered cleaner and tidier by Ida Letherbridge, who had removed all soup and coffee stains, yet he still gave the impression of one who either slept in or on his clothes. He had combed his hair; the gray mass was remarkably smooth on the surface but now looked like gauze over a clump of steel wool.

"Your Honor,"—he stared at the judge as though trying to remember his name and shuffled the papers on his lectern until enlightenment came—"Judge Conan." It was a bad start.

"Ladies and gentlemen of the jury, the counsels for the prosecution, Mr. Boyman, Mr. Marlatt, and . . ." he made a bow toward the defense table, "my client, Mr. Lawrence Pagels."

He paused to wipe his forehead. He had been talking for one minute.

"We are living in a time of revolution. It's not a revolution that we see. It is one that takes place in the hearts and minds of the people. It has taken place in me. I hope it is taking place in you. For only with this sense of inner revolution will the truth of this case be seen. And only then will Lawrence Pagels, an honest and good man, be acquitted and allowed to return to the life he has always known with his grandson in the peace and beauty of the hills above Chatsworth.

"This revolution will affect the way you see what's going on around you. It will also affect the way you look at the defendant and how you judge his actions on the night that John Nields was murdered.

"On the morning of April twelfth, Lawrence Pagels, together with his grandson, went to John Nields' house to discuss Nields' plan for building luxury homes on and around the site of Mr. Pagels' trailer, where he has lived peacefully and without incident for over thirty years. In fact he has lived in the Chatsworth area all his life. He is as much a natural part of Chatsworth as those big rocks at Stoney Point.

"Mr. Pagels and Mr. Nields had a discussion while Daniel Pagels went to play with the puppies in the kitchen. When Mr. Pagels left, was he spitting out fury and murderous threats? No. He left calmly with his grandson. Mr. Nields was an expressive man on all occasions. Nothing can be inferred from his energetic and expressive manner when the defendant left the house that morning. Mr. Nields could get excited about a bus route. That's the way he was. Everything was an event for him.

"On the journey home the only topic of conversation between Lawrence and Daniel Pagels was . . . the puppies. Daniel, like all five-year-old boys, wanted a puppy. He could think of nothing else. The puppies were then about three weeks old.

"That night the boy tried to sleep but the thought of those small puppies and the fact that John Nields had talked about having them put down because they were not pedigree . . . it was too much for him. At eleven thirty that night, after his grandfather was asleep, Daniel Pagels went to the Nields' house. He was seen by a witness at eleven thirty in his trailer with his grandfather and he was seen by another witness at exactly eleven thirty turning on the lights in the kitchen at the Nields' house ten miles away. He was wearing his pajamas. He was barefoot and showed no signs of walking along sidewalks or over rough hillsides. He was alone. His grandfather was not with him. No witness has come forward to say they saw Lawrence Pagels anywhere near the Nields' house that night.

"It is estimated that John Nields was killed between ten and midnight. The neighbor who witnessed Daniel Pagels arrival at eleven thirty became a little curious. She sat at her dressing table, removing her makeup, and watched awhile. She heard no commotion, she saw no bodies being dragged out of the house. And do you know why, ladies and gentlemen? Because the body of John Nields was already lying out there on the Winnetka off ramp.

"The killer had been to the Nields' house already. He or she was known to Mr. Nields, certainly, and he or she was known to the dog also. Because the dog did not bark that evening until Daniel Pagels arrived. The dog did not bark when the killer arrived because it was someone the dog must have known. It barked when Daniel Pagels arrived because it had only met the boy that morning and was still a little wary.

"The prosecution has offered no evidence to show that the murder of John Nields took place after Daniel Pagels arrived at the house. They have offered no proof that John Nields was not dead before the arrival of Daniel Pagels. They have offered no proof that Lawrence Pagels returned to the Nields' house after his morning visit. They have offered no proof to show that Daniel Pagels' presence at the house on the night that John Nields was killed was any more than a coincidence. They have offered no proof to show that they were not two entirely unrelated events.

"The prosecution has built its case on a small speck of blood and two coincidences.

"First, let's look at the blood. Let's imagine the picture. We have an excited, energetic man running down his driveway with his hand stretched out toward Lawrence Pagels. We have a witness who saw that.

"What did he do when he disappeared from sight behind the trees? We know that John Nields never took no for an answer. He was the kind of guy who'd grab hold of a truck if he saw it moving away from him. We know that Lawrence Pagels stopped his truck and John Nields spoke to him. We also know that the speck of blood left on the tailgate of the truck was far too small to have come from a body that was bleeding heavily from several grievous wounds. It came from a minor accident. The sort of accident that might happen when a hand comes into contact with a hard object that is pulling away from it.

"Now, let's look at the two coincidences that mean so much to the prosecution. The victim's body was found on a freeway near the defendant's home. And the defendant's grandson was in the victim's house.

"Because of this small speck of blood and these two coincidences, the prosecution is asking us to believe that an intelligent man would bludgeon and stab someone to death, have the presence of mind to remove the body from the victim's house, set the code on the burglar alarm (which he did not know), and yet at the same time be confused enough to leave his five-year-old grandson at the scene of the crime. Some people say the defense's propositions are impossible but what about that one!

"Can you imagine Mark Boyman getting together with Harvey Marlatt and saying, 'What d'ya think Harvey. Is it possible to throw a dead body over one shoulder, dust and wipe most of the fingerprints, tidy up, take a quick guess at the alarm combination, punch it out, forget to take your grandson with you and then go home and drop off into a calm sleep?' 'Oh sure, Mark. It happens all the time.'

"I ask you. Who's dreaming? Who's having the fantasies? If Lawrence Pagels had killed John Nields, would he transport the body to the other side of the San Fernando Valley and leave it just up the road from his trailer? Only a retard would do that and the prosecution has offered no evidence to show that Mr. Pagels is in any way mentally deficient."

Harvey Marlatt was listening with his eyes directed to a spot just in front of Stassen's feet. Mark Boyman, on the other hand could not hide his twitching fingers, the slight but constant tapping of his feet, and his darting eyes that would jump nervously from one juror to the next.

Stassen crossed over to the jury. "The prosecutor says that a five-year-old child cannot travel ten miles at night by himself especially if it does not take the generally accepted amount of time. We all have it fixed in our heads how long it should take to go that distance. It takes this much time in a car, it takes that much time on a bicycle, it takes a lot longer if you walk. The prosecutor says it's only possible to cover those ten miles in the way that everyone says you gotta do it. He says anything else is impossible.

"Well, you know, if you look at railroad tracks your eyes tell you that they converge at the horizon. But that doesn't stop you getting on a train. You ain't scared that the train will fall off the tracks once it reaches the horizon. You get on the train because your intelligence tells you something different. And that's what we're dealing with. Intelligence.

"We're relying on our intelligence. Or should I say, ladies and gentlemen, we're relying on your intelligence. . . . Now, you've been exposed to the kind of physics instruction that is a complete mystery to most people. If it wasn't for this case you could have gone on a lot longer in happy ignorance. But you are on this jury. What can I tell ya? You're gonna find out a little sooner than other people, that we're living at a time when not to know will keep you in the dark ages. This trial and its verdict could signify one of the first steps out of darkness into light. You could be part of it.

"Throughout the history of mankind there have been men who have shown us a new view—Copernicus, Galileo, Isaac Newton— great men who revolutionized science. Then at the beginning of this century certain men of genius began to make strange discoveries which completely turned around the way we looked at things . . . Einstein, Max Planck, Niels Bohr, Werner Heisenberg. They discovered that time was not absolute but relative, that we lived in an observer-created reality.

"These were earth-shattering, totally revolutionary discoveries. They make the Russian Revolution, which was taking place around the same time, look insignificant by comparison. So what happened with these great ideas? Did the world get turned around? Did the discovery of an observer-created reality fill mankind with awe. Did our schools and universities start digging deep into the act of observation instead of taking everything at face value? Not exactly.

"Scientists went on making toast in the morning. They thought to themselves I'm making toast, maybe this toast is a figment of my imagination but I'll eat it first and worry about the rest later. And, ladies and gentlemen, they've been doing that ever since. For one thing they don't want to be thought stupid, for another they're scared of stirring up a hornet's nest of strange ideas that'll be seized by every weirdo and loony tune on the block.

"Scientists have spent the last fifty years trying to make physics seem ordinary because they couldn't handle the idea that mankind was moving into another dimension. But the fact is that quantum mechanics has showed scientists another world, a world where the observer is not outside of things, he is part of it.

"One of the old Greek philosophers, Socrates, Plato . . . one of those guys, caught a glimpse of it. He said that life is like a cave where people are tied up unable to move. People have been tied up in this cave their whole lives and all they've ever seen are their own shadows on the wall. They watch the wall and think that the shadows are life itself.

"Then one day one of the guys in the cave gets untied and goes out. He comes back and says, 'There are people out there. They're moving about. What you've been watching are only shadows.' And they say, 'Nah. Don't be ridiculous. You're crazy. Come and sit down and watch the shadows. They're reality. Don't get carried away with paranormal fantasies.'

"Or, if you wanna bring it up to date. Life is like a computer screen. A kid sits in front of the computer watching this screen and he begins to think that life is all in that screen. But if he stops to think about it, life and reality are all in him. The computer is just a screen that he makes come alive.

"So, if you get what I'm saying, we're discovering that life is not on the computer screen. It is in the observer. We're the reality. We make it happen.

"So you might be thinking, that's no big deal. I know reality is in me. I know I make it happen. I know life is just the way you look at things. But then I'll say to you, put that to the test. If you believe reality is in you then why do you accept the idea that you're getting older? Einstein said there's no such thing as absolute time. So why don't you choose a nice slow-moving time? And if you want to get somewhere real fast why does it have to take you any time at all? Think about it.

"Once people believed that the earth was flat because it seemed flat. Once they believed that the sun went around the earth because that's how it looked until Copernicus told them otherwise. People have believed for a long time that we're stuck in certain definite strictures of time and space but now men who know more than we do tell us differently. It's the difference between living your life watching shadows on the wall of a cave or running outside and joining the people moving around.

"The last decade of the twentieth century will be the decade when we discover that the thinker is the thought and the thought is the thinker. That's pretty heavy stuff for us guys who've been tied up all our lives and I guess we'd prefer to give the whole idea a miss. But we have an obligation here to a man's life. A man is accused of murder who was not in the place where and when the murder was committed. The People say the only way that Daniel Pagels could have gotten all the way to the Nields' house is by going there with his grandfather. But we can explain how Daniel got there by himself. He went alone. No one helped him.

"He got there by simple thought. He got there because he didn't know enough not to know that he couldn't get there. Children learn foreign languages real fast because they're too dumb to take a long time. They can swim when they are born. They grow up a little, they forget, they have to be taught. They can do a lot of stuff that adults can't do. This child, Daniel Pagels, was untouched by the usual everyday influences that touch you and me. His thought was even more simple and uncluttered than the average five year olds'. He wanted to go. He went.

"And that's not the only amazing thing, ladies and gentlemen. I'll tell you something that'll really blow your mind. If you could get into that child's way of thinking, you could do exactly the same thing. We don't use one thousandth of the ability we have. We're walking around handcuffed and blindfolded.

"Now you might be asking, why doesn't every child who's lived a little cut off from society have the same ability as Daniel Pagels? I don't know for sure. All I do know is, we're living in an age of new thought, new movement. The knowledge is there. Go to your library. It's there. But people are acting like dinosaurs. They don't wanna know.

"It's scary to accept ideas as different as this. You have to loosen up your mind, throw out everything, and begin all over. Here we have an example of someone who's done something we consider impossible. We may consider it impossible now, but one day we won't. Almost everything we do today was thought to be impossible once. Satellite television, computers, airplanes, rockets. The high scores in the Olympics. No one ever thought that man would run so fast or jump so high.

"But you always find that once everyone's accepted the idea that one guy can do something impossible, then a lot of guys suddenly come out of the woodwork and they're all doing it all over the place. They're doing it over and over until people get bored with it and they say 'What's the big deal?'

"It may be hard for you to imagine, but one day, and that day may be sooner than you realize, people will be saying 'What's the big deal about traveling about the way Daniel Pagels did?' There will be so many people using that form of transport that it will be stale news.

"That's hard to imagine because we're still struggling with the idea that one little kid did it. Why a little kid? Why wasn't it an astronaut, a great scientist, a great athlete? It was a child because somehow this ability requires a child's thought. How do we get that kind of thinking? What thoughts do you keep in? What thoughts do you keep out? Well, I'll be honest with you. I don't know. There are various philosophies and religions, I believe, that say 'become as a little child' . . . I'm just throwing that out here because I can't say I know too much about that.

"I know that we begin to get an explanation in quantum mechanics; but this explanation can lead us to the less-explored areas of life. One great scientist said, 'To understand quantum mechanics deeply you will have to understand the nature of mind.'

"It may be, ladies and gentlemen, that you will be unable to accept any of this. It may be that no one of your generation will accept it. It's disruptive. It threatens just about everything.

"If you accept the idea that the observer and the action are one . . . then . . . then heck, it places a real big load of responsibility on your shoulders. You have to examine all your decisions, not just the ones you're making now, but all the ones you've inherited from past generations. We've all been told one thing and now we're finding it's something else. I'll tell you, it's a real can of worms.

"We're getting close to the twenty-first century. The time has come to take a new look, to think in a new way. If you cannot bring yourselves to do this then you are avoiding inescapable truths. You are joining the flat earth society. You're saying that the sun moves round the earth. You're relying on your eyes instead of your minds.

"And as I said, it may be that you can't accept this. It may be that this whole thing will remain submerged for a few more generations, but it can't remain submerged forever. The day will come when people will awake out of their long sleep and understand their full capacities. And that day will be a glorious day. It could be that day has arrived and that you ladies and gentlemen, by your vote, will lead the way. And the day could go down in history as the day that men saw the light."

Edgar Stassen paused and took a few deep breaths. He wiped his face and looked round the courtroom. Harvey Marlatt was staring at his spot on the floor. Boyman had his arms folded and his mouth gaping slightly. He was trying to figure Stassen out. It was beyond him. Max Haydn appeared embarrassed. He rarely took his eyes off the table in front of him. Only Ida was with Stassen. She would have breathed for him if she could.

Lawrence Pagels listened intently, but not with the same involvement. He was more impersonal than Ida. It was not a matter of life and death to him. It was a matter to be weighed and considered. At least that's how it seemed to the outside observer and that's how journalists were describing Pagels in their newspapers.

Edgar Stassen, like someone halfway through a street fight, pulled up the waistband of his pants so that they fitted over his stomach instead of under it, and he continued.

"So . . . let's recapitulate. In the double-slit experiment . . . Boy, you've heard so much about that, I bet you dream about it at night. In that experiment, which is so crucial to the understanding of quantum physics, you learned that a subatomic particle acted like a wave and went through two holes at once. This particle, being a basic part of a table or a cup or a human body should, logically speaking, behave like a table or a cup or a human body. It should stay put, just like we have to.

"That's why the fact that it goes through two holes at once is weird, it's one hundred percent weird. That's equivalent to our friend the prosecutor getting out of the elevator on this floor and getting out on the second floor at exactly the same time.

"And if that isn't wild enough for you, we discovered that in this same experiment, if you introduced an observer, the subatomic particles froze in their tracks and behaved like obedient Boy Scouts. They stopped zipping through both holes at once and went through just one. The inescapable conclusion is that in some way we affect what happens by the way we look at things.

"We know that subatomic particles jump. They disappear and appear in another place. Why can't we? Does it only require our consent for us to behave with the same freedom? This body of frozen, solid substance that we all carry around, it has arms and legs and a head, it grows fat and slow on some of us—what is it? How much does our action as observer affect it? In the light of what quantum physics teaches us, how should we change our attitude to our life and to our body?

"Does the act of observing cause it to be solidified into certain conventional ways of moving? If the act of observing has any effect at all, shouldn't we know a heck of a lot more about it than we do know? Why isn't observing and its effects taught in all the schools?

"The act of looking at something turns it from a wave into a particle. When we look at our life do we change it from a wave into a particle? Did Daniel Pagels, by not looking at things the way we look at things, manage to retain the wavelike nature which, we have learned, is common to all subatomic particles? Are we, each and every one of us in this courtroom, nothing more than waves? Are we solidified by thought? Did Daniel Pagels, in all the ignorance of extreme youth, bypass certain restrictions we place on ourselves?

"Lastly, I'll ask you to think about this. Why did this happen in the United States of America? What is it we have here that provides an atmosphere of thought where something like this can happen?

"We have a way of life based on the Declaration of Independence. What are people from all over the world escaping from when they come here? They're escaping from the old ways of doing things, its restrictions. They come here for freedom of thought, freedom of religion, freedom to live and work without the limitations they experienced before.

"And you could also ask, why of all the states in the union did it happen in California? I'll tell you why. Because California has always been the first to take up a new way of thinking. It's always been first to throw off the old and welcome the new. Things that might get laughed at anywhere else get an opportunity in California. The prosecution is laughing but this is not a laughing matter. This is a fundamental fact of life. The prosecutor does not show the true California spirit.

"I hope you, as true Californians, will open wide your thought and let in this new idea. And I hope you will fully comprehend that the defendant, Lawrence Pagels, is an honest and good man. I hope you will see that he is not only innocent of any crime but a man whose purity of thought has encouraged his young grandson in a great step forward, a step that will eventually be taken by mankind everywhere. Thank you."

———

In his closing arguments, the associate counsel, dry and desiccated Harvey Marlatt, worked from notes written out on small cards. His opening line "Ladies and gentlemen, 'Star Trek' is over," brought laughter and he held up his hand to subdue it. "It's been amusing but don't forget that at the end of every episode of a show like that, they write on your TV screen, 'series created by.' The little dramatic episode we've been entertained with in this courtroom has been created by a defense counsel who has nothing else to offer in defense of his client. Even as a smoke screen it's completely ineffective. It's got so many holes in it that it doesn't hide a thing, not even the desperation of the defense counsel. And it certainly doesn't hide the guilt of the defendant Lawrence Pagels who has had to sit through all this drivel, these inane claims that have been made on behalf of himself and his grandson. And by the way, what an assault on a young child! It makes you wonder if there shouldn't be some way of preventing innocent little lives being used as fodder for some kind of dream machine by desperate and ruthless people. Just out of respect for childhood I'd think you'd want to throw this garbage out."

After that Marlatt polished his reading glasses and descended into a long and deadening rehash of the material reasons and facts that incriminated Lawrence Pagels. The jury listened solemnly and without emotion except for revealing that slight quickening of intensity that resulted from the imminent end of the trial, the realization that a decision would soon be required of them.

"Look at the evidence and then ask yourselves, who had a motive for killing John Nields, who had a bitter argument with him on the morning of April twelfth, who possessed the only fingerprint found in Nields' study, who had the victim's blood on his pickup truck, who lived right by the Winnetka off ramp where the body was found, and who was responsible for the child left unattended in Nields' house? Are there several people who would answer to that? Is it difficult to make a choice? No it is not difficult because there is only one person to choose from, only one person who could have committed this murder. And who is this person? It is the man before us in this courtroom today, the defendant Lawrence Pagels.

"Let me end by noting that you, the jury, have been a solid and stable factor in this courtroom, you've been attentive and uncomplaining all through this long, difficult trial. I know that the decision you are about to make will not be hard if you simply weigh the facts. You've had a lot of fantasy thrown at you. But stick to the facts and you can't go wrong. Stick to the facts and you will serve the cause of justice in the State of California. An innocent man was murdered. Don't let a guilty man go free. Stick to the facts and you will reach an inescapable conclusion, that Lawrence Pagels is guilty of the murder of John Nields."

————

While Judge Conan read the instructions to the jury it was evident that the idea of deliberating the guilt or innocence of the defendant had begun to create a degree of tension among the jurors. They filed out of the courtroom, each one lost in his own thoughts. Even the two smilers—the pretty, plump Doria Rudell and the sometimes cheerful Fred Turner—had lost their smiles. The moment was upon them.

There was the one plus factor. They were almost through now. Get this decision made, they could all go home and life could get back to normal.

Not knowing where to begin, they concentrated their first efforts into a debate on the smoking issue. There were three heavy smokers on the jury, Antonio Rocha, Jane Sue Rodofsky, and Bill Perrott. And there were two, Brad Ryker and Doria Rudell, who indicated that they would like to smoke occasionally although they would not die without it.

The rest of them were against it, particularly Angela Barry and Elvie Richter, who felt that inflicting smoke on others was a kind of bodily assault.

"You want to make yourself sick, that's fine with me, but don't do it to me. I want to live." Angela Barry, from the start was the most outspoken.

Smoking became one of the paramount marks of division among the group, more so than race, class, age, or sex. Angela and Elvie, a young black woman and a white senior citizen, teamed up and formed an inseparable bond. They always sat together as far away from the smokers as they could get. They were frequently joined by Fred Turner and Donna Fabry.

Angela Barry, who had established herself as the talker, was close to being elected chairman but was finally pushed into second place by Brad Ryker. The smoking issue may have influenced the vote.

Angela was to say later things may have gone differently if she had been chairman.

Ryker, a religious man, asked them if they would agree to a

simple prayer at the beginning of each day's proceedings. As there was a preponderance of semibelievers and not one adamant atheist in the group, it was agreed upon.

Following the prayer Ryker suggested they start out with a first ballot to establish where they all stood.

"You mean we say if Pagels is guilty or not guilty right off without talking about it?" Elvie Richter asked.

"That's correct."

"What if we all agree?"

"We'll discuss that when we come to it."

"You mean," added Angela Barry, "That this could be it. We could be sending someone to jail for life by this vote?"

"Look, just vote. Let's see where we stand at this point."

The results of the first nervous, reluctant ballot were eleven guilty and one not guilty.

———

The jury deliberated for eleven and a half days. As one journalist, who spent that time playing cards on the plaza outside the Van Nuys court, jokingly remarked, "It took God seven days to create the world but twelve men and women needed an extra four and a half days to re-create man."

During the first few days the jury sent requests for specific details on certain forensic evidence relating to blood identification, fingerprints, and the type of wounds incurred by John Nields. On the sixth day they sent out a question to Judge Conan asking for clarification on the relationship of the law to quantum physics. After that it was quiet.

A journalist from a London newspaper reported that the Pentagon had sent out an observer to cover the trial, but when inquiries were made, the Pentagon denied the claim. During the eleven and a half days that the jury was out, a wire service reported that government officials were hanging around the courthouse and were questioning anybody who had met Daniel Pagels. It was even said that several of the major oil companies had investigators at the trial awaiting the outcome.

None of these claims was proved. But it was apparent that every day more people of unknown purpose and great curiosity were adding their presence to the crowd waiting outside the building. They sat in the cafeteria on the second floor drinking coffee and eating sandwiches, they bought cold drinks and pretzels from the stands outside. They offered no information about themselves.

———

While the jury was out, Daniel asked one recurring question.

"Can we go and see Grandpa now that he's not so busy?"

"No, honey, it's best if we wait," Sandy said.

"Why?"

"Because."

"Because why?"

"I'll be honest with you. I just don't want to take you there. I couldn't handle it."

"I could help you. You could stay with me the whole time."

"No, Danny, you'll have to wait. Be patient. You've been patient all along. You be patient now."

But he was not patient and he made the same request again and again.

———

By the tenth day that the jury was out, Stassen had gained some hope. It was a good sign that they were taking their time.

"Every minute they're out is another point to us."

Max was unconvinced but he kept it to himself. Stassen's summing up had been powerful. Even Max found himself wanting to believe it for a moment or two. But now they were in the cold light of day. And with every hour that passed he began to see that they didn't have a hope in hell.

It looked as though Ida realized that too, but she was saying nothing. There was nothing more to say. It was all conjecture now. She had used the break to get a little more sleep. She was looking healthier.

Stassen was not looking any better. Doing nothing but wait was even more taxing for him than standing up in court and mouthing what everyone considered to be ludicrous impossibilities. As the weeks went by he had almost grown accustomed to being the court wacko. It was like taking off all his clothes and walking down the street. It was embarrassing for a while but even the worst kind of embarrassment could not last forever. What was worse than embarrassment was waiting helplessly. That was the most difficult thing of all.

He was still not sleeping. Supreme fatigue had taken the strength out of all his facial muscles. Below his eyes there were deep drifts and hollows that seemed to go down to his chin. In the morning the face in the mirror looked like a Halloween mask.

"What about . . . er . . . are you taking exams or anything like that?" he asked.

"Hah!" said Max. "Did you hear that, Ida? He's taking an interest in our academic work."

Ida smiled. "We're a little behind."

"Behind! What a euphemism. But you know . . . we thought this past year was worth it for the invaluable experience we've had in handling ridicule. It was a once-in-a-lifetime opportunity. It's also given me time to pack up and change my name."

Stassen looked at him wearily. He had no idea where this cocky kid found the energy or the disposition to make jokes. He himself needed everything he had to sustain the simple act of waiting.

One thing he knew for sure. By the time he stood up to make his closing argument, he had become convinced in his heart that Lawrence Pagels was innocent. Yet that conviction gave him no comfort.

———

Lionel Brown also thought it was a good sign that the jury was still out.

He sat on his bunk in the Men's Central Jail and considered the situation. "You've got someone pullin' for you," he told Lawrence. "While you're doing your prayin' there, you'd better put in a word for a hung jury. Then you can walk out of this place a free man."

"I'm free everywhere I go, Lionel. In here or out."

Lionel looked at him skeptically. "If I didn't know you better, I'd say you're a dumb old man. But I know you're dumb because you wanna be and not because you don't have no choice. Now depending how you look at things, that makes you really dumber than most people or just plain crazy."

"And what do you think?"

"I'm still workin' on it."

———

If DeRosa had forced himself upon Rhonda he would have felt a familiar sense of guilt but since he had behaved well he was experiencing a new sensation—regret.

Late in the evening he went to Le Bon Café where Rhonda worked and sat at the bar watching her like an old man thinking of his lost youth.

Now that the jury was out she was anxious to talk to him. As soon as she noticed him she came over and asked "Any news?"

He glanced round at the black walls, mirrored walls, ficus trees, trailing plants, and black marble pillars and announced, "This place looks like a whore's bathroom."

"You wish."

She wore a uniform, a black dress and white apron. Her hair was tied with a white scarf in an unsuccessful attempt at tidiness.

"Any news?" she repeated.

"I've gotta tell you the chairman's against your dad."

"The ex-Marine. You told me that before."

Her face was tense with anxiety. Her days at court were now spent sitting on a wall near the front entrance, drumming her fingers and smoking cigarettes.

DeRosa looked at her with curiosity.

"Excuse me for asking, but . . . uh . . . have you always been so hard to get?"

Rhonda eyed him wearily. "I don't know. I guess it's a matter of timing. Now is a bad time for me."

He sighed. "So if the timing was different I'd see a different person."

"Maybe. I don't know."

"Wouldn't you know it! I come along. The timing's bad. I get the nun."

Rhonda gave him a disdainful, bored stare.

DeRosa sighed again. "It's just an accident of history."

"You act like you missed out on the Holy Grail or something," she snapped. "What have you missed? I'm here. You've got my full attention. You've got all of me as far as I'm concerned."

"There's something missing."

"No, there's not. If you want a good sensation, don't come sniffing around after me. Have a chocolate sundae."

DeRosa looked hurt. "How can you say that? There's no comparison. It's two people getting together. It's great. It's like poetry. It's what life is all about."

"Lawrence says life is much better than that."

"But you don't believe your dad, you've never believed him."

Some customers went by and sat down at one of her tables.

"I've got to go." She moved off.

DeRosa spoke quickly. "I talked to him today. I asked him if he wanted to give you a message."

She stopped.

DeRosa enjoyed the suspense. "He said . . . tell her she's O.K."

Rhonda turned the message over in her mind. Then she allowed herself a small smile and walked away.

———

The crowds outside the court grew even larger as the days went by, and curiosity as to the reasons for the length of the jury's deliberation increased. By noon on the twelfth day when the chairman of the jury, Brad Ryker, finally announced that they had reached a verdict, traffic around the municipal buildings had come to a standstill.

At 2:30 on December 19, 1989, the jury filed back into the courtroom on the sixth floor.

All of those who had waited outside in the warm winter sun for eleven and a half days were not rewarded. Only a small percentage of the faithful found their way back into the courtroom; only some of the press could cram themselves inside. The rest had to wait in the corridors or outside the press room, or even worse, outside the building. There simply was not enough room for them all. Joe DeRosa called Rhonda Pagels as soon as he could, and he found her a place.

The clerk read the verdict. "In the Superior Court of the State of California, in and for the County of Los Angeles, the People of the State of California versus Lawrence Pagels."

The old chestnut that the jury won't look at the defendant after a guilty verdict was not applicable here. It seemed that half the jury was looking at Lawrence Pagels and half was not.

The clerk went on, "We, the jury in the above-entitled action, find the defendant guilty of the crime of murder of John Wilson Nields in violation of section 187, Penal Code of California, a felony, as charged in Count One of the Indictment, and we further find it to be murder of the first degree."

After the Trial

19

There was a free-for-all in the halls and corridors as some reporters ran for the phones and others competed for interviews with the attorneys and members of the jury.

Harvey Marlatt and Mark Boyman staged a press conference in the hall. Ida Letherbridge hid behind a white and nervy Edgar Stassen, who talked edgily of an appeal. He offered no comment on the nature of his defense.

Max Haydn spoke into any microphone thrust into his face. He said that it had been a daring and historic defense and had stirred debate. He said working on the defense team had been an opportunity of a lifetime.

Few members of the jury were willing to speak to reporters. Brad Ryker read out a statement signed by the entire jury that stated they never had any doubt in their minds that Lawrence Pagels had killed John Nields. He made no mention of the so-called quantum defense and the testimony of the various physicists. When pressed to comment Ryker would only say that they had considered what they had heard and that one member of the jury had been prepared to believe Stassen's explanation for Daniel Pagels' means of transport to the Nields house. He would not divulge who that person was. He also said that particular individual was not willing to discuss it with the media.

Angela Barry was the only other juror who spoke to any reporters. She was caught in the elevator.

"Hi, Angela. How are you feeling?"

"O.K."

"Can you tell us about the decision. Who held out?"

"I can't say."

"Did you discuss the quantum defense?"

"Sure, we discussed it."

"How long were you discussing it?"

"Not too long."

"Was it ever an issue?"

"Not really."

"What do you personally think of the quantum defense?"

"It's interesting."

"Did any other jurors think it was interesting?"

"Oh sure. But most of them were really against it."

"So what happened to the juror who was holding out? Did this person get pushed into voting against it by the others?"

"I guess you could say that, yes."

"Is this person now convinced that he or she did the right thing?"

"Well, this person was reluctant but it was hard for ... er ... this person to go believing in something like that under the circumstances."

"What circumstances?"

"Well you have eleven people saying two and two make four and you got one person saying two and two make five."

"Are you happy with the decision?"

"It was hard."

"Why was that Angela?"

"He didn't look like a murderer. But the evidence showed that he did it."

The day after the guilty verdict, white T-shirts emblazoned with bold black lettering went on sale in various small boutiques throughout Los Angeles and were worn in the halls of high schools and colleges by students, in shopping malls by mothers with babies, by retired people taking constitutional walks, they were on the beaches at Malibu and Santa Monica, one was worn by a homeless person living in a cardboard box, and another was seen flashing around the courts at the Beverly Hills tennis club. The T-shirts read "Lawrence Pagels Is Innocent."

———

Daniel was unfazed by the guilty verdict. Don Leutwiler said the child was like someone watching a movie. He just watched, he wasn't in it.

Sandy had brought him back to Granada Hills. They had been there for two days, and so far Daniel's presence there was a secret. He was not allowed to go out to play or even go near the front windows. It was like a jail sentence but Don said it would all blow over very quickly and he could go back to school in a couple of weeks.

It had not been easy to keep him from hearing the news reports that had been flashed on television all afternoon. And when Sheila and Greg came in from school, bursting with the news, they were immediately sent out to spend the evening with friends.

Don was the one chosen to tell Daniel. He took him out to the pool just before bedtime. The boy was wearing pajamas, just as he had been the night he was found at the Nields' house. They sat on a bright, cushioned swing seat with a polka-dotted fringed awning and swung back and forth, listening to the crickets and watching the shimmering blue underwater lamp in the pool that turned the water a bright, fluorescent turquoise. Don had also switched on the colored Malibu lights hidden behind shrubs throughout the backyard; now the place was lit up like Disneyland. The palm trees glowed orange and green, the ferns shone yellow and pink. They were in a magic grotto. And Daniel was thrilled to be regaled by such glory.

Don did it in one sentence. "Your grandpa's been found guilty of murder, Danny, and they're going to keep him in jail till he's a very old man."

Daniel changed the subject.

"He changed the subject?" Sandy cross-questioned him afterward.

"Yeah, I told him, and he kind of nodded and then he said if people put salt instead of chlorine in their pools they could keep sea bass in them."

"He's holding it inside. He's hiding it from us."

Don shrugged. "If he's hiding it, he's hiding it real good."

Sandy broke a five-year abstinence and started smoking again. She had known what she was taking on when she agreed to foster Daniel but she had not been prepared for the helplessness she was now experiencing. She wanted to protect the child from any feelings of anguish but nothing she said or did was effective.

Daniel did not seem to go through a period of mourning. He was calm and cheerful, fighting with Jason as usual, a typical seven year old battling his wits against a nine year old.

Two days later Sandy heard that Daniel had told Sheila he would soon be with his grandfather again in their motor home up in the hills and that Lawrence had applied for him to attend the Balboa Boulevard Elementary School. This particular school was a magnet school for gifted children.

Sandy decided to say nothing. If silence was how Daniel wanted to handle it she would not try to interfere anymore. The child was avoiding reality in his own way.

———

Sharon Nields phoned Mark Boyman and asked how long Lawrence Pagels would have to stay in jail.

"That hasn't been decided yet," he told her.

"Do these kind of decisions ever get overturned?"

"Not in a case like this."

"Oh."

"Are you going to take a vacation now, Mrs. Nields?"

"I don't know."

"Have you tried Hawaii? Sit out on one of those islands and you forget everything."

"Will he get parole?"

"I don't see why not."

"I know how the little boy feels losing his grandfather like this. I wouldn't want to be by myself. I've lost John. I couldn't stand it if I lost Ray as well."

———

The press reaction to the guilty verdict was relatively subdued. On the day itself, it was headline news, the big story on the national evening news, flashed instantly around the world.

But there was not much follow up. Reporters were quick to distance themselves from what appeared to be a wild con trick that had not paid off.

The *Washington Post* allowed itself some reflection on the nature of belief versus reality. Its editorial said that Lawrence Pagels, in his brief moment of fame, had caught the imagination of the entire world. It also said that even his most ardent opponents may have nurtured a sneaking doubt about his guilt. "There is part of all of us that wishes Lawrence Pagels were right."

On the whole, however, there was a general sense of misgiving that so many members of the media could have been caught up in the wild dreams of an overimaginative old man and his gullible attorney.

"Media madness" was a term frequently used to describe the jostling crowds of cameramen and reporters who had fought for positions in the Van Nuys courthouse. The usually unself-critical media went no further than that and made amends by dropping the story as quickly as it had picked it up.

There were passing references in some papers and on television news to the "Lawrence Pagels Is Innocent" movement. But few news editors allowed themselves to be caught any longer giving coverage to a crazy convict's philosophy.

Leon Ferguson, however, was permitted to write a short epitaph in the Los Angeles *Daily News*. "The convicted murderer Lawrence Pagels is an unusual man. He used his trial to teach the world some unusual ideas. As he sits in his cell in Men's Central awaiting sentencing, he may receive some comfort from the fact that he started a debate which may go on. Through him we took new steps in examining the nature of mind as it applies to our daily life. As we approach the new century and dig deeper into the nature of mind, we may discover that guilty or not, in some small way Lawrence Pagels was right."

———

A week after the guilty verdict, Jennifer and Bruce Perry arrived back home, dragged their suitcases out of their car, and resumed their normal activities.

When Leon Ferguson telephoned to ask why they had departed so suddenly, Bruce Perry told him, "My wife didn't want to be hassled by guys like you."

———

Over Christmas vacation Don Leutwiler took Daniel to visit his grandfather.

On their way into the visitors' room they passed Rhonda, who was on her way out. She paused for half a second, thoroughly startled by the unexpected meeting. Daniel, however, was intent on seeing Lawrence and walked straight past her.

The meeting with his grandfather was emotional but it did not disturb Daniel unduly.

"Can you get out of this place, Grandpa?" Daniel asked.

"No." Lawrence put his hand out and touched the glass that divided them.

"That's too bad." Daniel looked around at the guards. "There's a lot of policemen about."

"Yes, they're all over the place."

"Are you allowed out for walks?"

"Not too much."

"Because if you went out for a walk you could run off when they're not looking."

"I'll think about that."

"I know it's cheating but they haven't played fair."

Lawrence smiled. Don Leutwiler, sitting next to Daniel, appeared uncomfortable and did not smile.

When they were on their way out of the visitors' room, Daniel persisted in discussing, in a theatrical hushed whisper, various ways of escaping from the jail.

Don hustled him out.

The Leutwilers explained to Daniel that his grandfather would soon be sent to another jail that would be a long distance away. Even so, they agreed to take him on regular visits after that as it seemed to be the thing that mattered to him most.

———

Shortly after Christmas Lawrence Pagels was sentenced to twenty-five years to life. As soon as the news was out, a vociferous group of "Free Lawrence Pagels" supporters arrived outside the Men's Central Jail. They had banners, placards, leaflets, and bullhorns that boomed over the noise of the traffic. A group of women from the valley who had initiated the T-shirt drive had stepped up the campaign by picketing the jail; they were quickly joined by a variety of students, working and retired people, anyone who could find the time to stand and shout, which included a group who arrived in a psychedelic painted bus, long haired and barefoot; they appeared to have been preserved in aspic since Woodstock.

In order to avoid this rapidly expanding group a black police van, transporting Lawrence Pagels from Men's Central to Chino, left through a back exit at 10:30 at night and took a circuitous route to the freeway.

A drought-breaking storm had whipped up the warm, dry air of downtown Los Angeles and doused it with rain that fell in dense, wet lumps. The rain swept the dust off the sidewalks and gushed it into the parched storm drains. Water swamped the gutters, spilled out onto the roads and formed sizable rivers that forced the traffic into slow, baptismal lines. The storm scattered the "Free Lawrence Pagels" supporters in every direction. They sought refuge in doorways and coffee shops.

The unmarked police van chose this moment to move quickly toward the freeway. Lawrence Pagels, an armed guard at his side, sat handcuffed in the back. In an effort to avoid a traffic jam caused by flooding on one street, the police driver turned on to Olive Street and was caught in a crowd of first-night operagoers coming out of the Dorothy Chandler Pavilion at the Music Center.

The driver looked in his mirror and saw what he thought was a press photographer running along the sidewalk in pursuit of the van. He stepped on the accelerator, pulled out into the oncoming traffic, and attempted to speed toward a gap in the traffic about three cars ahead. He raced along the waterlogged street sending up a fountain of spray. When he pulled in he was confronted by a party of first nighters in tuxedos and long gowns crossing the street to their cars. They were half ducking under large striped umbrellas so that their view was restricted and they did not see the van immediately.

The police van swerved to avoid them and was confronted by an RTD bus coming straight at him. The bus took evasive action and pulled in toward the curb. The police van braked and spun around three times, mounted the sidewalk, sending opera lovers scuttling in all directions, and, falling on its side, crashed tailfirst into the concrete wall of the Music Center. It lay on the wet sidewalk steaming, its wheels spinning while the rain suddenly chose to increase its ferocity and fell with demonic force.

On the other side of the street the bus with one wheel up on the sidewalk had crashed into a series of newspaper-vending machines and nosed them along until forced to a halt by a steel bus-stop sign.

The elegantly dressed theatergoers had been flattened against the

Music Center wall by the dual force of the weather and the accident. There was a moment of paralysis while the upturned wheels of the police van went on spinning helplessly and the back doors flapped loosely, the lock smashed and useless from the impact of the crash.

The only other movement came from the traffic, which continued forward and piled up around the scene of the accident. The oncoming cars solidified into one unmoving mass that spread outward in every direction. The entire area became one gigantic traffic jam.

Drivers jumped out and ran to the two crashed vehicles thus breaking the paralysis of the watching pedestrians. The first to approach the police van was a woman in a long white evening gown who, in later reports, was likened to a ministering angel. She ran over to the van, her pale hair soaked and flattened against her head, and attempted to pull the unconscious driver out on to the sidewalk. She was quickly aided by several men in evening dress who were shouting to each other about the danger of explosion and fire.

One who said he was a doctor instructed them how to lay the man on the ground, his head cushioned on jackets and coats.

The bus driver across the street was not unconscious but was bleeding from head and facial cuts. And many people inside the bus had suffered minor head and body injuries. They were predominantly black and Mexican workers traveling home from a late shift. They were somewhat suspicious of the people in the fancy evening clothes who insisted on lifting them out of the dry bus and sitting them on the cold sidewalk in the pouring rain.

It was a minute or two before anyone approached the flapping doors at the back of the police van. Two men who looked inside found a guard suffering from concussion, a broken arm and cracked ribs. A handcuffed prisoner in a dazed state lay slumped on top of him.

Lawrence Pagels was lifted out. By this time someone had produced some cushions for the victims to rest on. Pagels and the guard were placed together by the curbside while a woman held an umbrella over them. The sound of police cars and paramedics, sirens blaring, could be heard all round the Music Center as they tried vainly to push their way through the solid block of traffic.

Performing artists with makeup half removed, musicians, and stagehands, hearing the commotion, ran out of the stage doors and rushed to help the remaining passengers out of the bus until the area was jammed with bewildered victims and curious onlookers.

The accident took place at 10:41 P.M. The first emergency vehicle pushed its way through the traffic and arrived at the accident scene at 10:52. Officer Ron Mathias had been stuck at the corner of First and Hope for over five minutes and finally drove the rest of the way along the sidewalk.

It was Officer Mathias who checked the limp and bloodied figures lying prostrate or half propped by the roadside and discovered that one person was missing. That person was Lawrence Pagels.

20

Max Haydn was used to being awakened in the middle of the night by Edgar Stassen. He'd originally thought that the mean bastard woke him up like that for reasons of personal antagonism but now he was not so sure. Stassen chose to disturb him at night not only when they had spent the day threatening each other with bodily harm but also when their relationship was going through a rare calm patch.

The same went for Ida Letherbridge. Stassen was no sexist as far as waking people up at night was concerned. He'd phoned Ida at two or three A.M. at the outset of the relationship when she was still Little Miss Dream Girl who could do no wrong, and he'd continued the practice when she'd descended to a little bossy rich kid, a disturbed bitch, a confused necromancer. After her rehabilitation, when Stassen became a slow convert to the Letherbridge school of thought, he continued to wake her up.

So Max read nothing into it when Stassen called him at 3:30 in the morning. It was only when Stassen announced that Lawrence Pagels had escaped that Max attempted to open his eyes.

"He's what?"

"He's escaped. The son-of-a-bitch escaped!"

Max lived in a studio apartment in a student block on Zelzah Boulevard. His room was uncarpeted and unfurnished apart from a bed which was an unholy mess of unwashed shirts and underwear, half-finished essays, dictionaries, and law reviews.

The news had the effect of galvanizing Max into uncharacteristic action. He sat on his bed for the next half hour saying "God Almighty" and "Jesus" repeatedly and assembled his clothes, books, and papers into neat piles around him. From out of the tangled mess he produced a photograph of Ida which he set up in a place of honor on top of the books.

———

Ida was in her parents' guesthouse, a small cottage hidden from the main house by a cluster of apple trees. Her law books and notes were arranged in stacks at the foot of her bed and a framed photograph of three men hung on the wall above her head. The three men were Edgar Stassen, Max Haydn, and Lawrence Pagels.

"If he's escaped," Ida told Stassen, "He'll go and get Daniel."

"He can't do that, they'll have police cars ten deep around the kid, they'll be coming out his ears."

Ida expressed her doubt that Lawrence Pagels would be deterred by that.

"He'd better be. If he's not he'll be on his way to Chino before you've cleaned your teeth."

Stassen called the Leutwilers and spoke to Don, who answered the phone on the first ring. He was still up, sitting in the den smoking a cigar after returning from the restaurant. He roared with laughter, a big belly laugh.

"You're kidding! That old guy. You've got to be kidding. Holy shit! Incredible. Well, you tell that old guy not to come here. We don't want any trouble."

"He ain't dressed for making social visits."

Another big belly laugh.

"Thanks for letting me know, Ed. I'll tell Sandy. You guys . . . you guys put on a show. You shook up the valley. You shook up the world. You got everyone going."

"Yeah. I guess we did."

———

Stassen went and stood outside his Winnebago. It was by now 3:55 A.M. There was a big, clear moon in the sky. A freight train went by, momentarily endless, an infinity of freight cars jangling and rattling, then it disappeared into the night, and never was.

Where was Pagels? Stassen had imagined many scenarios for Lawrence Pagels but not one of them had involved his escaping from custody. Men of that age did not escape. What did men of his age do? They rotted, Stassen supposed. Most men of his age did, in or out of jail. But he was not most men. Lawrence Pagels was an original.

But whichever way you looked at it, the old man's chances were not good. Where could he go?

At least the rain had stopped. A few hours ago the storm drains had been unable to cope with the sudden deluge and rivers of water swamped the Chatsworth streets. But now the storm was over, the air was losing its moisture, oil slicks were reforming on the road. Things were getting back to normal.

Stassen was tired. His mind was blanking out. By rights he should be back in Sacramento getting on with his life. There was no real reason for him to stay in this trailer on a burned-out lot in the San Fernando Valley. But he had put his life on hold. He'd been thinking about finding a beach to lie on; maybe he could try it again. No that wouldn't work, beaches made him restless. That's how the whole thing had started. He'd been on a beach when the idea came to look into an odd case he'd read about in the paper.

It was past four A.M. He couldn't go back to sleep. He decided to make a few more phone calls. He flipped through his address book for Mark Boyman's number.

———

Lawrence Pagels had lain prostrate by the side of his police guard while a woman in a long white dress held an umbrella over him. As the large, unwieldy umbrella waved unsteadily back and forth he would catch occasional glimpses of the sky. Even in its dark and stormy state it reminded him of the free life he once had and caused him to make an effort to sit up and look around him.

Immediately a solicitous man threw a tuxedo jacket round Pagels' shoulders. He was Wes Taylor, a wealthy real-estate dealer from Pacific Palisades, who felt no concern in giving away an expensive jacket. Not at that moment anyway: he had made full use of the lengthy intermissions during the evening at the opera to put away a considerable amount of brandy. Wes was a large man with a considerable girth and his jacket had been cut accordingly.

Investigators who reviewed mistakes made at the scene of the accident concluded that the size of the jacket played a vital part in the prisoner's escape. The voluminous jacket fell loosely round the convicted murderer's broad shoulders and concealed the fact that he was wearing handcuffs. When he staggered to his feet and wandered away, the woman holding the umbrella paid little attention, as she was more concerned about the bleeding and unconscious guard at her feet who seemed in greater need of her care. She was also distracted by the sirens of the approaching police cars and ambulances.

As she later protested, she was not a policeman, it was not her job "to hold the man by force."

Wrapped in his protective tuxedo jacket, Lawrence Pagels walked through the crowd. In general people were moving in the direction of the accident; Pagels was one of the few going away from it. He walked into the lower level of the Music Center complex and came to a door in the back wall of the Ahamanson Theatre. It was the stage door, momentarily left unmanned when the stage doorman had run out to take some towels to the accident victims. Pagels slipped through the door.

Once inside he was ignored by actors and stagehands, who were scurrying to gather first-aid boxes, blankets, and more umbrellas, which were rushed outside. Those who remained behind were either performers preparing to leave or stagehands involved in closing the theater down for the night. They paid no attention to a man in a tuxedo jacket wandering around. He was considered to be somebody's guest, a friend of an actor perhaps who was waiting for him to finish dressing. There were visitors there every night. It was always difficult to get past the stage door but once past, few questions were asked.

Pagels found a dark, empty dressing room and waited there until past midnight, when all the lights were out and the theater was deserted. Then he wandered from one dressing room to the next, his footsteps on the stone floor echoing around him dangerously until he realized he'd better take off his shoes. He rummaged through makeup boxes that looked like toolkits in the hope of finding a file, but the most he could come up with was a pair of nail scissors. They had little effect on the handcuffs. He attempted to smash one of the cuffs against a door handle, but this did nothing but cause pain.

Pausing for a while he drank an abandoned glass of mineral water and ate several Mother's Pride chocolate chip cookies. The meal seemed to give him the strength to continue.

It was then that he found the workshop with its complement of hacksaws and sharp chisels. It took less than ten minutes to file through the steel around his wrists.

In another of the dressing rooms he found a smart gray suit that fitted him, except at the waist where it gaped open. This was easily corrected with a belt. There was a good-quality striped shirt to go with it, too large around the neck but otherwise fine. The stylish gray shoes that completed the outfit were too small for Pagels so he was obliged to retain the worn dark brown pair he had worn in jail. The gentleman who emerged from the Ahamanson Theatre at one A.M. with a bundle under his arm bore no resemblance to the one who had gone in.

Pagels threw his prison uniform into a trash can and draped the tuxedo jacket over a bench. He headed toward the freeway just as the police driver taking him to Chino had done a few hours before.

The area was quiet now. There were still a few cars around but nothing like the chaos earlier. He did not stop to look at the scene of the accident, nor did he glance up when a police car cruised by. He moved in step with a small group of well-dressed laughing diners who were walking back to their car from a restaurant in Chinatown. Then he slipped past them and walked casually toward the Harbor freeway.

The storm was over. The black marble clouds that covered the night sky were gradually sliding away and the air was clean, washed free of smoke and grime. Downtown Los Angeles looked born again.

Pagels had been standing near the freeway entrance thumbing a lift for about twenty minutes when a white Cadillac limousine with dark windows swung over and stopped. The back window rolled down and a young man with tangled, bleached-blond hair leaned out.

"Where ya goin'?"

"Chatsworth."

The young man turned to the chauffeur. "Charlie d'ya know where Chatsworth is?"

There were giggles in the back of the car as the chauffeur looked at Pagels and then muttered to the passengers in the back.

The young man put his head out the window once more. "He says he's never heard of Chatsworth. Can you tell him how to get there."

Pagels obliged. "You go north on the Golden State and west on the 118. That's the Simi Valley Freeway."

"Great. We're goin' to Chatsworth."

The door opened and Pagels was ushered inside to join the young man and his companions, a man with dark hair tied back in a skinny ponytail, and two teenage girls who sat awestruck and giggling, clinging to each other rather than the young men.

Pagels assumed that the young men were some sort of celebrities since they had a limousine and what appeared to be two fans with them. The young men were called Tom and Rudi; the girls, who were not introduced, had apparently been selected at random to join them in their travels in the limousine. Pagels settled himself between the girls and the men like a chaperone.

"So where is this place? Is it like Oxnard? We were in Oxnard. Don't know why the hell we were in Oxnard." Rudi was slurring his words.

"It's in the valley." Pagels informed him politely.

"Down in the valley, valley so low . . ." Tom and Rudi crooned together and made the girls giggle some more.

"Are you a snake-oil salesman? That's why we stopped. I said to Tom we gotta stop because that guy looks like a snake-oil salesman."

"And," added Tom, the one with the ponytail, "we wanted to buy some snake oil." Giggles all round.

"Charlie doesn't like snake oil." Rudi indicated the chauffeur. "He's a whiskey and soda man with three children."

"Yeah, they asked him what he wanted and he said I'll have a whiskey and soda with three children."

Rudi grinned. "They asked me what I wanted and I said what you got?"

Charlie concentrated on finding the 118. It was his second day with the limousine company. The downtown freeways were a maze, one slip and it might take him twenty minutes trying to get back on course. And the 118 was completely foreign to him, right outside his territory. A few hours later when he was asked by police about the conversation in the car he could remember nothing. All he could tell them was that the hitchhiker had a fancy gray suit on that looked kind of old-fashioned, like a suit that the men wore when ladies had long dresses with hooped skirts.

When they were finally on the Simi Valley Freeway and passed a sign indicating they were in Chatsworth, Rudi got curious.

"What you gonna do in Chatsworth?"

"I'm going to fix up my motor home and then I'll pick up my grandson."

"What street are you on?" Charlie called out.

"Here. Stop here."

"Here?"

"Yes, right here. This will do fine."

"You mean just pull over?"

"Sure."

Charlie pulled the limousine over to the side of the freeway and stopped.

Lawrence Pagels stepped out, paused to look cautiously up towards the hills, then he turned and bowed. "Thanks very much. I really appreciate your kindness. Many many thanks."

"Forget it man. It's a big deal for us comin' to Chatsworth."

They watched as the man in the quaint gray suit started to walk up into the stark empty hills. He reached a summit, paused to look around once more and then climbed down the other side, disappearing from view.

In their intoxicated state, Rudi and Tom were unable to distinguish between a romantic notion and a stupid idea. The sight of Lawrence climbing up the mud-soaked hillside was incredibly tempting to them. It seemed to offer adventure.

"Come on! Let's go with him!"

Rudi and Tom started out after Pagels. They were unsteady on their feet and getting through the rough undergrowth and up a steep incline was close to impossible for them. They staggered and fell repeatedly, cursing and singing as they went.

The two girls watched fearfully for a few seconds and then, not wanting to be abandoned, set out after them. They were wearing spindly high heels that dug into the soft, rain-soaked earth, and mesh tights that ensnared them on tumbleweed and bushes. They toppled over every few steps and giggled hysterically together.

Charlie stayed in the car, got out a cigarette, and turned on the radio to drown out the odd sounds coming from the hills. He sat and waited.

Two policemen from Devonshire Division, Jerry Cook and Leonard Ortiz, were sitting in a squad car positioned close to the bushes alongside Lawrence Pagels' motor home. When they heard the hullabaloo they turned on their headlights in the direction of the noise and went to investigate. They saw two men coming down the hill toward them.

"Freeze! Police!"

When Rudi and Tom saw the headlights go on and heard the police screaming at them the muscle control in their legs went completely and they fell and rolled the rest of the way down the hill. This seemed to be like a form of assault. Rudi and Tom were a fraction of a second away from being blasted to pieces by two extremely nervous officers. The appearance of the two girls, who screamed and waved as they tottered precariously on the ridge above, saved their lives.

The officers found the two girls and their semicoherent boyfriends unable to explain why they had climbed up the hill toward Pagels' trailer. By some silent agreement not one of them mentioned that they had picked up a hitchhiker near the Music Center.

The girls acted in both a flirting and insolent manner as they made their way back to the freeway.

"Move it!" Ortiz nudged the girl forward.

"I can't walk in the mud. You don't prod me!"

It was not until the officers confronted the bored Charlie sitting yawning in the driver's seat that they were told about the hitchhiker who had climbed up the hill and disappeared from view some thirty minutes before.

Officers Ortiz and Cook raced back to their car at a speed that broke most records for running on mud-soaked hillsides. They had been away from their car for exactly fifteen minutes.

———

Lawrence Pagels had observed the police officers sitting in the patrol car next to his motor home. He had dropped down onto his stomach and crawled through the long ferns and waited. He had been prepared to lie there for a week if necessary, whatever it took until they went away. It took no time at all.

When the headlights were switched on and the officers moved up the hill toward the sound of raucous singing and laughter, Pagels ran to the police car. One of its front wheels was pressed against a cluster of small rocks piled one upon the other. Pagels removed the top two rocks and recovered a set of keys that lay in a hollowed-out stone.

He ran to the front of the motor home, lifted the hood, and connected the battery. Then he went round to the side, unlocked the door and slipped inside. He paused for a millisecond to look at Daniel's drawing on the wall, and inspect the tidy interior with its homemade wood paneling and counters, then he dropped to his knees and crawled toward the driver's seat. The cabin was not only illuminated by the headlights of the police car but also by a bright moon. Any movement past a window would have been clearly visible.

Outside he could hear the officers' voices shouting at the intruders. Then he heard the two girls screaming, then more shouts. Then the voices went away, up the hill, and over the other side. The voices gradually faded out.

Quickly he tried the key in the ignition. Nothing. He tried again. The battery was dead.

A few seconds later Pagels was moving furtively toward the police car, holding jumper cables. He lifted the hood, fitted the cables and then leaped inside the car, started the engine and moved it closer to the motor home. With the engine going he could no longer listen for the sound of the returning police officers. Consequently he began to move at a well nigh manic speed, like a pit-stop mechanic in the Indianapolis 500.

In no time he had the cables attached to his engine and when he turned on the ignition it coughed into action.

Officers Ortiz and Cook reached the second ridge a few seconds before 2:18 A.M. and looked down onto the grove of fan palms that encircled Pagels' home. They saw that their vehicle had been linked as though by an umbilical cord to the motor home and had given it life. Lawrence Pagels had his foot on the accelerator, listening to an increasingly healthy roar from his engine and was smiling with delight. The smile vanished when he looked up the hill.

In the thirty or so seconds that it took the two officers to slide down the muddy, precipitous slope toward him, Pagels jumped out of the motor home, hurled himself at the police car, pulled the key out of the ignition and threw it with massive force into the tangled shrubbery at the bottom of the hill. When the police engine stopped, Pagels' engine continued coughing once but not cutting off completely.

Pagels raced back to the motor home and made some desultory kicks at a pile of rocks around the front nearside wheel. The motor home was jacked up on rocks which were stacked around each wheel, lifting the front wheels a couple of inches off the ground. The rocks around the back wheels were buried in heaps of soil and debris, leaving the wheels resting on small hillocks. Pagels found he was unable to dislodge the rocks in the one second he allotted himself and left them, jumping back into the driver's seat without shutting the door.

As he stepped on the accelerator and raced the engine again, Cook and Ortiz reached the bottom of the hill and instead of running along a path chose a short cut, pushing their way through the bushes and long dry grass in a straight line toward the motor home.

Pagels put his vehicle into gear. The back wheels revolved uselessly for a couple of seconds then they gripped the soil and debris underneath and the motor home shuddered and jolted forward. The front wheels toppled off the rocks and crashed onto the ground; the vehicle rocked violently from side to side. The battery cables snapped away from the police car and with his hood still raised, the cables dangling, and the door flapping and banging, Pagels swung the vehicle round in the direction of the path.

By now Ortiz and Cook had reached the motor home but the door was facing away from them. Otherwise it might have been remotely possible for one of them to have hurled himself through the doorway into the cabin. Ortiz managed to jump onto the back bumper but as Pagels continued to swing around, the officer fell into the bushes and sprained his ankle.

Officer Cook fired four shots in the direction of the driver. One appeared either to hit Pagels or get close, the other three shots went over the top of the roof.

Pagels rattled over the bumpy track, and took a long, circuitous route to the freeway. There was no direct route for a motor home such as his. It could not go up and down the hills, it had to go round them and descend in a variety of S-shapes to the flat land below. Pagels crashed through a line of bushes and then drifted out into the sparse traffic that traveled the freeway in the early hours. He headed toward the Simi Valley and was not discovered by any of the police teams who combed the freeway for the rest of the night.

———

The escape caught the media by surprise. It had not been prepared for this.

A few minutes after hearing that Pagels was floating free on the California freeways, phones were ringing all over the state. Reporters, who had made the mistake of going to bed, hastily dragged on clothes and jumped into their cars. Farther afield, news teams who had arrived home on planes from Los Angeles a few weeks before began packing their bags and heading for the airports again.

Photographers and film crews converged on the bare patch of ground in Chatsworth where Pagels' motor home once stood. One of the first to arrive there was Leon Ferguson who stood on the side of a hill and greeted fellow reporters whom he had not seen for a few weeks. There was a slightly festive air about the proceedings.

The unfortunate police officers Cook and Ortiz spent the entire night giving statements and had to undergo some ridicule at being outfoxed by an old man.

———

The morning after Lawrence Pagels' escape, Sandy Leutwiler received a visit from Mrs. Joan Briese of the County Department of Social Services. Mrs. Briese had not heard the news and was disturbed when Sandy told her. She looked around nervously as though she half expected to see Lawrence Pagels jump out from behind a curtain.

"Where is Daniel now?"

"At school."

Daniel had gone back to school three weeks after the trial was over. By then the story was a dead issue and the child had been left in relative peace, with only the occasional snide remark from the other kids to torment him.

Now the whole thing had been stirred up again. Sandy had worried that reporters would follow him to school and she had walked him all the way into his classroom that morning.

"Will you meet him after school?"

"You better believe it."

Mrs. Briese advised Sandy that it was not only the media she should keep away from Daniel.

"His grandfather is a very confused man. He needs to be protected from that guy."

"I guess so. You try explaining that to Danny."

"How do you feel about your future with Daniel?"

"I've discussed it with Don and we'd like him to stay. We've even been thinking about adoption."

"How does Daniel feel about that?"

Sandy smiled.

"Daniel's getting used to us and we're getting used to him. It took a while. But he's a dreamer. Like he tells the kids at school that his grandpa's coming to get him."

Mrs. Briese looked around her again.

"He might come here."

"I doubt it. The police have been driving past here all morning."

As if on cue, a police car drove up and slowed down as it came into view through the window."

Mrs. Briese picked up her briefcase and shuffled through her papers. "I have a report here that a woman came up to our office who claims to be Daniel's mother."

"His mother!"

"Yes, but she had no proof. She filled out half a form and then she left. It says here she didn't look like the motherly type."

"Is she going to take Daniel back?"

"I don't see how she could." Mrs. Briese studied the report on her lap. "In any case, she's unmarried. She was living in a motel and now she's sleeping on someone's couch. That can't last forever. Where does she go after that? She said she has a temporary job as a waitress. She had a car and then sold it to pay for her room at the motel. Police records say she's been arrested twice for drug possession. If you want my opinion, Daniel can say good-bye to the Pagels family. The poor kid's got a bunch of really disturbed relatives."

————

When Lawrence Pagels had swung his battered motor home around onto the freeway, the jumper cables still dangling from his engine, he had headed west. But not for long. He pulled off at the next exit and drove up a narrow winding road to a partly constructed luxury estate where monster Gothic and mock Tudor palaces were towering up out of the naked earth. One or two of the houses had been completed and were already inhabited. Around them small, well-watered bushes and skinny, leafless trees sat in the soil, waiting to grow larger and conquer the vast acres of dirt.

A dog barked as the motor home clattered by. Pagels drove to the far side of the estate through a gathering of ancient oaks and onto a construction site where the skeleton of a small castle rose up out of a heap of timber and bricks. A four-car garage lay at the end of what would one day be a drive but was now a mud-soaked track. The main garage door was already in place, but the end section was gaping open. Pagels drove up the muddy track with some difficulty, his wheels turning uselessly at times, but eventually he was able to squeeze the vehicle through the opening and pull it behind the main garage door so it was hidden from view. By that time it was 2:50 A.M.

He wasted no time but set out immediately to investigate, going from one building site to the next. It was some time before he found what he was looking for. In fact at one point he paused and fell to his knees, his head sunk deep in his chest. When he did find what he needed he said a quiet "Thank you."

He had found several containers of off-white, weather-resistant paint, rollers, and brushes in a house that was in the process of being decorated. He took them back to his hiding place in the garage.

Pagels' motor home had spare planks of wood and pieces of plastic tacked all over its sides and roof; it looked like an old, broken-down shed on wheels. It seemed a miracle that this heap of driftwood could move. In fact its appearance was deceptive.

Many of the pieces of wood and plastic had been hammered into place by Pagels to give his home added protection from the fierce winds that blew through the Chatsworth hills. This was not to say that underneath that outer cover there was a streamlined, modern motor home, but it did have a conventional shape, and it was this that Pagels brought to light when he prized off the old timber and pulled away the sheets of plastic.

In a drawer, Pagels found some masking tape that he placed around the outer edges of all the windows. The bodywork was a mass of scratches and rust on a surface that was once a creamy yellow. This he covered completely with the dull white paint, giving it a fresh, clean coating that was not too bright or shiny. He applied a second coat and although he was not using the right paint it still gave the appearance of a reasonably professional piece of work.

By five A.M. Lawrence Pagels emerged from the garage and watched the first, faint morning light growing brighter behind the trees. Far in the distance he could hear the hum of the early commuters on the freeway. He took a deep breath of the morning air and stretched gratefully just as if he were a man on vacation testing the air before spending a day fishing.

After removing the license plates from his motor home, he started up his newborn vehicle, pulled out of the garage and drove down the hill toward Chatsworth. He turned onto the street where George Lejeune's vine-covered house was situated on a corner behind a fringe of silver birches and pine trees. A long wall backed up by a row of teetering Italian cypresses stretched along the side of the house, the backyard and the swimming pool, and ended with double gates. Pagels stopped here and went to examine the padlock on the gates.

A neighbor getting an early start backed out of his driveway and gave Pagels a searching glance, and a jogger stared at him as he shook the padlock. Pagels ignored them both and went back to the vehicle in search of a screwdriver. He returned and unscrewed the hasp on the gate and released the padlock. Within seconds he had opened the gate, slipped inside, and closed it behind him.

Beyond the gates was an uncovered trailer park where George kept the small camper he used for occasional weekend jaunts. Pagels crouched down and removed the license plates from George's vehicle. He replaced them with his own number plates, produced from a hiding place inside his jacket.

As he went back through the gates the lights went on in George's kitchen and his dog was let out into the backyard. The dog, a young German shepherd, dashed to the far end of the backyard and sniffed the fence round the trailer park. He found a loose board, pushed his head through, and came eye to eye with Lawrence Pagels, who was by now halfway out of the gate.

The dog let out a surprised yelp, followed by a joyful bark as he recognized the visitor. He began to whine and scratch as he made frantic attempts to squeeze his body through the small gap.

"Ssh!" Pagels held his finger to his lips, a sign the dog did not understand. He yelped and whined all the more.

When Pagels closed the gates behind him and began screwing the hasp back into place, the dog tried to jump over the fence, barking loudly. Disturbed by the noise, George emerged onto his patio to investigate.

Pagels climbed into his motor home and flicked on the ignition. After several attempts the engine had still not turned over, and it did not sputter into action until he released the brake and slid backward down the incline into the street. He was backing his vehicle around the corner when George put his head over the side of the wall and caught a glimpse of Pagels' retreating front wheels.

A time-and-motion study expert reviewing Pagels' actions after his escape from custody would have approved some of his efforts but criticized others. Stealing George Lejeune's license plates was dangerous and inefficient. He could have taken the license plates from one of the trucks left on the building site where he spent the night.

The logic behind taking George's plates was that George did not use his camper frequently, therefore Pagels' own license plates would not see the light of day for some time. Also George was a friend, or at least a good acquaintance, and might be less likely to be disturbed by this action. Pagels felt that if he was driven to steal, he should steal from someone he knew.

At 7:30 A.M. Pagels called the number shared by Jason and Gregory Leutwiler from a public phone on the corner of Balboa and Devonshire Boulevard. Jason Leutwiler answered and then handed the receiver to Daniel.

Jason, who made a conscious effort to ignore everything connected with Daniel, did not tell his parents about the phone call. When Sandy Leutwiler walked Daniel into his classroom later that morning, she was in blissful ignorance of the child's conversation with his grandfather.

At 9:30 A.M. Daniel excused himself from his classroom and then walked casually out of school. At 9:35 A.M. Lawrence Pagels drove past the school and picked Daniel up.

The child's disappearance was not reported by the school until ten A.M., by which time Lawrence and Daniel Pagels were in an antique store on Sherman Way near Canoga Avenue, selling several items of old Indian jewelry and two Indian rings. Lawrence Pagels insisted on cash rather than a check and he accompanied the antique dealer to the bank, where he was paid $950. They walked to the bank and the antique dealer did not see Pagels' motor home.

The bank teller who saw reports of Pagels' escape on TV later told the police that Lawrence Pagels appeared calm and was dressed in a smart gray suit and clean white shirt. She observed him shake hands with the antique dealer who was grinning broadly. The dealer, on the other hand, told the police that he could remember little about Pagels' appearance. This may have been because he had made an excellent purchase and was in fear of having it taken from him. His haul consisted of several intricate pieces crafted by Zuñi Indians as well as two Navaho rugs, worn but beautiful. He sold them for five times what he paid.

At 10:15 A.M. someone from the District Attorney's Office called Daniel's school and advised them to keep a close watch on Daniel Pagels. The caller was forty-five minutes too late.

———

Max Haydn and Joe DeRosa arrived within minutes of each other at Rhonda's apartment on Sherman Way. DeRosa was running up the stairs to the main door of the building when Max drove past on the other side of the street and made a sudden U-turn.

Max jumped out of his car and ran toward DeRosa.

"What are you doing here?" Max shouted.

DeRosa did not explain but pushed the door open and ran inside the building.

By the time Max was in the lobby, DeRosa was halfway up the stairs to the second floor. By the third floor Max had caught up and the two men emerged on to the landing together.

They raced toward a door at the end of the corridor. While Max rang the bell, DeRosa slapped the door with his fist.

A girl in a white terrycloth bathrobe came to the door. DeRosa recognized her as one of Rhonda's co-workers from Le Bon Café.

"Is Rhonda here?"

"Yes," said the girl. She put her head back inside the door and called, "Rhonda."

DeRosa pushed his way past the girl and Max followed him. Rhonda was pulling a blanket off the couch where she had slept. The radio and the television were both tuned to news stations, loudly competing with each other.

"Where is he?" asked DeRosa. He was panting from the exertion on the stairs.

"I don't know. I just heard it on the radio." Rhonda threw the blanket back on the couch as though her arms were too weak to hold it.

"If he tries to contact you," said Max, "Tell him to call Stassen."

"How did he do it? Did he get any help?" DeRosa was walking round the room looking through doorways.

"It was an accident, wasn't it?" She looked thoroughly shaken.

"Leave her alone," the other girl said. "She's really upset."

DeRosa went off to search the bathroom and the bedroom. It was a small apartment and it took very little time.

"He might get killed," Rhonda said to Max. "Why did he do it? Why did he drag Danny into it?"

Max was looking curiously after DeRosa. "What's he doing here?"

DeRosa, no smile in his eyes, came back into the room.

Rhonda ran her fingers through her uncombed hair. "Lawrence doesn't believe in accidents. I always used to say to him, how can you not believe in accidents? He thinks there's no such thing as fate or chance."

"Yeah," said Max. "That sounds like him all right."

He walked to the door. "Well, I guess there's nothing I can do. Sorry to burst in on you like this. Call me if you hear from him or if you want some help. O.K.?"

DeRosa followed him to the door and then stopped. He looked over his shoulder to see if Max was out of hearing.

"She's back. My wife's back."

Rhonda looked at him blankly. "Uh huh."

"She came back last night."

"Tell her I said hi."

DeRosa shuffled uncomfortably. "I had to give out your address."

"To her?"

He smiled awkwardly. "I'm sorry, Rhonda."

She said nothing.

"Well," he clapped his hands together. "Gotta go."

As Max and DeRosa made their separate departures the sound of approaching police cars, sirens blaring, grew louder.

Before the first police officer was in the building, Rhonda had gone out the back way.

21

John Starbeck had questioned Lawrence Pagels when he was first taken into custody at the Devonshire Division Police Station. A former pro football player who had been with the Los Angeles Police Department for fifteen years, Starbeck saw himself as a paid witness to the garbage element of life, and his fellow police officers, be they saints or sinners, as the only human beings he could trust.

He had followed the Pagels trial with half an eye and had slotted it away as another example of the perfidy of ambitious attorneys. He saw it as a flagrant waste of public money, a science-fiction sideshow put on solely for the benefit of attorneys and of no use to the defendant, the jury, or the cause of justice. As far as he was concerned, attorneys would wear pink tutus and roller skates into court if it would get them some attention.

Pagels' escape was a major embarrassment for the L.A.P.D. lessened only by the hope that the old man would be picked up within hours. Instead, with every hour that he remained at large it was growing into an even larger embarrassment.

During the latter days of the trial the old man's face had been seen on television across the United States. There weren't many members of the public who didn't know what he looked like, and who didn't have a pretty good idea of what the old motor home covered in decaying panels looked like. So there was no reason why the guy hadn't been picked up five minutes after he ran off.

In John Starbeck's opinion there was no way the guy would still be driving that battered old vehicle. It'd be like standing under a spotlight. But, he reasoned, once you discounted the motor home you still had an old man with a small boy. If he was dumb enough to pick up the kid then he'd have to resign himself to a short vacation from jail. The police may have slipped up but they weren't going to make the same mistake twice. That dumb old Indian had had it.

Unless he was being hidden by someone. There was a growing number of people joining the "Pagels Is Innocent" campaign, a growing number of loonies and weirdos as far as Starbeck was concerned. One of them could be hiding Pagels, thinking himself a big shot because he was helping the cause.

What amazed Starbeck was the jury being out so long. It was one of the reasons that all these loonies had come out of the woodwork and found themselves a movement to attach themselves to. There was a certain element in Los Angeles that seemed to have nothing to do but support weirdo causes—your liberal, astrology, homosexual, health-food, ecology nuts. He had nothing against them personally; he believed in free speech, but it got him in the gut when these people interfered in police work, in bringing a murderer to justice. It made him want to puke.

What was the point of policemen risking their lives to get evil men locked up if these sickos, and he included the attorneys here, did everything they could to get them out of jail so they could be a threat to society all over again.

If Lawrence Pagels was looking for publicity then he certainly knew how to go about it. Apparently he was the one who set the attorney up in the first place. Acting like a dumb old man, then getting a top attorney to defend him for nothing, and getting him to tap dance in court like no other attorney had done in LA legal history. And then when he'd got himself convicted and there wasn't one reporter left hanging outside Men's Central, then he staged an escape in a thunderstorm and got himself on the front pages again.

Starbeck had noticed that about a lot of dumb people, no matter how lacking they were in the brain department, they often had a skill close to genius for looking after number one.

Pagels had been on the TV national evening news, all three channels, for the last two nights and some idiot rock star was singing a song about him. Get the guy locked up again and all this malarkey would stop in an instant. Starbeck knew the public, they were very fickle.

The tide was about to turn. There wasn't a policeman in the country who wouldn't like to gain a little extra kudos by capturing Lawrence Pagels.

———

Daniel was disappointed by the appearance of the motor home. He didn't comment on it in the first joy of seeing his grandfather but later, as they drove south on Route 5, he spoke up.

"It doesn't look like itself anymore, Grandpa."

"Its outside's of no account. We don't get attached to outsides that are shiny and new and we don't get attached if they're beaten up and old."

"It was like a pagoda. It was all layers."

"That may be so, but we don't get attached to it. It's only a place to live."

"The Leutwilers are attached to everything. They love their things so much, Grandpa."

"We won't hold that against them."

They stopped at a gas station in Anaheim where Lawrence made another phone call. Daniel watched him as he spoke earnestly and at some length.

Back on the freeway, deliberately driving at average speed to avoid drawing attention, his grandfather warned him.

"They'll be after us, Danny."

"I know."

"If we get caught I want you to go on ahead to Harry Buck's."

"O.K."

"Do you want me to tell you how to get there?"

"Sure."

"He has a real small place about two hundred miles south of the border. He has horses and some vegetables. You'll like it. I'll draw you a real good map and you see that drawer there, there's a photo of his place. Real Mexican-looking place. Long dirt track leading up to it. You study that photo real well. His dog's called Holly. You'll like Holly. Last time I went down to see Harry was before you were born."

Lawrence Pagels had few living relatives apart from Rhonda and Daniel; so in his time of need he was turning to Harry Buck. Harry had been a partner in a short-lived gardening business in the fifties. In 1961 Buck had gone off to Mexico, preferring to work for himself rather than others.

"You turn up that dirt track. Holly'll come up making a noise. If Harry doesn't come out right away you knock hard on the door. Say your grandpa's been held up but he'll be there soon. They're not going to keep me in jail anymore because I don't like it."

"Why did it take you so long, Grandpa?"

"Because I thought I could rely on the law. But I guess you learn that there's no such thing as law where human beings are concerned. There's a bunch of opinions. And these opinions didn't swing my way."

"I won't let them take you away again. I want to stay with you. I'm not going back to the Leutwilers."

"The Leutwilers were doing their best."

"They have a piano. I played it a bit."

"You played the piano? . . . Maybe one day we'll get a piano. It'd be nice to have some music around the place."

"They say a lot of bad stuff."

"Like what?"

"Mr. Leutwiler calls Jason a schmuck and Sheila says that me and Jason are retarded and Mrs. Leutwiler says that Mr. Leutwiler is a fuck up."

"She said that?"

"Yes."

"Why?"

"I don't know exactly. I think it was something he was supposed to do, something he forgot."

"Uh huh."

"And Jason says I'm dumb all the time."

"You're not dumb."

"He says I'm dumb because I don't know much."

"Like what?"

"I dunno."

"You don't even know that, huh?"

"Did you know there are eighty new stores at the Northridge Mall and there's a new Robinsons and a new May Company. It's a big deal."

"No, I didn't."

"Now you know."

"Thanks for the information."

"I told Mrs. Leutwiler—"

"You call her Mrs. Leutwiler?"

"She asks me to call her Mom or Sandy, but I don't call her anything."

"Just, hey you?"

"No, I'm very polite."

"I bet you are, Danny."

"I told Mrs. Leutwiler that you wouldn't stay in jail and she thought I was crazy and Jason said I was mentally retarded."

"Mentally retarded again. They throw that term around a lot."

"Uh huh. They say I'm slow. I guess me and you, Grandpa, we're not too smart."

"No, we're not too smart. I didn't know about the Northridge Mall. But I knew I would get out of jail and so did you. And we were right. So we're not dumb."

"No I guess not. We may be dumb but we're not too dumb."

"The voice that speaks to you and me, Danny, is the one that speaks to all men, but they don't listen."

"No, Grandpa. They're too busy. The Leutwilers are real busy. They're rushing around all day long and when they're not rushing they watch TV. Are they in trouble?"

"No, they're O.K. The minute they stop running they'll hear it just like we do. We don't have exclusive rights, you know, Danny."

"Why didn't you bring the pickup? This old motor home rattles."

"Because it's in some police garage in Van Nuys."

"They should give it back to you. It doesn't belong to them."

"It'd be real hard to get them around to that way of thinking right now, Danny."

They continued south on Route 5, the Santa Ana Freeway, moving beyond dusty commercial towns to perfect, crystal-clean coastal communities of San Diego County. Just before the county line at San Clemente they stopped at a supermarket to buy supplies.

As they pushed their loaded shopping cart across the parking lot an elderly couple watched them closely and whispered to each other. Lawrence said, "Hi, how you doing?" as he went by and they smiled back awkwardly, pretending not to notice as the two Pagels continued on their way to the back of the supermarket. They waited there for some time until the old couple had gone. Then Lawrence made a quick dash to the motor home and drove it behind the store, where they loaded up quickly and secretively in the obscurity of trash bins and delivery trucks.

Back on the highway Daniel reached into their purchases and brought out the floppy white hats and sunglasses they'd bought which were to serve as flimsy disguises. He busied himself with a black crayon, drawing dark eyebrows and an ever-thickening black mustache, which he was ordered to wash off.

"Will we get caught, Grandpa?"

"Let's put it this way. They won't catch us like they caught us before. When they come next time we'll be ready for them."

———

Within hours of the word that Pagels had escaped, Pagels-spotting became a national preoccupation. He was sighted in most states: in New York three people saw him go into an X-rated movie theater on Forty-second Street; a logger saw him in a canoe in Oregon; he was even seen pushing a wheelbarrow in a village in the Dordogne, France, in a café in Bogner Regis on the south coast of England, and driving a truck through downtown Sydney, Australia.

A sighting by an elderly couple, Jim and Dora Wiley, in San Clemente was taken seriously: at least they offered a correct description of the man and the boy. Jim and Dora, who lived in Pasadena, were visiting their son in San Clemente when they noticed a man and a small boy who looked like Lawrence and Daniel Pagels. They did not see what kind of vehicle the two were using but did confirm that there was no battered motor home covered in weather-worn slats of wood anywhere in the supermarket parking lot or vicinity.

Orange County and San Diego County sheriffs departments immediately sent out patrols on Interstate 5. San Clemente was soon awash with police; John Starbeck was sent along with another detective from L.A.P.D. to search the San Clemente parking lot, by now a pointless exercise.

It was not too difficult to work out that Pagels was heading for Mexico down the I–5. The challenge was not only to apprehend him before he crossed the border but also before he took fright at the large posse of pursuers and headed inland toward the desert.

———

A number of reporters turned up on the doorstep of Stassen's Winnebago looking for information about Pagels' whereabouts. They pushed their way in, sat down, and helped themselves to coffee.

Stassen assured them he hadn't a clue.

"Why are you still here?" one reporter asked suspiciously. "Isn't your office in Sacramento?"

It was a sensitive point. Stassen was annoyed. "Sure, but I'm hanging out here to help the old guy with his getaway. We're heading out to Las Vegas as soon as you assholes clear off."

"Come on. Didn't he tell you he was planning to do this?"

"No he did not. He had no idea the driver was going to take an alternative route. He had no idea it would rain. He had no idea an RTD bus would come along at that moment. He had no idea someone would put a tuxedo jacket round his shoulders. It was a surprise."

"Will he contact you?"

"Not if he's smart."

"Did you know he was going to pick up Daniel?"

"No."

"Do you think it's right for him to involve the child in this?"

"It's his grandson."

"What do you think of his chances? Do you think he'll get caught?"

"Your guess is as good as mine."

———

After San Clemente they drove along the freeway and were beguiled by the shimmering vision of the Gulf of Santa Catalina and the Pacific Ocean, a rippling blue-gray satin quilt dropping from the sky.

Immaculate town houses, perfect cardboard cutouts sitting on the hills, gave way to the bleak desolation of the San Onofre nuclear plant and its multimillion-dollar sea-front location. The great bulbous dome squatted like an ugly bullfrog overlooking its beautiful captive, the treasured California shoreline.

No homeowner had sunk his life savings into building in the shadow of this giant nuclear generator. No developer had cut back the rough grasses on the hills around this nuclear plant. Like a leper it was free from companions.

It was at this spot that twenty-two-year-old Robert Jeffries, a rookie with six months experience in the San Diego County Police Department, and John Harter, his thirty-eight-year-old senior partner, began trailing the freshly painted cream-white motor home coming from the direction of San Clemente.

It was a hunch on Bob Jeffries' part. He was looking out for any vehicle with a school-age child in it, figuring that it was a school day and most kids would be in class.

He was alerted by a small face that looked through the curtains on the back window of the motor home and then ducked down when it saw the sheriff's car. The face was of a small boy somewhere between six and nine years old.

John Harter didn't read too much into that but he didn't want to squelch a rookie so they checked out the license plates and discovered they belonged to a George Lejeune of Chatsworth. Further checks revealed that the motor home ahead of them conformed in make and size to the one belonging to Lawrence Pagels, although its surface appearance was different. And the driver answered the description of the escaped, convicted murderer who had slipped out of police custody the night before.

By the time the two Pagels reached Oceanside, police vehicles were converging from the north and south in a pincer movement on the shiny, freshly painted trailer.

Lawrence Pagels could see four police cars heading north in his direction on the other side of the freeway.

"You see those guys, Danny. They're getting off at the next exit and they're going to turn around and follow us. There's already one police car about a hundred yards back. It's been following us for several miles. That's five police cars all trying to catch us."

"That's a lot of policemen, Grandpa."

What they didn't see were four more cars from the San Diego Sheriff's Department forming a corps de ballet in a steady procession behind them. They had not yet cleared a bend in the freeway and come into view.

"I've seen car chases on TV." Danny peered through the window and assessed the situation.

"Car chases?" Lawrence was alarmed. "You want me to get involved in a car chase with five police cars?"

"Nine. There are nine."

The other five cars had loomed into view.

"You'd better do something fast, Grandpa."

"O.K., Danny, we're gonna bail out."

"Now?"

"No. I'm going to pull off and we'll run. How close are they?"

"Not too close. Not as close as they get on TV."

"Good. That's good."

"Will you get into trouble for this, Grandpa?"

"No. They haven't told me to stop so I'm not doing anything wrong."

"But you stole George's license plates."

"I gave him ours in exchange."

"So will they take our motor home? Like if we leave it, they might take it away for good."

"Son, we're gonna have to say good-bye to this vehicle. Don't worry about it."

They were now close to an offramp leading to Oceanside. Pagels signaled his plan to turn off and then headed toward Oceanside at an unhurried pace. He ignored the right turn that led into Camp Pendleton, and took the curving road that led into the Oceanside marina. When he saw the bobbing rows of yachts and cabin cruisers, he took off "like a mad rhino" as Bob Jeffries later described it to a reporter from the *San Diego Union*.

The posse of police cars swung off the freeway, sirens blaring, and pursued Pagels along the harbor road. Pagels had a sufficient start on them to be able to pull into the marina parking lot and park his vehicle quite tidily at the far end before the police came through the entrance.

"Let's go, Danny."

"What about your books?"

"Leave them. Let's go."

"The police won't throw them away?"

"No. Let's go."

The size of the motor home was a plus factor. It obscured their exit and the police, guns drawn, were surrounding it and sidling cautiously toward the door for a good minute and a half before they realized it was empty.

By the time it had been ascertained that neither Pagels was in, under, or behind any vehicle in the parking lot, the two Pagels had blended into the tourists at the harbor edge and were standing among a group of men and small boys who were dangling fishing rods into the water. This temporary camouflage served them reasonably well while Lawrence looked around for a safer situation, as more police sirens wailed and more policemen swarmed up and down the harbor road.

Lawrence could see that the harbor was mercifully provided with row upon row of boats, all white with splashes of bright royal blue, many of them providing a possible hiding place for an escaped felon such as himself. They also provided the police with an almost innumerable supply of places to investigate. But it was clear, if he and Daniel hid in one of these boats, tethered and vulnerable, they would be found in due course. No, he would not choose one of them.

To his left a fisherman sat half hidden by the pile of nets he was mending. He looked oddly antique in contrast with the people around him in their crisp, sporty beach clothes. Lawrence watched as the fisherman gathered the nets into a neat pile and then went off in the direction of the parking lot where two police officers questioned him briefly.

"Danny, see that big pile of fishing net?"

"Yes."

"I'm going to pick it up and walk around the harbor, that way."

He pointed in the direction away from the parking lot filled with police.

"O.K."

"You grab a piece of the net and we'll try to look like fishermen."

Lawrence moved over to the fishing net and lifted it high onto his shoulder. Much of it dropped around his feet.

"Grab it, Danny. Pick it all up and carry it on your shoulder. Hide your face just like I'm doing."

Daniel picked up as much as he could and followed his grandfather.

They walked in brisk procession around the curve of the harbor, past elegant gift shops and ritzy T-shirt boutiques until they came out onto the coast road.

On the other side of the road, winter swimmers and sunbathers dotted the beach. About one hundred yards up the road, three carloads of police officers were emptying on to the coast road. In the other direction another police car had come to a halt by a boat trailer park.

"Just keep walking, Danny."

"Which way?"

"That way."

They headed toward the boat trailer park and inevitably closer to the police car.

"Hide your face, Danny." Pagels voice was muffled under the net.

"I'm hiding my face!"

They were about ten yards from the two police officers. The large, dark fishing net hung over their heads like a thick wedding veil. The officers watched them go by but showed no real interest, apparently assuming they were two fishermen.

"Go up that ladder, Grandpa."

"Where?"

"There."

Through the shroud of net Daniel pointed to a cabin cruiser lodged high up on a boat trailer.

"There's no ladder."

"There's a place for our feet."

On the side of the cabin cruiser were footholds and a handrail.

"O.K., let's look like we know what we're doing."

Lawrence moved to the side of the cabin cruiser that was hidden from police view. He dropped the net to the floor and looked up at the boat.

"Danny, do you think it just arrived or is it just going?"

"Why don't you ask someone?" Daniel glanced around for a helpful face.

"I can't ask someone."

"I'll ask."

"No, you can't ask either."

Lawrence lifted Daniel onto the metal frame of the boat trailer and then pulled himself up after him.

"I hope it goes on the ocean, don't you, Grandpa. Wouldn't that be great!"

"Anything as long as it doesn't stay here—Come here, Danny. I'll give you a leg up. Act like it's your boat."

Lawrence lifted the boy up onto the trailer and then hauled himself up after him. Standing gingerly on the steel frame of the trailer, they edged their way round to the handrail and footholds which were in full view of the police officers.

"Up you go, Danny. Jump casually onto the deck. Whatever you do, don't duck."

With studied casualness Daniel languidly pulled himself up and stopped to admire the view of the harbor, alive, as it was, with the drama of police presence.

"Don't overdo it. Hurry up!"

Daniel jumped down onto the deck. Lawrence began to climb up after him.

"Grandpa, you left the nets down there. Will the man be able to find them? He can't go fishing without those nets."

"Yes, I'm sure a police officer will see them or someone will, and he'll get them back."

"We didn't steal them, did we, Grandpa?"

"We inconvenienced him. There's no getting around that."

Two children, a boy and a girl, roughly Daniel's age, stopped to observe Lawrence's ascent into the boat, but they were distracted by the sound of a police helicopter that was descending over the harbor. Forgetting the Pagels, the children craned their necks upward to watch its circular motion.

Lawrence used the moment to take Daniel's arm, lead him across the deck, down the steps to the cabin below and out of sight.

It was 2:05. They remained undisturbed in the cabin cruiser until 3:20 P.M. at which time the owner Frank La Firenze returned.

The Pagels could hear him complaining loudly to a fellow boat owner about the steepness of the launching dock.

"My father lost a motor home in the water last week. Backed down there and his brakes wouldn't hold."

"Yeah, it took a real asshole to build that."

La Firenze's boat trailer was adjoined to a pickup truck. The Pagels heard him throwing things into the truck, then they heard him start the engine and they felt the boat trailer shudder forward.

"We're going somewhere, Danny."

Within minutes La Firenze and his cabin cruiser were heading inland along Route 76 toward San Luis Rey. There he stopped briefly to fix a loose coupling on his tow bar and moved on toward Bonsall.

The first stretch of the journey led through hot, airless country, many traffic lights. Construction sites abounded: the developers were moving in from the coast.

As the trailer headed up to a higher elevation the buildings thinned out. Through Bonsall and over the I–15 freeway he passed Lancaster Mountain and the Pala Indian Reservation, a bleak area that offered no sights of an Indian village. Giant cactuses grew by the roadside, rocky hills, bare earth, palms, and dry creeks.

About thirty miles farther inland they approached Pauma Valley, signs of humanity increased. They passed orchard upon orchard of trees heavy with ripening oranges. Neat farms hemmed by white picket fences and beyond them, on either side, big hills or small mountains. They came to the heart of Pauma Valley, a post office, a real-estate office, a Chevron gas station. Next to it was Melba's Market and Peg Henry's restaurant and beyond that nothing but more road and lots of country.

La Firenze stopped at the gas station and filled up.

"What's he doing now, Grandpa?"

"He's gone over to the market. Come on, Danny!"

Frank La Firenze was coming out of the market with a can of 7-Up and a pack of cigarettes when he saw a man and a small boy climbing down from his cabin cruiser. The boy jumped down and the man, athletic for his age, jumped down after him. Then they walked slowly down the road in the direction they had just come. They did not pick up their pace until Frank La Firenze yelled, "Hey you!"

In his report to the police La Firenze stated that the man and boy ran off the road and headed somewhere up a track behind the post office. It may have taken them in the direction of a church that was in the area but he could not say for sure.

The Mexicans who were sitting on the porch outside Melba's Market rose nervously to their feet when a stream of police vehicles descended upon Pauma Valley. A group of locals sipping coffee in Peg Henry's restaurant came to the door and stared as their quiet watering hole was invaded by every type of law-enforcement officer including a SWAT team carrying high-powered rifles.

The officers made jokes about the surrounding reservation being "a brier patch for that old Indian." They spat on the road, talked incessantly into their radios, and crunched soda cans.

John Starbeck, tired from his 130-mile trek down the Santa Ana Freeway from Chatsworth, and Bob Jeffries of the San Diego Police Department were among the many who hung around the Chevron gas station in Pauma Valley that late afternoon. They were privileged to witness the sun gently fall behind Weaver Mountain but neither of them gave it a second's glance. They cleaned out the soft drinks at Melba's Market, studied maps of the area that showed a patchwork of Indian reservations to the north, south, and east, and debated how much of an Indian remained inside Lawrence Pagels.

22

Edgar Stassen met Ida and Max at Carrow's Coffee Shop on Devonshire just after midnight.

"I'm going down to Pauma Valley tonight," Stassen announced.

There was a silence. Almost an embarrassed one.

Ida spoke first. "I don't think I can come."

"I'm not asking you to come." Stassen was hostile, defensive.

Max grinned. "Who would have thought that old guy could pull off a stunt like this?"

Stassen looked gloomy. "Yeah."

There was another silence, a silence that said the two students wanted to distance themselves from the Pagels' case, the one reluctantly, the other gratefully, glad to get out of the whole mess.

Stassen's face had not relaxed after a few weeks of rest. It had dropped permanently into a set mold of lines and sags, all of them pointing downward. He stared out of the window at the cars making midnight journeys along Devonshire.

Ida touched his hand. "There's nothing you could have done. You did everything in the world you could do."

Max looked at them curiously. It always amazed him that Ida seemed to know what Stassen was thinking. If he made a stab at guessing what was on the guy's mind he was wrong ninety-nine percent of the time. Max's success in life, if there was to be any, would not be based on intuitive leaps.

If the purpose of the meeting was not to be for inviting them on a jaunt to Pauma Valley and for further analysis of the Lawrence Pagels' mystery then it would be a wake for their dead defense, a ritual cup of coffee in Stassen's local eatery, a last good-bye. Max whispered to Ida that he was surprised the old bastard didn't bring out commemorative medals.

"What are you going to do in Pauma Valley? He's probably hitched a ride to El Paso by now." A crass Haydn question.

"I'm gonna see for myself. I owe it to the guy."

"You don't owe him anything. Why don't you just admit you're going because you . . ." Max stopped and winced.

Stassen smiled for the first time. "I didn't know people really did that. She kicked you under the table. That's great!"

"There's nothing like a little pain to cheer you up."

"Your pain, Haydn. Your pain cheers me up."

"Anyway. Don't ask me to come. I'm writing papers all weekend."

They talked again about Lawrence Pagels' chances and what future lay ahead for Daniel. The discussion was careful, restrained, and exhausted. There was no more to be said about Lawrence Pagels.

And then Max was the first to get up and bring it to an end.

They went out into the cool air of the parking lot where they made weak promises to keep in touch.

"I can't say I like you any better," Stassen told Max. "You're an ugly son-of-a-bitch."

Max retaliated. "Let the guy go, Stassen. You did your best. It's dumb to go chasing after him."

"He's right," Ida added. "It's the first time he's ever been right. Give him credit for that."

Stassen studied their youthful, unlined faces. "That's what I get for trying to economize and not employing professionals. I get two punk college kids."

Ida and Max watched the slumped shoulders of their former employer as he walked away across the parking lot.

"Ida, did he believe any of that stuff he said in court?"

"You were there. You were in it. You were part of all the discussions."

"So he didn't believe it?"

"No."

"He didn't believe it?"

"No. He didn't believe it. He was just saying it . . . to begin with anyway."

"To begin with? What do you mean, to begin with?"

"Just what I said. To begin with."

"And what about you?"

"Me?"

"Yes. What about you? You were the one who talked him into it."

"No I wasn't. My God."

"Now, come on, Ida."

"I just told him what Pagels had been telling him for weeks, that's all. Nobody would listen to what Pagels was saying."

"Then did you believe it?"

Ida sighed. She looked up at the brightly lit Carrow's sign and the equally bright moon beyond it.

"My feelings about it are . . . that I do and I don't believe it. The jury didn't believe it, so now no one believes it. All those people who were getting interested in the idea, all those phone calls we used to get . . . they're all gone. It's yesterday's news. I believe that it never was true for me or you but I believe it is true anyway. I want it to be true."

"You were just wishing then?"

"Kind of."

"Because you had me fooled. I was thinking on some days you looked like somebody who'd got religion or something. You looked like you were really gung ho."

"Did I?"

"And how about Pagels? Does he believe it?"

"I don't know, Max. You were there. You heard him."

"Sure I heard him. He said he believed it. He said it. But what did you really think about that? You always know what people are thinking. You must have known if he was telling the truth."

"No. I took him at face value. He said he wasn't lying. I believed him."

"If you believe Pagels then you must believe the whole thing."

"I didn't say that. I believe Pagels believes it."

"Then you must think he's deluded."

"Haven't we had this discussion before?"

"Yeah, we had it every morning for a year but I never got a satisfactory answer. To me the whole thing was like . . . well, you were like one of those ladies on a rock luring sailors to their death. And Stassen was the poor sucker. And I just kinda watched it. I couldn't believe what was going on. And now look at him. He looks broken. He can't face going back to Sacramento and he's going off to chase Pagels across the desert."

Ida shrugged. "So . . . that's how it looks to you."

"You must realize you have certain sirenlike abilities. You can talk anybody into anything and you don't even look like you're doing it."

"I do not."

"You're going to make one hell of an attorney. You'll seduce juries . . ."

"You're just saying that because you refuse to wrap your mind around anything to do with Pagels' defense. It was too weird for you. You didn't want to make that leap. I'm no siren. Geez, what a dumb remark."

"O.K., O.K., O.K. I apologize."

He walked her over to her Mustang, an inevitably sleeker, more costly automobile than his.

"This is it, I guess." Max came the nearest he would ever come to being shy and awkward. "You don't want to see me anymore because I'm too short and ugly."

Ida studied him and added before jumping into the driver's seat. "You're short. But you're not so ugly."

"I'm not asking for a romance or anything . . ."

"No. You're too short for a romance."

Ida had started her engine and was backing out of the parking lot when Max ran after her and hammered his fist on her window. She rolled it down.

"What d'you say? Shall we go to Pauma Valley?"

Within the hour Edgar Stassen, Ida Letherbridge, and Max Haydn had set out together in the Winnebago. It took them two hours and twenty-five minutes to reach Pauma Valley. They arrived there at 4:25 A.M., a short time before dawn.

————

At one A.M. Rhonda phoned her friend DeRosa to ask for a ride to Pauma Valley.

Mrs. DeRosa answered the phone and handed it immediately

to her husband. DeRosa was self-conscious and monosyllabic. He indicated that he was unable to help.

At 1:15 A.M. Rhonda left the Sherman Way apartment, went to the corner, and thumbed a lift.

By ignorance or the grace of God she not only made her way unharmed down to Oceanside, but she made the journey in two hours and fifteen minutes.

The first car to pick her up was driven by Angie Brownlow, a mother of five from Woodland Hills. She took Rhonda as far as the I–5 freeway where she was soon picked up by Ron Tunick, a truck driver hauling a consignment of refrigerated dairy products down to San Diego. He dropped Rhonda off at Oceanside where she proceeded to walk inland along Highway 76.

She was a conspicuous sight with her white-blond flossy hair, pale pink blouse, and denims. A San Diego police officer stopped his vehicle and took her to her destination where she was welcomed by all the law-enforcement officers hanging out at the Chevron gas station in Pauma Valley.

———

After the sun went down it was very dark in Pauma Valley. Lawrence and Daniel could see shadows and shapes and hear the familiar sound of police helicopters overhead and a new sound, the barking of dogs on the lookout for fugitives.

Lawrence and Daniel ran together through black citrus groves, ate oranges to give them strength, and then ran up a steep hill that seemed, according to Daniel, to go up miles into the sky. They ran in spurts, rested a while, and then ran again. By midnight they were on top of the hill that looked down on Pauma Valley, now faintly lit by stars and the headlights of the police cars gathering around the Chevron station. The lights grew brighter with the arrival of two television news crews.

"I'm going to take a little nap, Grandpa."

Lawrence was about to say no and then changed his mind.

"O.K., son. Now remember what I said. If we get caught I want you to go on to Harry Buck's. He's expecting you."

"I won't leave you."

"You won't have to for long. I'll come and get you real quick. They're not going to put me away this time."

"O.K., Grandpa."

Daniel lay down by a lone creosote bush that lay isolated in a large bare patch of dusty hillside, while Lawrence sat and watched. The flashing lights below bobbed this way and that, crossing one another, and making intricate patterns in the deep black darkness.

"You know, Danny, people say everything has to have a beginning and an end. They say you've got birth and death, a start and a finish. They say that because they like things in neat little packages. They say the finish is there because of the start but they don't know how the start got there. And if you tell them the start and the finish are the same thing and they were always there because they couldn't have gotten there any other way they look at you like you're kinda crazy."

"You're not crazy."

Daniel fell asleep and Lawrence prayed. Toward dawn he too fell asleep for an hour and then woke to see the sun edging up over the mountain, and a veritable army of police officers coming up the hill.

"Danny. Wake up."

Daniel woke up and looked down the hill. As if in unison with his awakening, two helicopters began circling overhead. The police dogs set up a loud barking that echoed and snapped against the side of the hill.

"Come on, Grandpa. They're getting close."

"No, Danny. We're not going to run."

"How come?"

"Because there's too many of them. But we're not afraid."

"So what are we going to do?"

"I'll stay here. You go on to Harry Buck's."

"Will you come and get me?"

"Absolutely. No doubt in my mind about that."

Daniel looked doubtful. His jeans and T-shirt were crumpled and dusty from lying on the hillside. Clumps of soil and gravel stuck to his hair and face. In spite of the dirt the immaculate newness of his hair and skin and the stark clarity of his eyes gave him an impeccable freshness.

Lawrence looked, as he was wont to look, like one carved out of granite, his deep-set eyes and his angular cheekbones, at one with the lines of the rock and boulders around him.

A row of police officers appeared over the brow of the hill above them. Guns drawn, they descended with military precision toward the boy and his grandfather.

Below them another line of officers moved carefully up the hill.

And then behind them came the reporters, Leon Ferguson among them, followed by the television crews, stumbling over bushes and pebbles as they carried their heavy equipment.

Accompanying them were a few curious local people and, Lawrence could just make out in the faint morning light, his attorney, Edgar Stassen, with Ida and Max. And far behind them he caught a glimpse of the bright, white-blond hair of his daughter. It was like a party or a funeral, they were all there.

An officer spoke through a bullhorn, "Come away from that bush, Pagels. Move slowly forward with your hands up."

"Go, Danny. Now!"

Daniel looked up at his grandfather, his face full of pain and reluctance. "I don't want to leave you all alone, Grandpa."

"It will help me if you go. More than if you stay."

"Really?"

"I promise."

"O.K."

Daniel stood up and edged backward and sideways so that he disappeared behind the creosote bush. He was no longer visible from the top or the bottom of the hill. There were no more bushes or trees in the vicinity; sandy soil and gravel stretched over a hundred yards in every direction around the bush.

"Tell the boy to come out, Pagels. We're not going to hurt him."

"He doesn't want to come out." Lawrence walked slowly away from the bush, his hands held high in the air.

"Daniel!" the police officer yelled, his voice booming and reverberating. "Come down the hill. We want to see you."

Lawrence moved further down the hill until he was surrounded by police officers. He offered no resistance and allowed himself to be handcuffed without any struggle.

There was a momentary silence on the hillside. No applause, no celebration, just a quietness. All eyes turned toward the solitary creosote bush, a small scrubby piece of vegetation, hardly enough to hide a boy.

"Why did Pagels choose this place?" asked one of the officers climbing down the hill to pick up Daniel. "There's no cover. He must have known he'd get caught if he stopped here."

As they approached the bush the police, and the crowds gathered further down, had a clear view of the bare hillside all around. Not even a bird could have moved out of that bush without at least ninety people seeing it.

There was no way of escape for Daniel. To get to the next boulder or bush that could shield him, he had to run across a hundred, maybe a hundred and fifty yards, of open ground.

The officers circled the bush. The police dogs sniffed and whined at its roots.

The scent of Daniel was in that bush but that was all.

The child had gone.

———

Helicopters circled the spot where Daniel was last seen and the dogs continued to sniff at the creosote bush. There was no trail to follow.

In desperation the dogs followed the earlier trail Daniel had taken to the bush. Quite logically it led to the spot where he had slept and then right back to the place in front of the gas station where Lawrence and Daniel had jumped down from Frank La Firenze's cabin cruiser. There was no trail leading from the bush in any other direction.

"Where is he, Pagels?" John Starbeck pulled the handcuffed Pagels out of the back seat of a police car where he had been roughly pushed minutes before.

Lawrence Pagels stared up at the hillside with about as much curiosity as all those around him.

"He's gone." He spoke with a touch of amazement in his voice. "He's gone. Daniel's gone."

"Gone where?"

"Gone."

"What kind of a stunt is this? Where did he go?"

"I told him to go and he went."

Lawrence turned as if heading back to his seat in the back of the police car. Starbeck swung him around.

"What the fuck are you playing at, Pagels? Where's the kid?"

Lawrence gave him a hard, beady look. "I don't have him." He held up his handcuffed wrists. "See. There's nothing here."

Behind him the crowds of police and reporters moved up and down the hillside like dozens of ants. Up and down. Up and down. Halfway up the hillside, the figures of Edgar Stassen, Ida, and Max could be seen staring up at the creosote bush. They were very still.

Rhonda Pagels emerged from the crowd around Lawrence Pagels and pushed her way toward him. She stood before him, her face smudged with perspiration and dust. No police officer attempted to stop her as she fell toward her father. She threw her arms around him and sobbed her heart out.

——

Harry Buck was an early riser. When he heard his dogs barking and came out to see a small figure running down the path to the front door of his small ranch house in northern Mexico, he had already been up for a couple of hours.

The sun had just risen and revealed the small figure to be, as it drew closer, a young boy.

Harry was not a tall man himself. Half Mexican, half Irish, with a leathery bald head and slightly bowed legs, he was smaller than most of the people he had worked with in California, especially Lawrence Pagels who towered over him by over a foot.

For that reason when Pagels had called and said he was sending his grandson down, Harry had expected to see a tall California-surfer type, someone old enough to make the long trek south. He had not expected to see a small boy running down the dusty track toward his gate. His ranch was, after all, thirteen miles from the main highway; it could be reached only by rutted dirt tracks. Buck lived alone and did not get many visitors.

"Harry Buck, Harry Buck," the boy shouted. "Are you Harry Buck?"

The boy said he had come from the San Diego area by himself, but could not explain how.

It was not until a week had passed and Harry went into town that he read in a newspaper about the capture of Lawrence Pagels and the disappearance of Daniel.

Harry was amazed to discover that Daniel had vanished from Pauma Valley in San Diego County just after seven on Saturday morning January 13. This was exactly the same time that Daniel had appeared in Mexico, running up the path toward Harry's front door. There was a distance of over two hundred miles between the two locations.

Harry hung around the town pay phone for a couple of hours, making calls to find out if the newspaper story was correct. It was.

"Is this a miracle?" he asked Daniel.

The boy shook his head and seemed embarrassed.

23

Lawrence Pagels continued his interrupted journey to Chino and once incarcerated there was not permitted to make any statements. Thwarted from seeing Pagels, the combined forces of the media turned their attention upon his attorney.

There were TV vans, trucks loaded with film equipment, mini-buses, and cars, double and triple parked around the block, waiting for Edgar Stassen when he returned to Chatsworth. The Winnebago showed its fragility when reporters jumped on the roof and climbed through the windows.

The motor home was definitely no fortress and Stassen was a sitting duck.

Ida and Max were quick to call in help from fellow law students who acted as bodyguards and bouncers. For many, their first employment in the field of law was in pushing reporters off the roof of a Winnebago.

"Where's Daniel, Mr. Stassen?" "How did you do it?" "Do you think this shows you were right, Mr. Stassen?" "Does this prove Pagels isn't guilty?" "Is it a hoax?" "Come on, tell us how you did it?"

When a man called Harry Buck, two hundred miles away in Mexico, came forward and announced that Daniel Pagels had arrived at his front door, the media troops headed south.

They found not only Harry but twenty farm workers in a field who had all seen Daniel arrive at Harry's front door early in the morning. They all swore they saw him just after seven on the morning of January 13. This was the same time that police records showed Daniel vanished from the hillside in Pauma Valley.

———

While Lawrence Pagels sat and waited in his new cell, Edgar Stassen lodged an appeal, declaring that the disappearance of Daniel Pagels in full view of over ninety members of the press and police in San Diego County and his simultaneous appearance at Harry Buck's ranch in Mexico, was clear evidence that he was capable of traveling alone to John Nields' house, as stated by the defense in Lawrence Pagels' trial.

The judge ruled that a phenomenon such as this, which could be the result of hysteria or trickery, did not constitute grounds for an appeal.

There was no legal reason for releasing Lawrence Pagels. He would have to remain in prison and serve out his sentence.

———

Rhonda retreated from the world. She did not want to talk, to be looked at, to be judged.

She wrote letters to Lawrence, which she mailed. Letters to Daniel, which she threw away.

She also wrote letters to herself.

"My son has blue-gray eyes and fair hair, not blond, but fair. When he walks he rolls a little from side to side. I don't know, a kid like that with his abilities, you'd expect him to be real graceful but he rolls. To me his face is very beautiful. Others may not think so.

"His skin looks soft, though I haven't gotten to touch it. I imagine stroking his cheek and feeling its softness. I imagine making him laugh. I'm a funny person. He'd laugh at my jokes.

"When he talks his cheeks flush a little as though his thoughts are shining through.

"I would like to hold him. Children run to their mothers. I would like him to run to me.

"I don't tell anyone this. I'm not going to tell Lawrence. He'd say 'Go see him.' But I know that I could never in a million years be what Lawrence is to that child. And I know that even locked away in jail, Lawrence is a stronger presence and comfort to Daniel; just the idea of him is more than I can ever be.

"I saw Danny interviewed on TV along with Harry Buck, who was kind of delirious. He looks like he doesn't know what hit him.

"The whole world descended on Harry Buck's place and old Harry has told his story so many times his voice is hoarse. On some interviews he looks like someone who's won the lottery and on others he looks scared to death.

"And I'm scared to death too. Who am I in all this? What's my connection? Can I be part of this? Is it in me?

"I guess I've seen Daniel about twenty times in the last two days. I flick around the stations and catch him. He looks real calm. He could teach me a lot.

"What could I do for him? I could tell him all the best places to buy cocaine between here and Seattle. I could tell him my cloud floated down to earth just a little too late.

"I notice children now. Once there was not one child on the entire planet. Now I see them everywhere. I hear their voices. And I see that they all have eyes like Daniel, seeing the invisible, knowing the unknowable. I'd like to have eyes like that."

———

Lawrence wrote to Rhonda, "Forget the past. What you think and do now are the only things that define you. You are not your past. You are your present. The past and the future are locked in the confines of time. The present is infinity.

"You have always looked for freedom, Rhonda. Your motives were not bad.

"There is nothing in you that I cannot find to love."

———

Sharon Nields made yet another phone call to Leon Ferguson.

"Did I tell you about my car?"

"No, I don't believe you did. Can you tell me quickly, because I'm expecting a call."

"I won't take a second. It was the roof. It was covered with sap from the trees. I went out and had it cleaned in the afternoon and then in the morning it was covered in sap."

"It must have been a real mess. Could we chat about this some other time because . . ."

"It was the night John died."

"I beg your pardon?"

"The afternoon before he died I took my car to the car wash and when I got back to the house I drove it straight into my garage because I didn't want it to get dusty. And I didn't use it till the next morning."

"What are you saying, Mrs. Nields?"

"I'm saying that it had sap on the roof the next morning."

"Maybe you caught the sap as you went along the drive."

"No way. We don't have any trees over the drive in Palm Desert."

"You have them in Bell Canyon?"

"Yes, we do. Big trees. They drop that stuff on the car roof and it's hard to get off."

"So maybe you caught it when you went up to Bell Canyon."

"I didn't go to Bell Canyon that often. I hadn't been up there for a couple of months before he died."

There was a brief silence then Leon said quickly, "Why don't I come over and we'll talk about this."

———

Lawrence Pagels wrote to Daniel, "All is consciousness. You have proved that to the world and they do not see it. Say to those people who feel trapped by their beliefs, have courage. Tell them to hold on to those small moments when their consciousness clearly affects the world around them and then take those moments and use them. Tell them to exercise them and have more success until they see that all is consciousness."

———

On February 15, 1990, Raymond Nields went to a police station in Palm Desert and confessed to the murder of his father, John Nields. He gave himself up at the instigation of his mother.

According to Raymond Nields his father had made unjust and constant criticism of perceived failings in his behavior, first as a student and then as a businessman. He said that his father had threatened to take away a trust fund that had been established in his name.

He had reached the point where he could no longer reason with his father and was fearful of a drastic change in lifestyle.

Sharon Nields told the police, "When I saw the sap on the roof of my car I knew he'd been up to Bell Canyon. He used my car because the trunk is bigger. I remember the inside of the trunk was all wet where it had been hosed down. I didn't want Ray to go to jail. John had made Ray the man he was. But I didn't want Mr. Pagels to stay in jail either.

"It had to come out because Ray couldn't go on much longer the way he was going. He was driving himself so hard. He was trying to be like John. He was trying to prove himself to John. I don't know why it turned out like this. Ray's always tried to please us."

———

On March 9 Lawrence Pagels was released from prison.

Postscript

Lawrence Pagels returned to the site in the hills above Chatsworth although the area is now under a new threat of massive industrial and domestic development by ambitious builders that could flatten all the ground around Pagels' trailer. Chatsworth residents are fighting this plan which they say will destroy the beauty of the hills, cause pollution, overpopulation, and gridlock on the already overburdened Simi Valley Freeway.

Pagels has little time for his work as a gardener, as he is in frequent demand as a lecturer.

Daniel Pagels lives with his grandfather and attends a magnet school for gifted children in San Fernando Valley.

Rhonda Pagels is working as a counsellor at a drug rehabilitation center in Orange County. She visits her father and son at the weekend.

Dr. Irving Walkman is heading a team at Stanford University to research quantum physics as it applies to human mental and physical ability.

Edgar Stassen defended Lionel Brown in court. He was freed on a technicality. Since then Stassen has given up his law practice and is writing a book.

Max Haydn is working for a law firm in Century City.

Ida Letherbridge is assisting Edgar Stassen in the writing of his book and is frequently seen in the company of Max Haydn.

Jason Leutwiler meets Daniel Pagels at baseball practice on Thursday evenings in Mason Park.

Contrary to Lawrence Pagels' wishes, the creosote bush on the hill in Pauma Valley has become something of a shrine for pilgrims and an attraction for curious tourists. It has been examined by the Pentagon, and oil and pharmaceutical companies for special properties, but so far has proved itself to be exactly like all other creosote bushes.